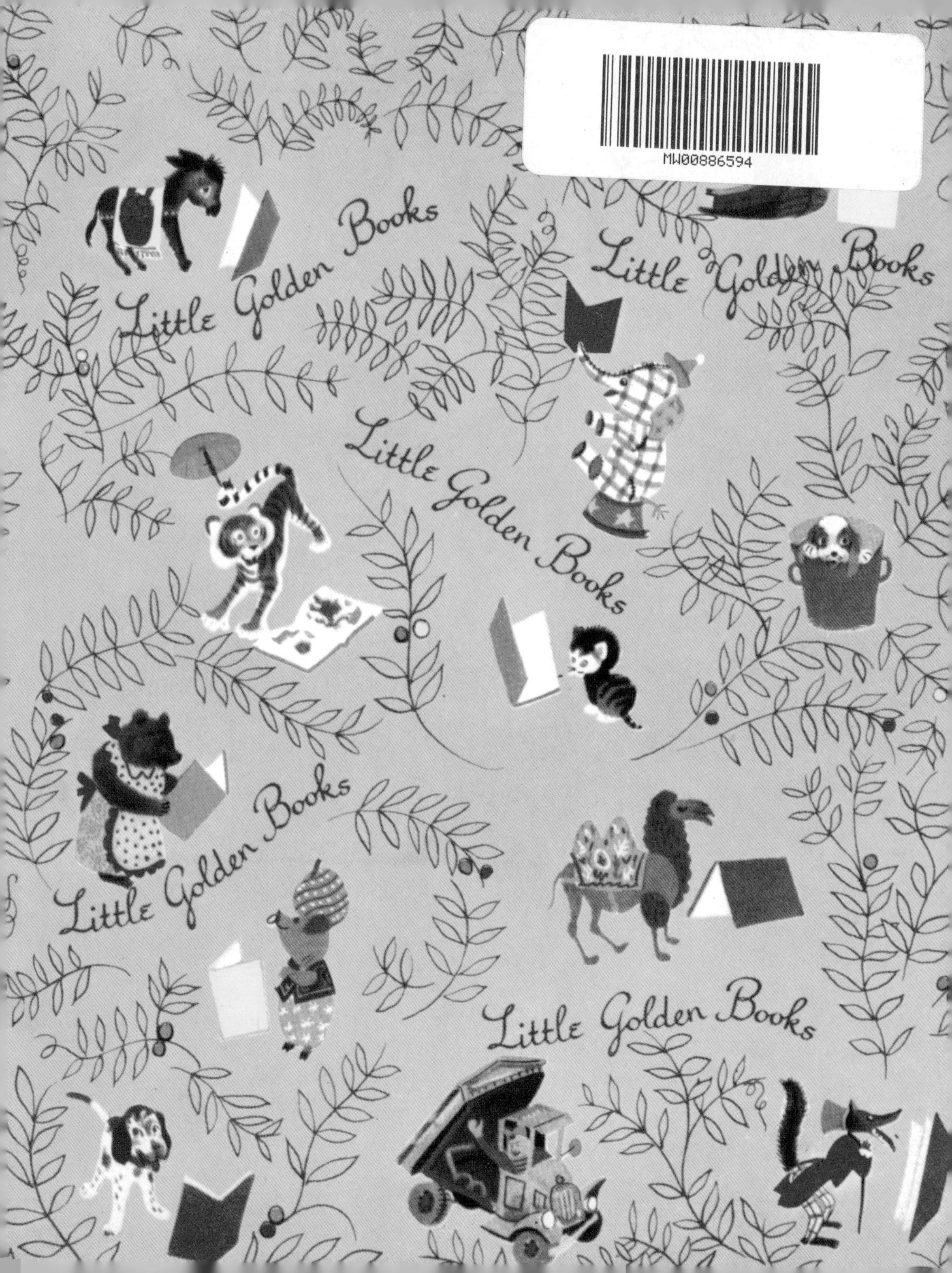
Little Golden Books
Little Golden Books
Little Golden Books
Little Golden Books
Little Golden Books

MARVEL

Marvelkids.com

 Published in the United States by Golden Books, an imprint of Random House Children's Books, a division of Penguin Random House LLC, 1745 Broadway, New York, NY 10019, and in Canada by Penguin Random House Canada Limited, Toronto. The stories contained in this work were originally published separately by Golden Books as *Guardians of the Galaxy* in 2016; *The Mighty Thor* in 2011; *The Incredible Hulk* in 2012; *Eye of the Dragon* in 2012; *Trapped by the Green Goblin!* in 2013; *Lights Out!* in 2013; *High Voltage!* in 2014; *High-Stakes Heist!* in 2014; and *Ant-Man* in 2016.

randomhousekids.com

ISBN 978-1-5247-1783-4

MANUFACTURED IN CHINA

10 9

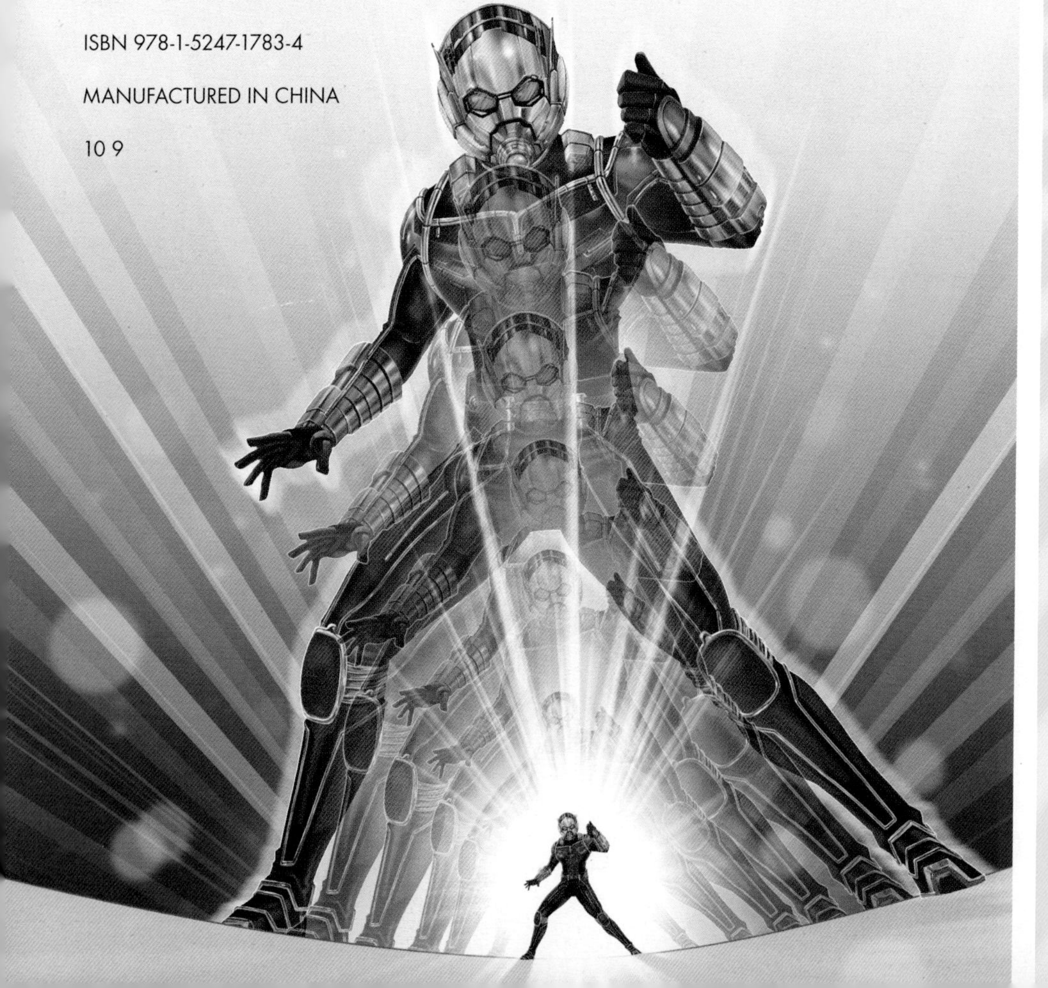

NINE MARVEL SUPER HERO TALES

FEATURING STORIES FROM

AVENGERS

SPIDER-MAN

GUARDIANS OF THE GALAXY

A GOLDEN BOOK • NEW YORK

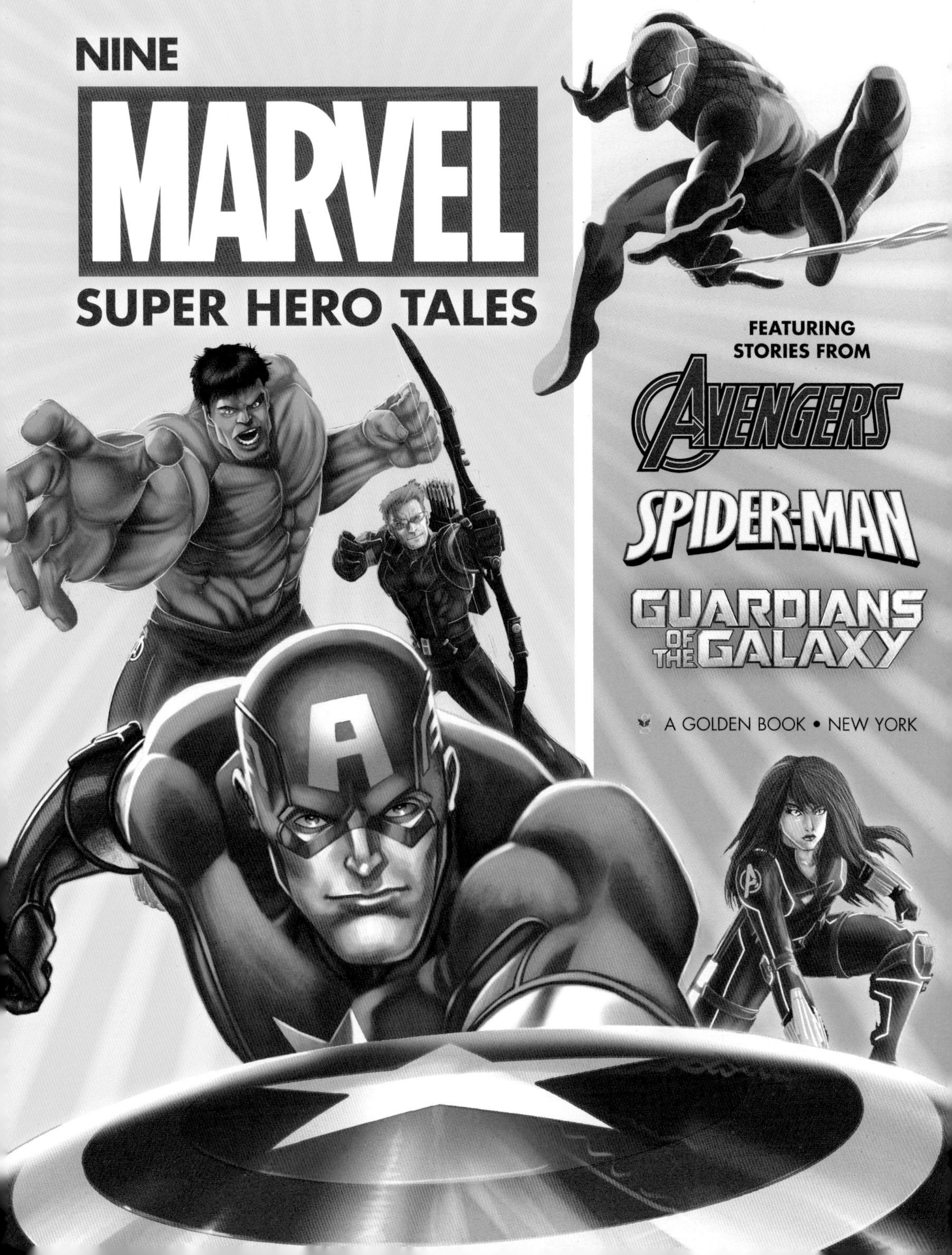

CONTENTS

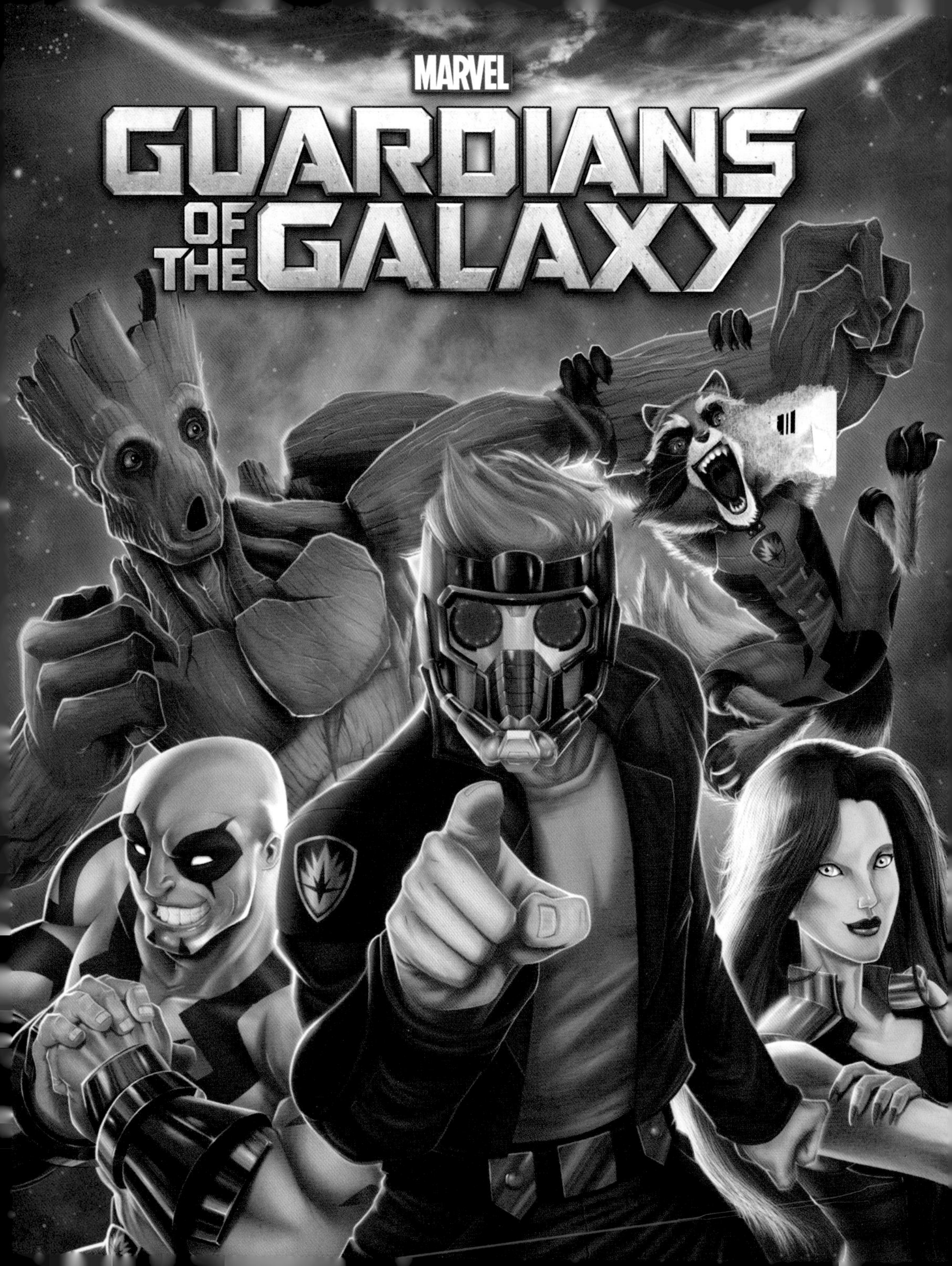
MARVEL
GUARDIANS OF THE GALAXY

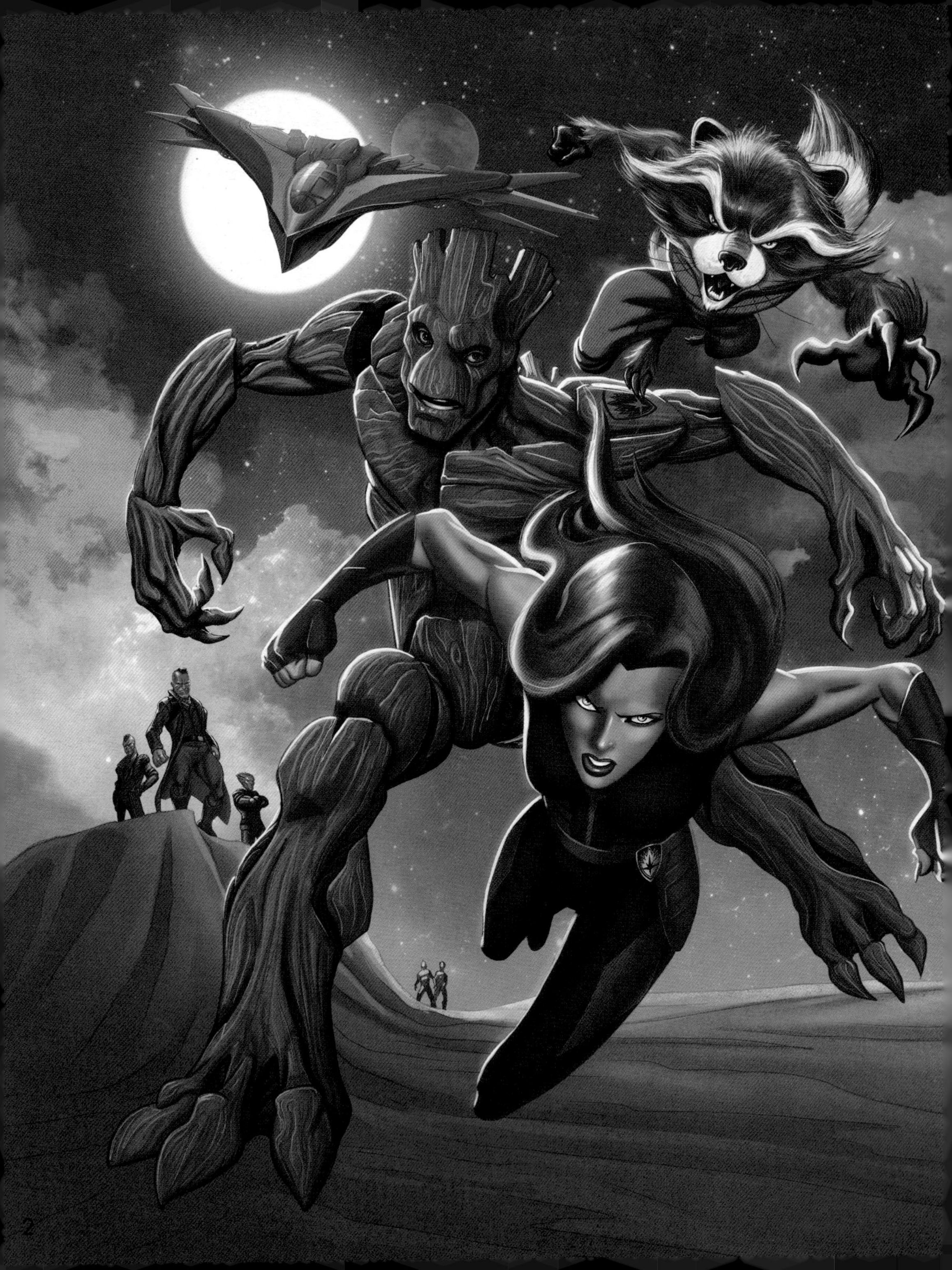

Deep in outer space, the **GUARDIANS OF THE GALAXY** are always ready for action! This ragtag team of heroes protects the universe from all sorts of interstellar threats.

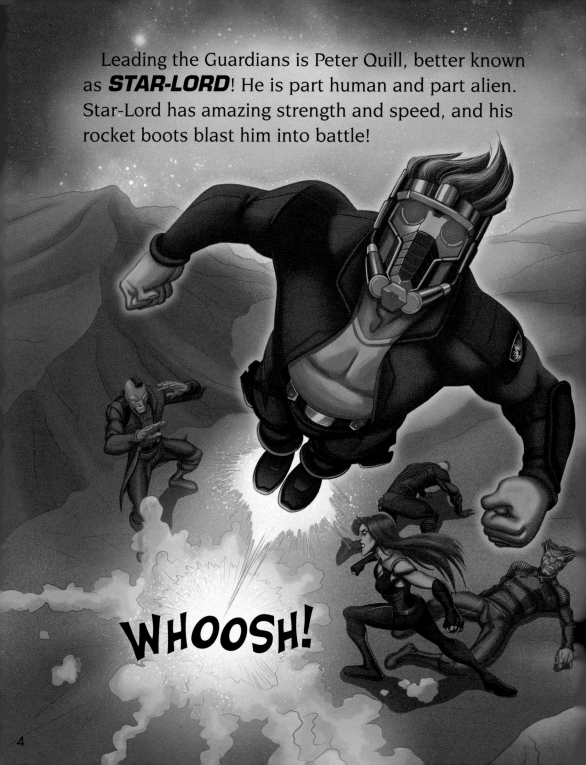

Leading the Guardians is Peter Quill, better known
as **STAR-LORD**! He is part human and part alien.
Star-Lord has amazing strength and speed, and his
rocket boots blast him into battle!

WHOOSH!

Fighting alongside Star-Lord is the green-skinned **GAMORA**. She is the last of her species—an alien race called the Zen-Whoberi. Gamora is a skilled warrior who can heal very quickly from any injury!

ROCKET RACCOON is an expert pilot. He may look cute and fuzzy, but he's no house pet! His sharp claws and enhanced senses make him tough to beat.

His best friend is **GROOT**. He is a tall, treelike creature who can control plants and grow to an immense size.

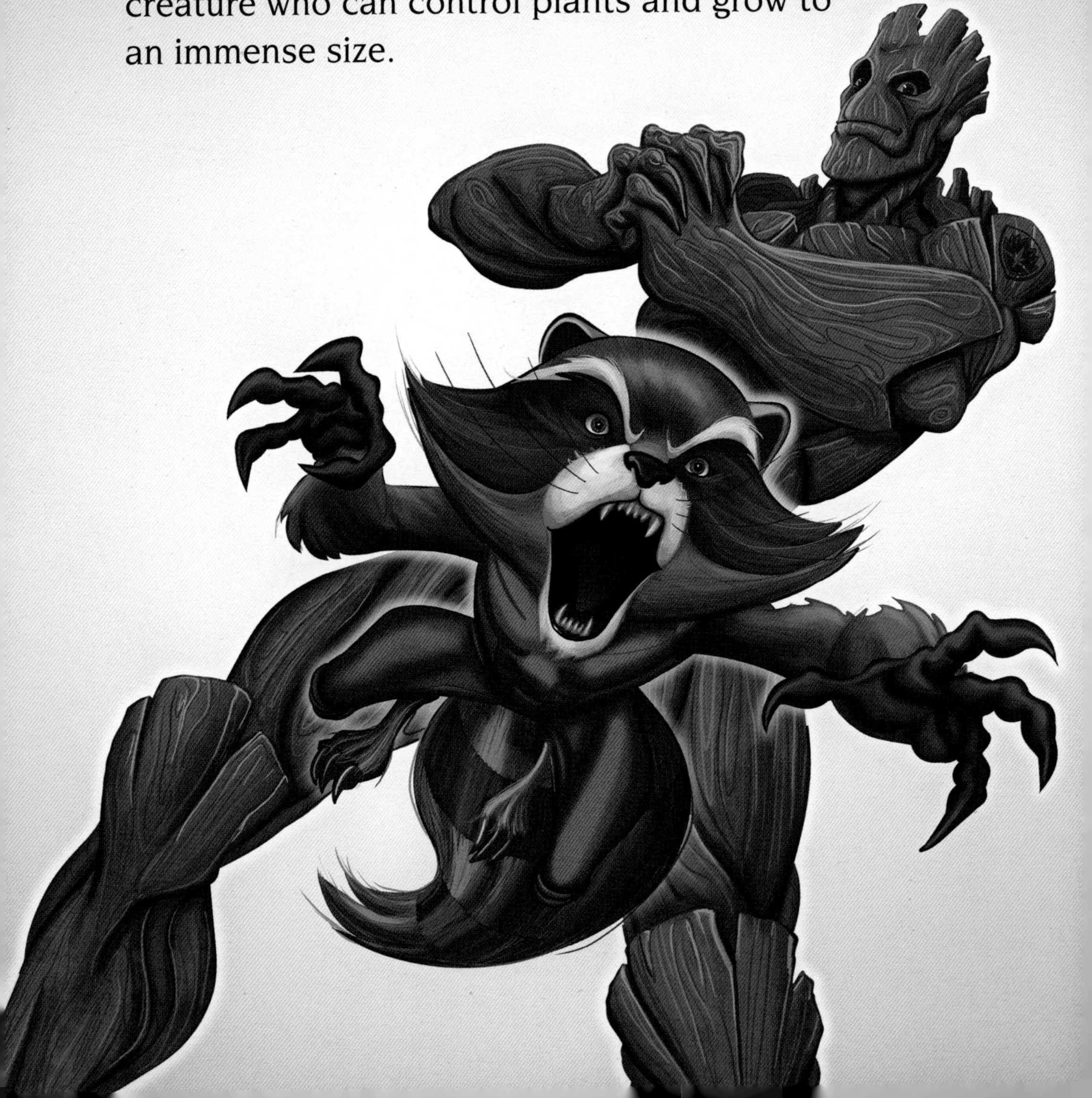

This odd couple is a powerful pair!

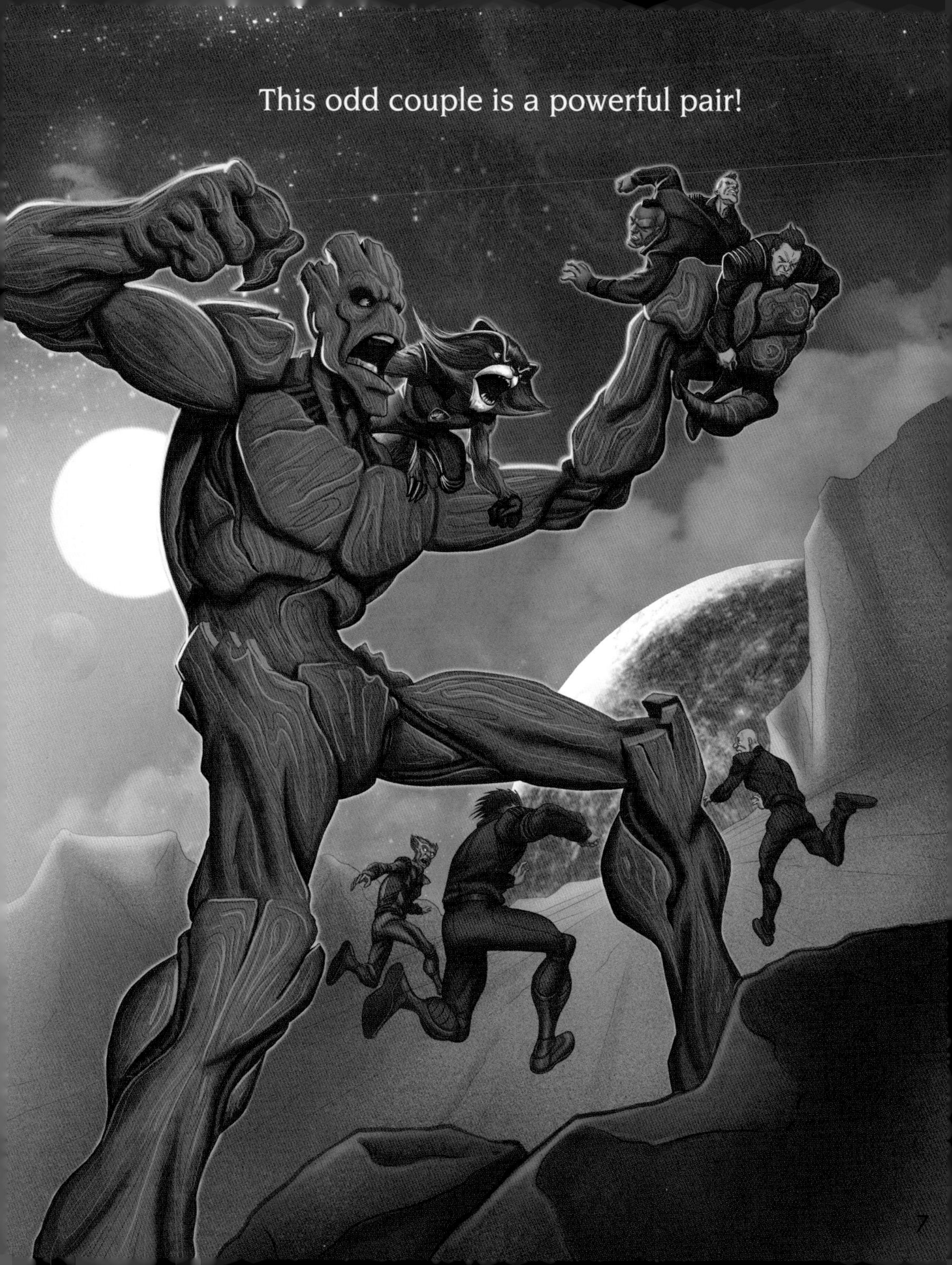

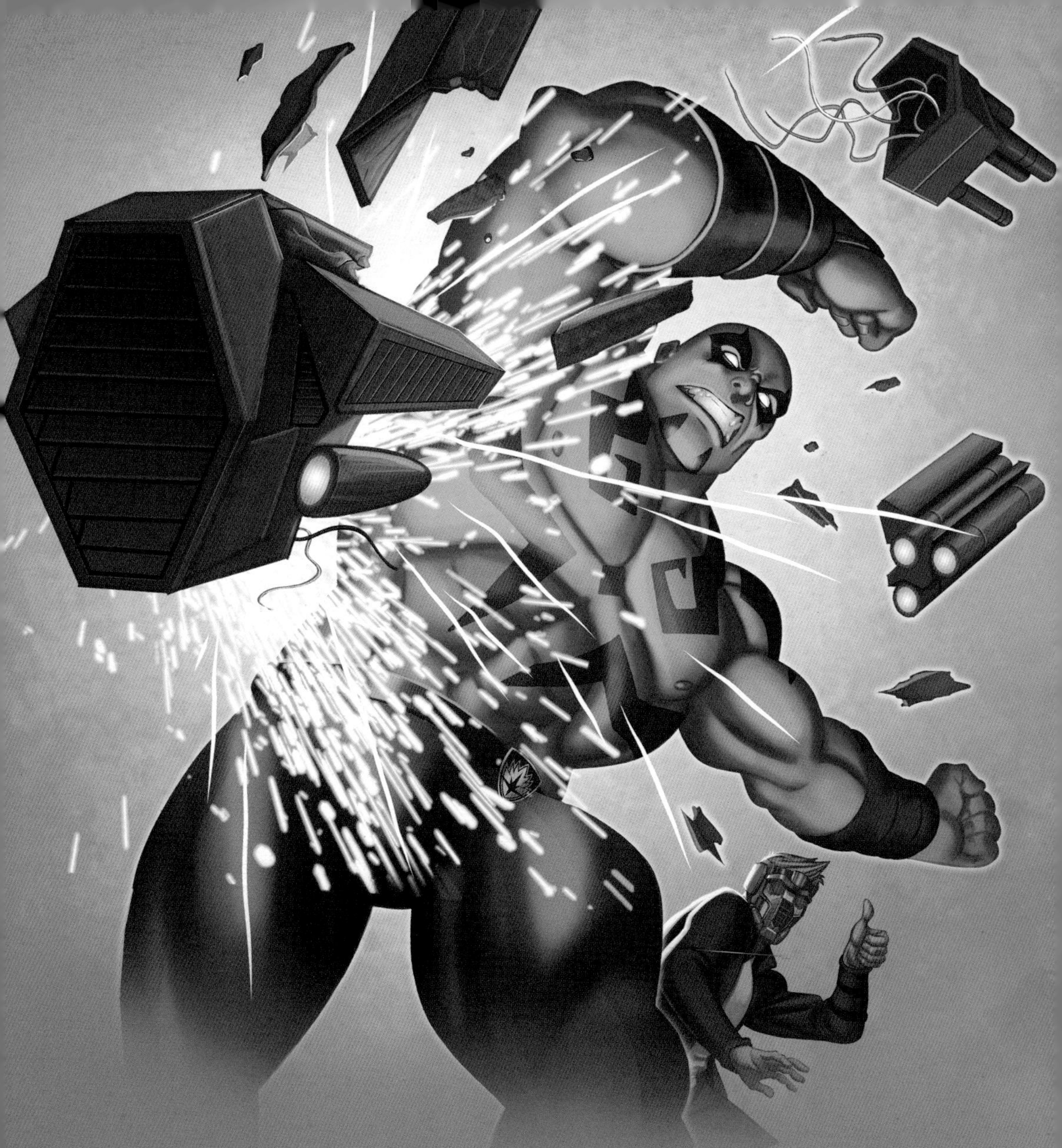

The last member of the Guardians is the super-strong **DRAX**. He is so tough, he can survive in the extreme cold of space without air, food, or water!

The Guardians of the Galaxy search the universe for adventure in Star-Lord's spaceship, the ***MILANO***.

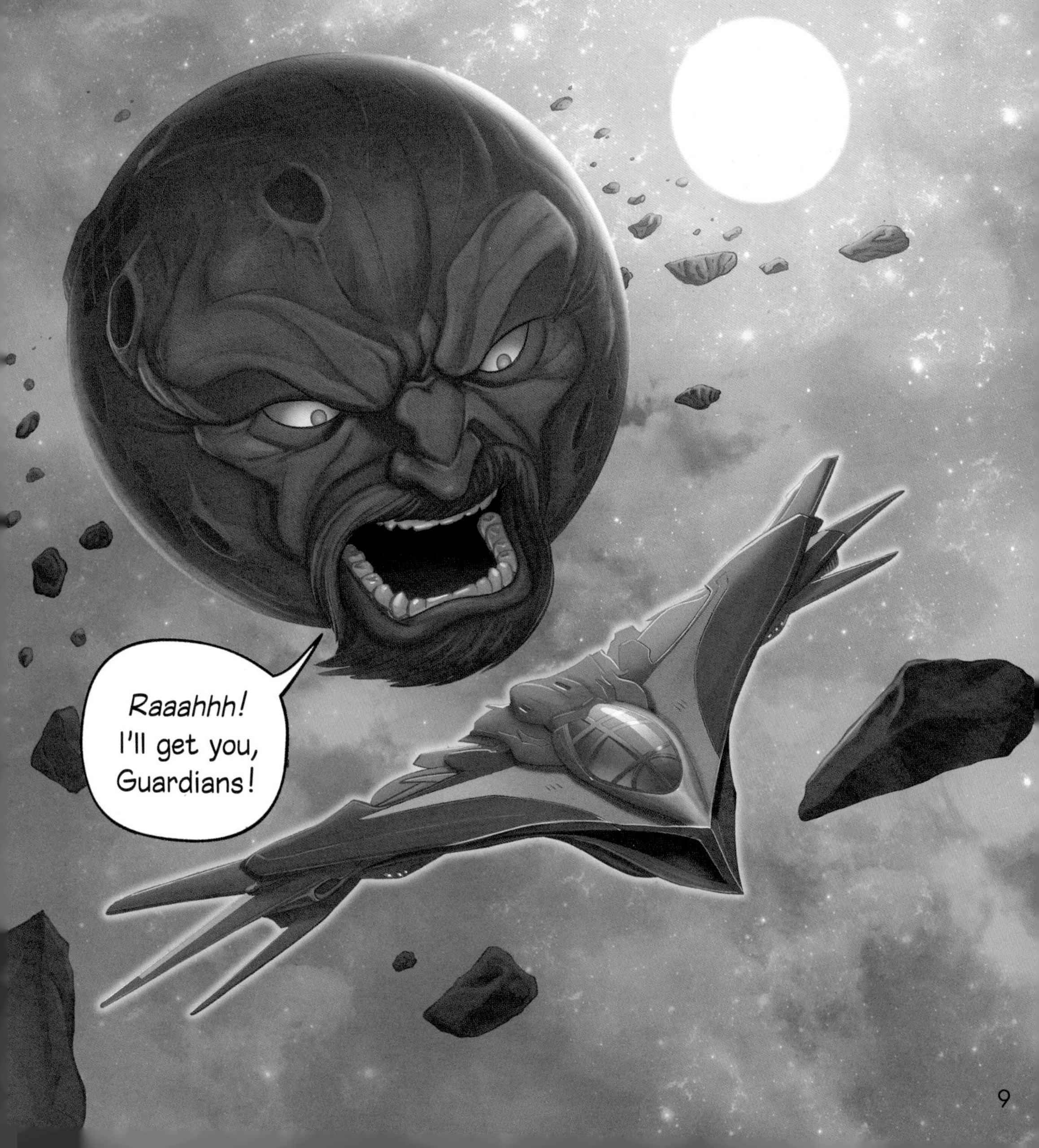
Raaahhh!
I'll get you, Guardians!

The Guardians' home base is called **KNOWHERE**, and **COSMO THE DOG** is their chief of security. Cosmo helps them sniff out trouble!

The Guardians have many different frightful foes throughout the galaxy.

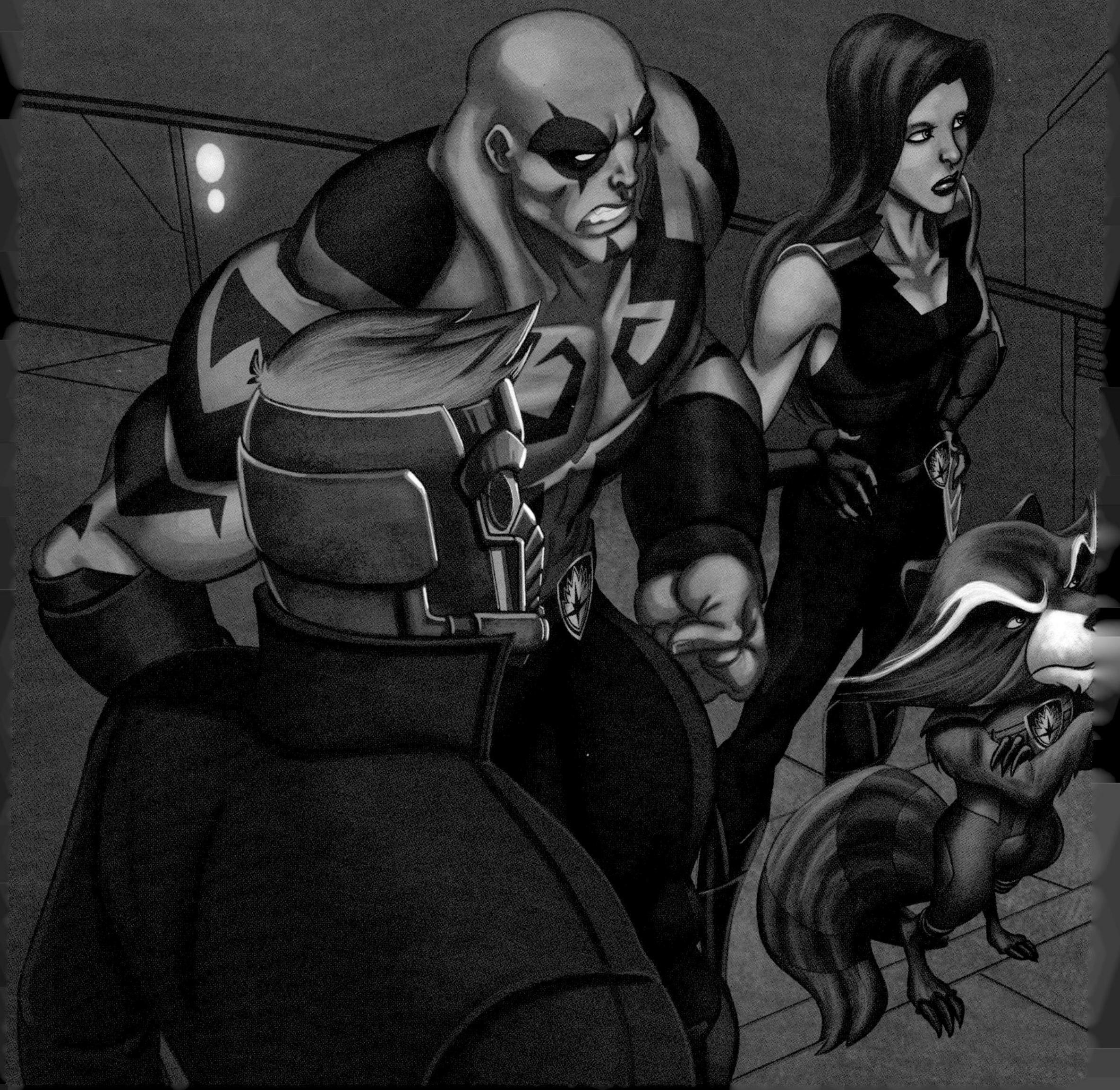

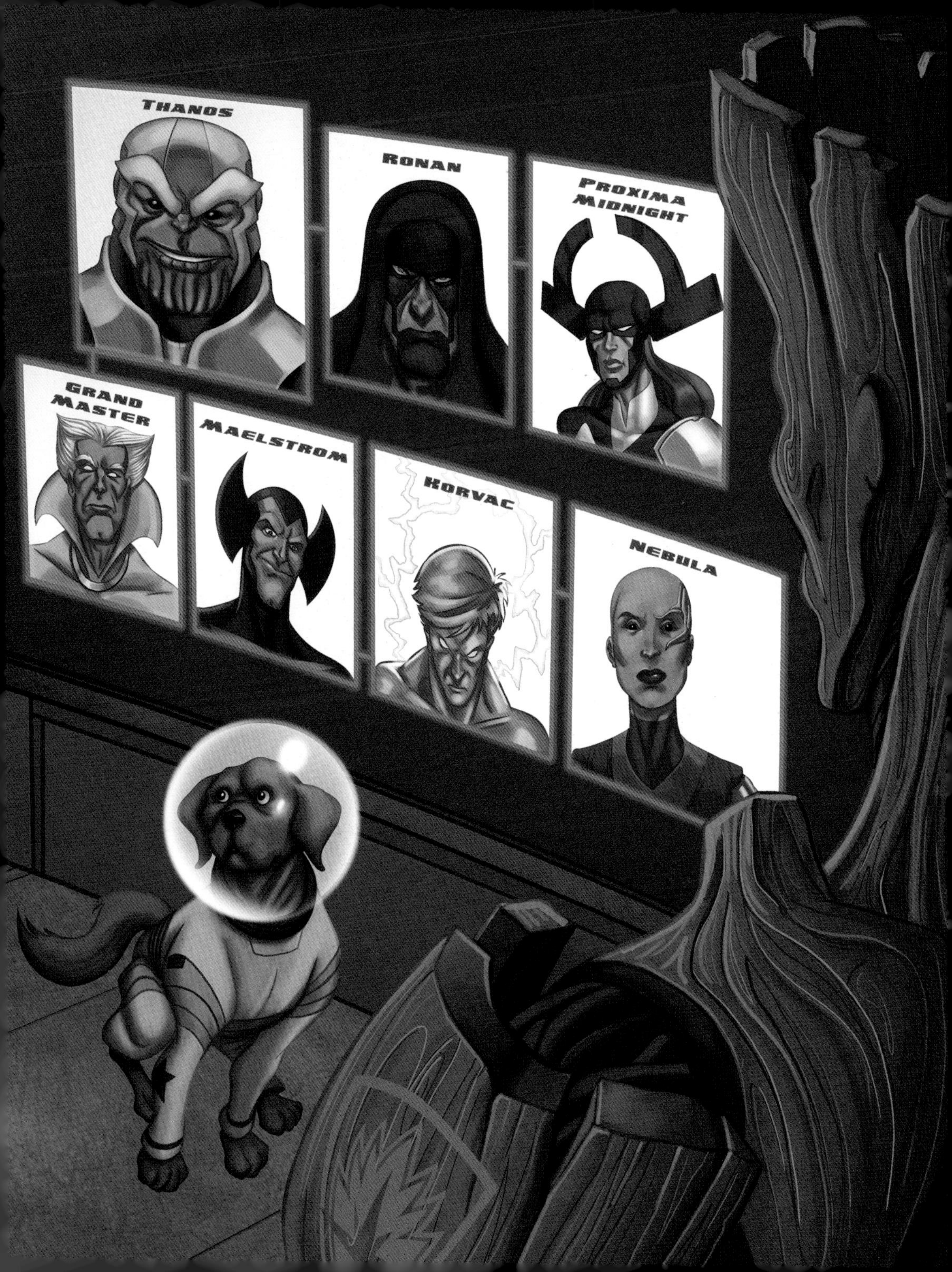
THANOS
RONAN
PROXIMA MIDNIGHT
GRAND MASTER
MAELSTROM
KORVAC
NEBULA

RONAN THE ACCUSER is a sinister soldier with super-speed, super-strength, and quick reflexes. He wields a giant hammer called the Universal Weapon. He can use it to crush almost anything!

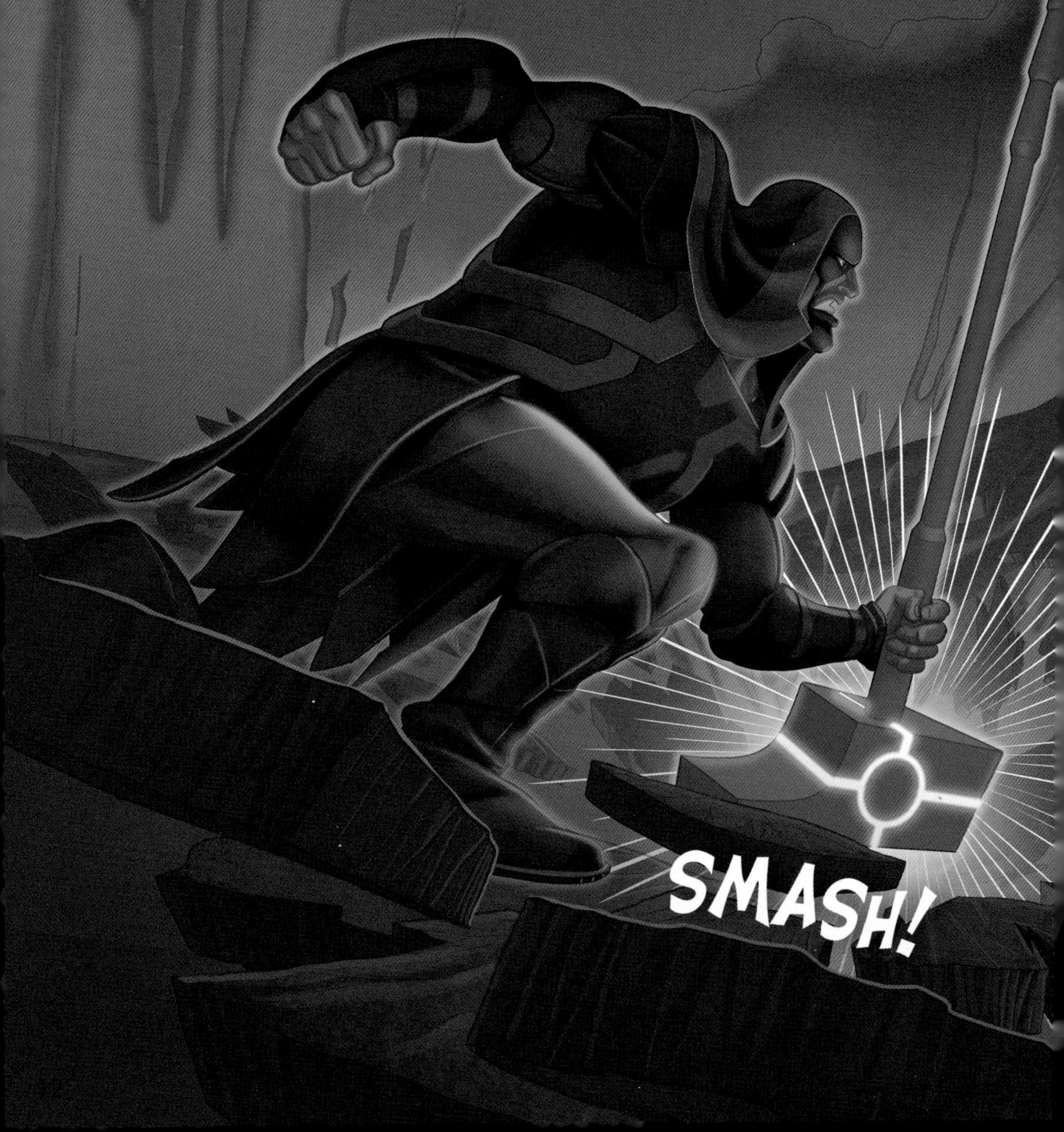
SMASH!

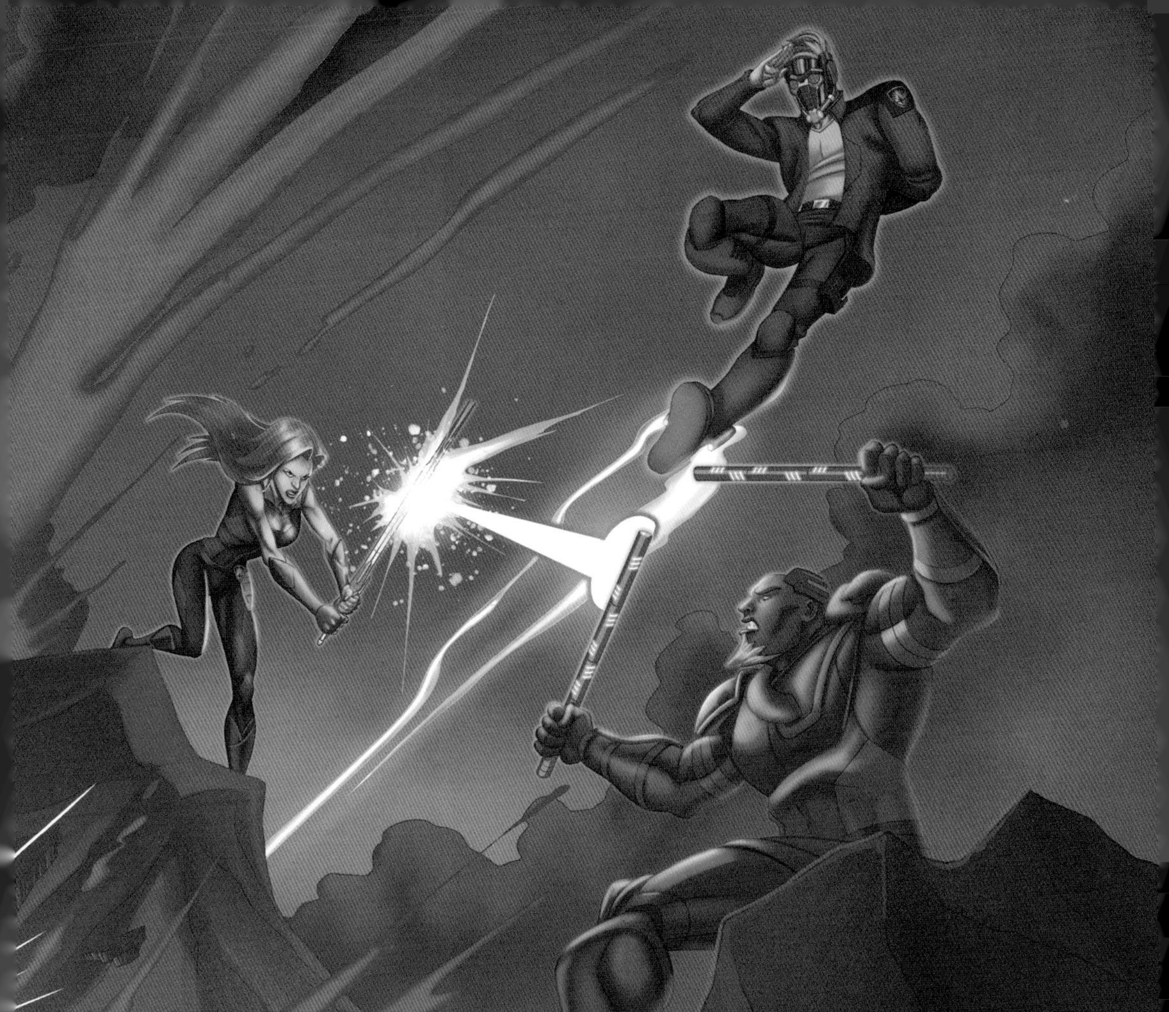

Like Ronan, ***KORATH THE PURSUER*** is a member of the alien Kree race. He carries two batons that fire powerful bolts of energy.

The **COLLECTOR** is an ancient being who travels the universe acquiring alien artifacts—especially those with great power!

Unfortunately for the Collector and the fearsome tiger man **TITUS**, Rocket Raccoon and Groot don't play by his rules.

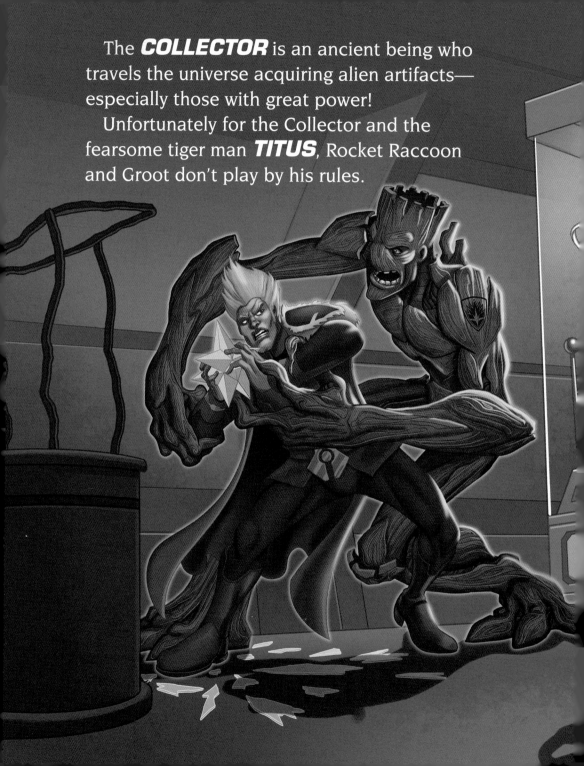

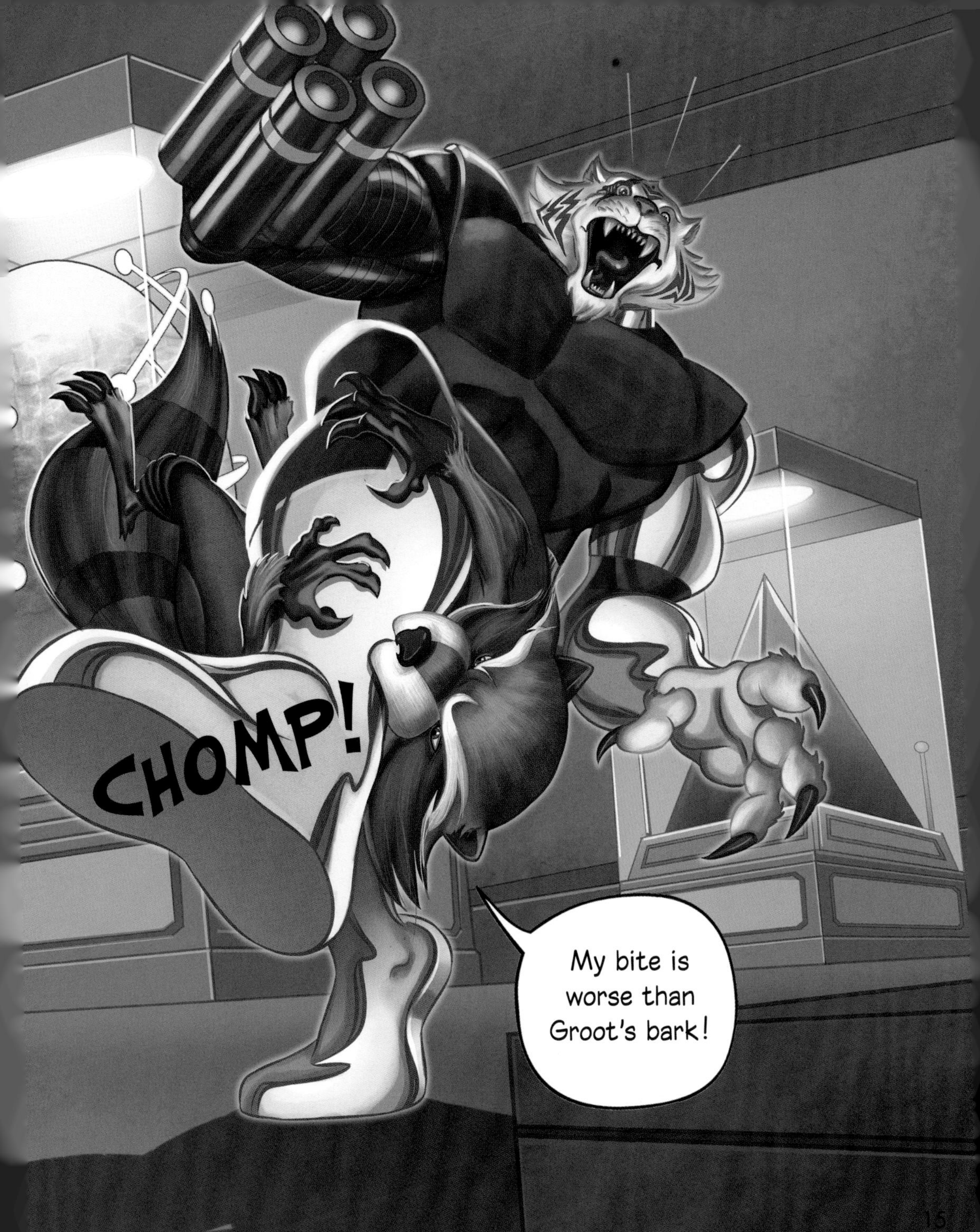
CHOMP!
My bite is worse than Groot's bark!

Feared across the galaxy, the space pirate **NEBULA** is a cyborg. She may be part machine, but she's *all* trouble for the Guardians—and the bad guys, too!

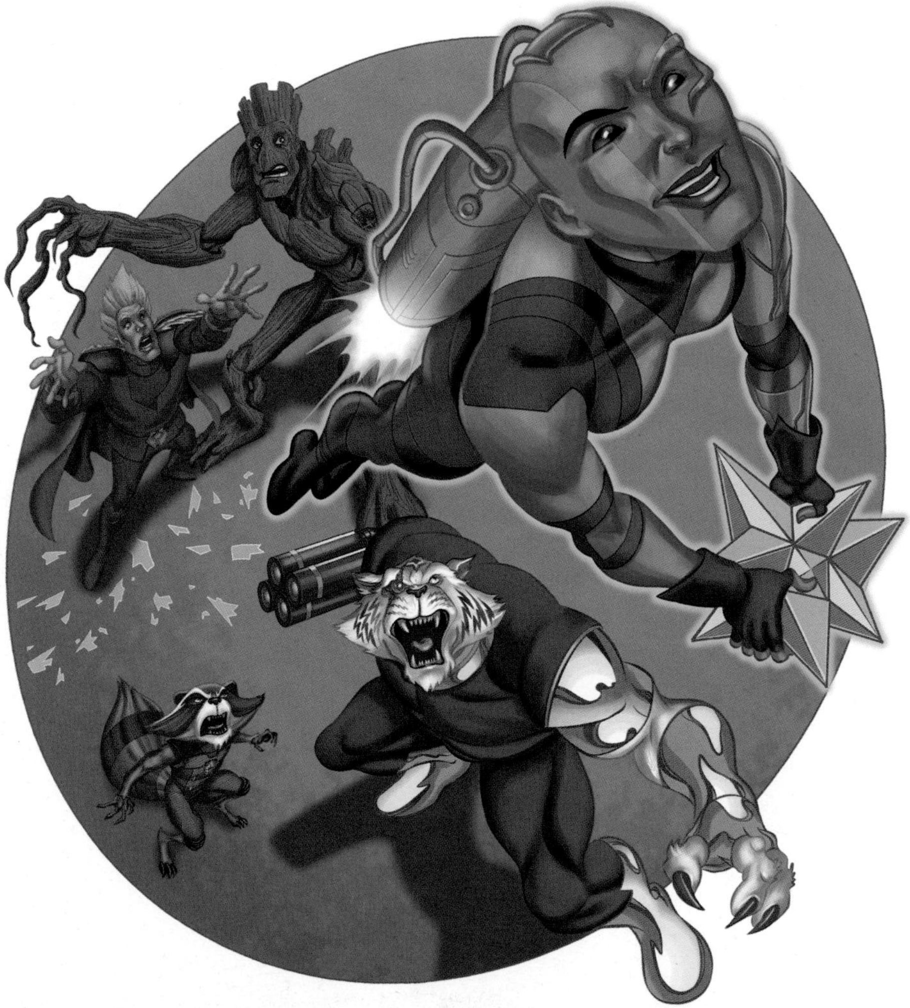

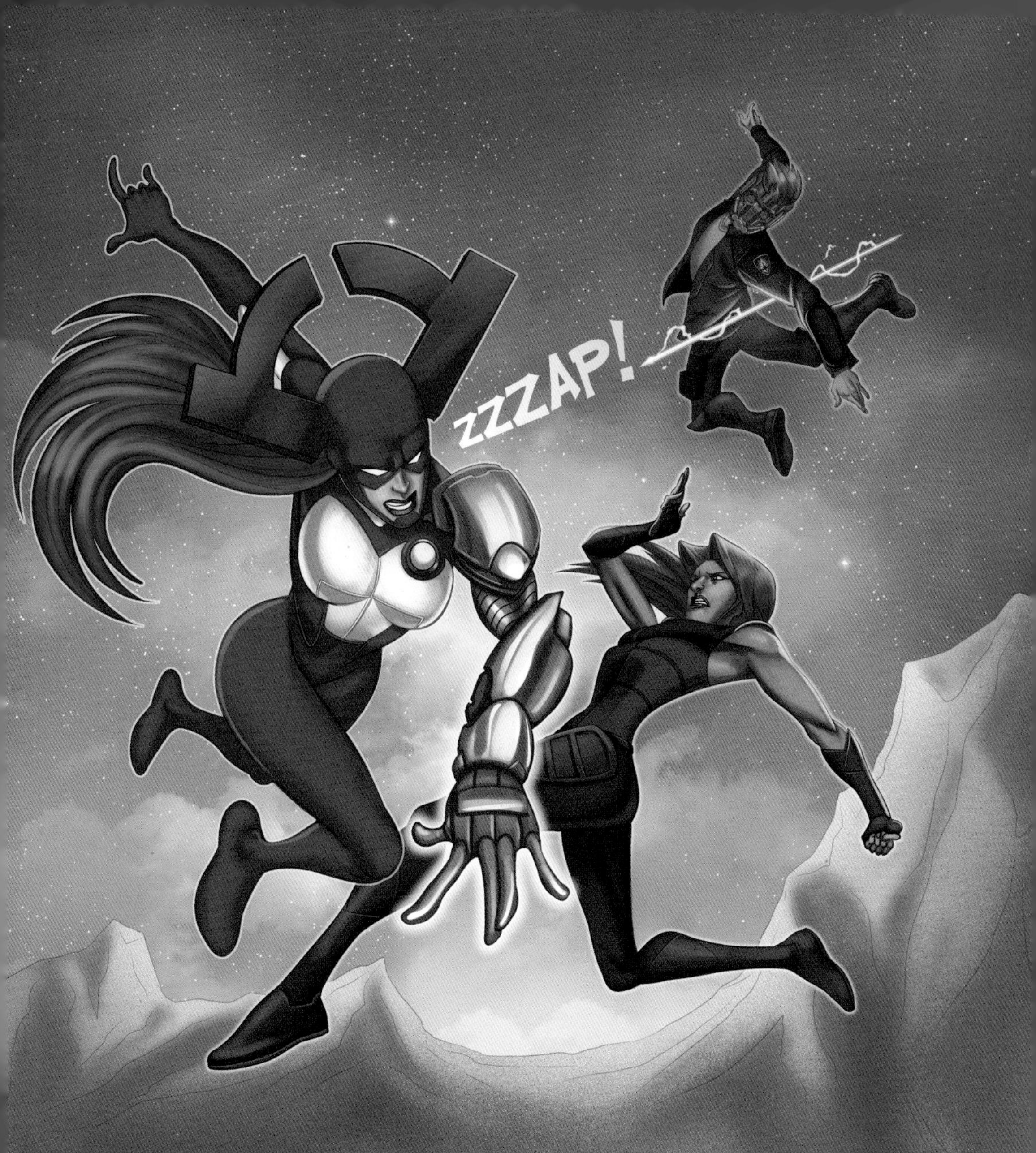
ZZZAP!

PROXIMA MIDNIGHT is a master of hand-to-hand combat. Her deadliest weapon is a spear made from pure star energy.

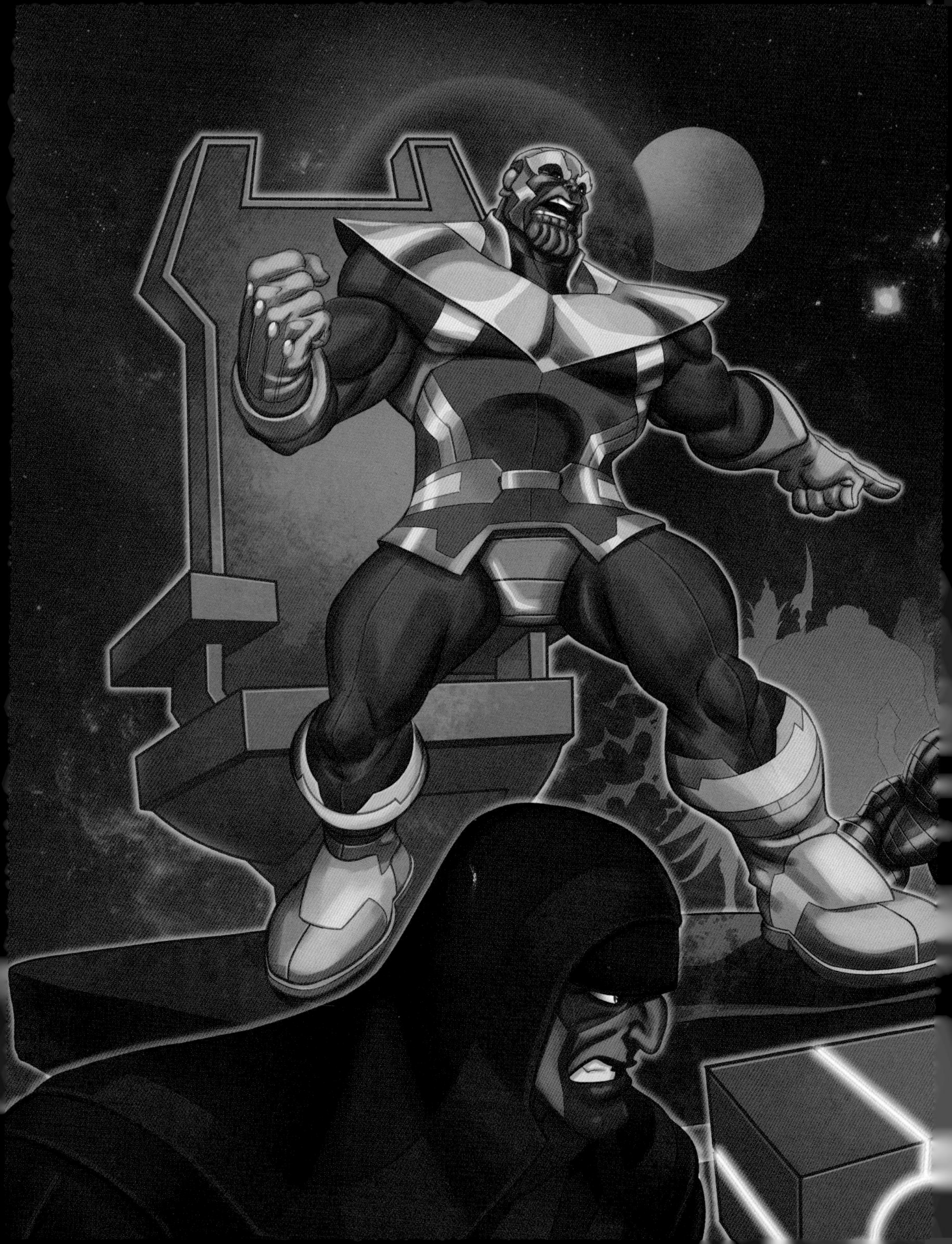

Possibly the greatest menace to the galaxy is **THANOS**. His life's goal is to control the entire universe!

Thanos has teamed up with other villains to try to defeat the Guardians of the Galaxy.

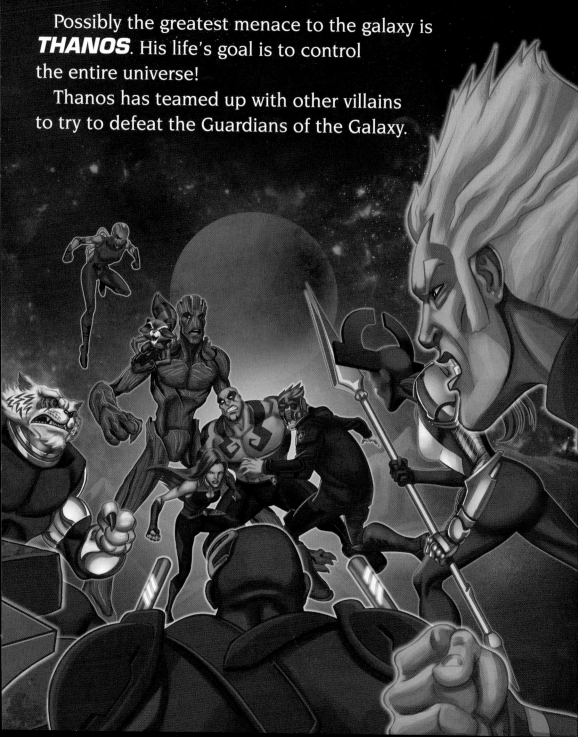

The monstrous **BLACK DWARF**, the energy-blade-wielding **CORVUS GLAIVE**, and the mind-eating telepath **SUPERGIANT** are also minions of Thanos.

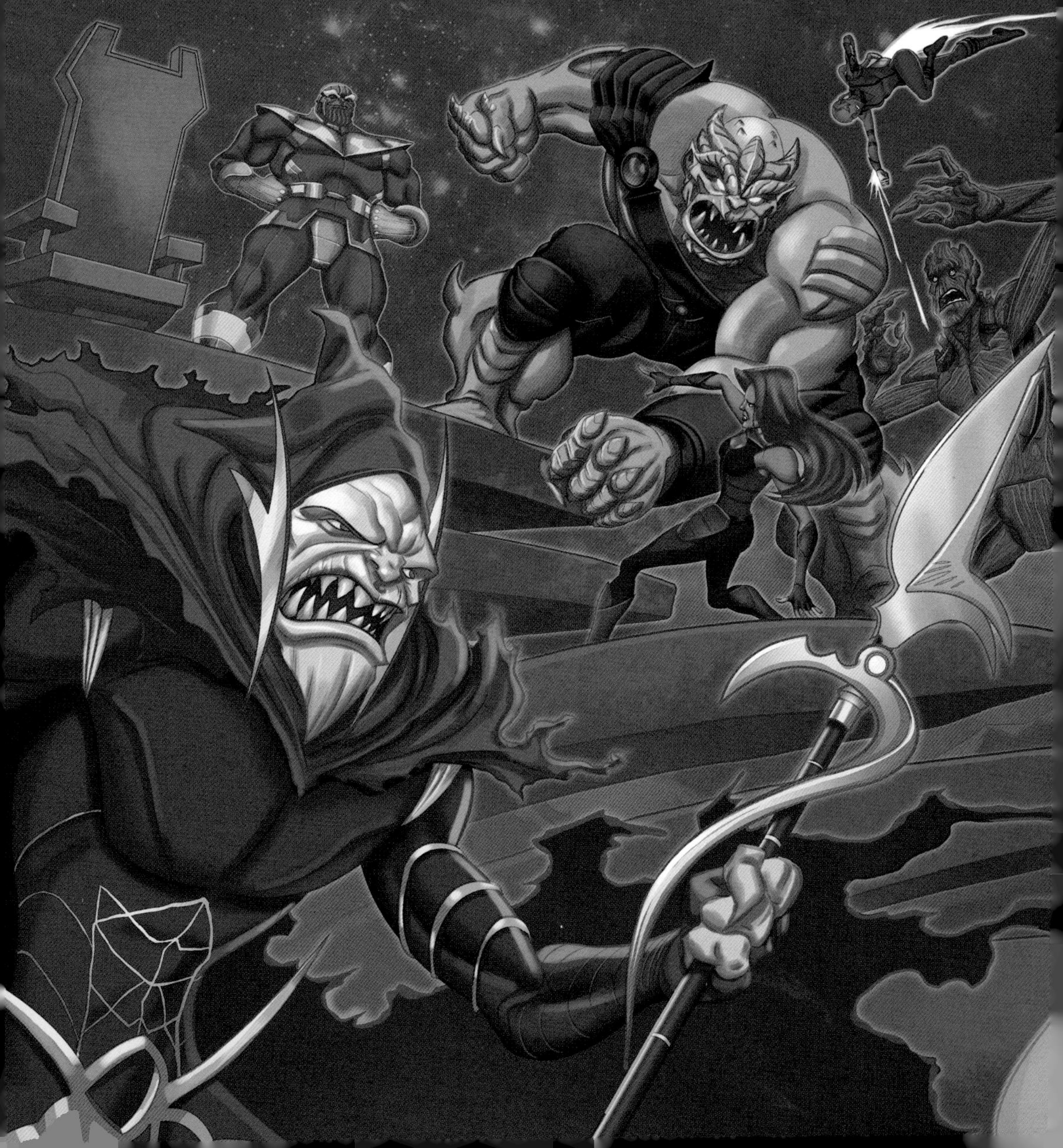

With all these powerful henchmen at his side,
Thanos thinks he is invulnerable . . . but the
Guardians plan to prove him wrong.

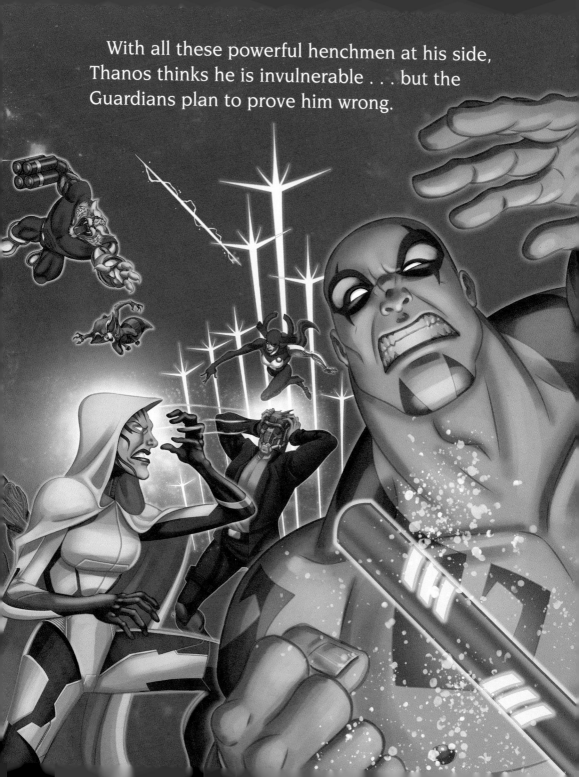

When the Guardians of the Galaxy face off against Thanos and his terrible team, the fight is fierce, but good ultimately overpowers evil.

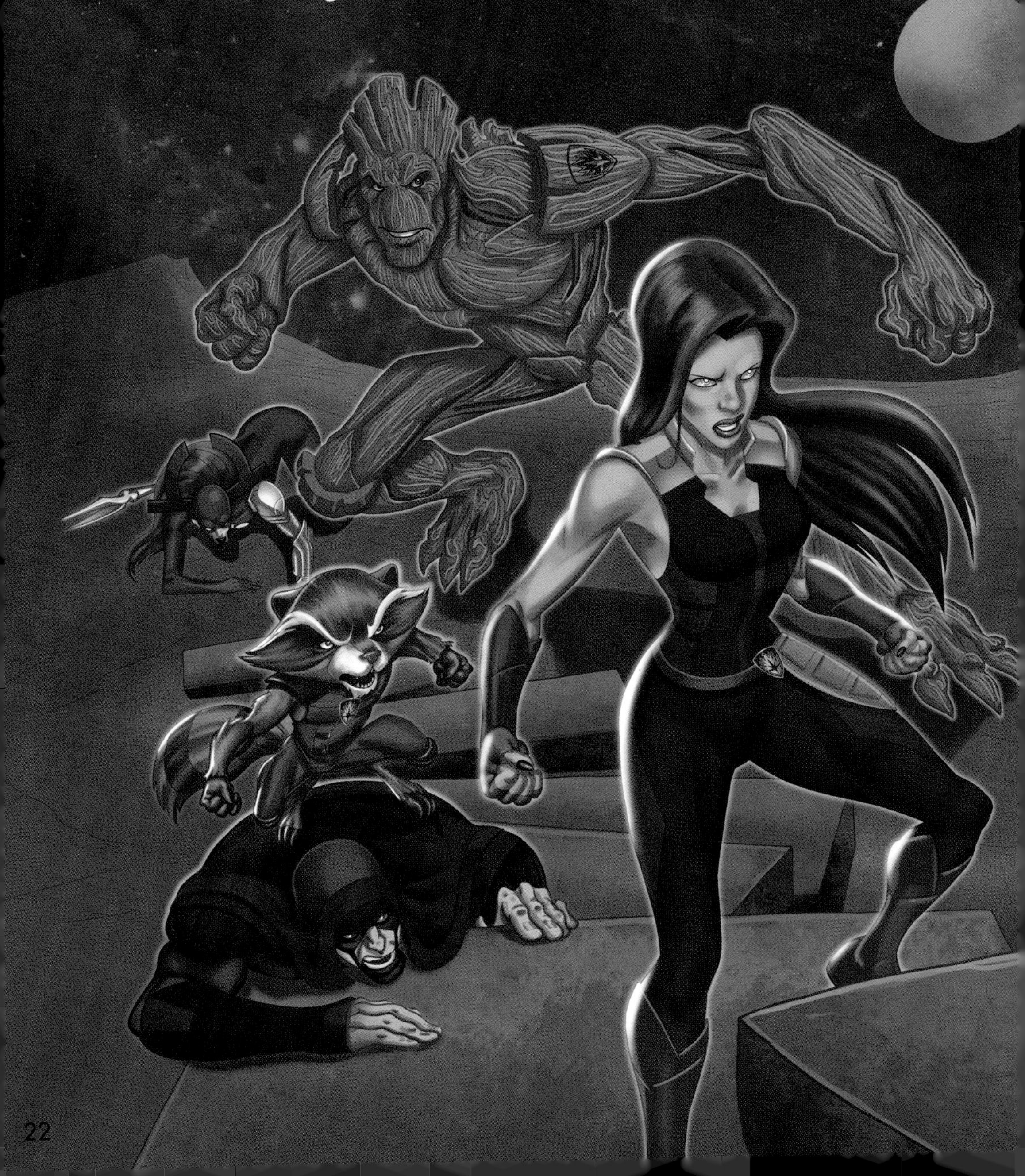

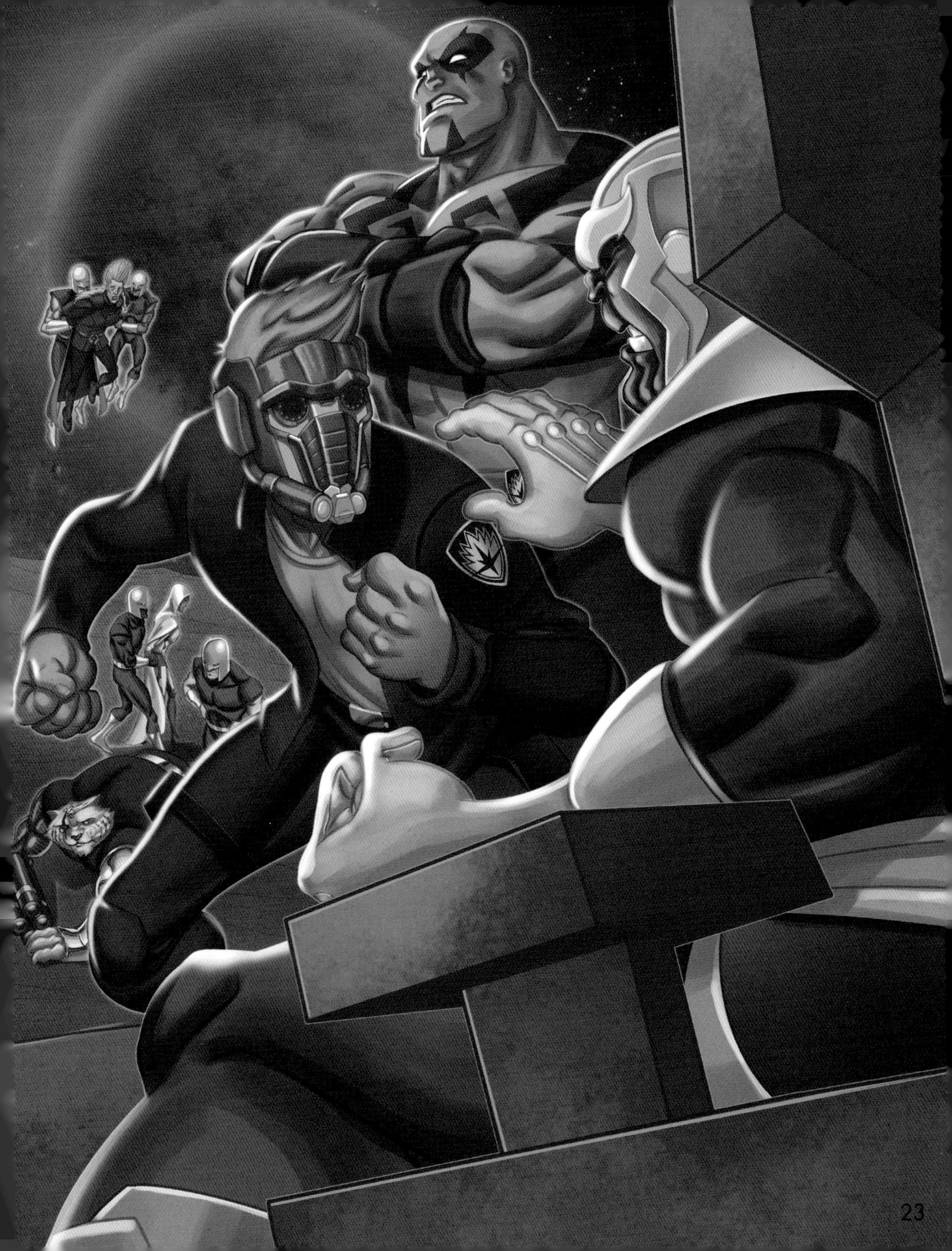

With the battle won, Star-Lord and his friends head home. The universe will always be safe under the protection of the Guardians of the Galaxy.

GO, GUARDIANS, GO!

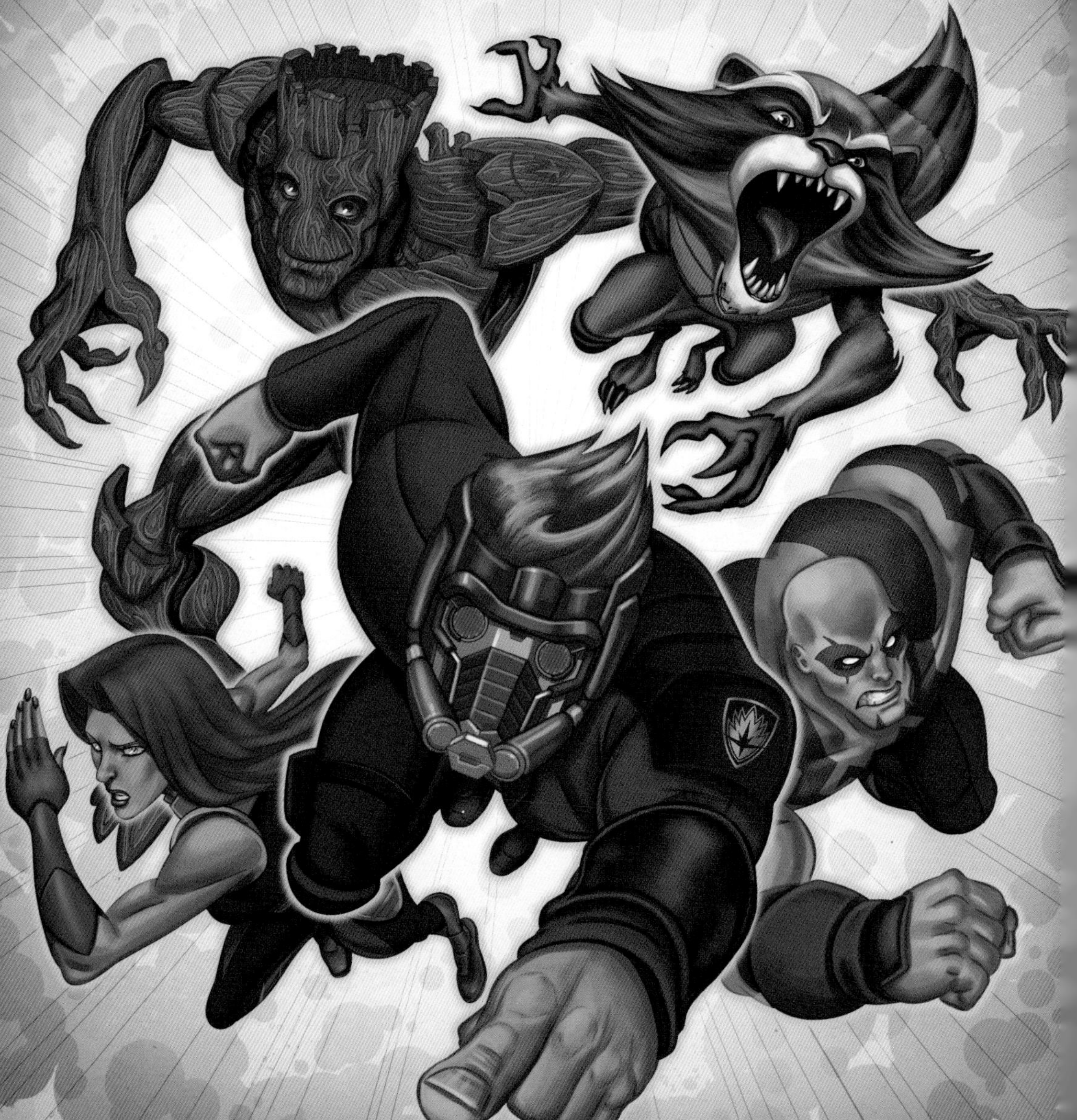

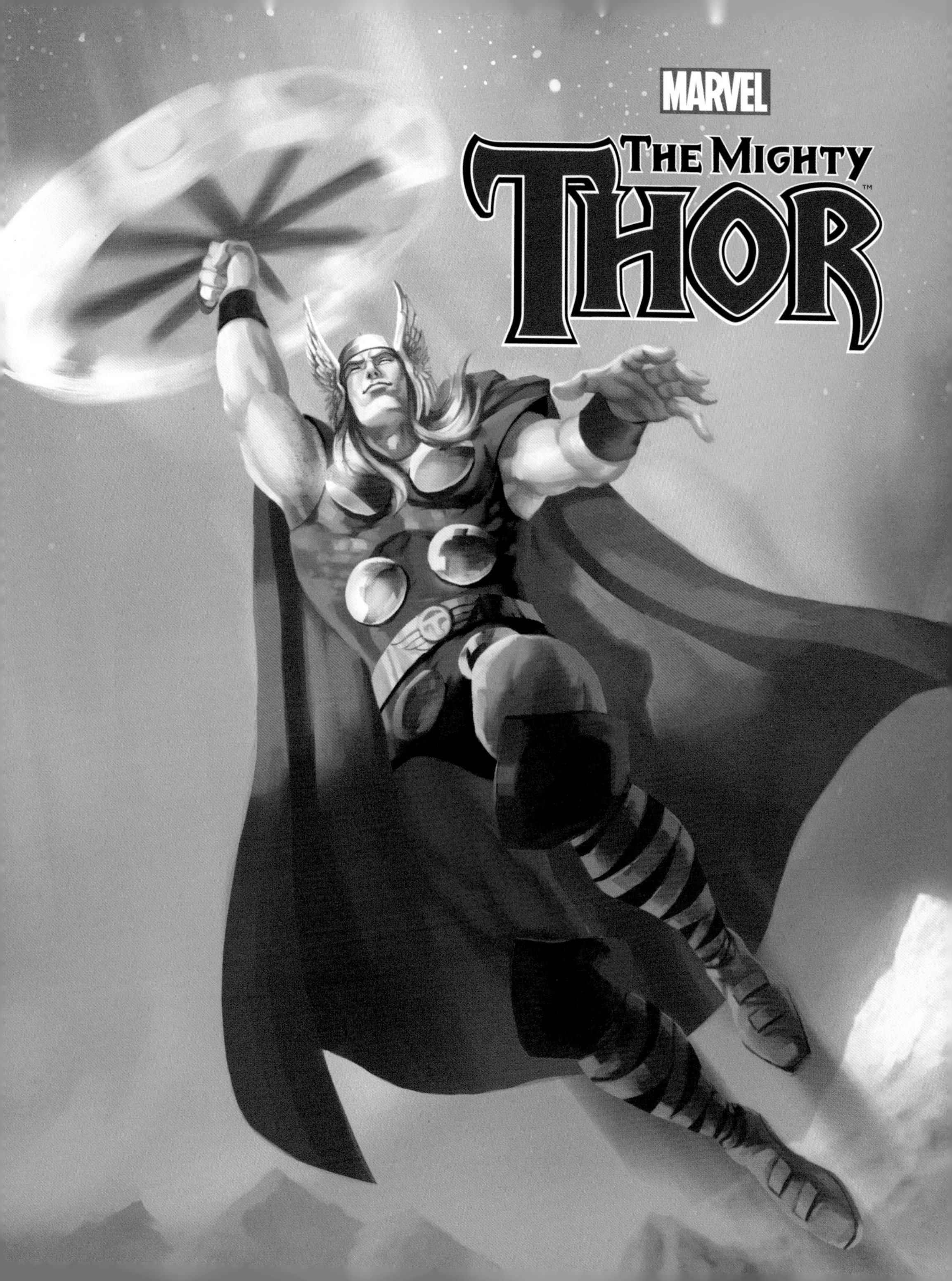
MARVEL
THE MIGHTY
THOR™

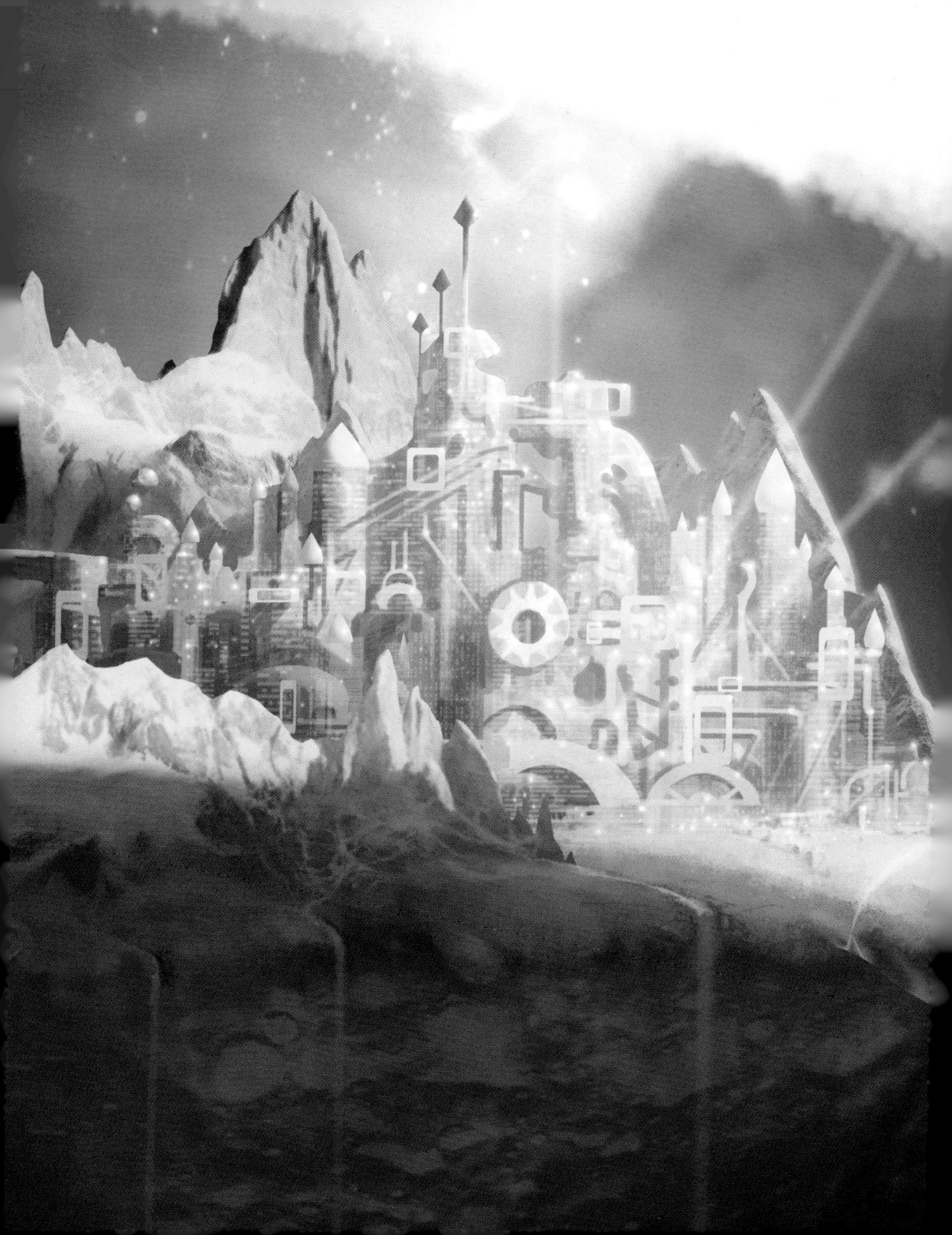

Far away, in the land of *Asgard*, brave warriors fought ogres, trolls, dragons, frost giants, and monsters of all kinds.

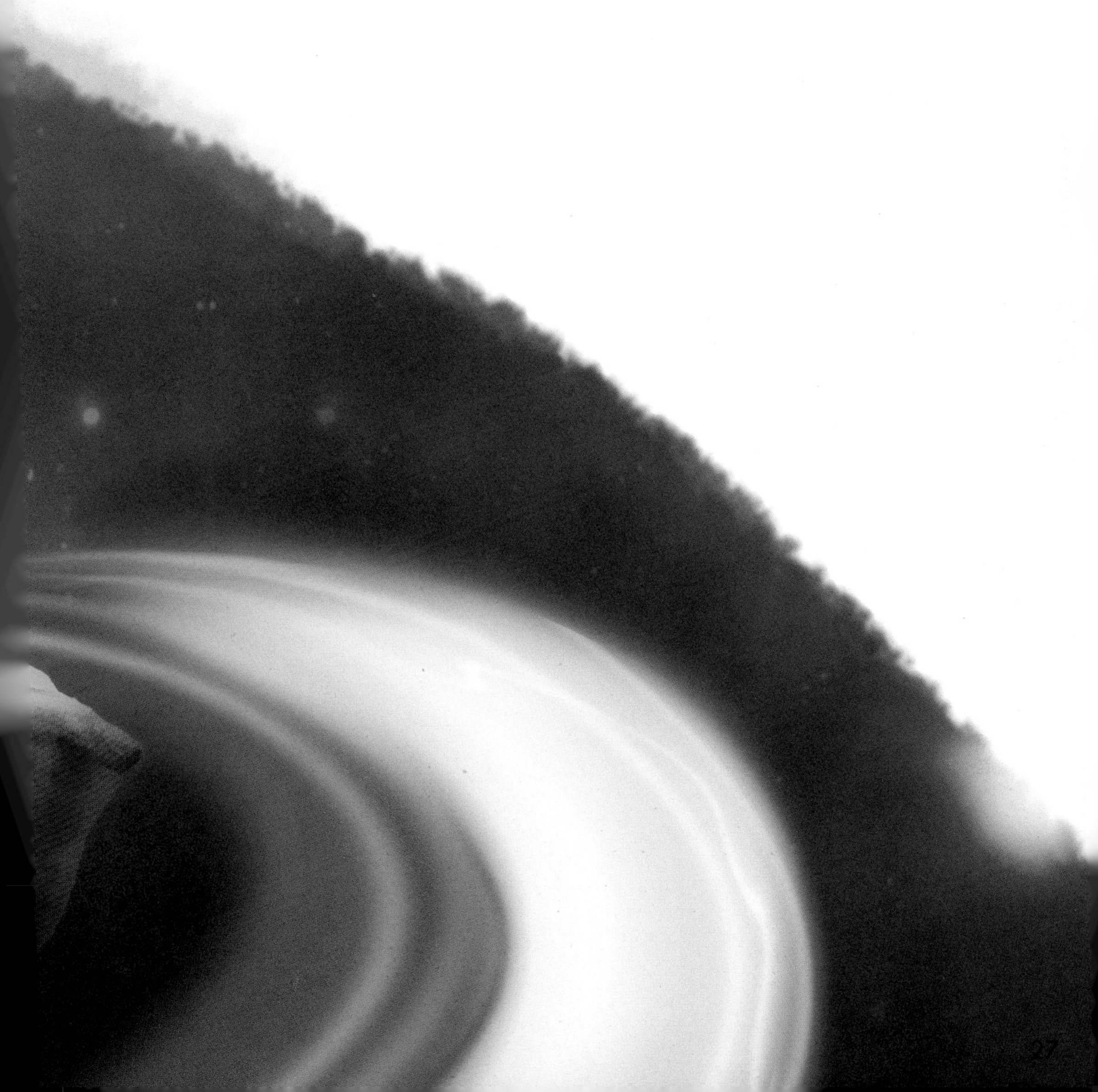

The bravest, **strongest** warrior in all of *Asgard* was named Thor. No monster could withstand his **might**!

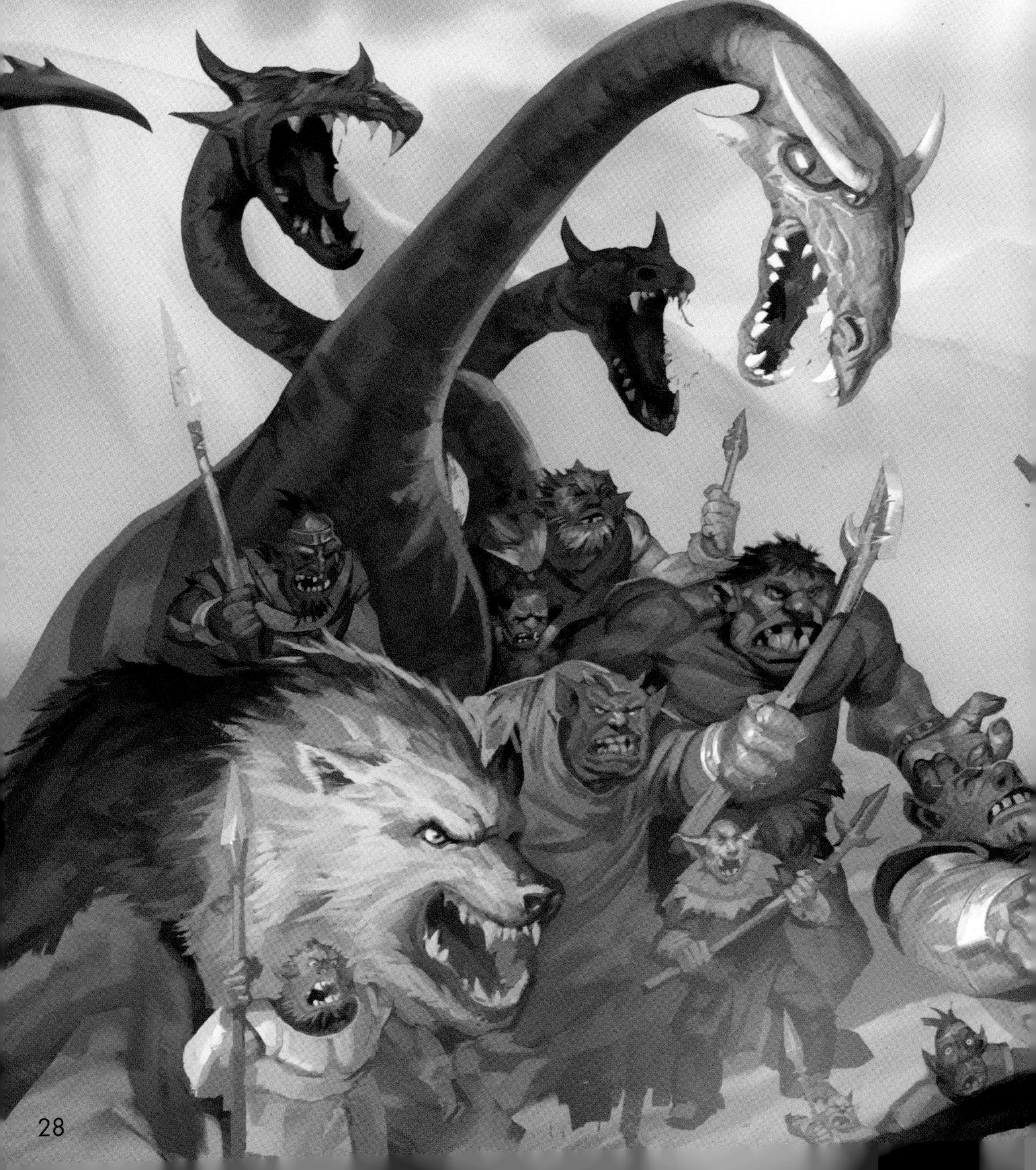

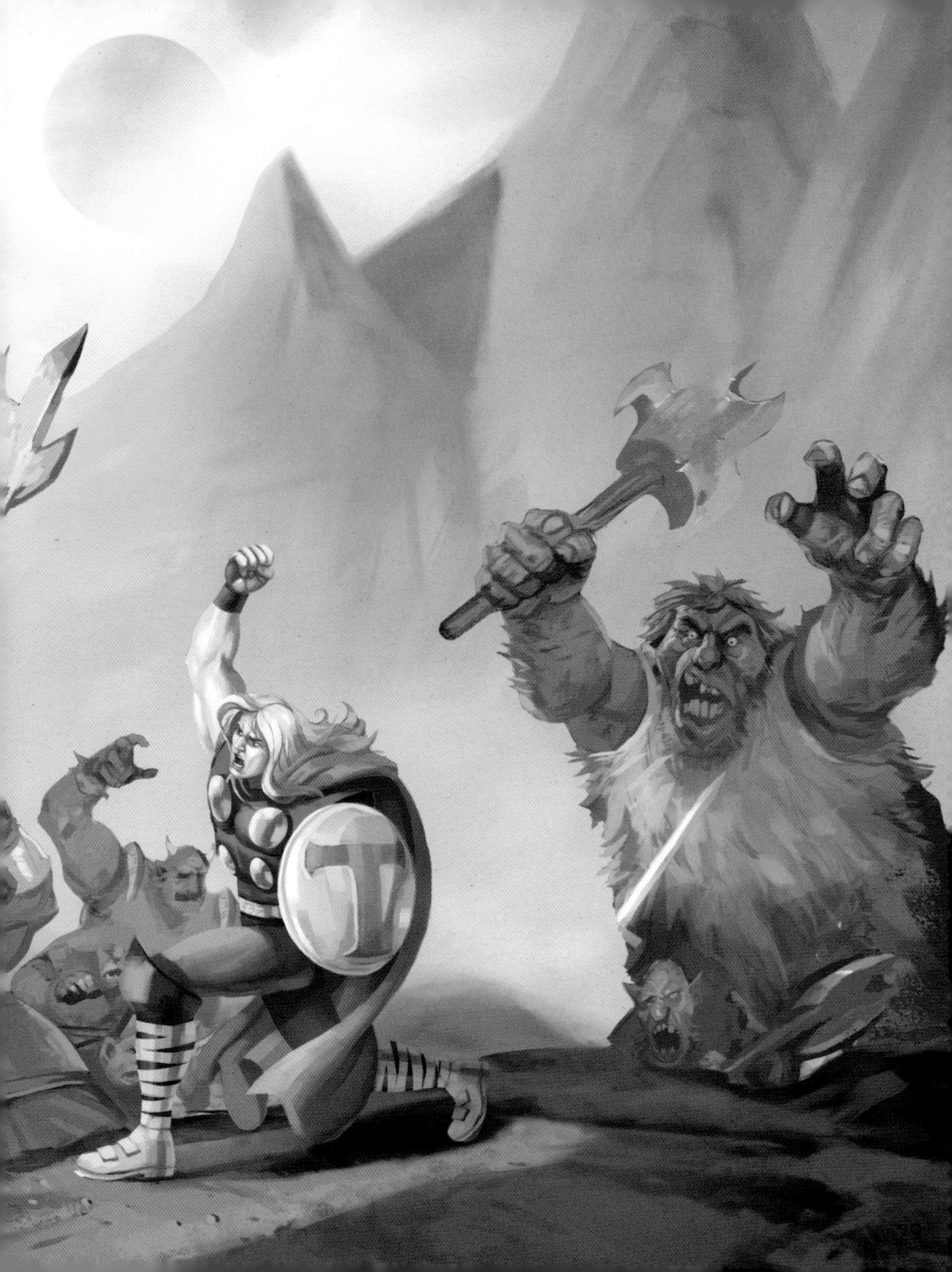

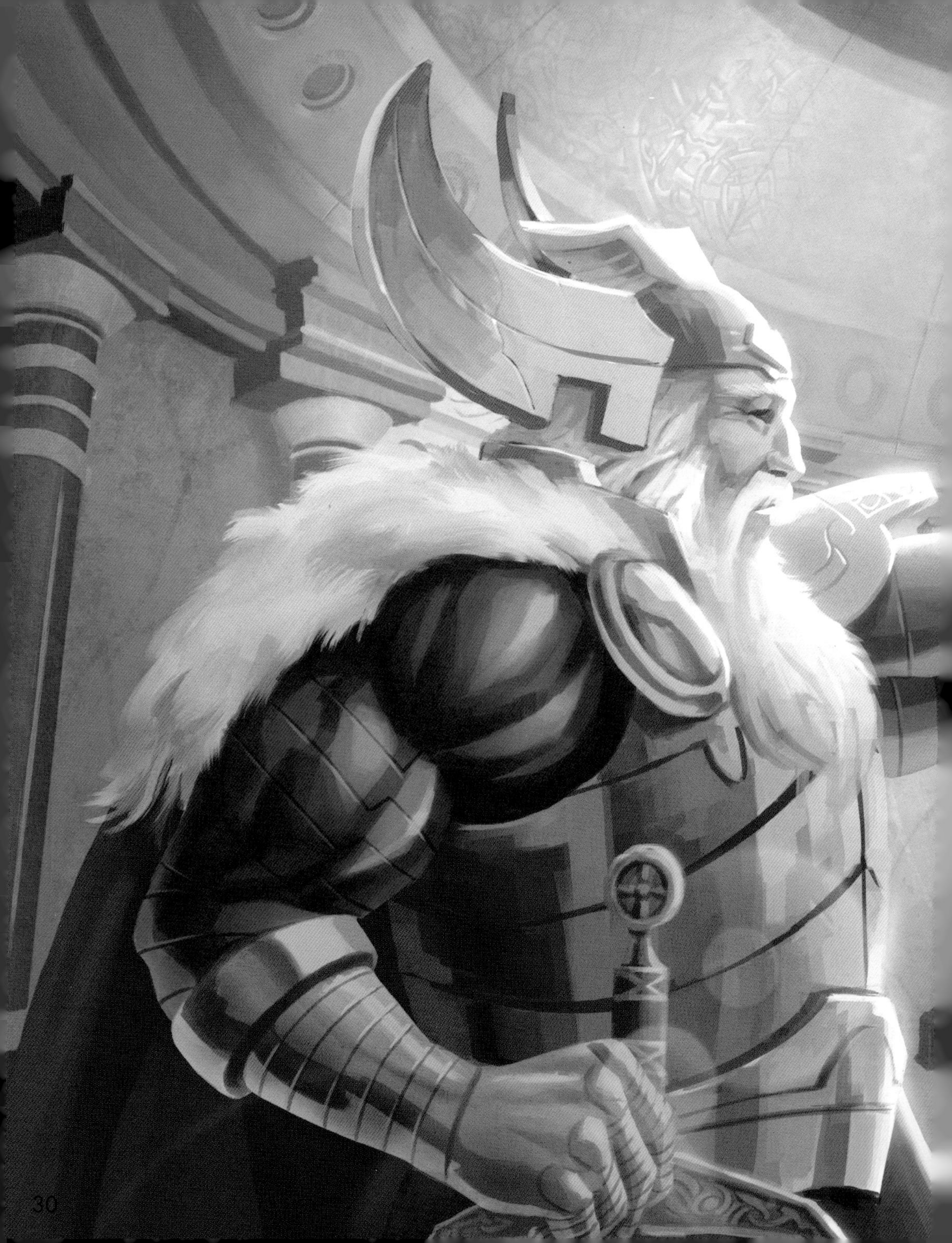

Thor's father, Odin, was the king of Asgard! Odin was proud of his brave son.

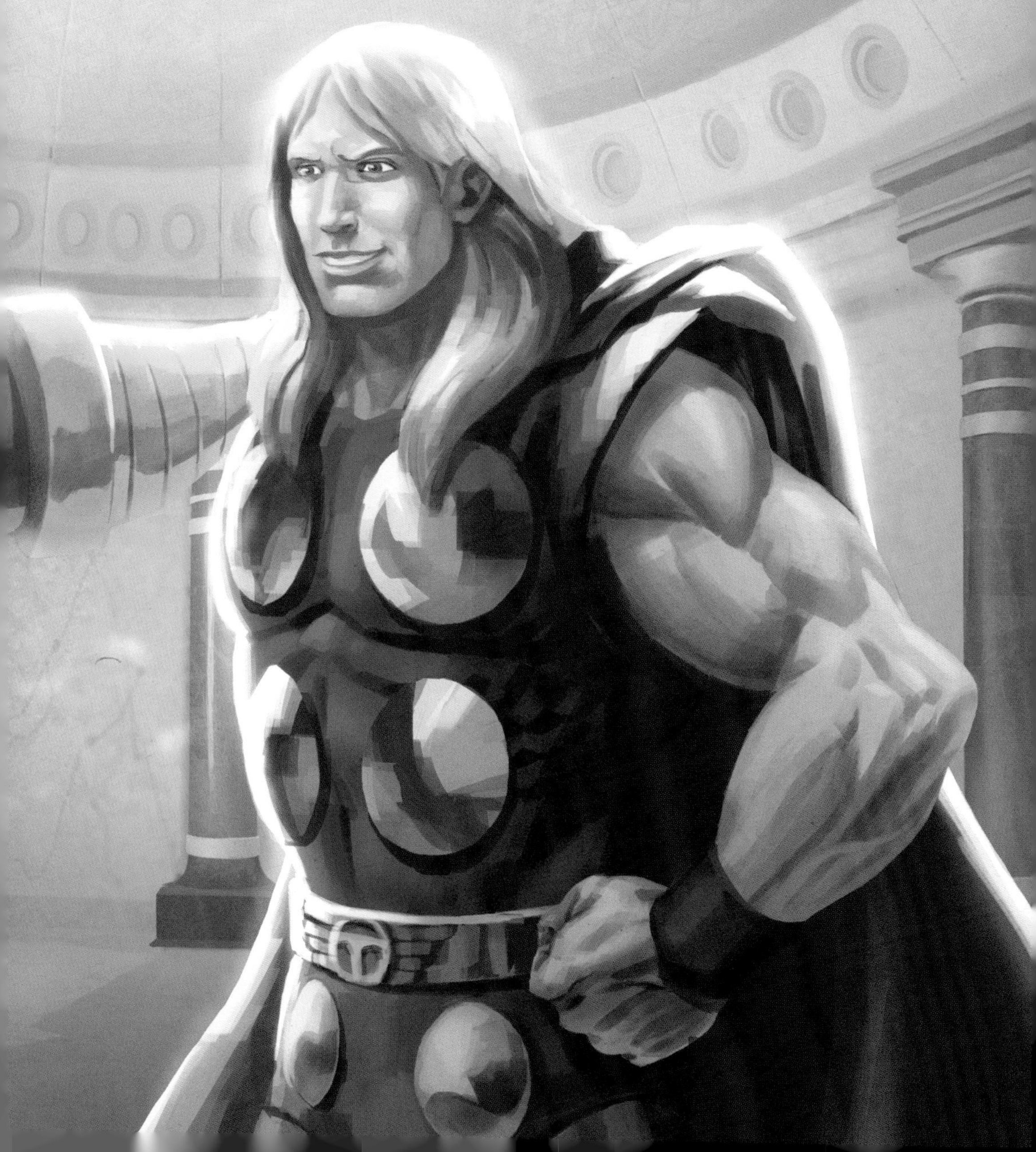

Odin showed Thor the most **powerful** weapon in the land . . .

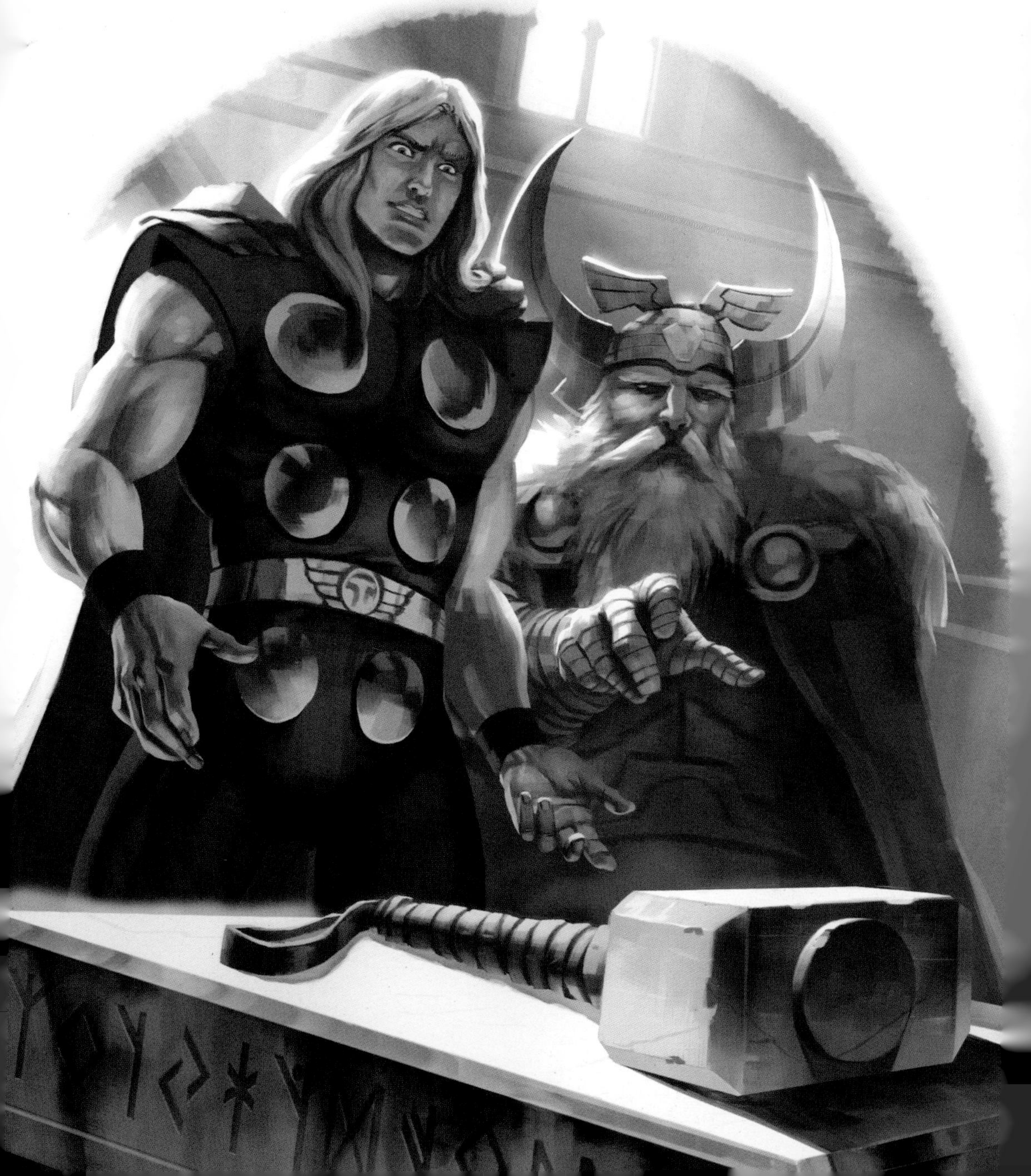

a magical hammer called Mjolnir (pronounced *mee-ALL-neer*).

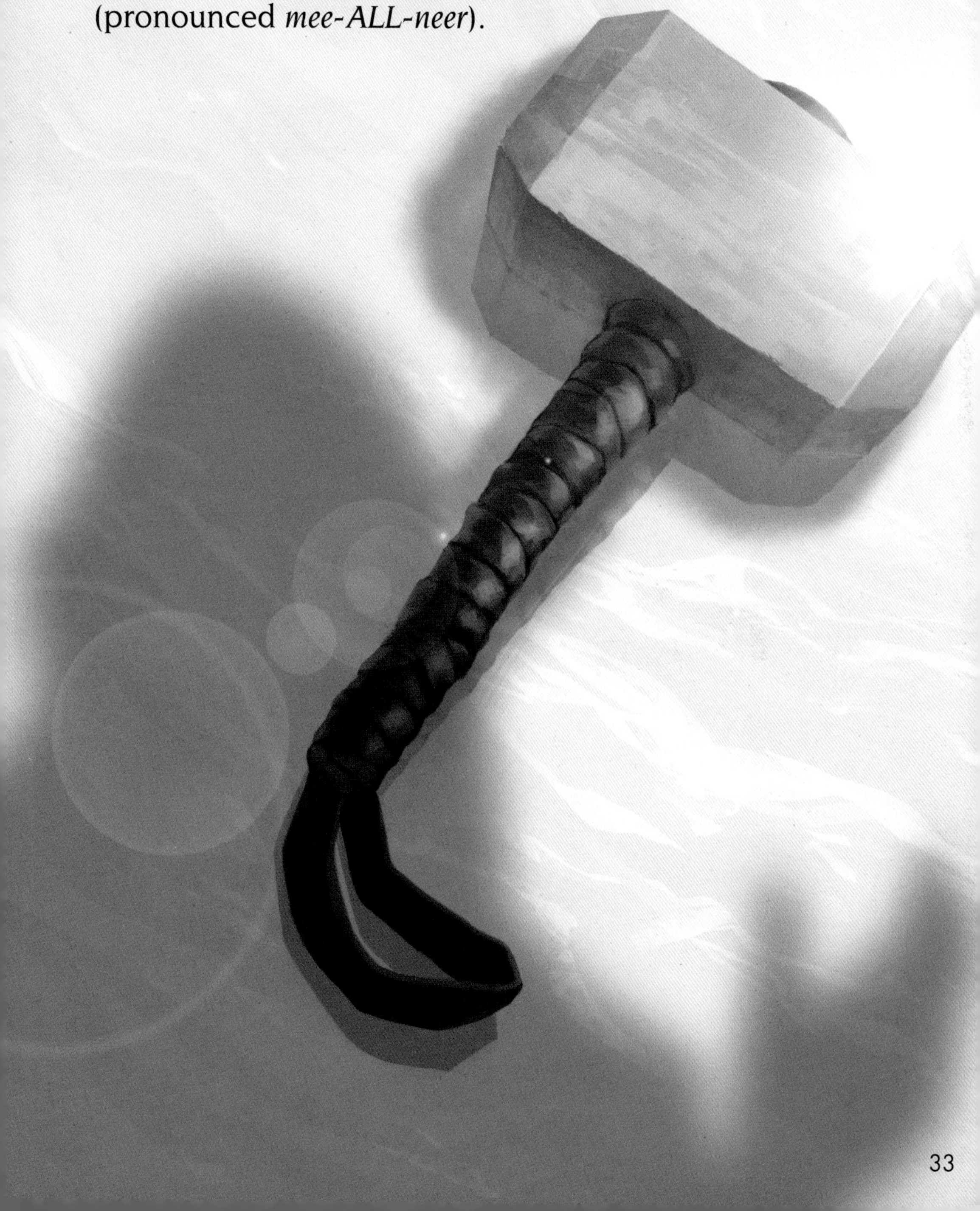

Thor tried to lift the hammer. But even with his great **strength**, he could not!

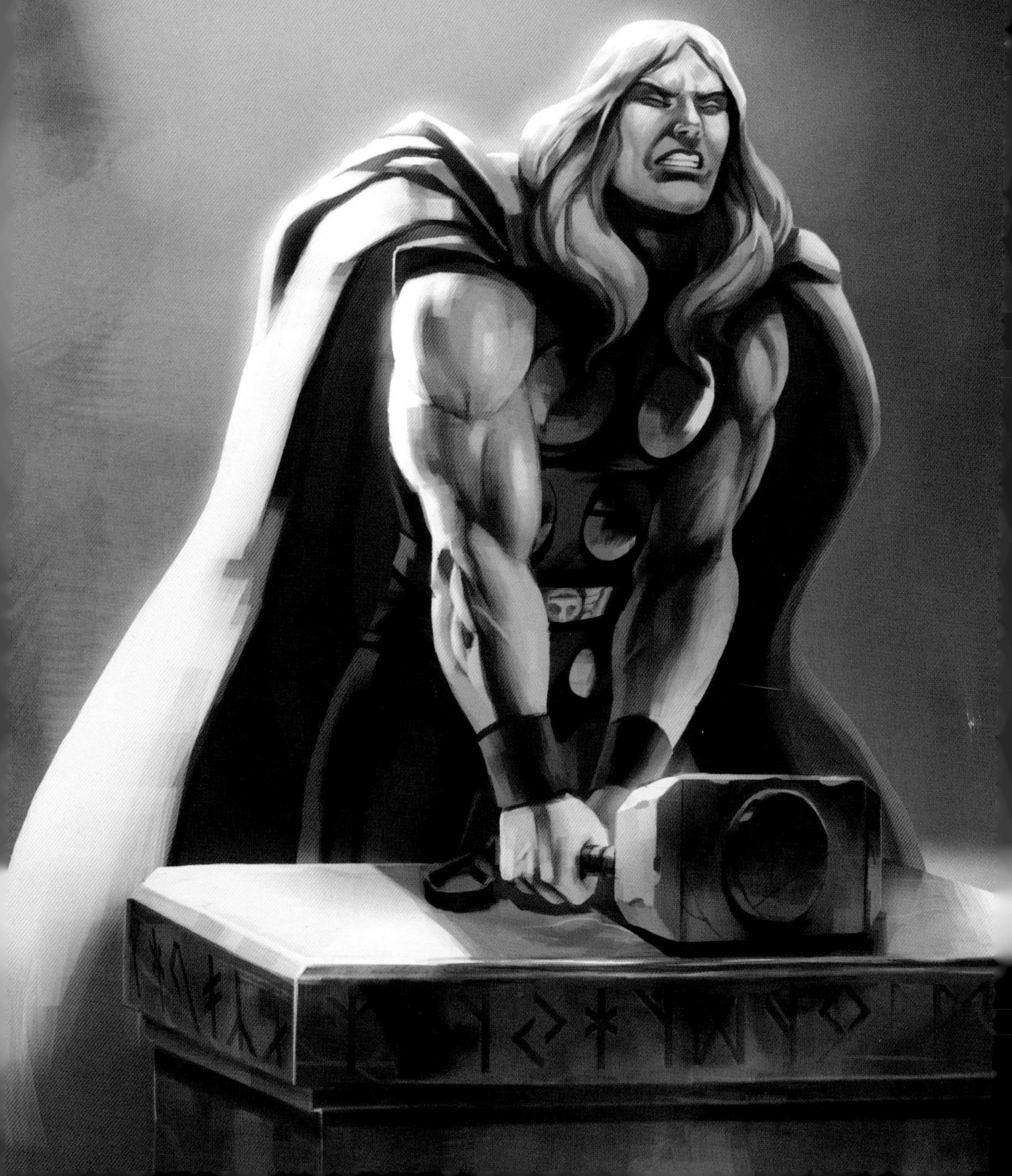

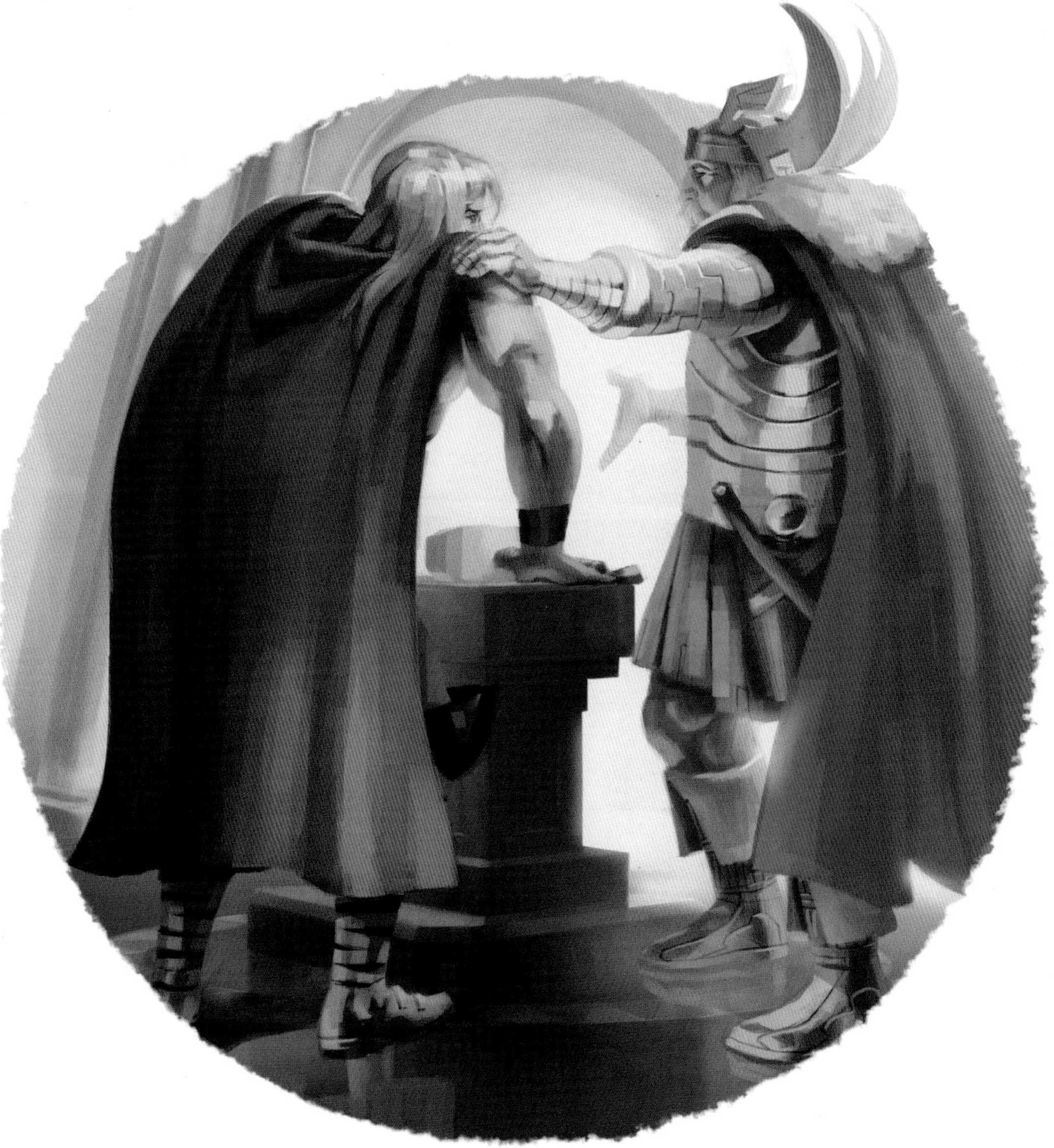

Odin told Thor that only a truly **valiant** warrior could lift the hammer.

Thor vowed to become
a hero worthy of the
mighty hammer.

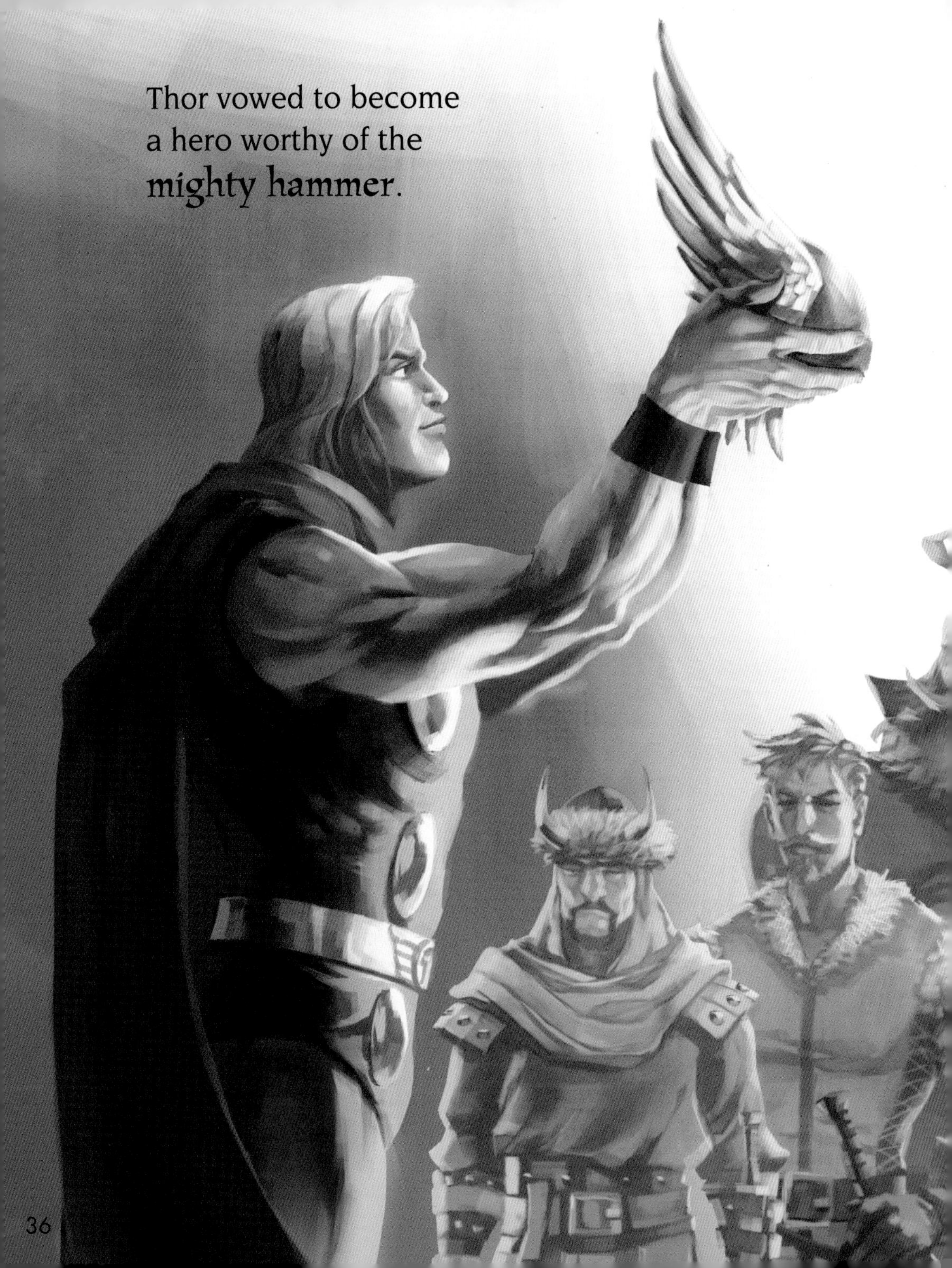

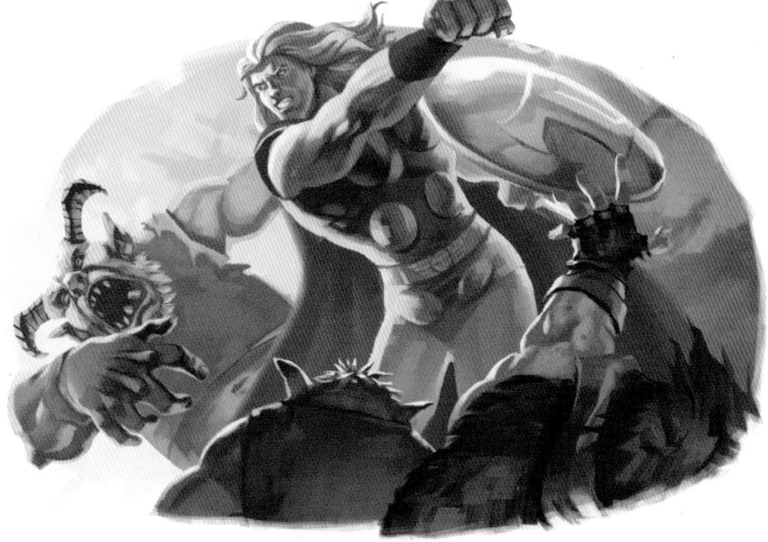

Thor fought many **powerful** foes . . .

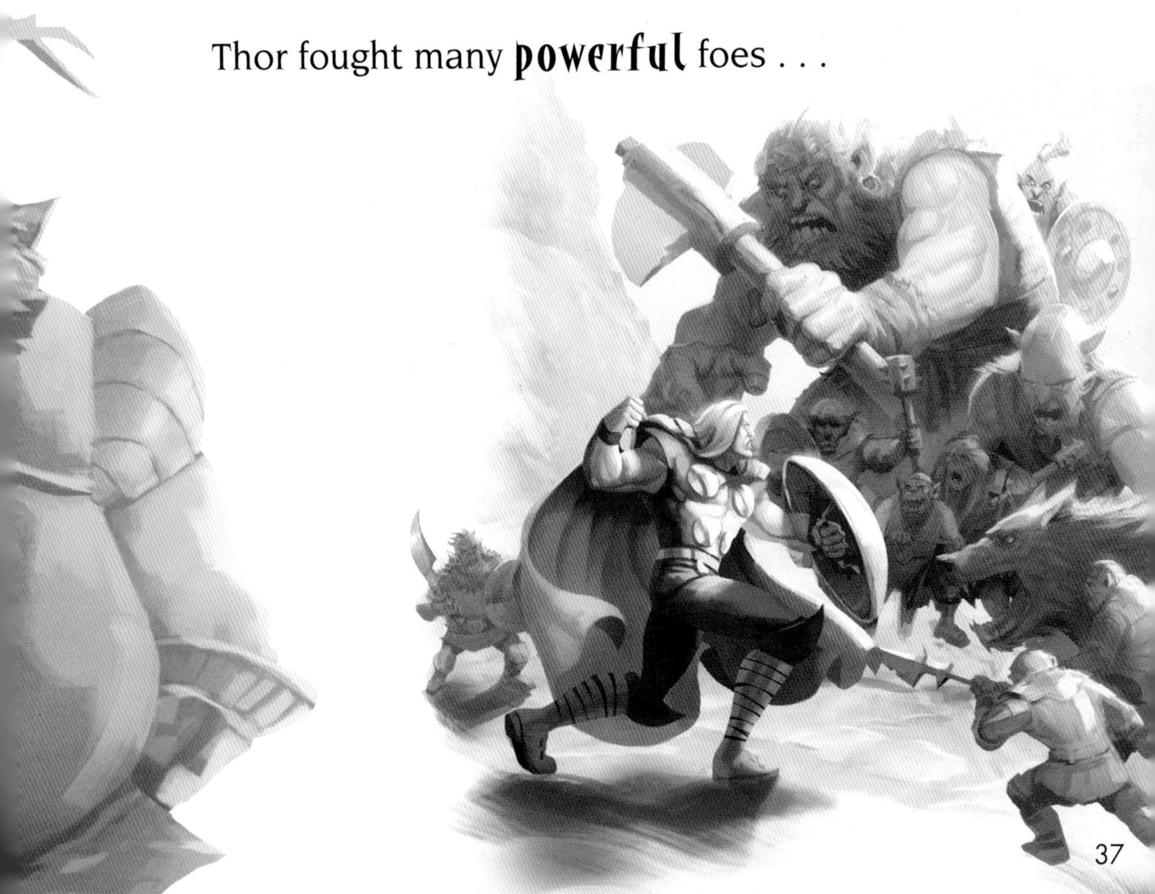

. . . and he was **VICTORIOUS** in every battle.

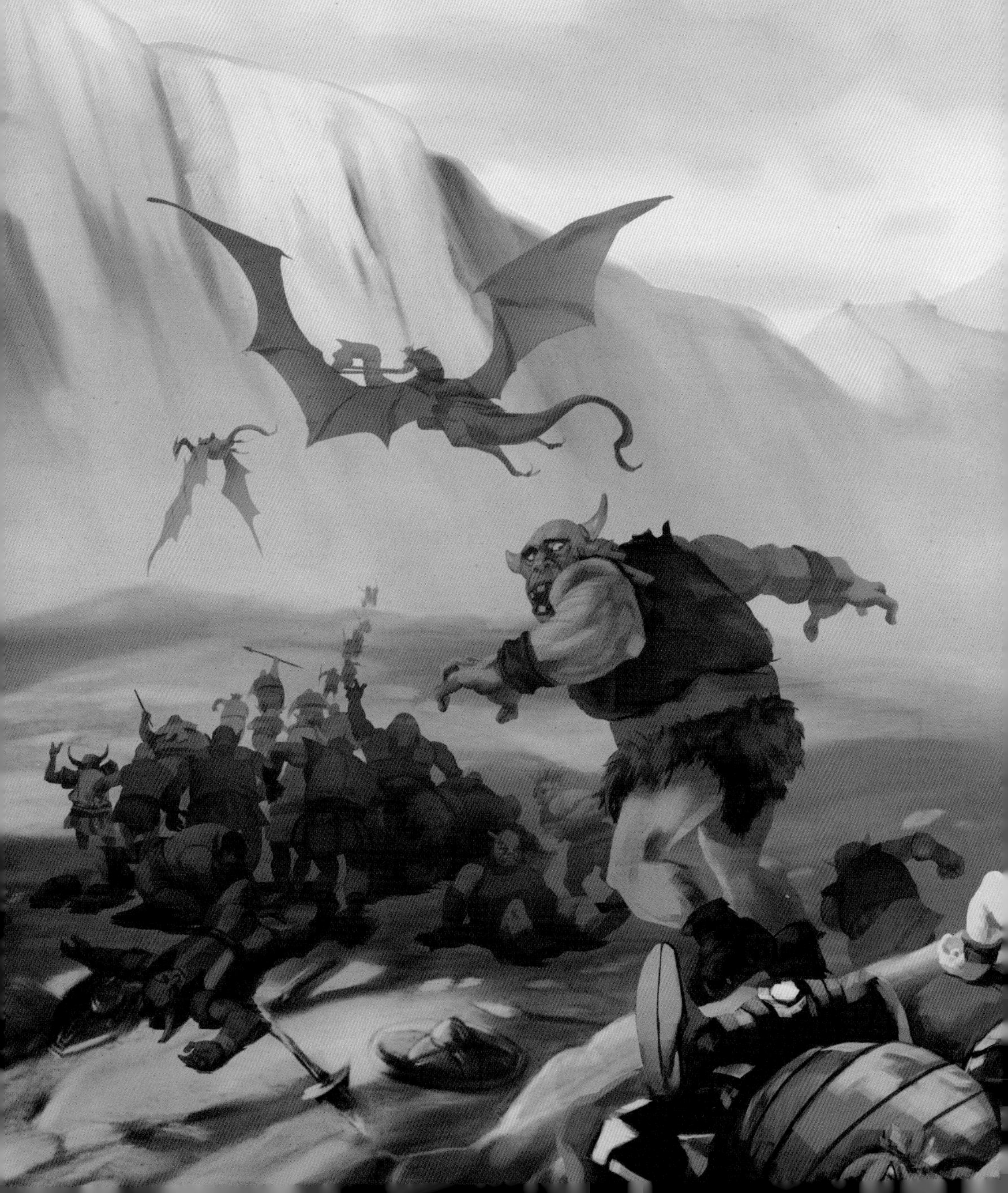

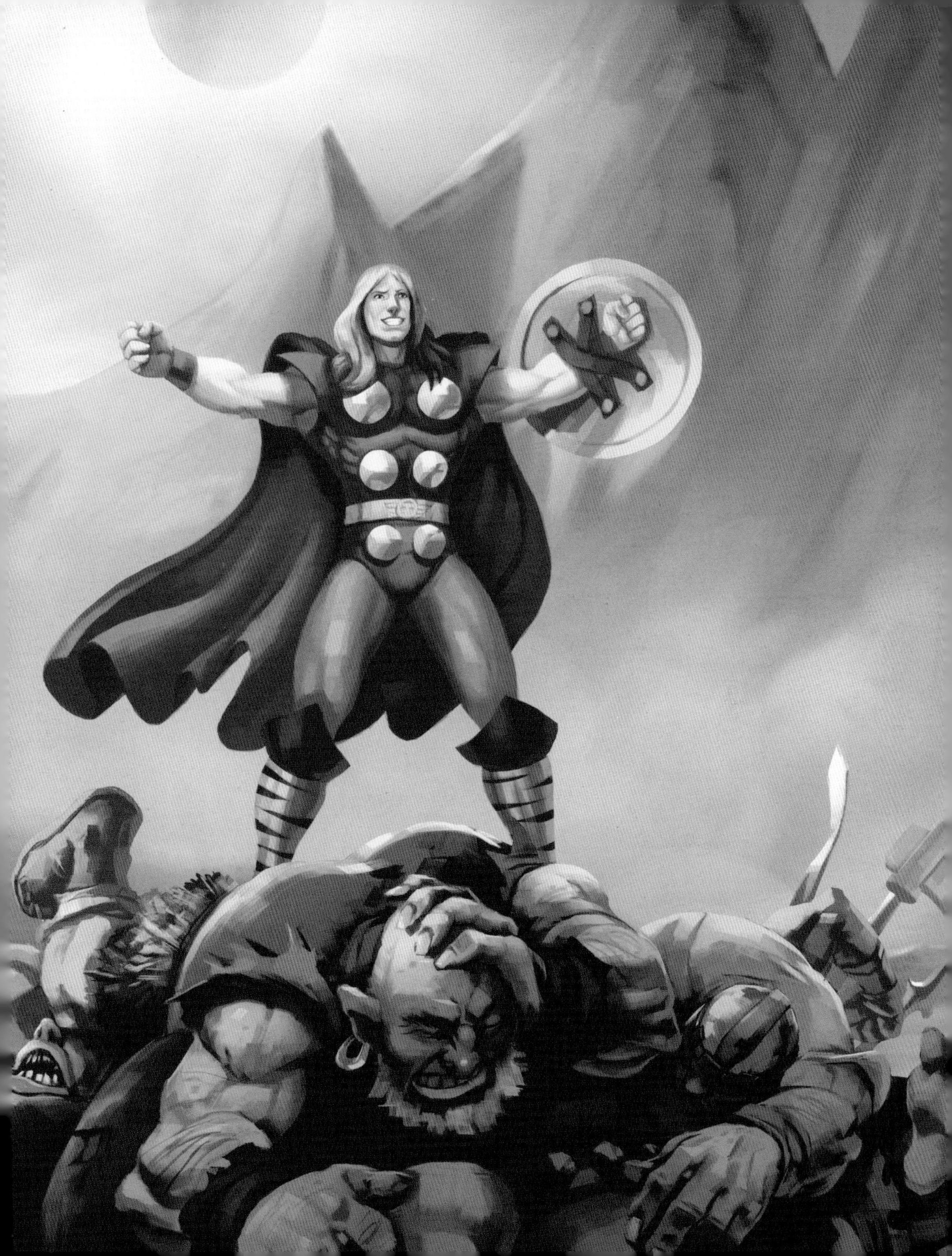

He even fought a *dragon*.

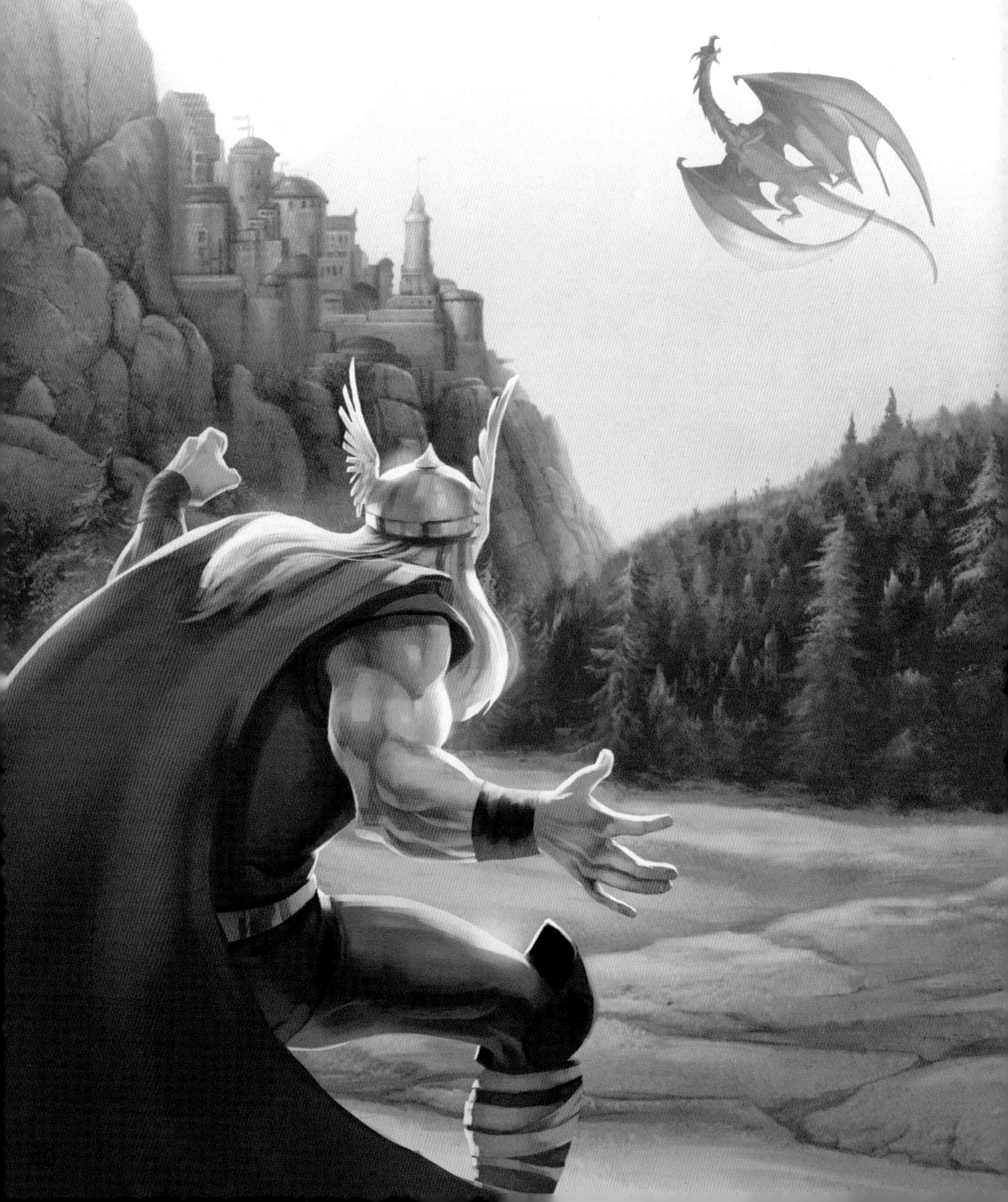

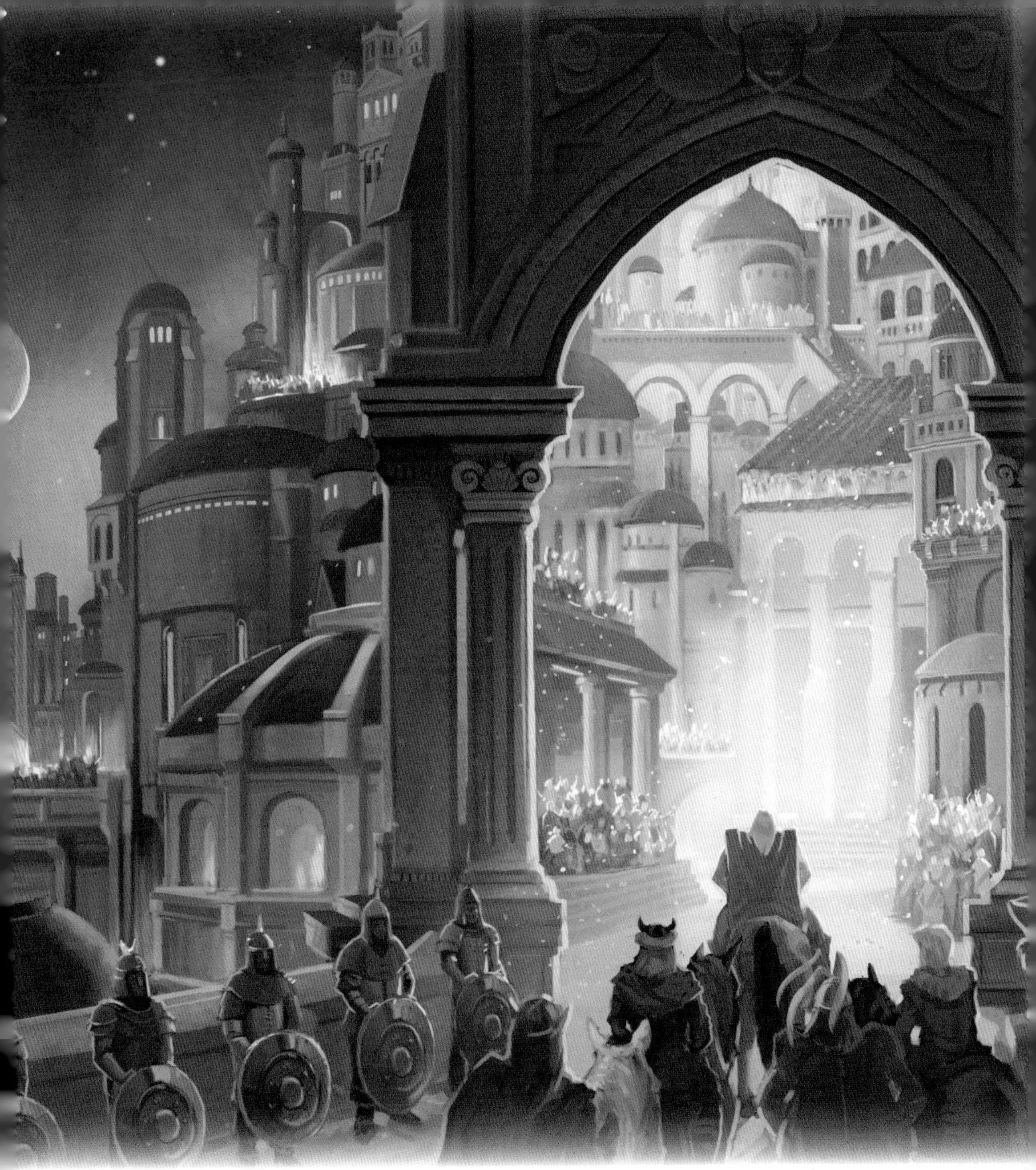

After many adventures, Thor felt he was a worthy **warrior**.

Thor went to Odin's palace and told his father that he was ready to try to lift **Mjolnir** once again.

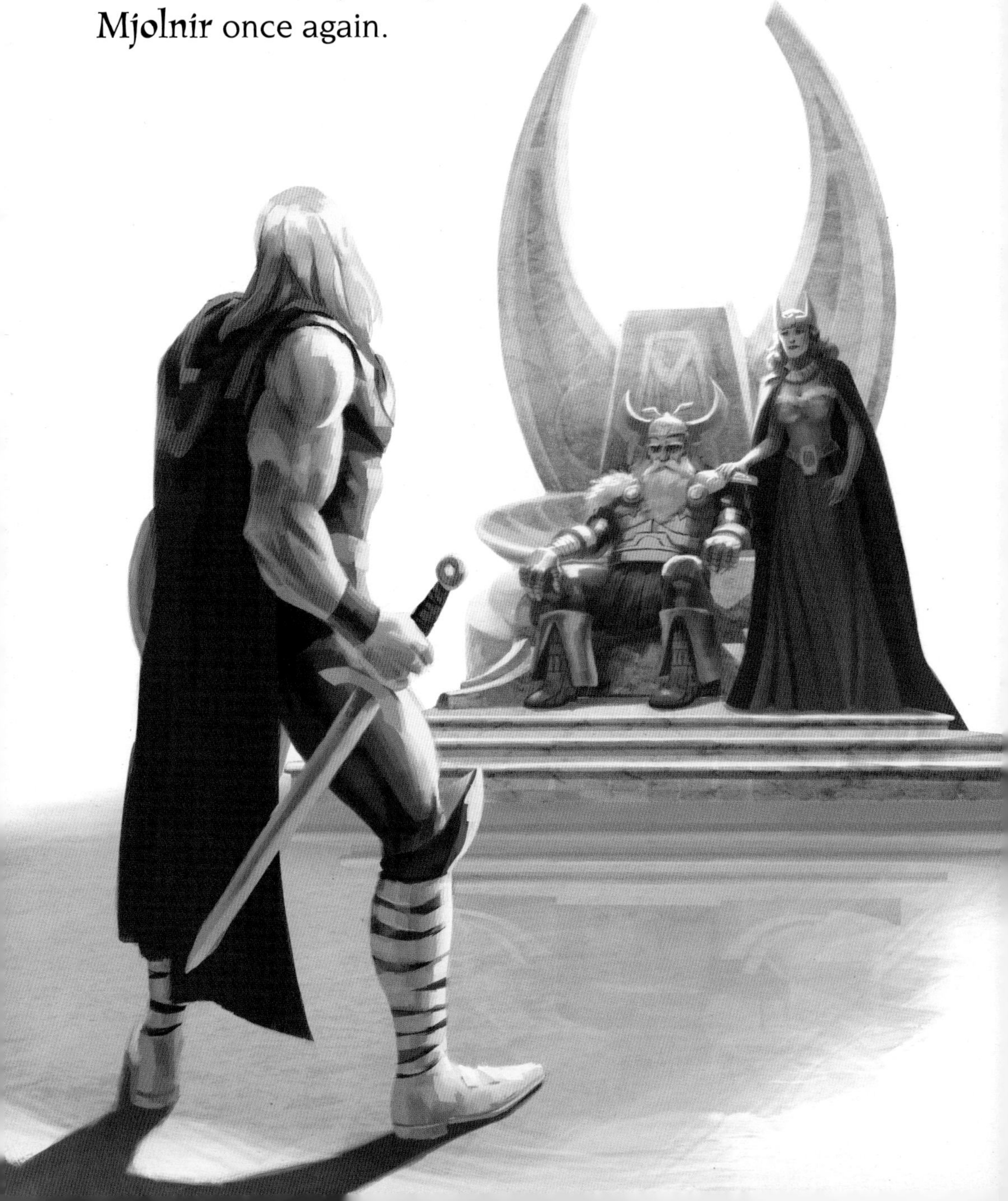

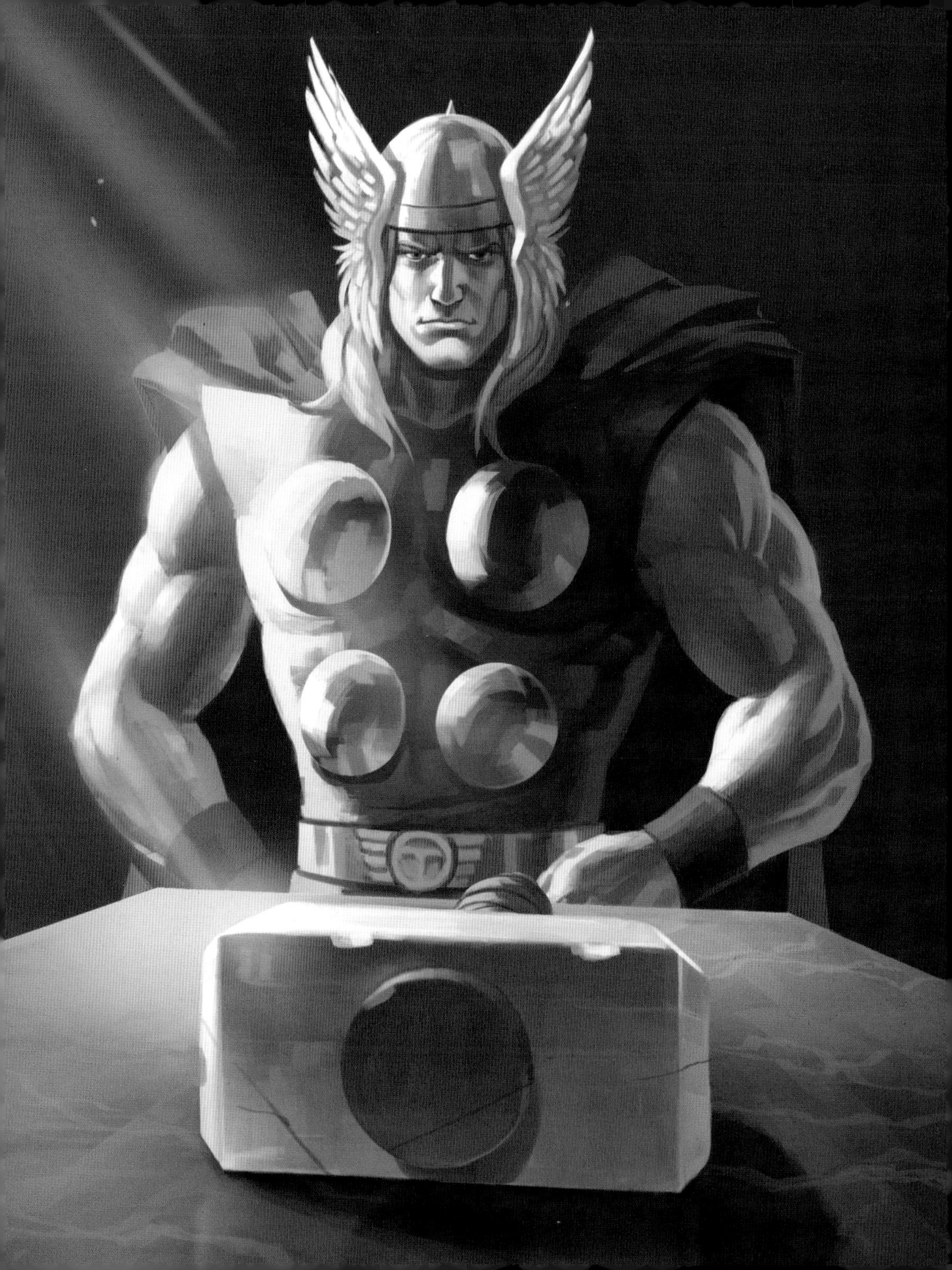

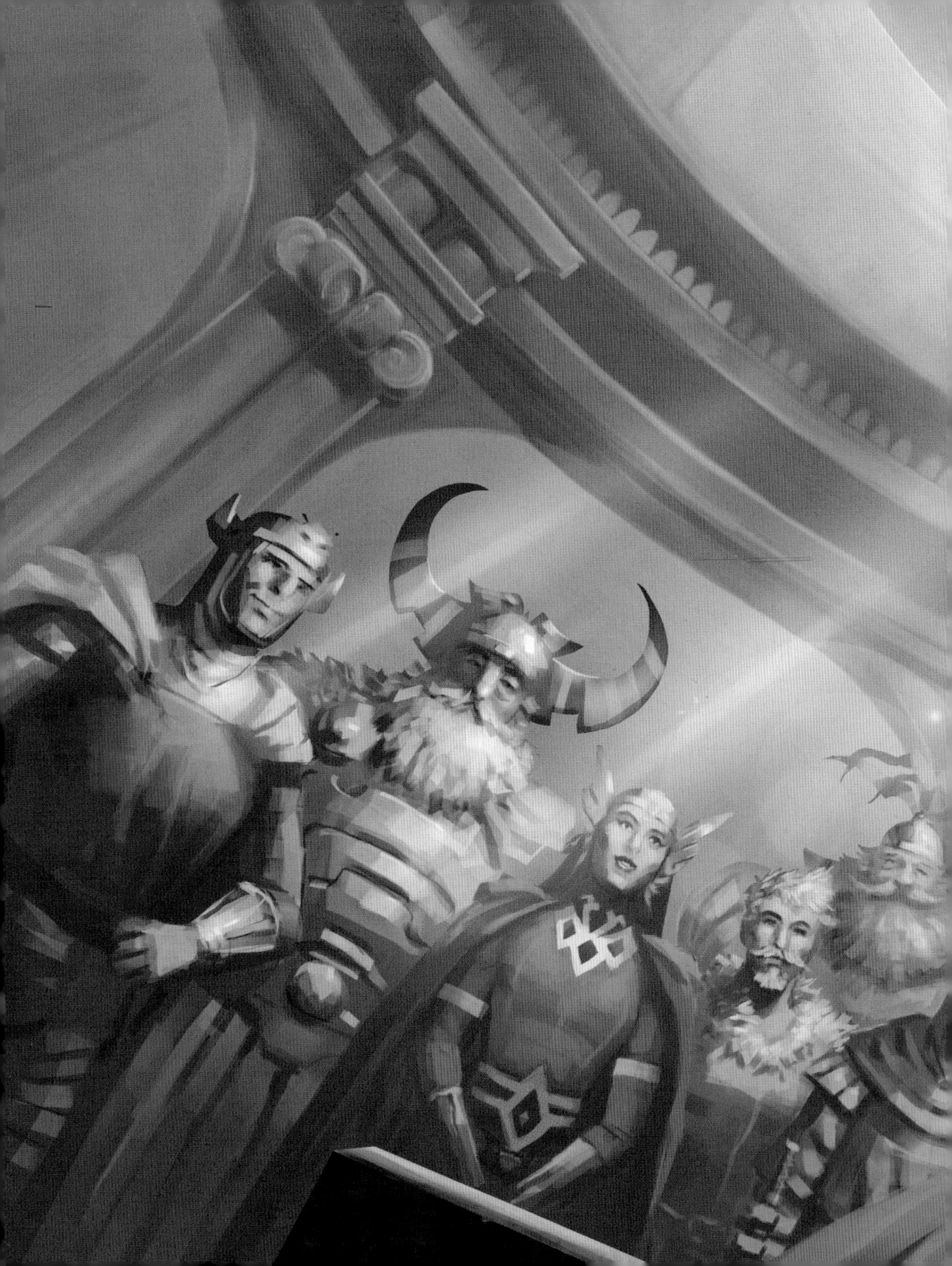

As the people of Asgard watched, Thor lifted the **heavy** hammer into the air. He *was* worthy!

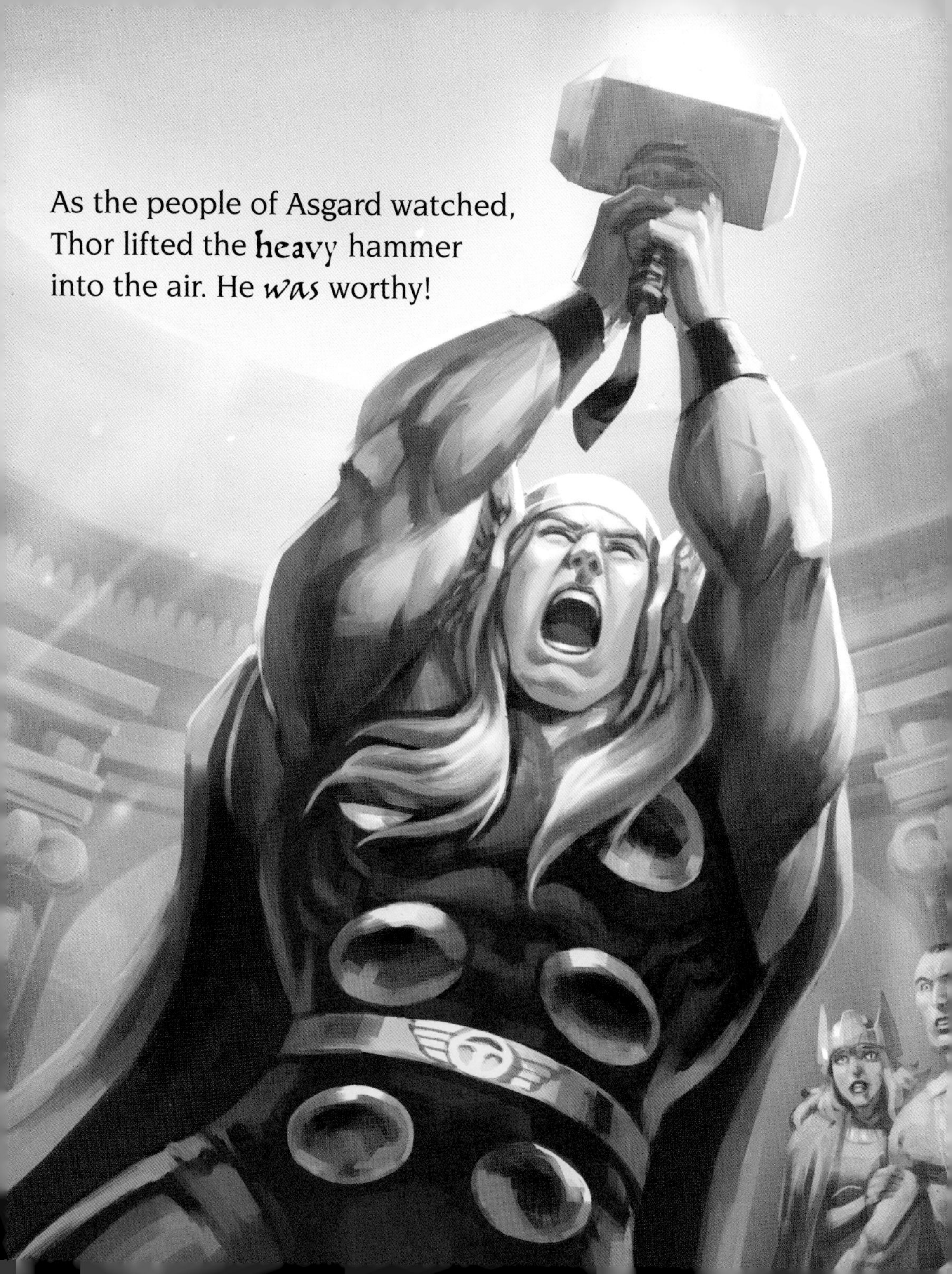

With the magical hammer,
Thor could control
thunder,
lightning,
and **wind**.

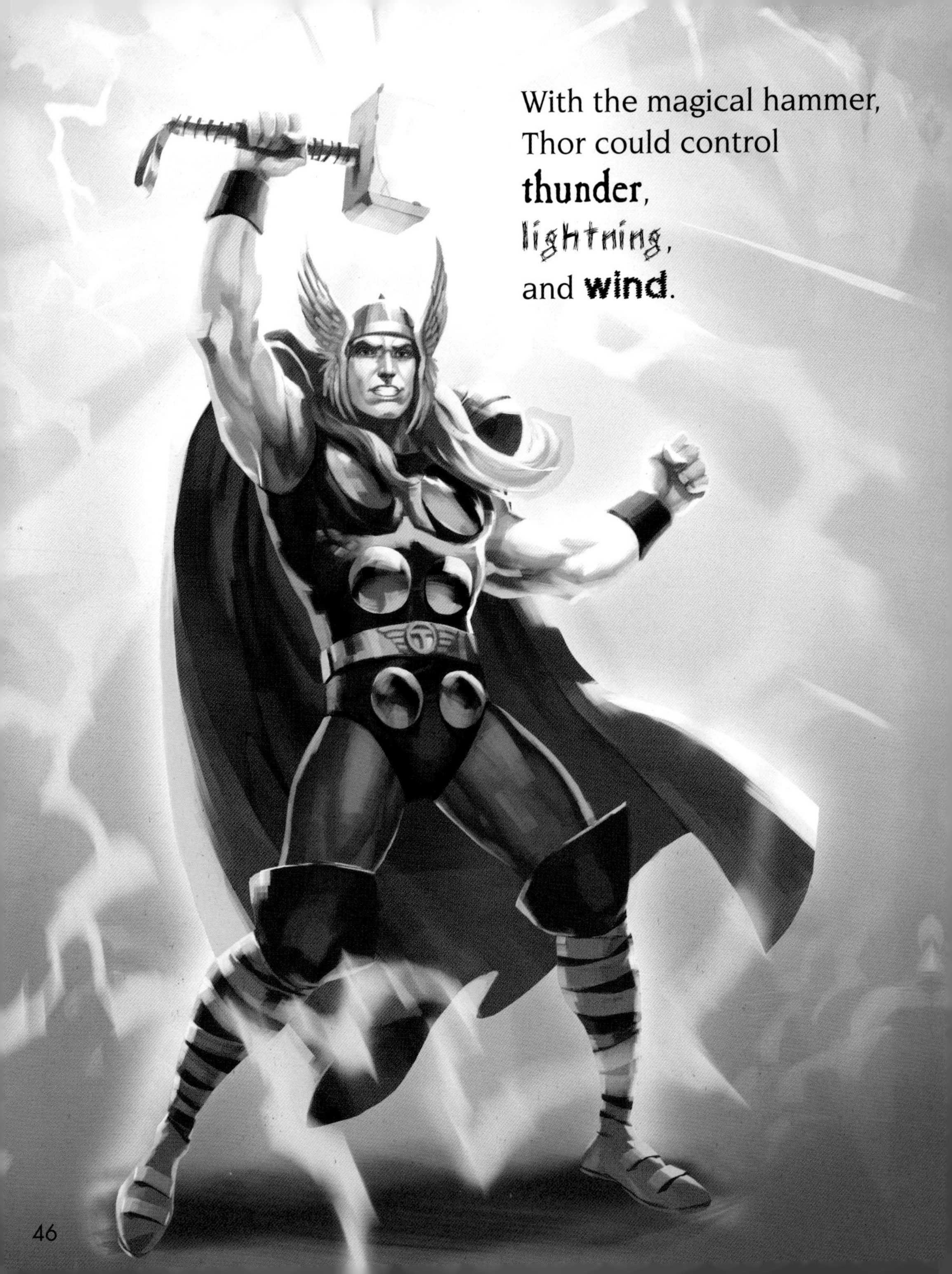

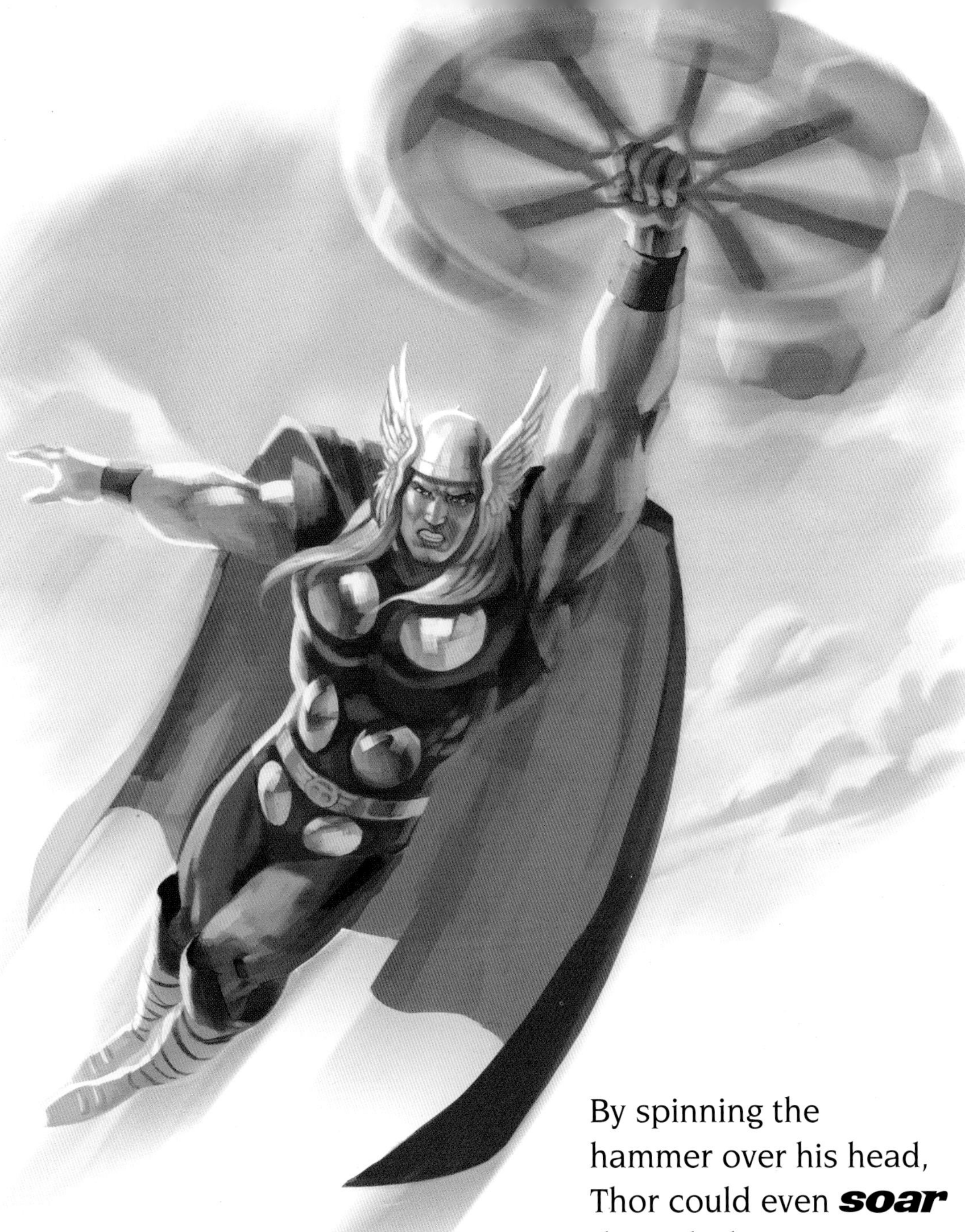

By spinning the
hammer over his head,
Thor could even ***soar***
through the air!

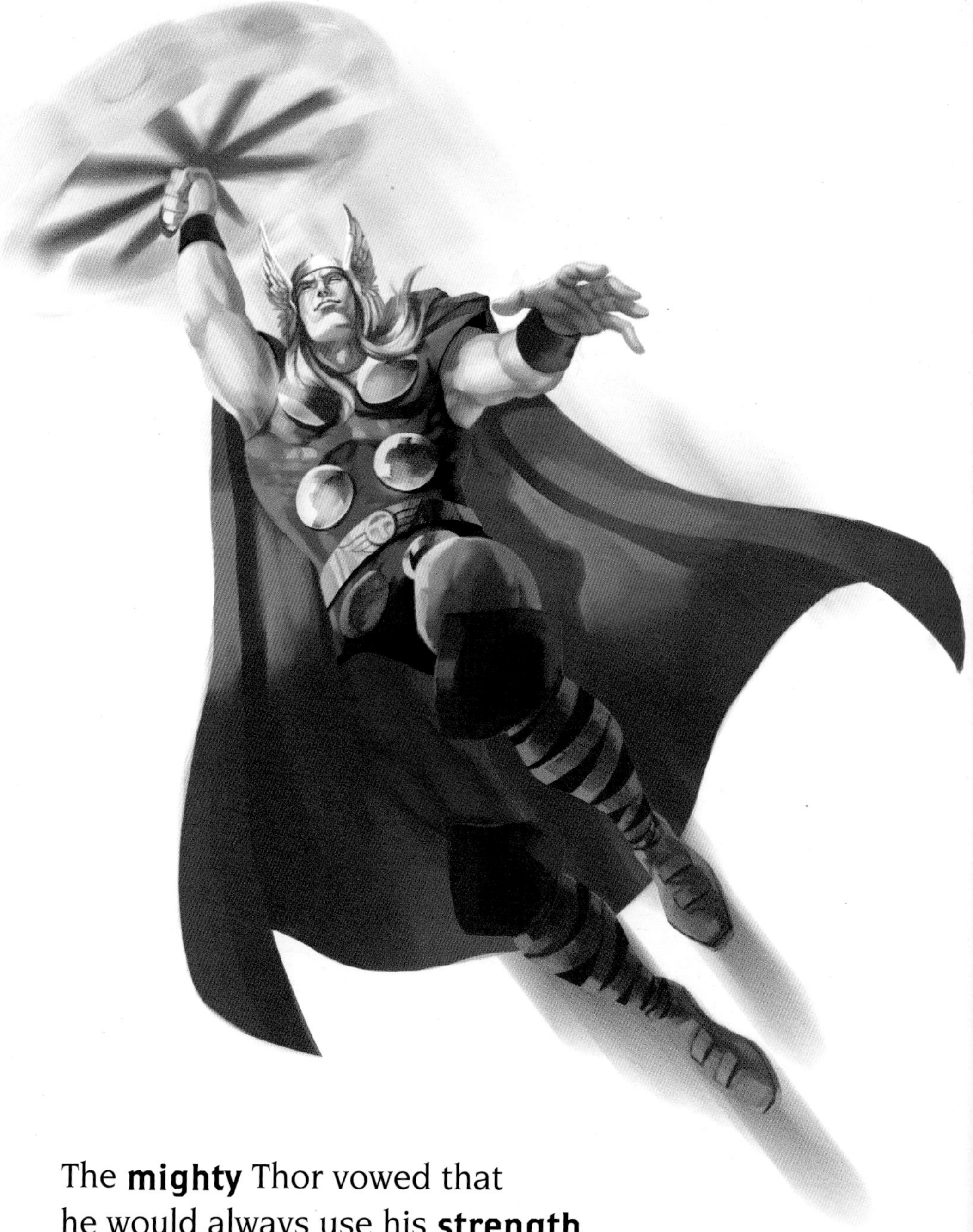

The **mighty** Thor vowed that
he would always use his **strength**
and his **powerful** hammer to fight for good.

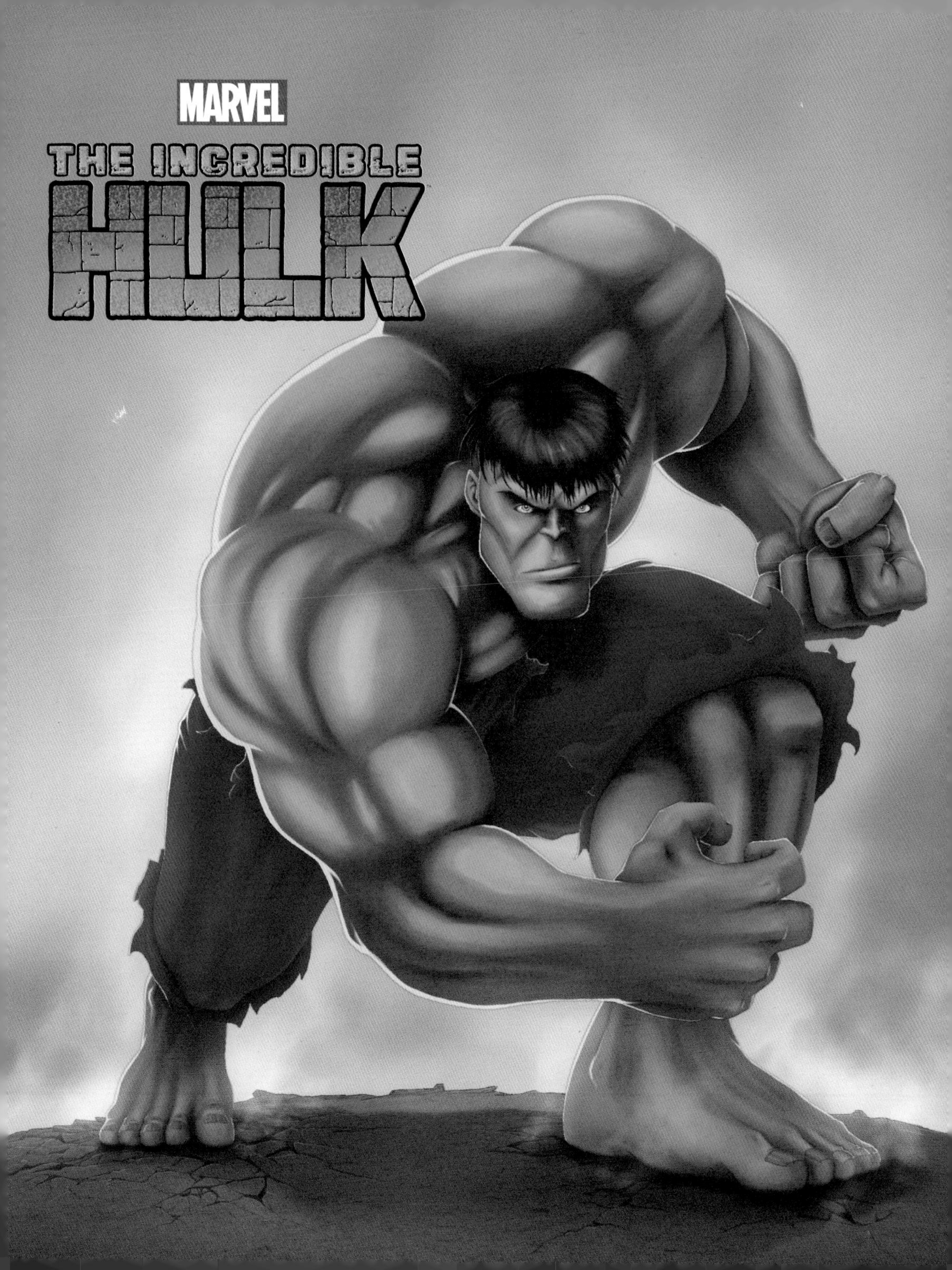
MARVEL
THE INCREDIBLE
HULK

He's huge. He's green. And he's a hero who can smash anything. He's the Incredible **HULK!**

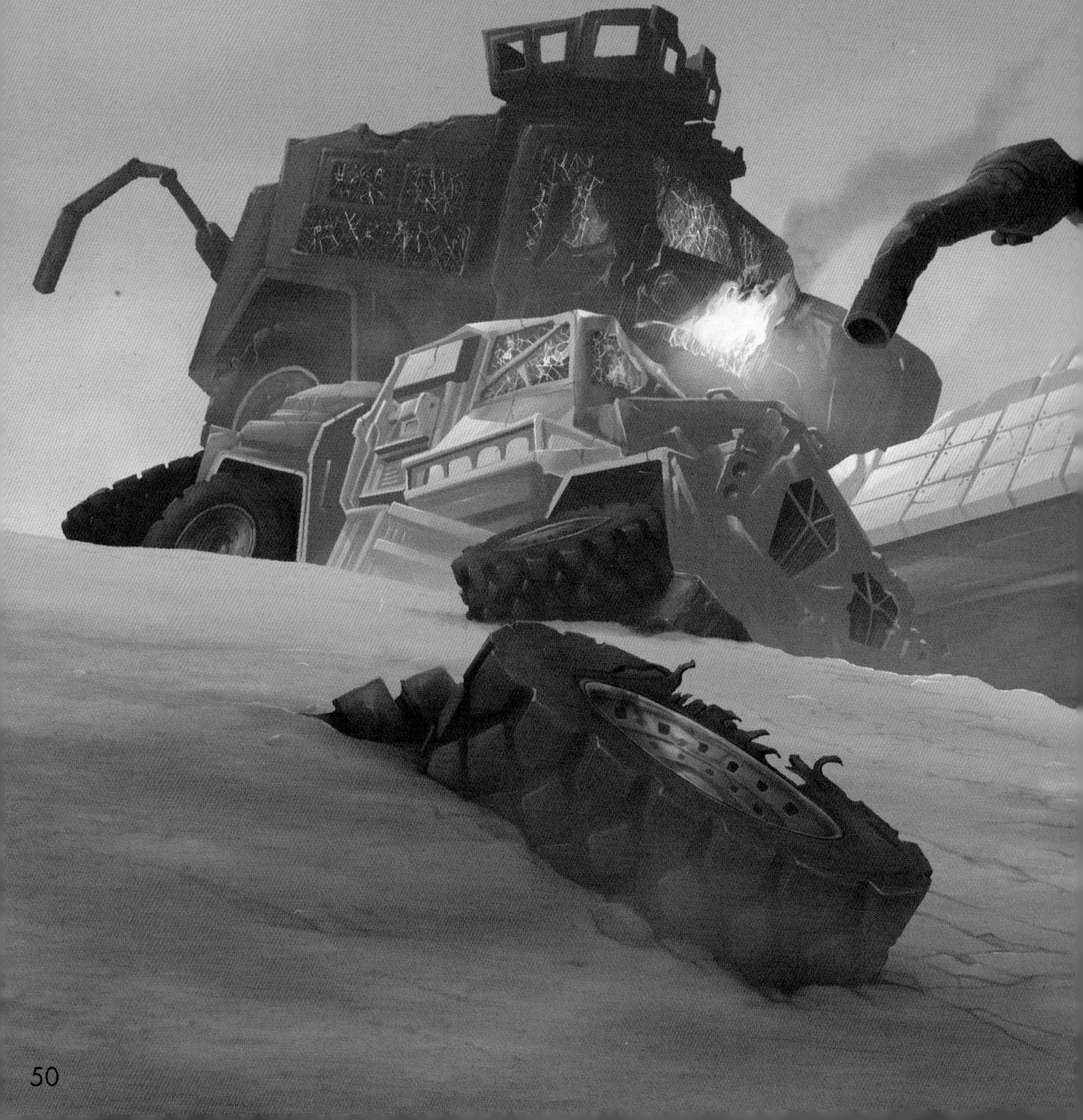

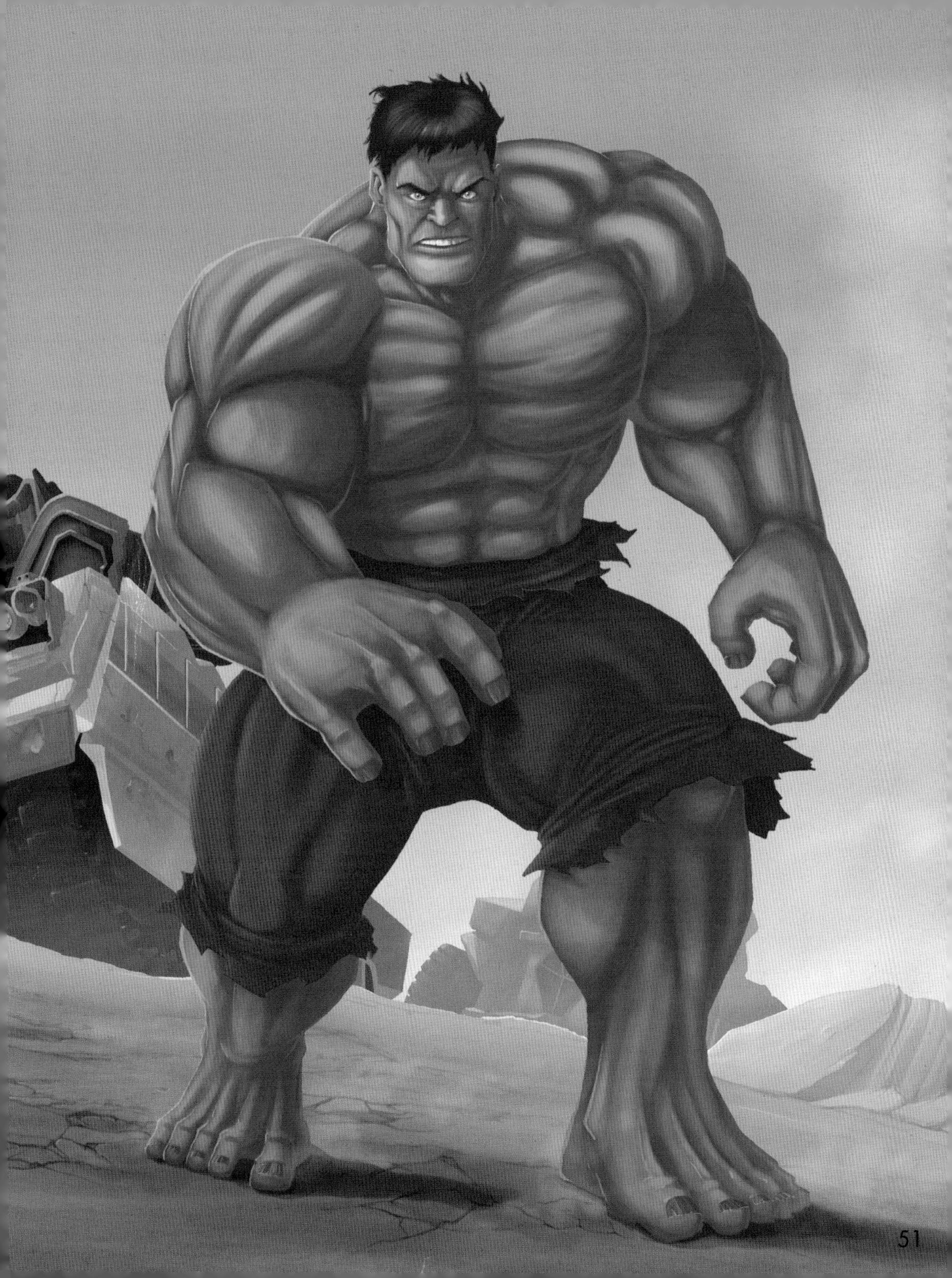

When a scientist named Bruce Banner was accidentally bombarded with gamma rays . . .

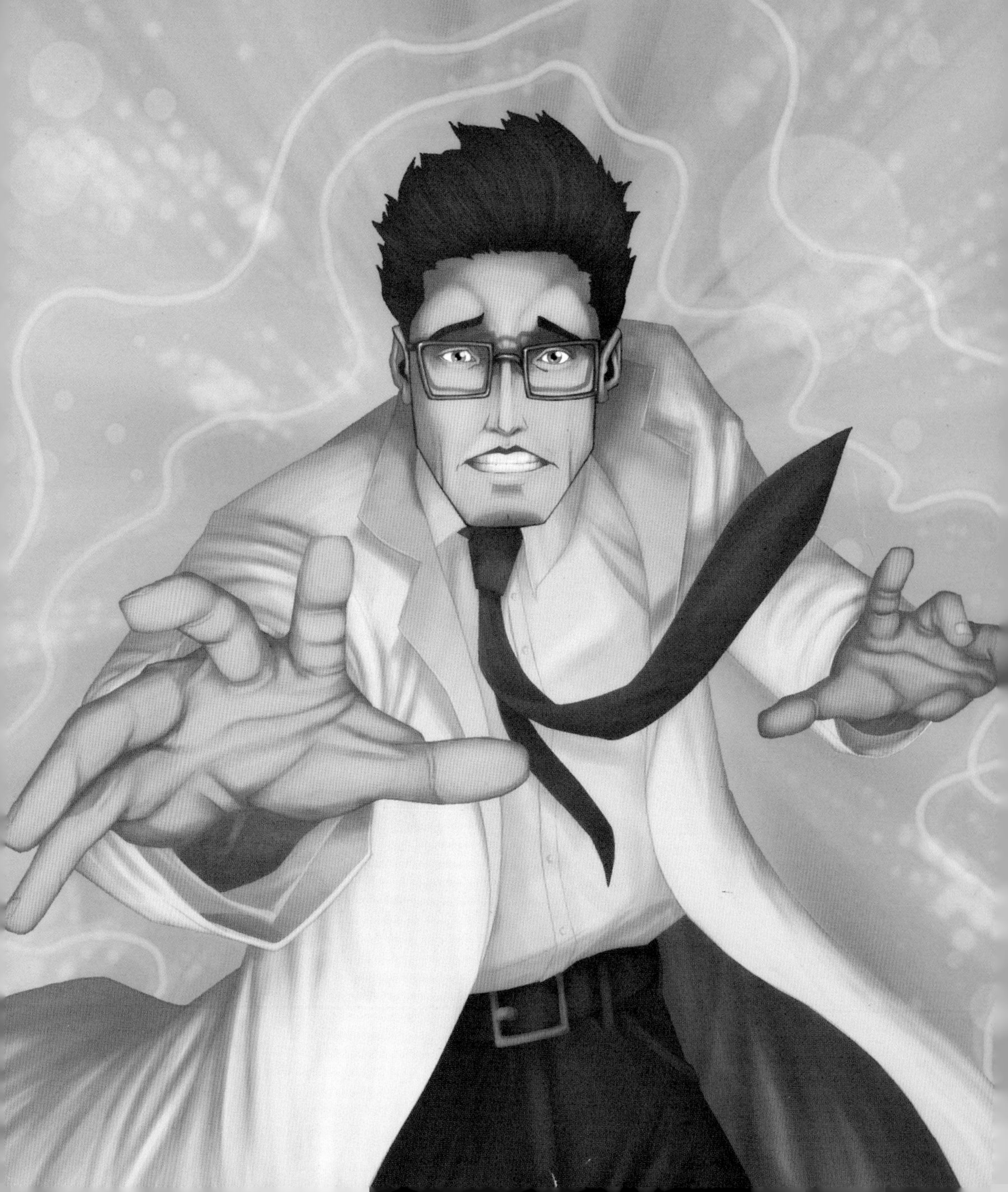

. . . the powerful energy turned him into an incredible green-skinned giant—the Hulk!

ROAR!

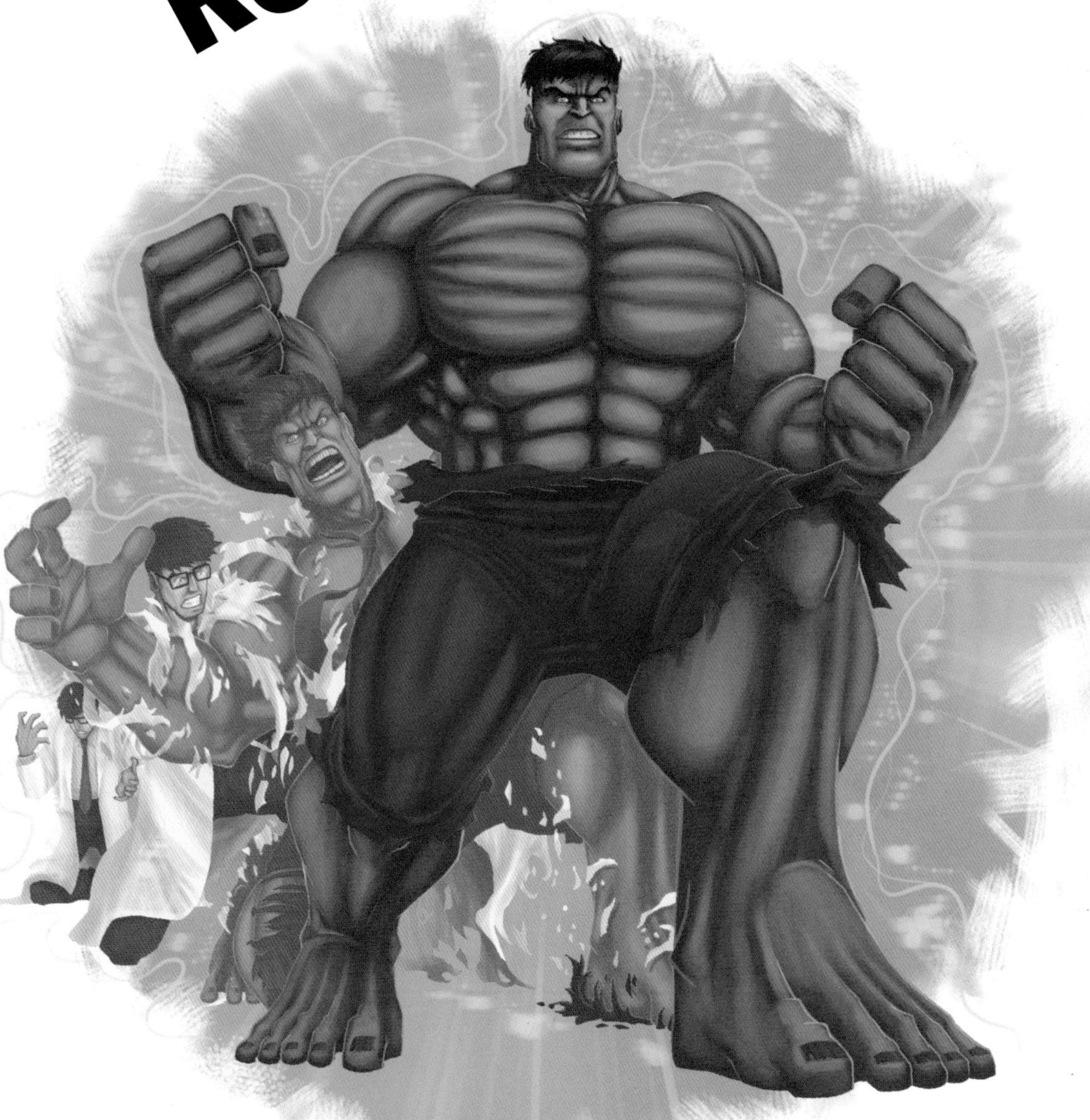

Hulk is super strong, and almost nothing can hurt him.

The madder Hulk gets, the stronger he gets. No enemy is too big for him to tackle!

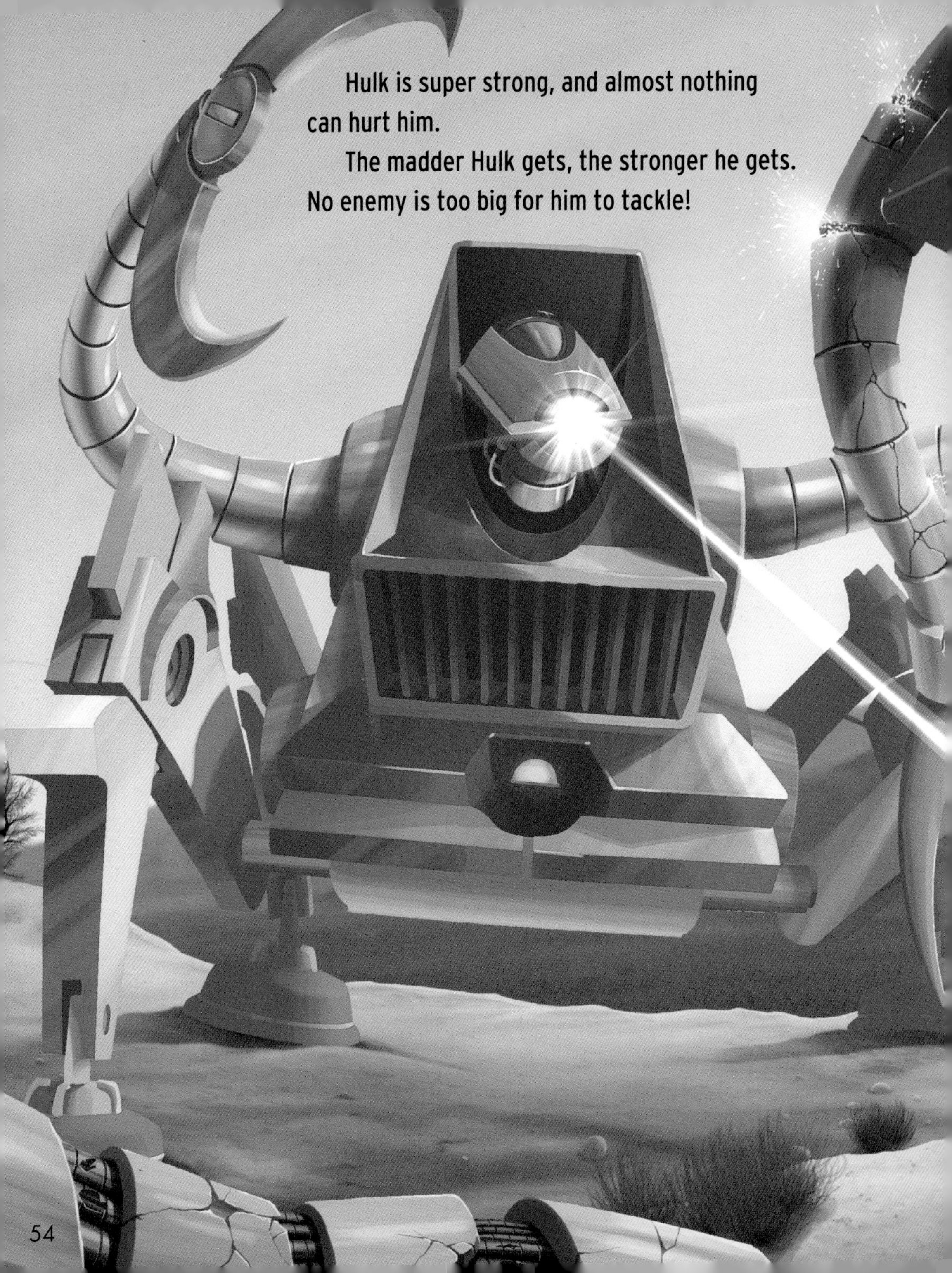

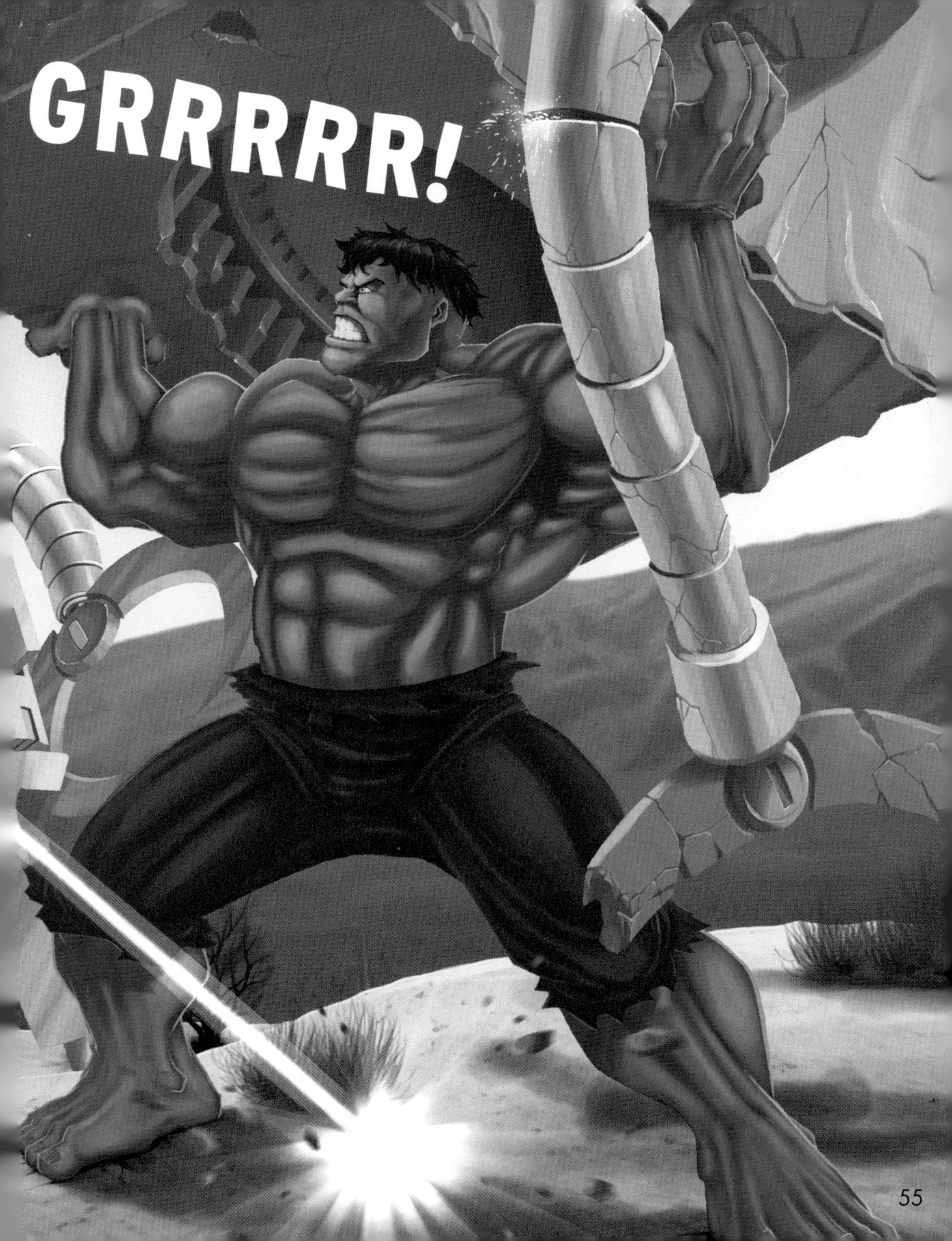
GRRRRRR!

Hulk can leap miles with his mighty leg muscles.

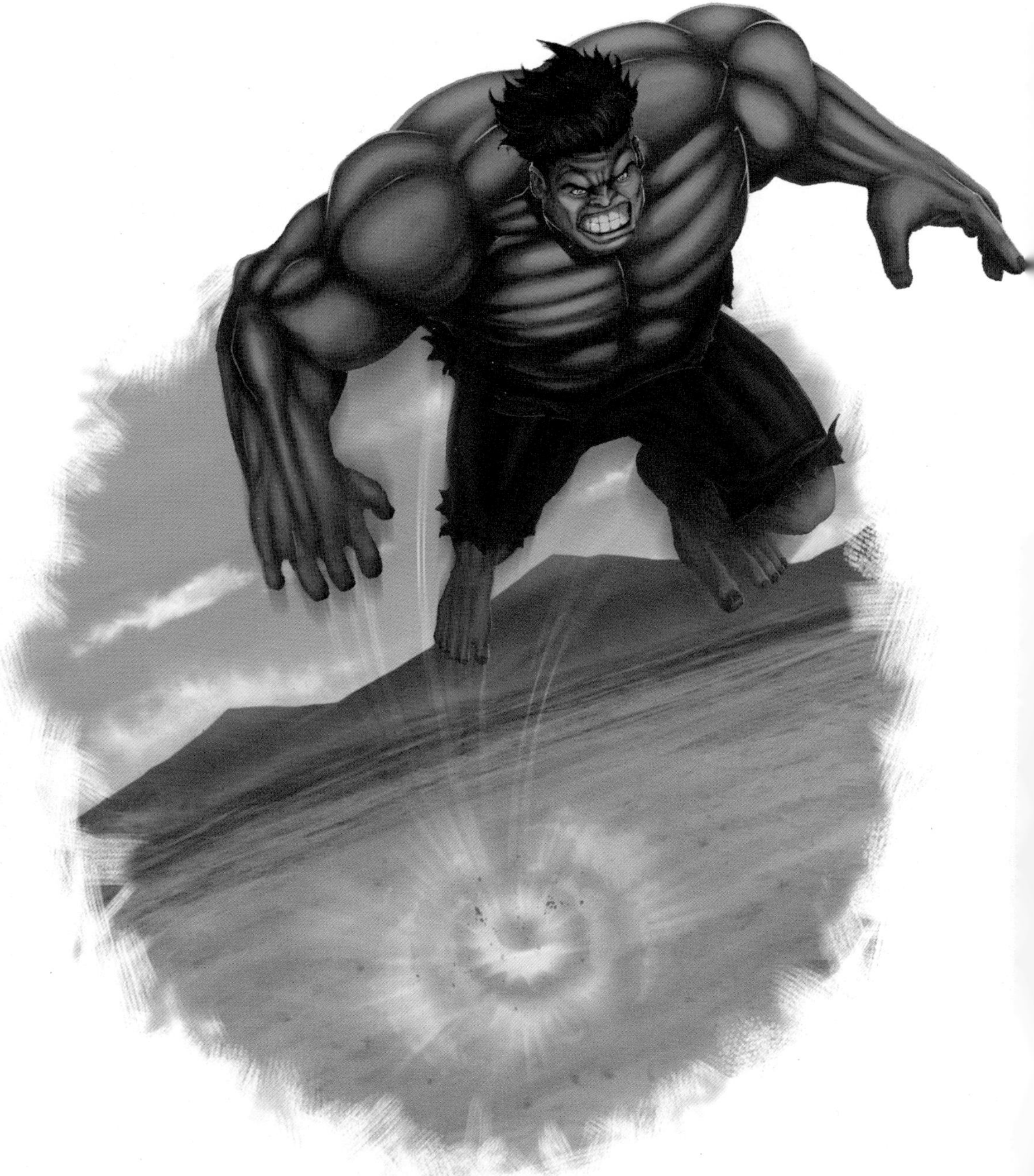

And he can create powerful sonic booms by clapping his hands together.

CRACK!

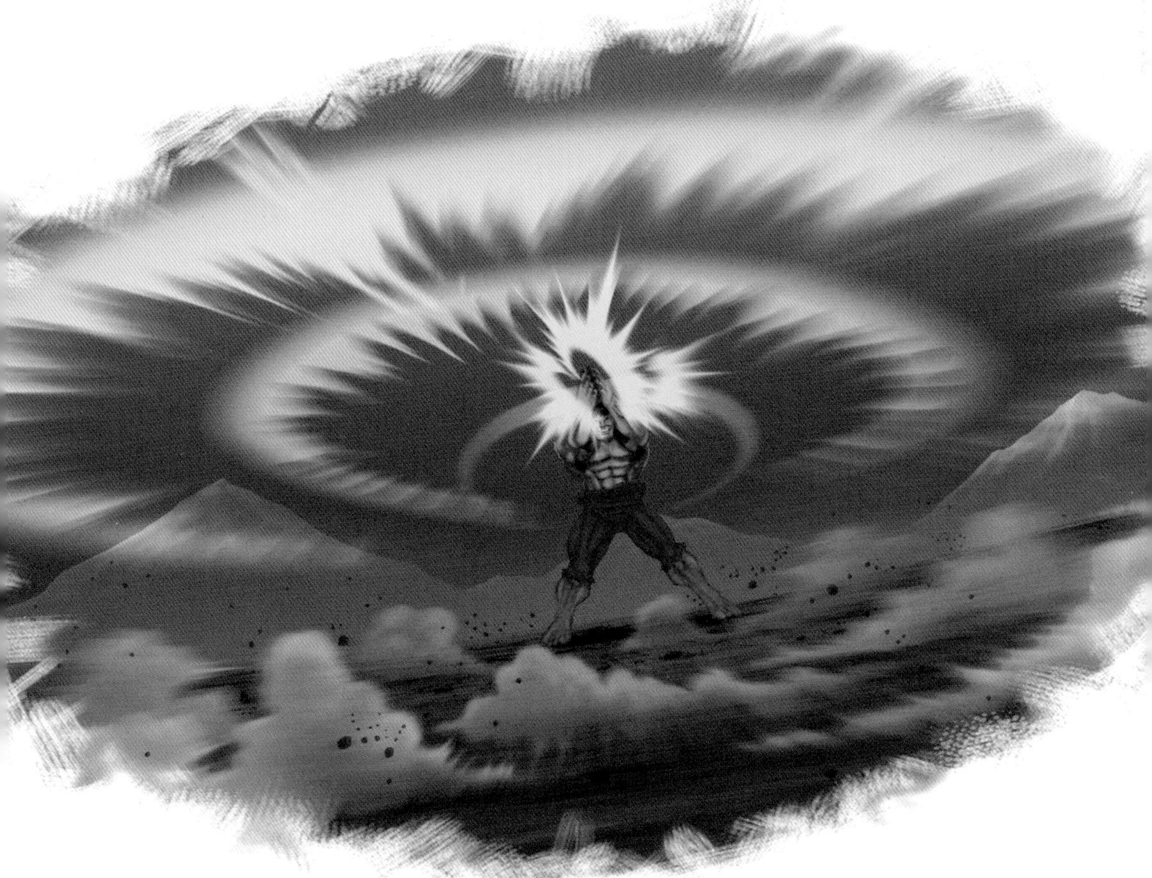

The Hulk is a hero, but some people, like General "Thunderbolt" Ross, think he is a monster. Ross wants to capture the Hulk—but he and the army can never hold Hulk for long!

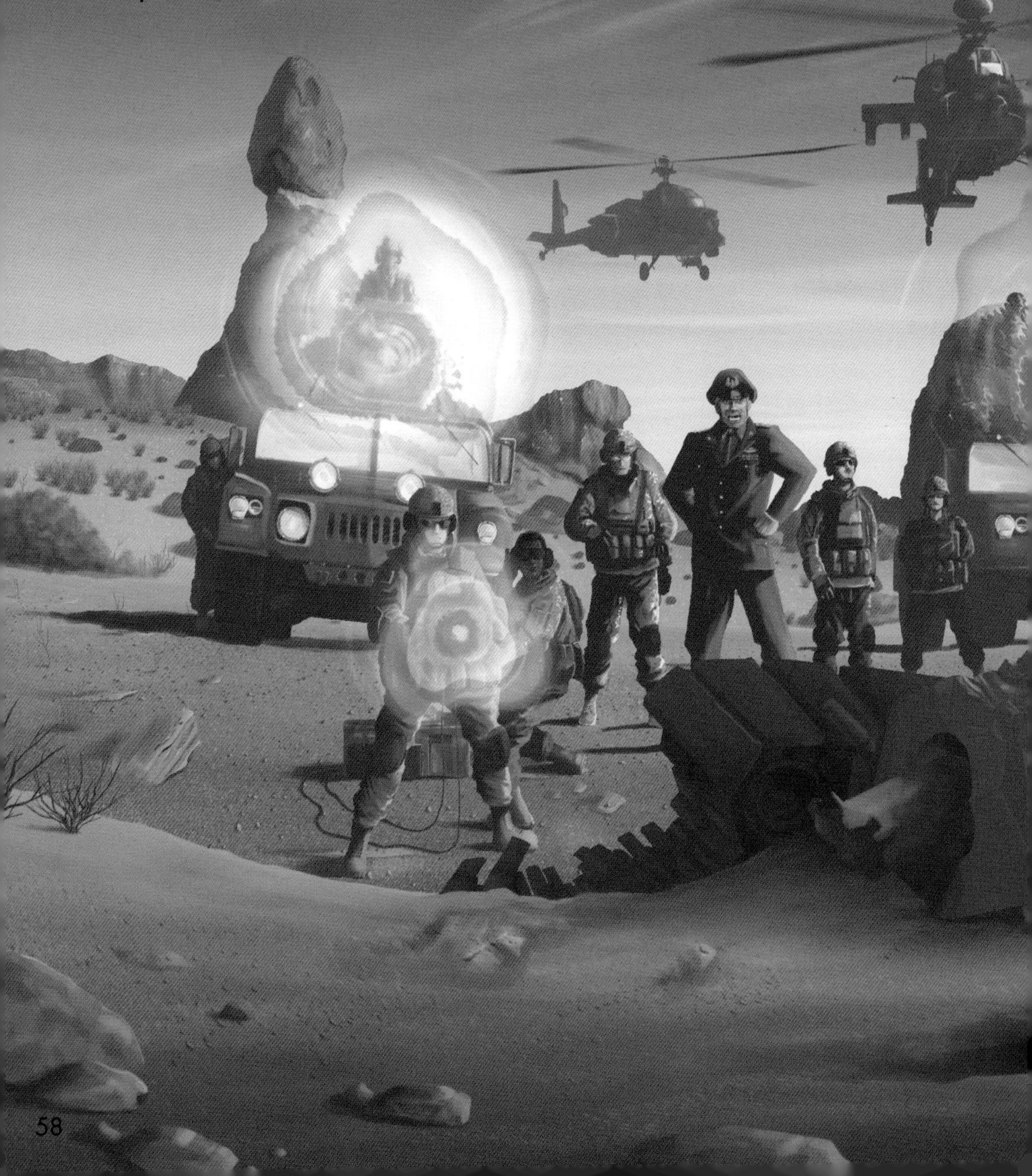

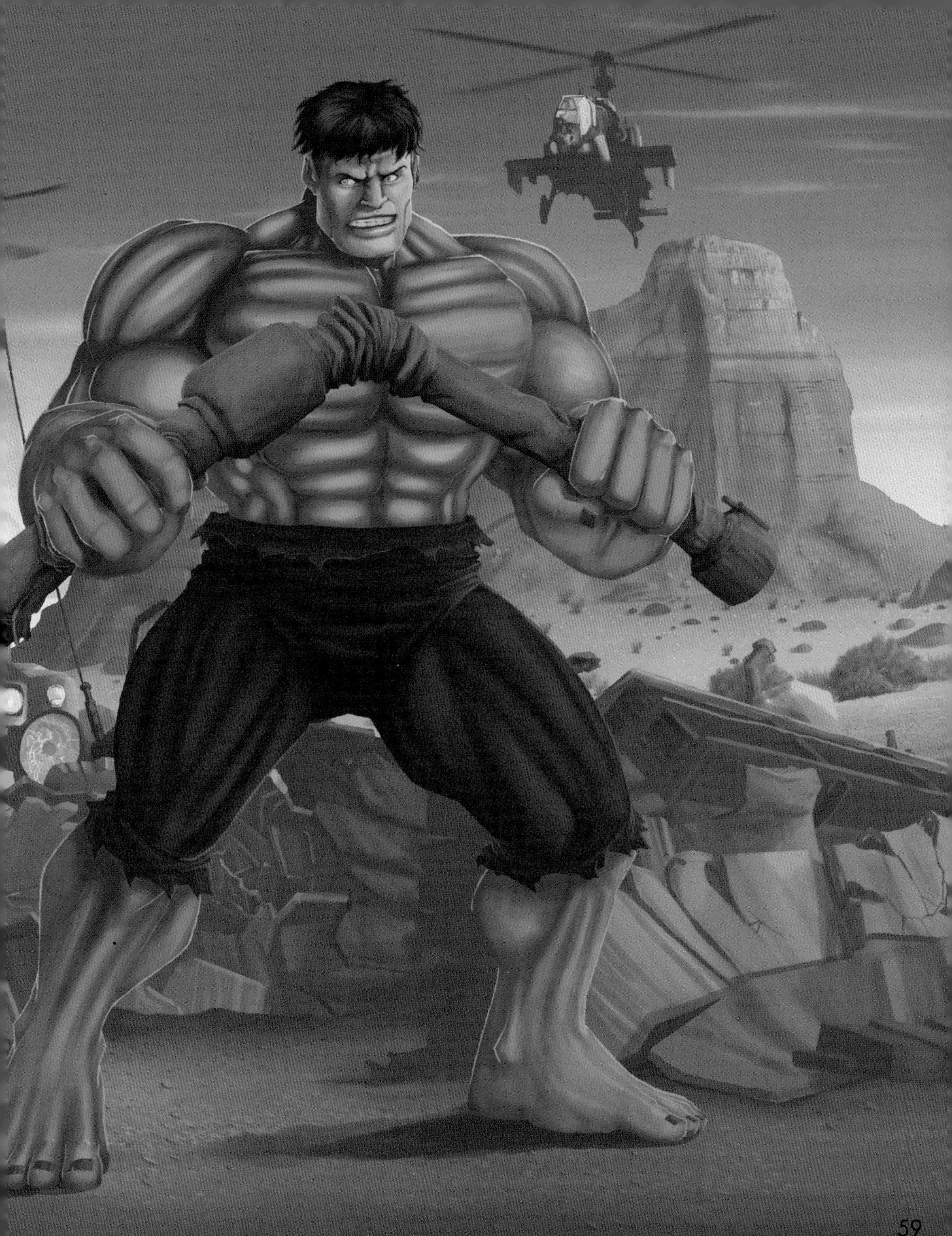

Hulk faces many fearsome foes. . . .

Abomination is a scaly, gamma-powered monster who is as strong as the Hulk. **Rhino** has a sharp horn on his head that he uses to ram his enemies!

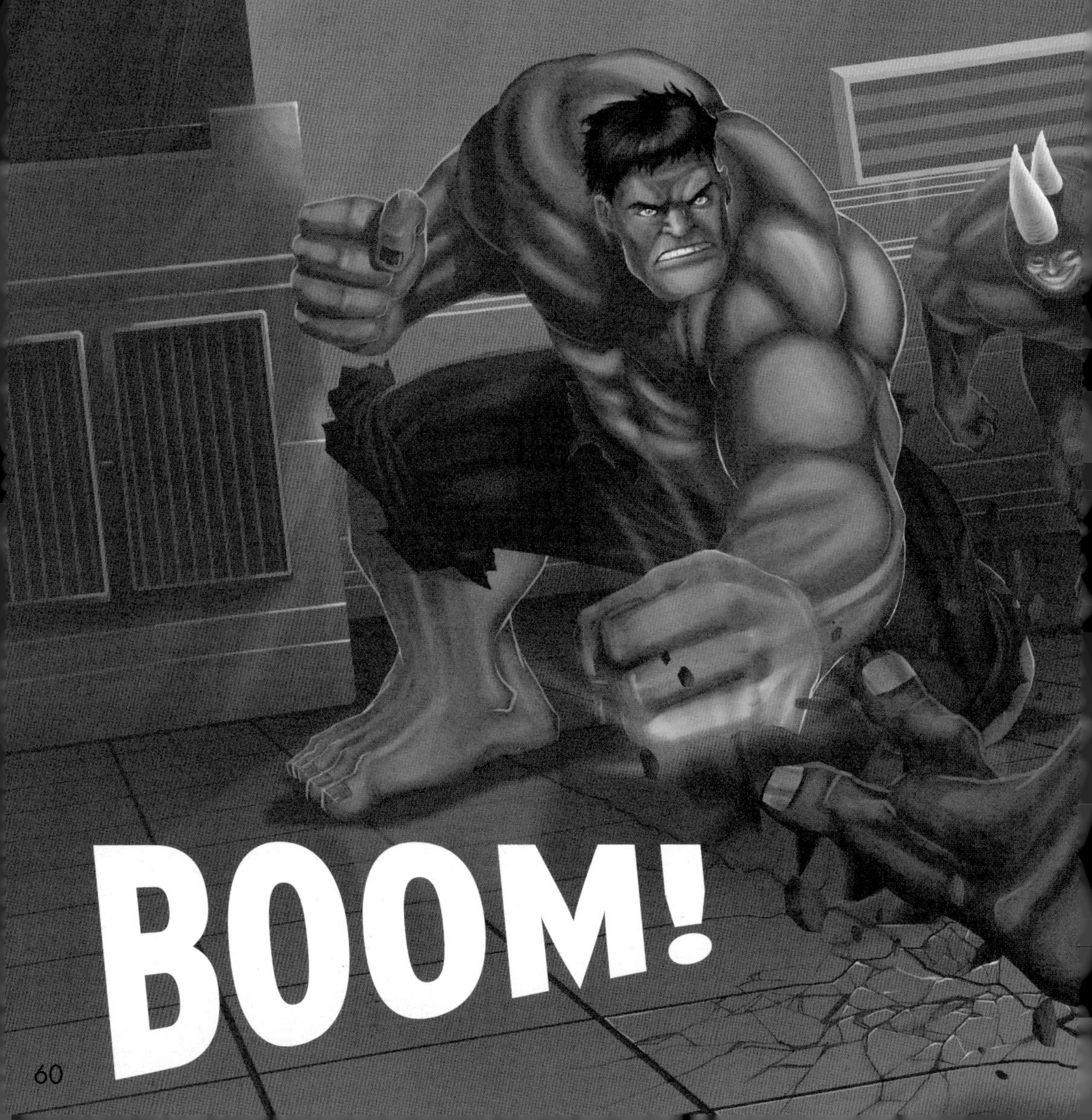
BOOM!

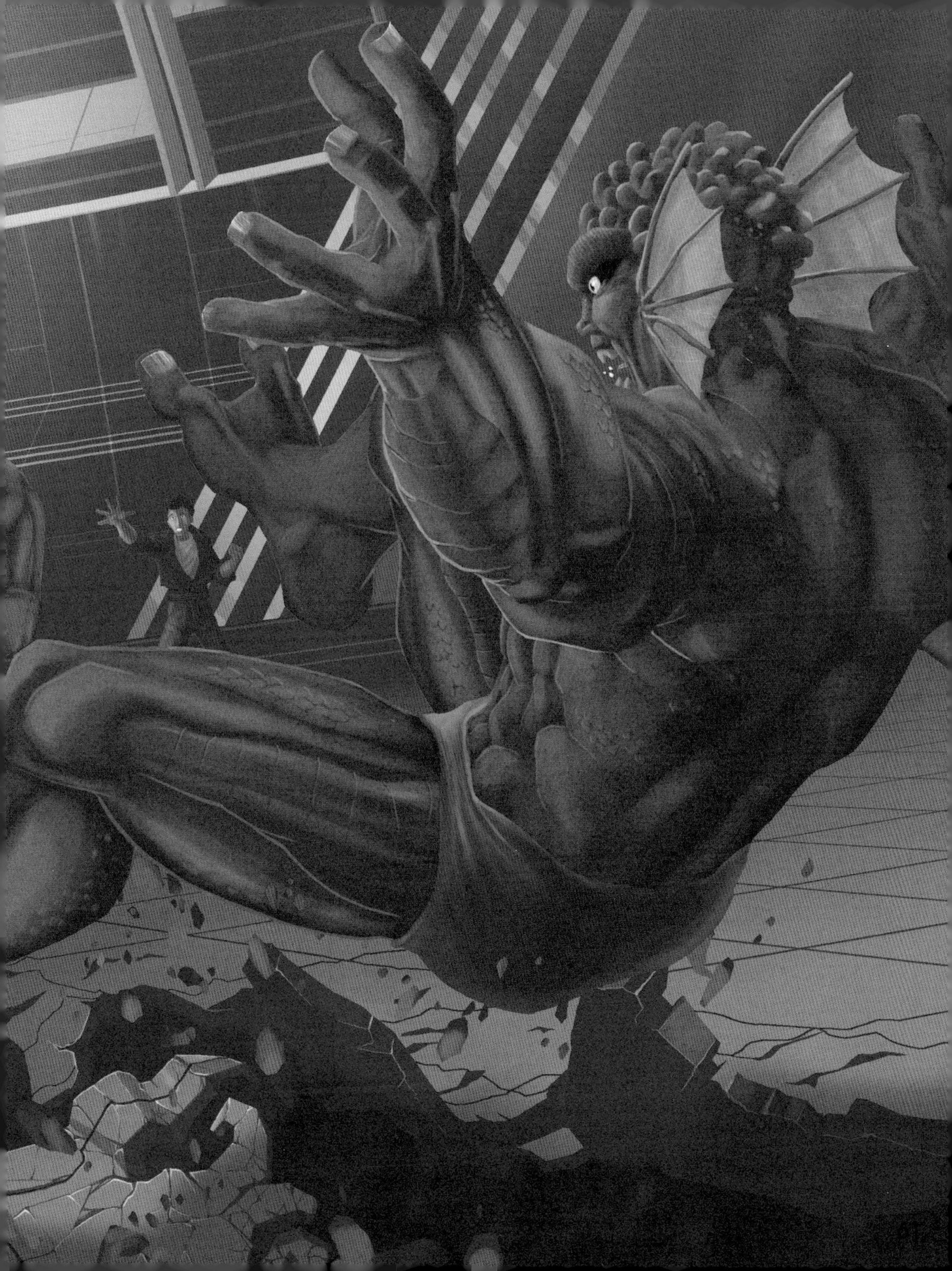

The **Leader** has a big mutated brain that makes him super smart. But instead of using his intelligence to help people, the Leader is always coming up with evil plans to take over the world!

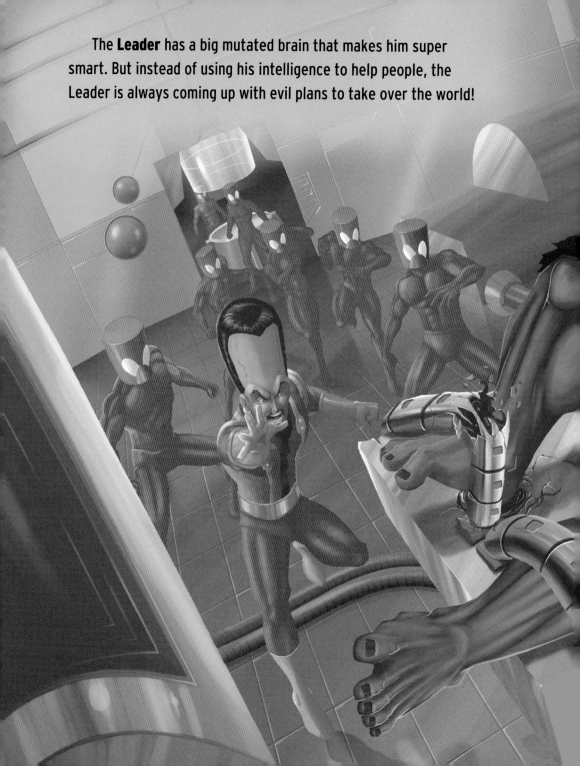

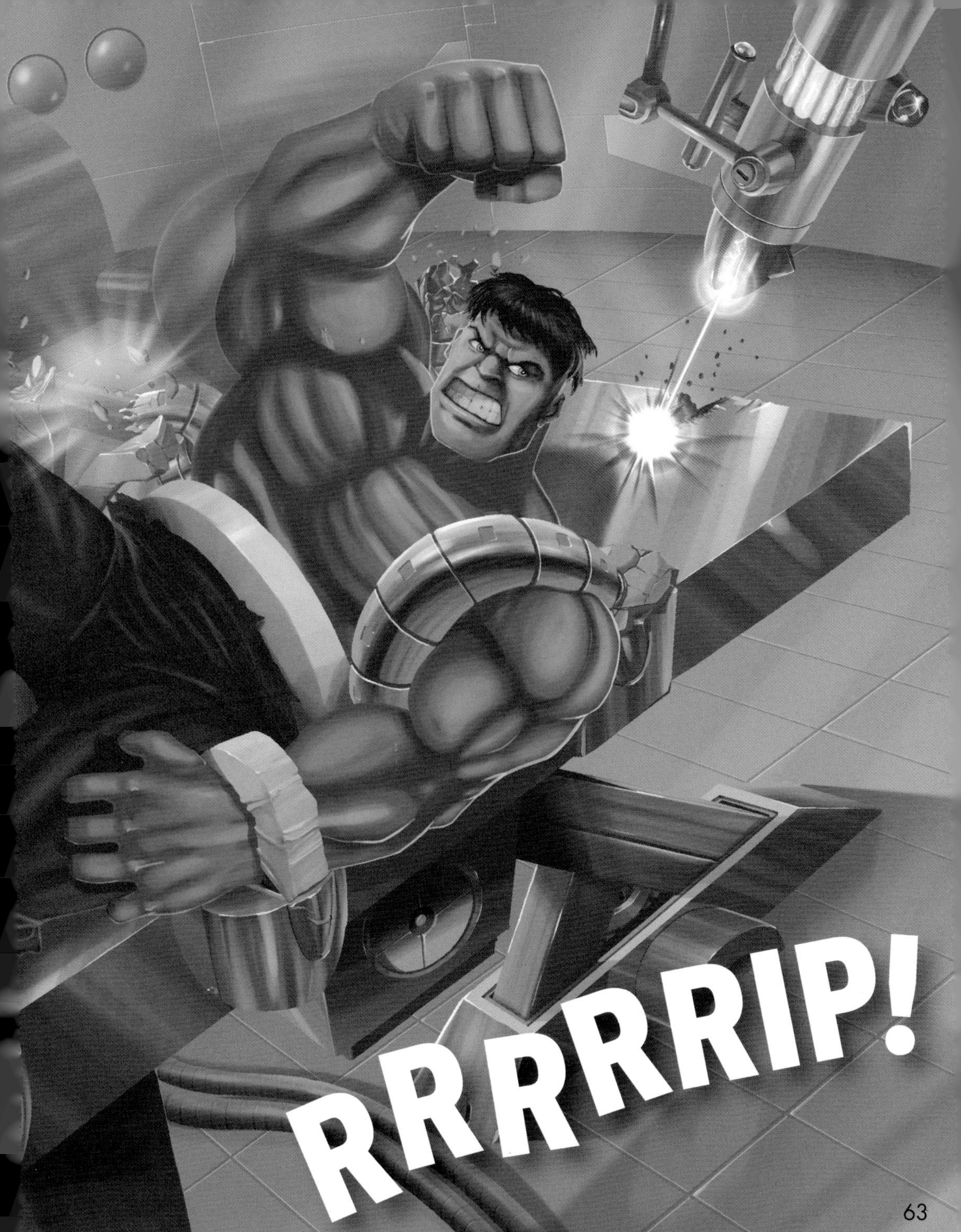
RRRRRIP!

Zzzax is a monster made of pure energy. This power-hungry creature wants to absorb the Hulk's life force to make itself invincible.

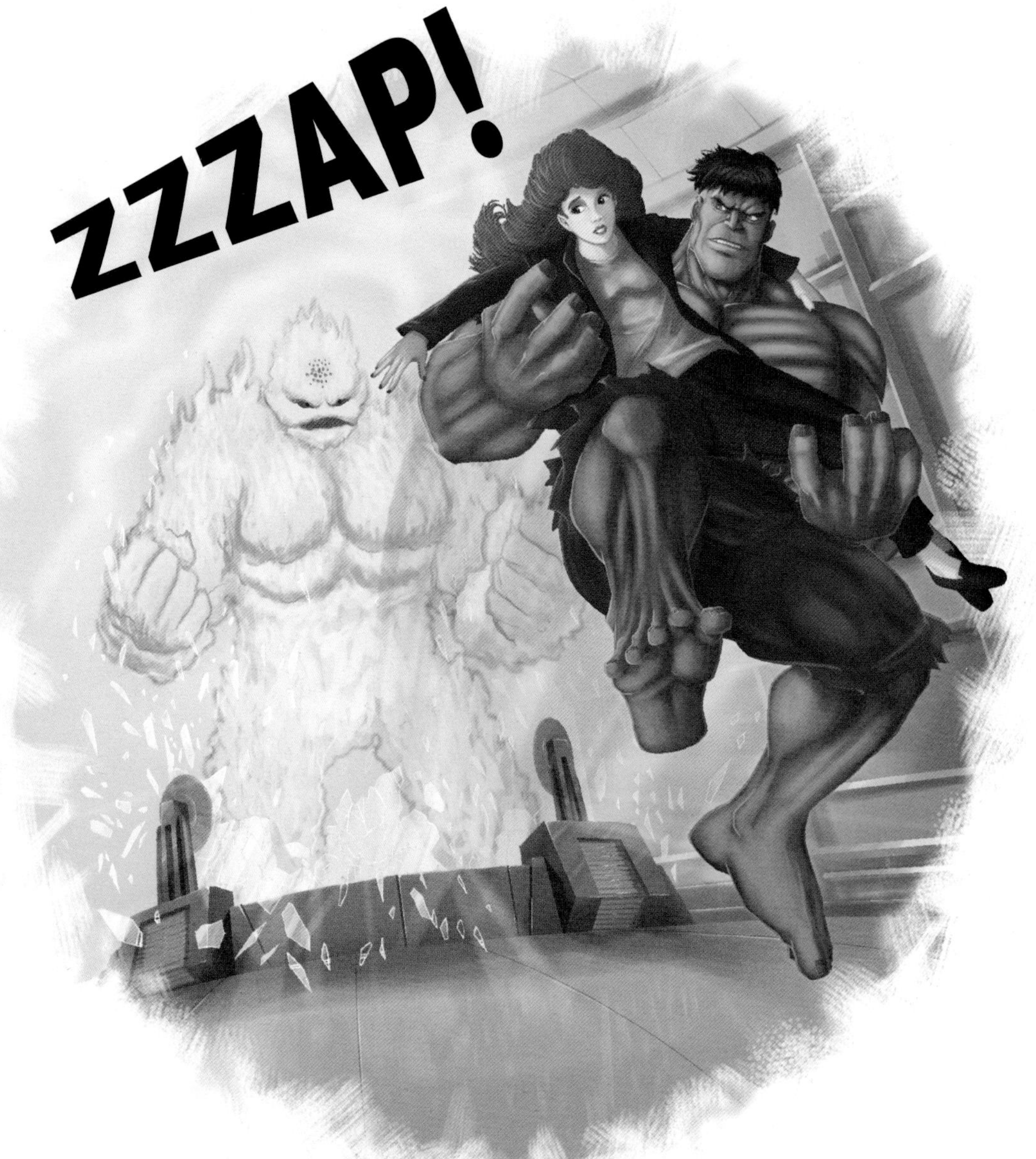
ZZZAP!

Absorbing Man is a thug with the ability to become anything he touches. He can be as slippery as a puddle of water or as strong as steel. But Absorbing Man is still no match for the Hulk!

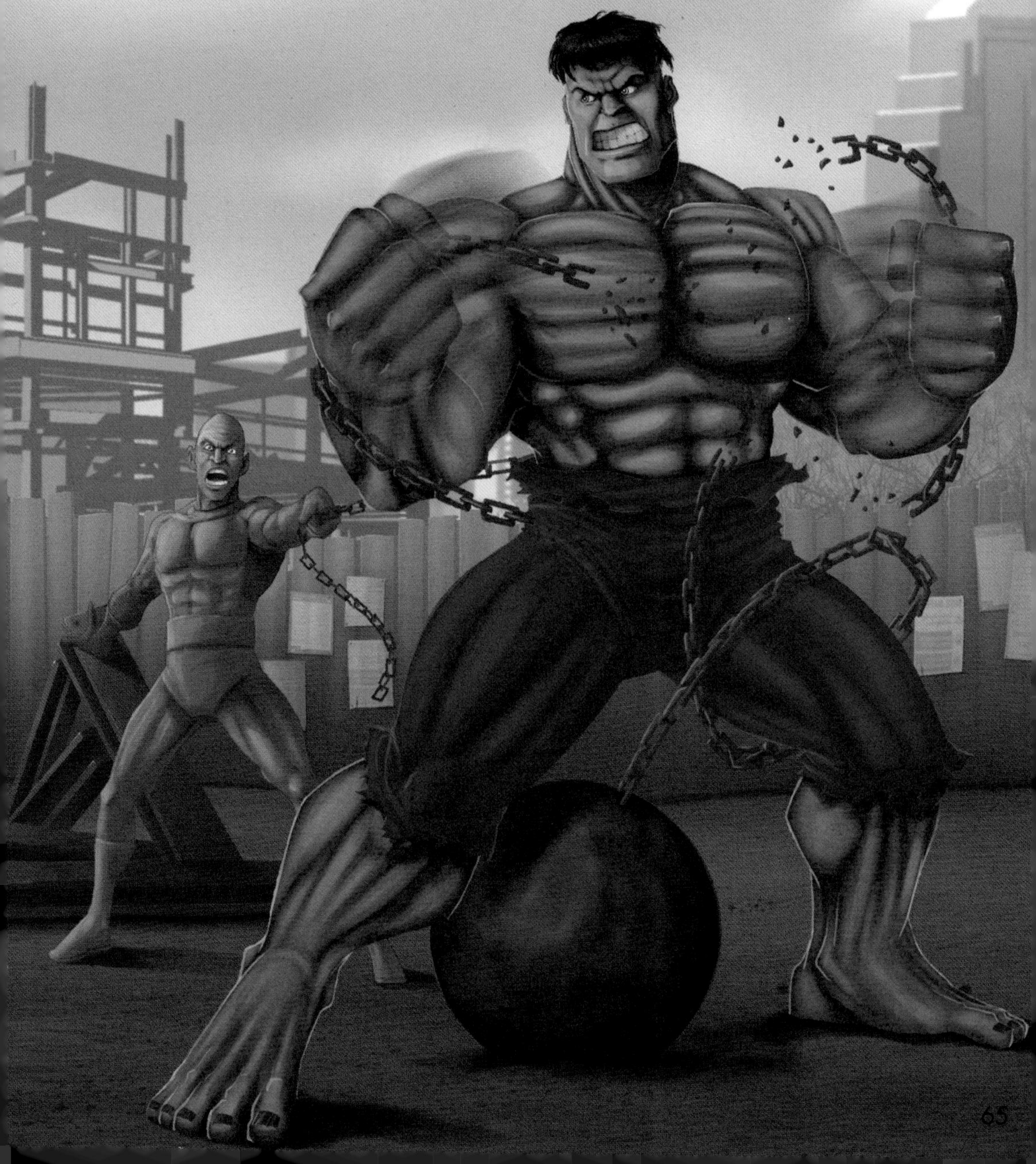

No one has fun when the **Circus of Crime** comes to town. These performers use their astounding circus skills to break the law. But when they try to make the Hulk part of their act, he brings the big top down on them!

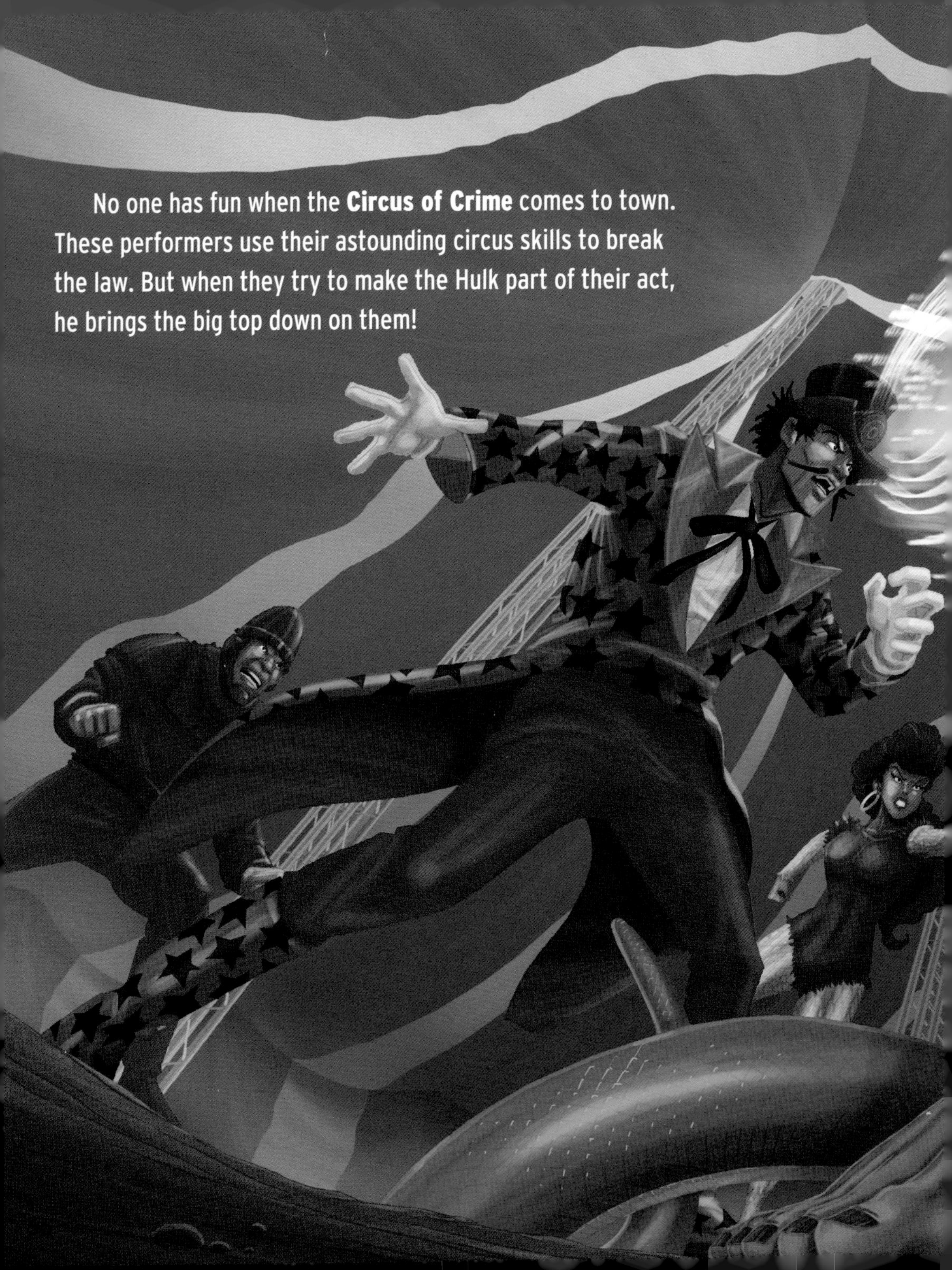

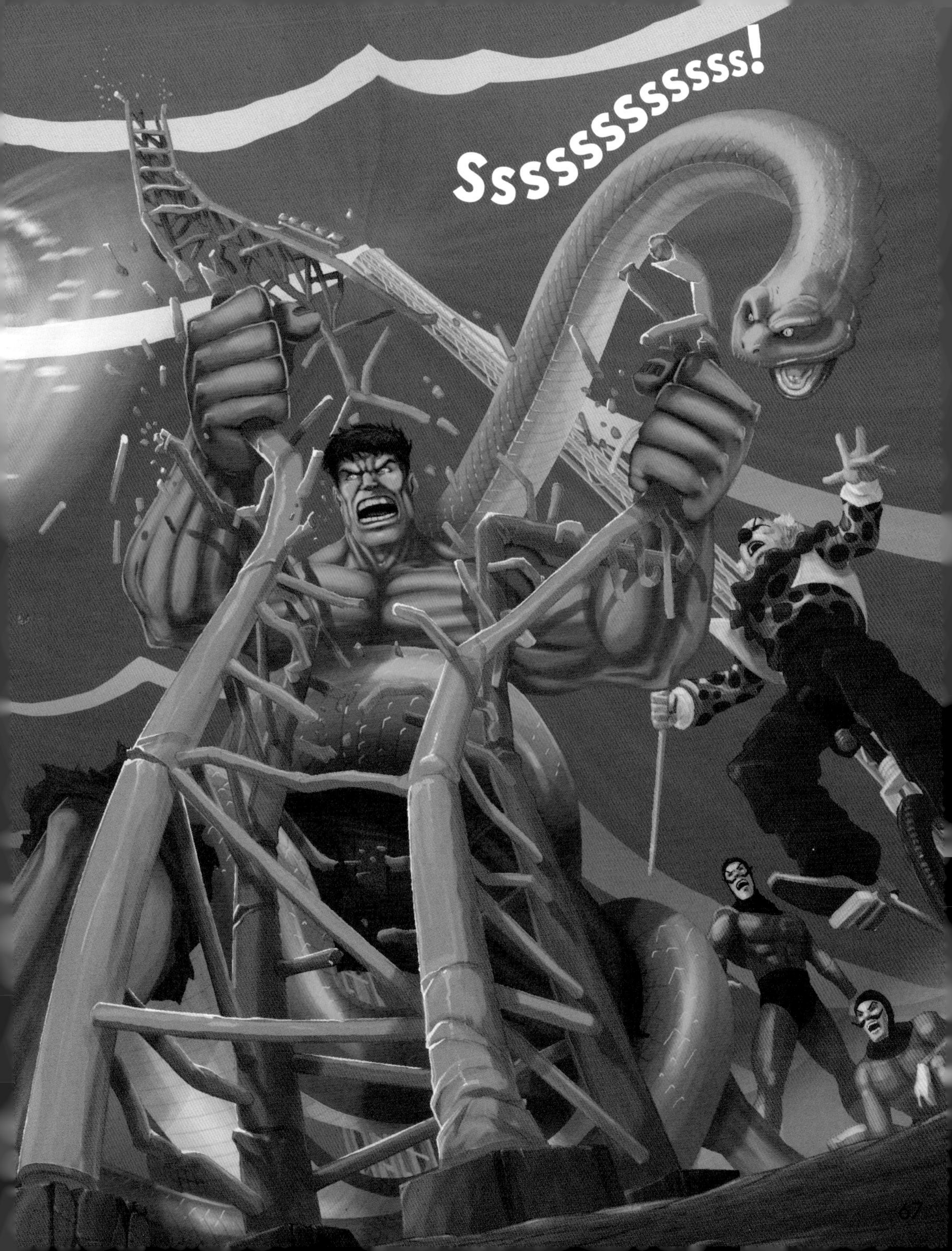
Sssssssssss!

The Hulk also fights alongside other Super Heroes, such as the **Avengers**. No matter which foes they face, the Hulk is always ready to help them save the world . . .

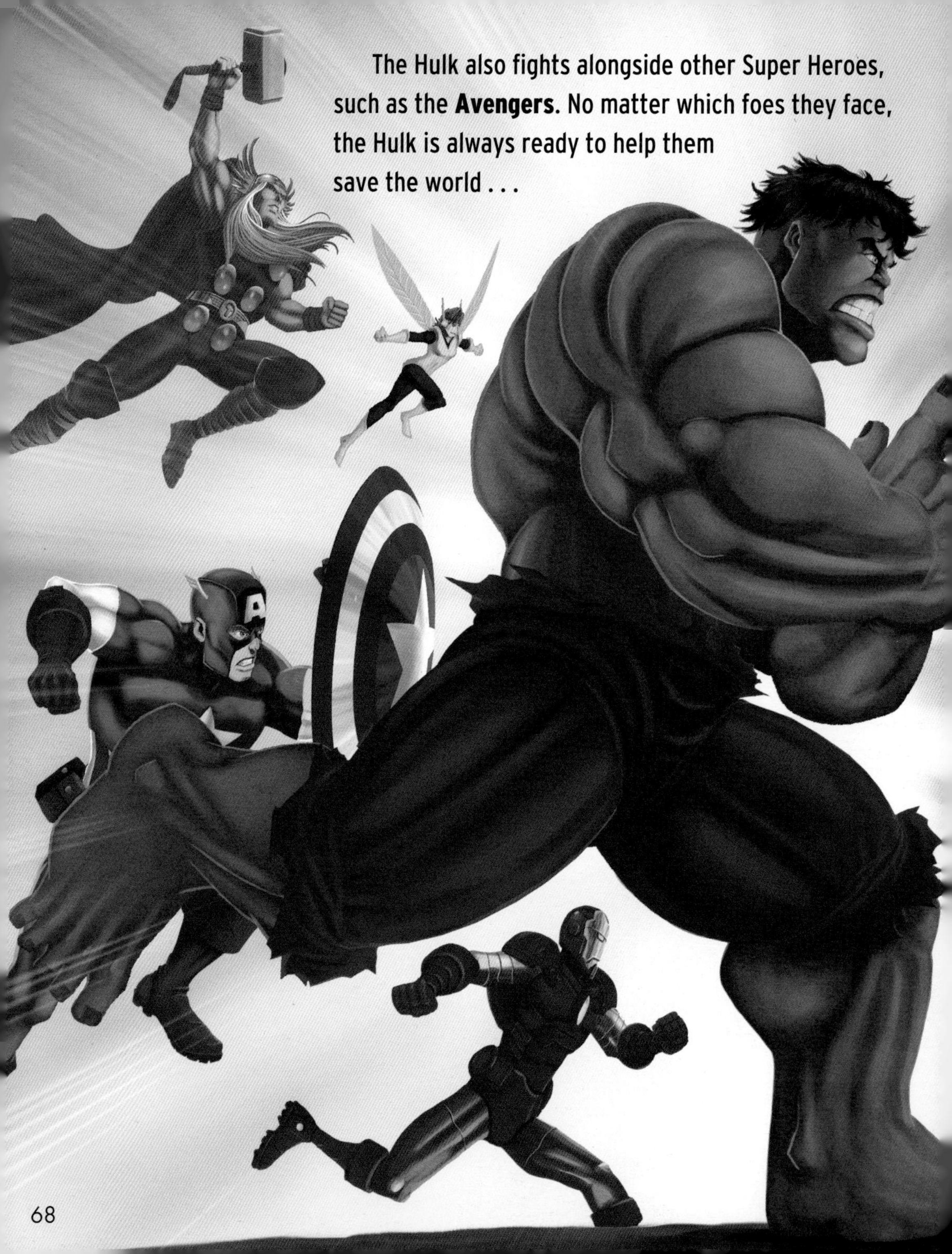

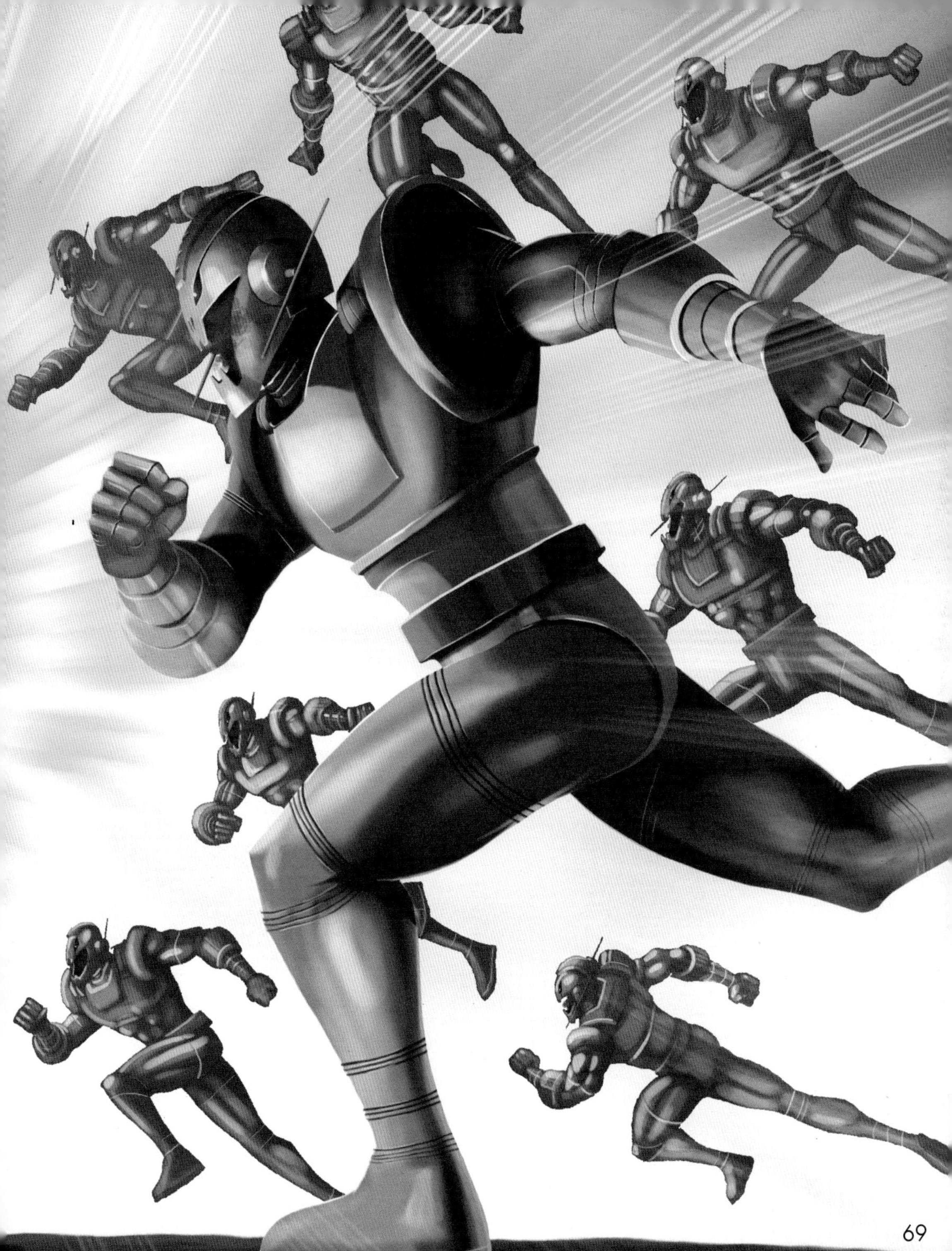

. . . and the Hulk always wins!

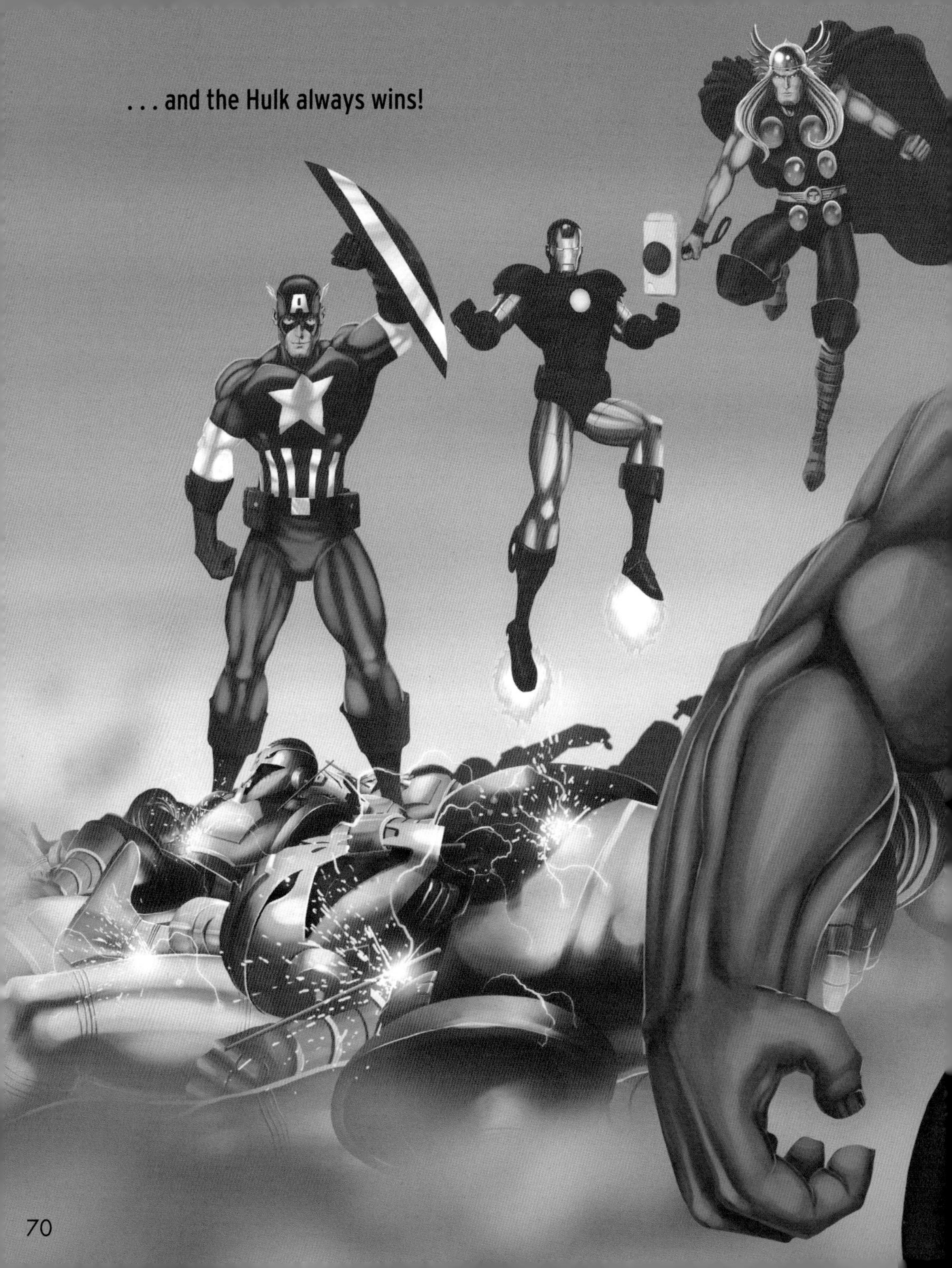

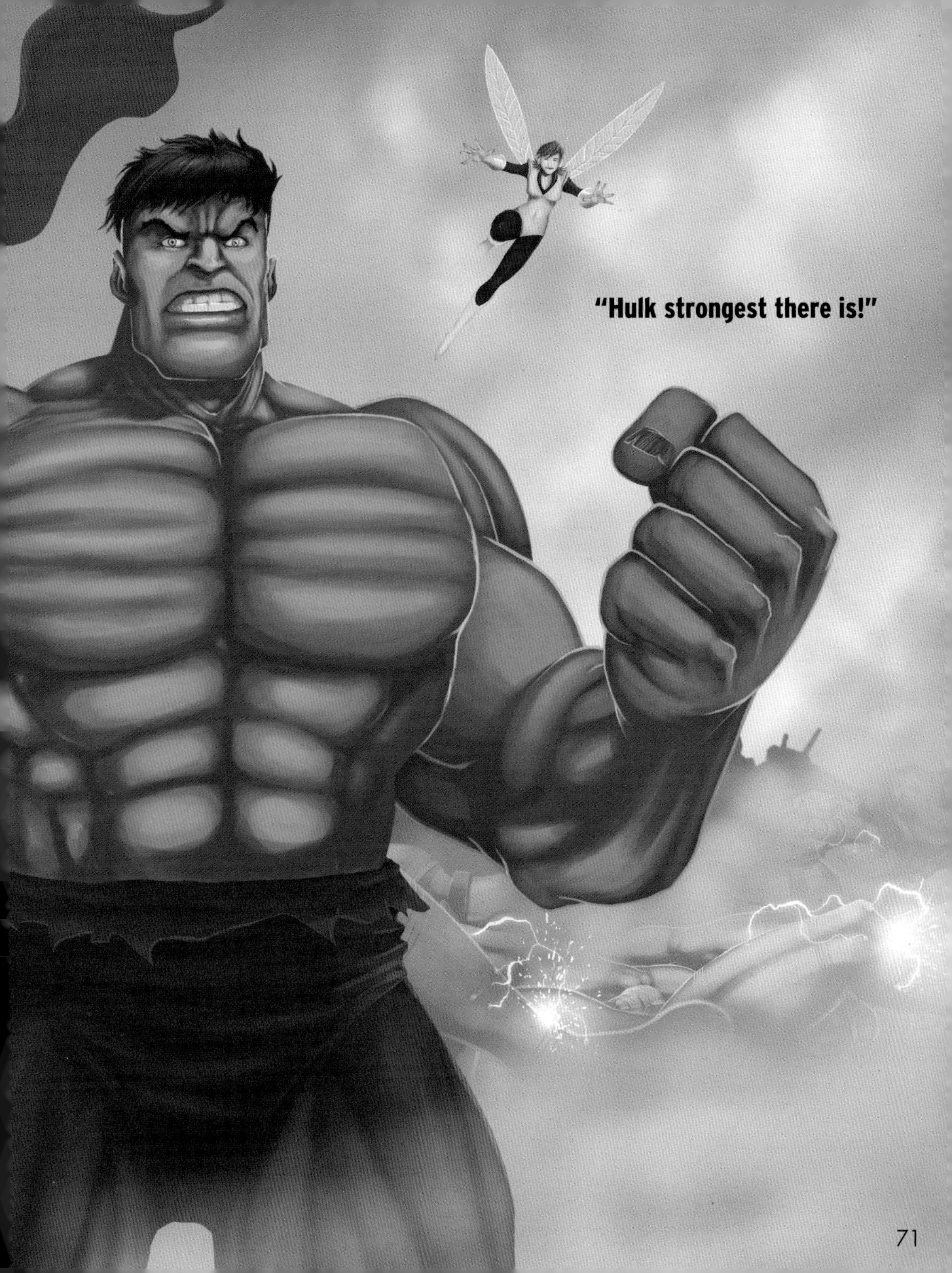
"Hulk strongest there is!"

The Hulk is an incredible hero and a gentle giant. Just don't make him angry!

Go, Hulk!

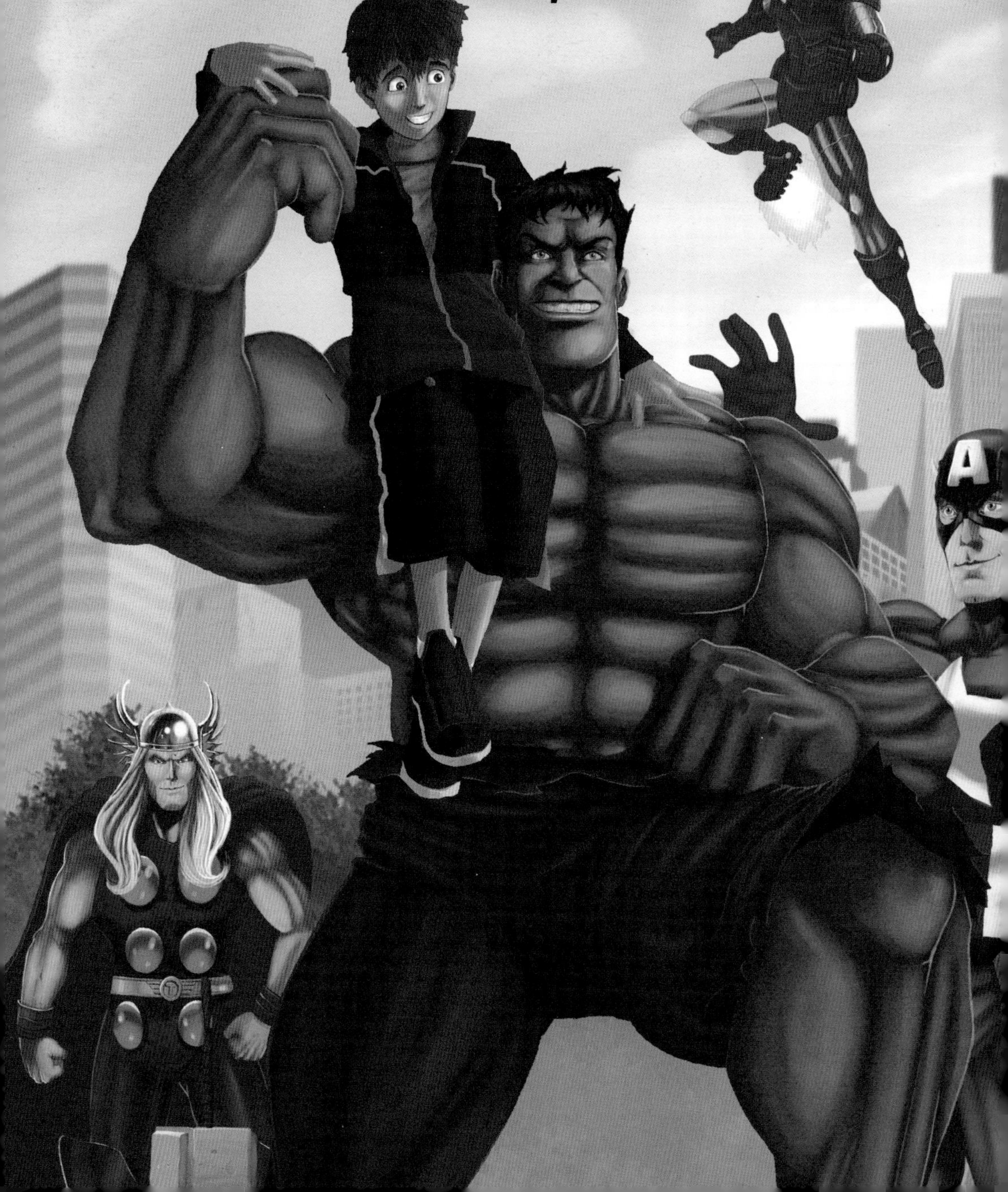

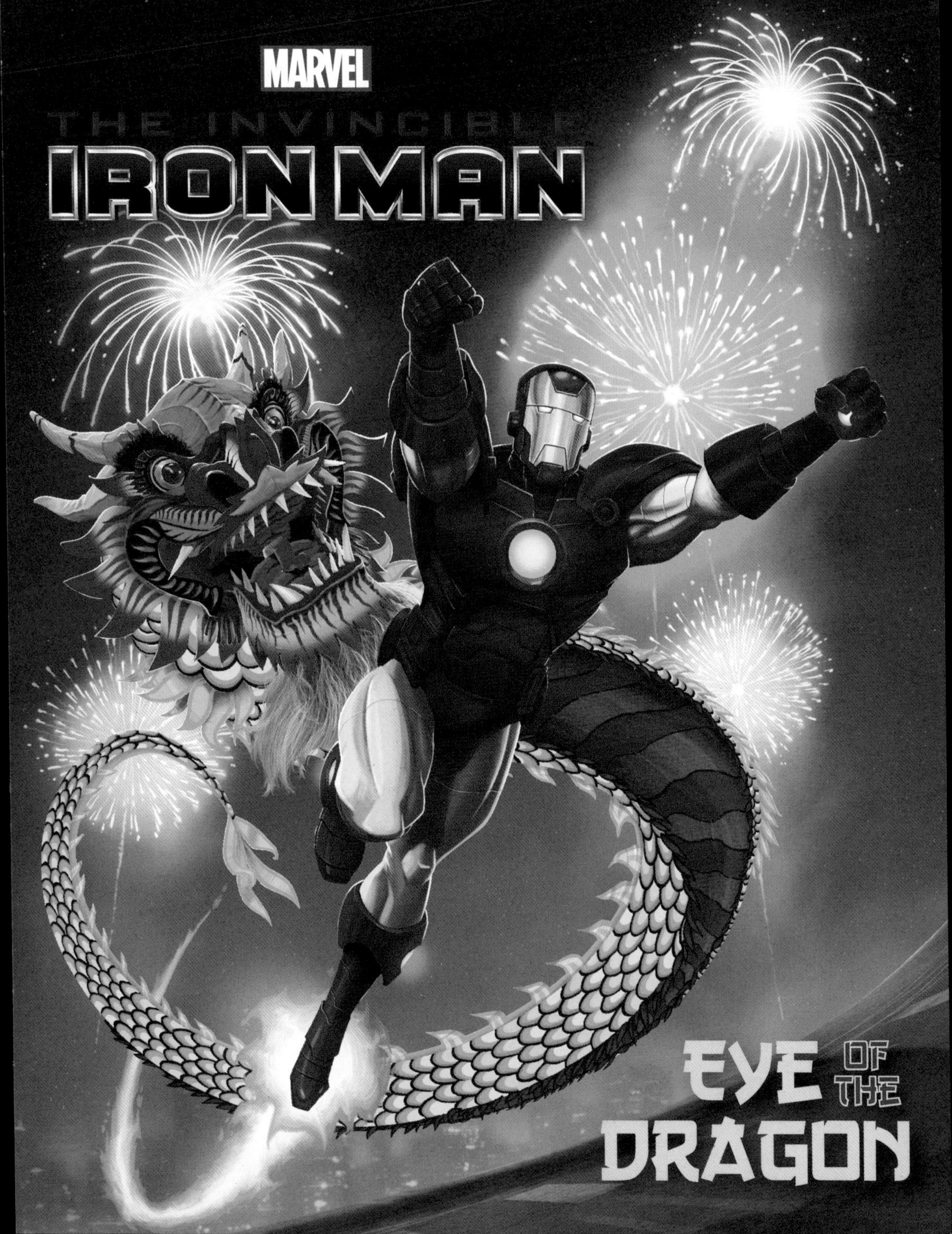
MARVEL
THE INVINCIBLE
IRON MAN
EYE OF THE
DRAGON

World-famous inventor Tony Stark is the guest of honor at a festival in New York City's Chinatown. Tony cuts a ribbon and starts the parade. Fireworks pop, dancers twirl, and acrobats leap.

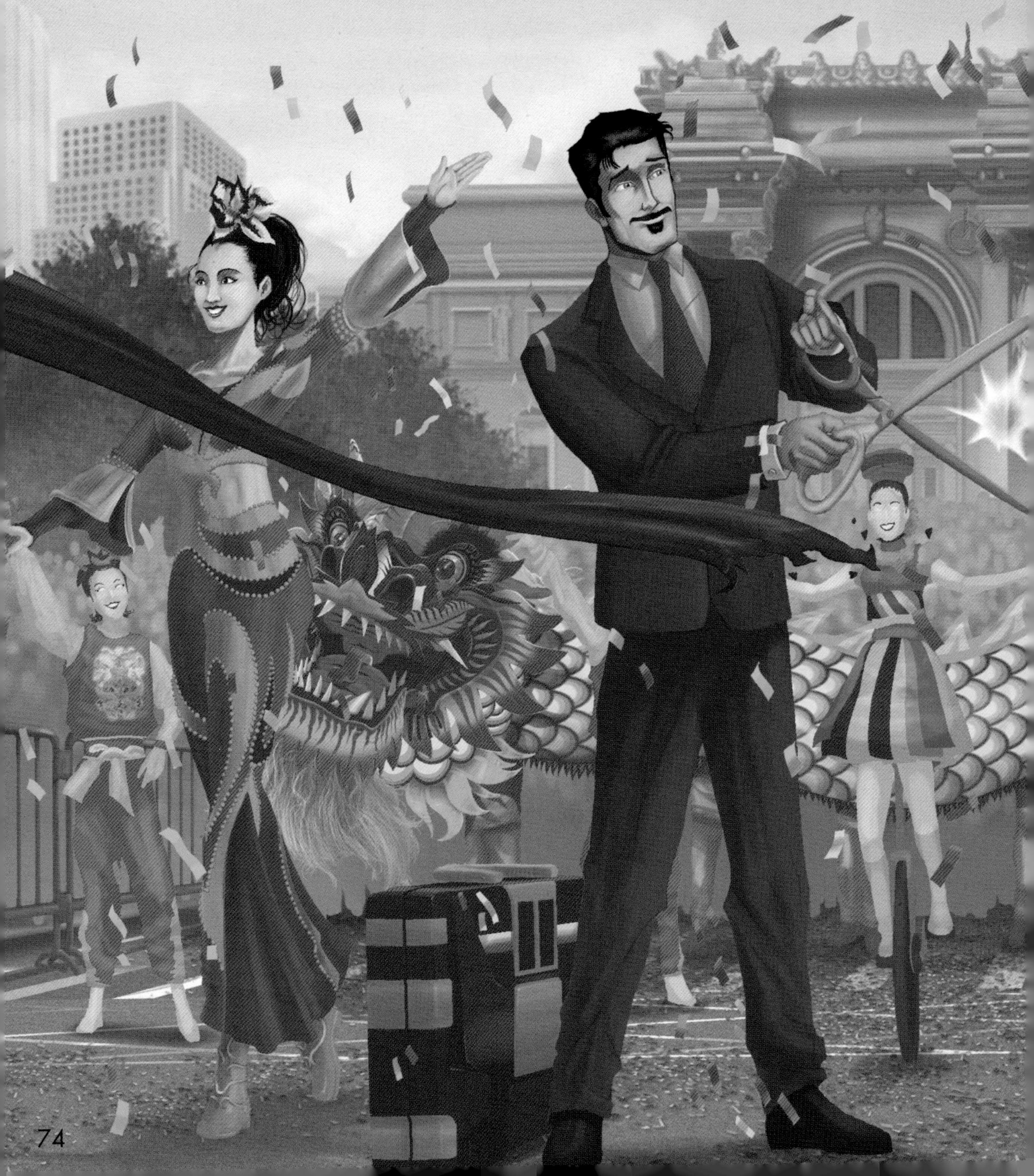

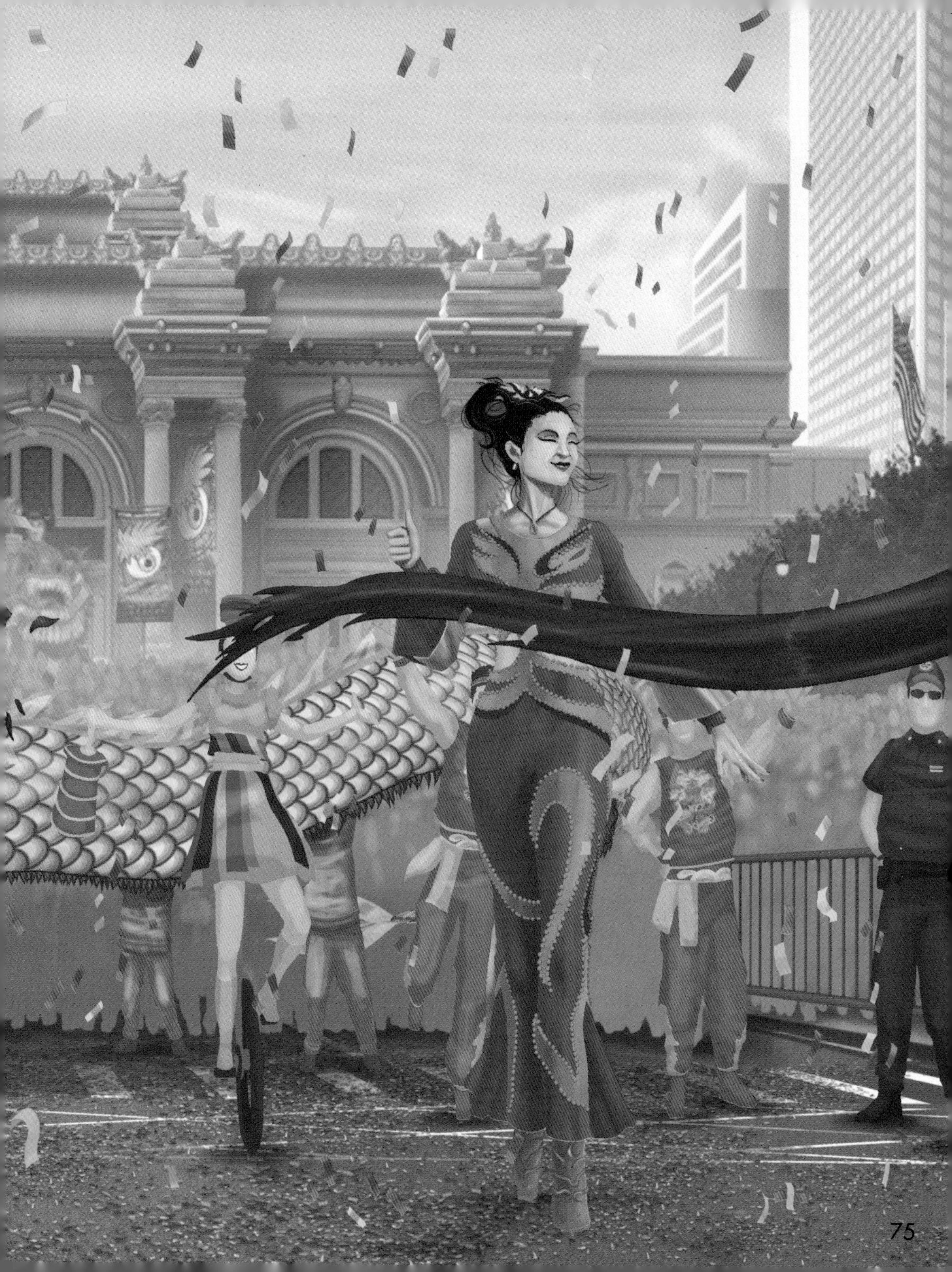

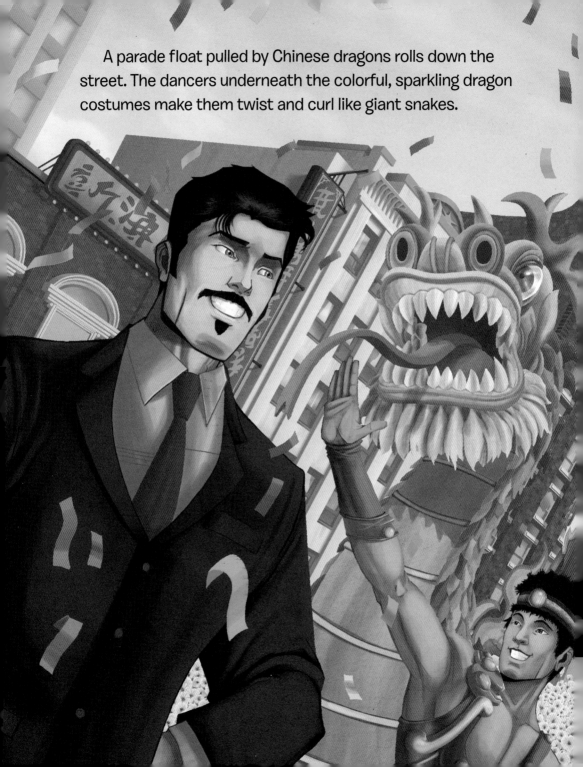

A parade float pulled by Chinese dragons rolls down the street. The dancers underneath the colorful, sparkling dragon costumes make them twist and curl like giant snakes.

The float carries a priceless gem called the Eye of the Dragon. The gem will go on display in a museum when the parade is over. Tony and the crowd cheer as it passes by.

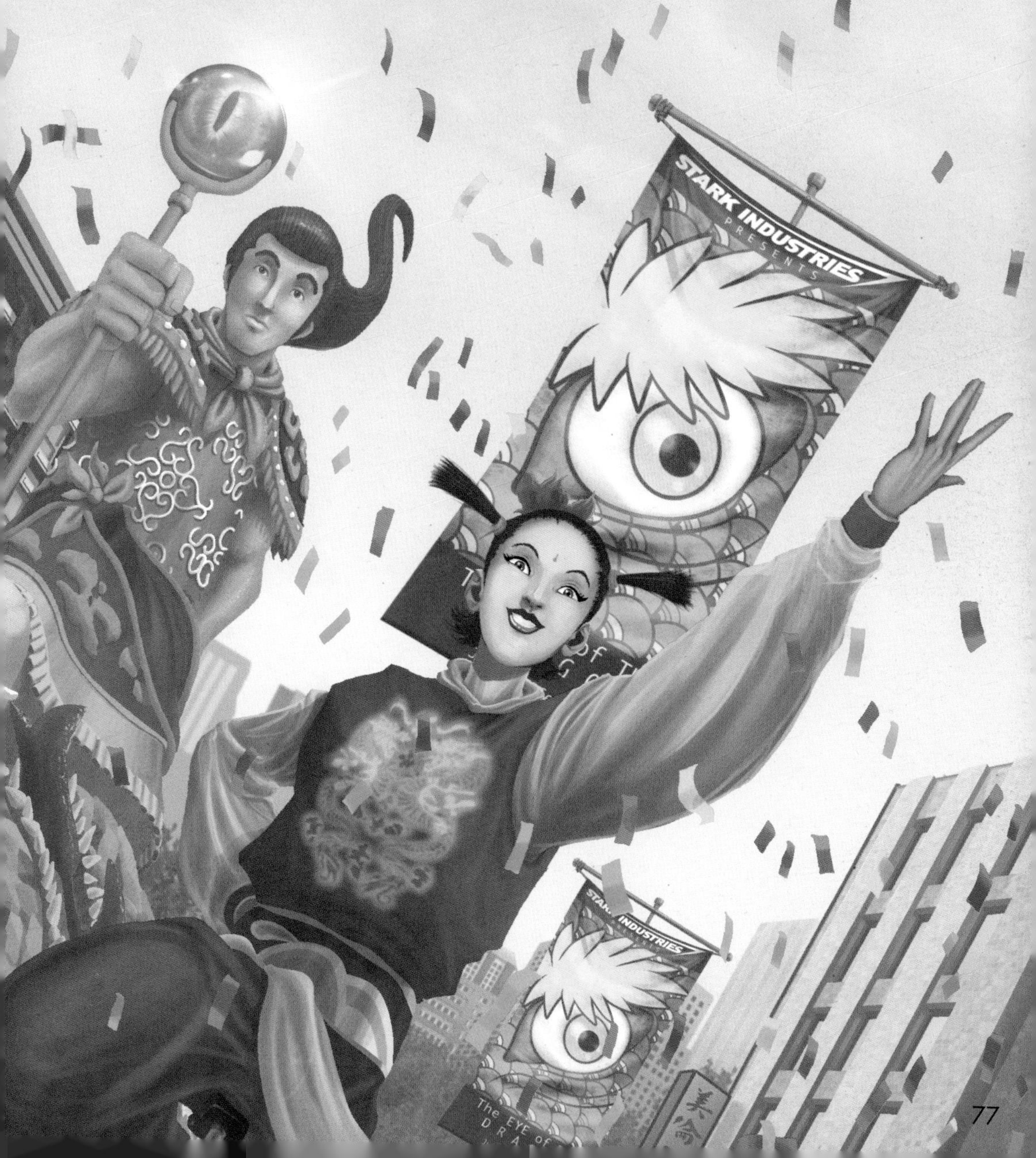

STARK INDUSTRIES
PRESENTS
STARK INDUSTRIES
The EYE of
DRA

Suddenly, the villain known as the Mandarin appears! He is armed with ten powerful energy rings.

"The Eye of the Dragon will be mine!" the Mandarin exclaims as he uses his Ice Blast ring to freeze the parade float in its tracks.

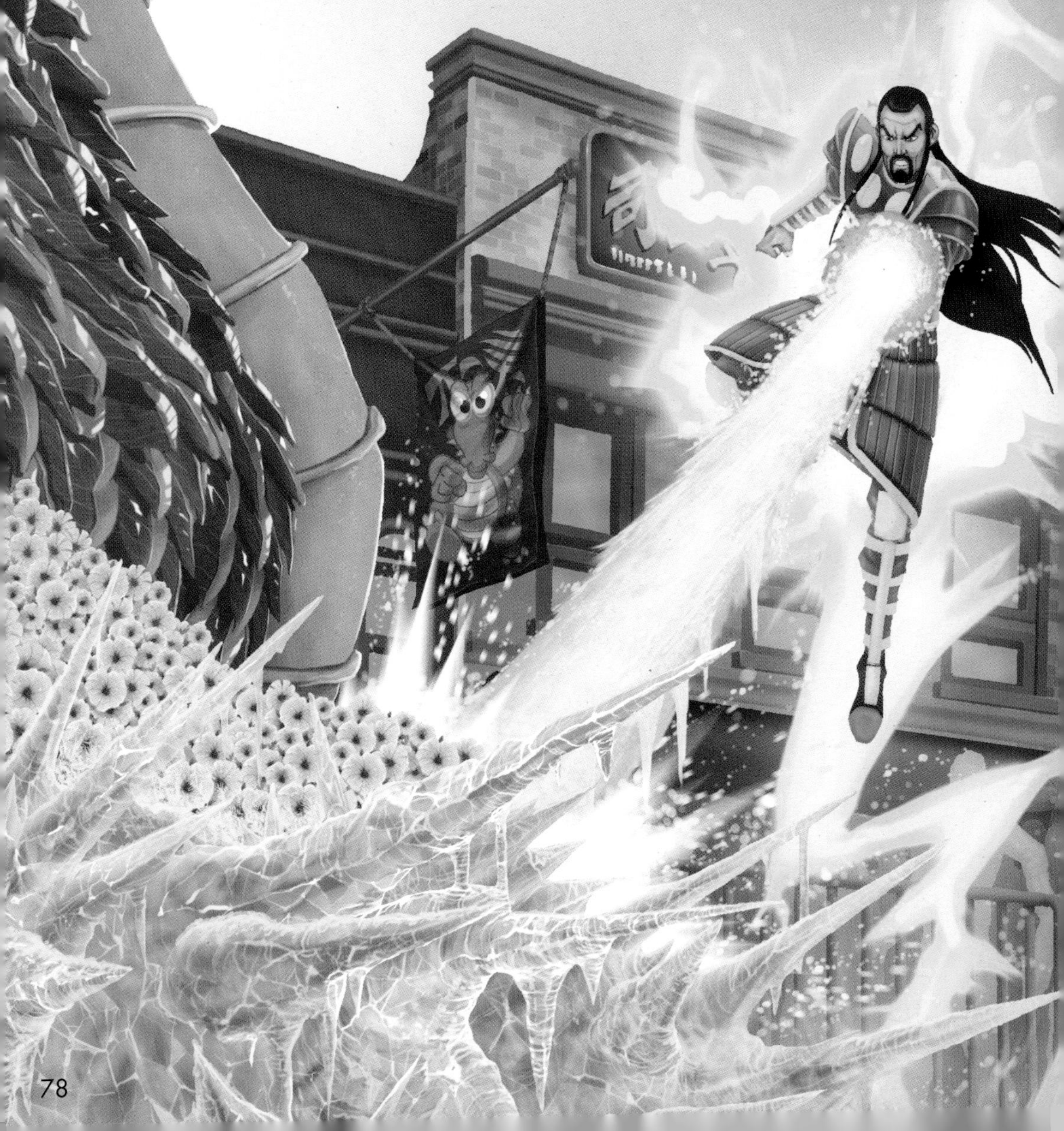

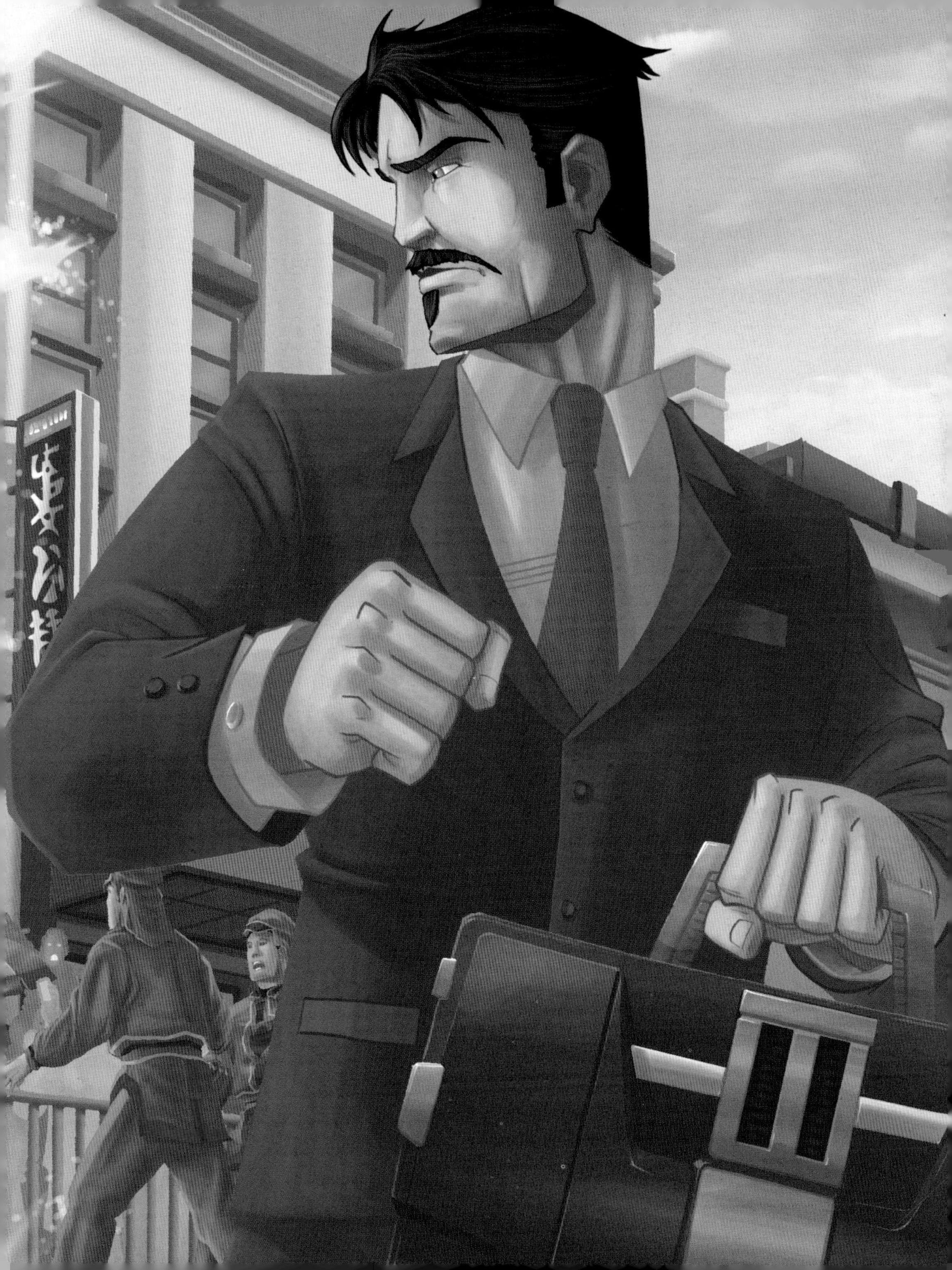

Tony Stark runs to an alley. Hidden in his briefcase is powerful high-tech armor that he puts on to become . . .

THE INVINCIBLE IRON MAN!

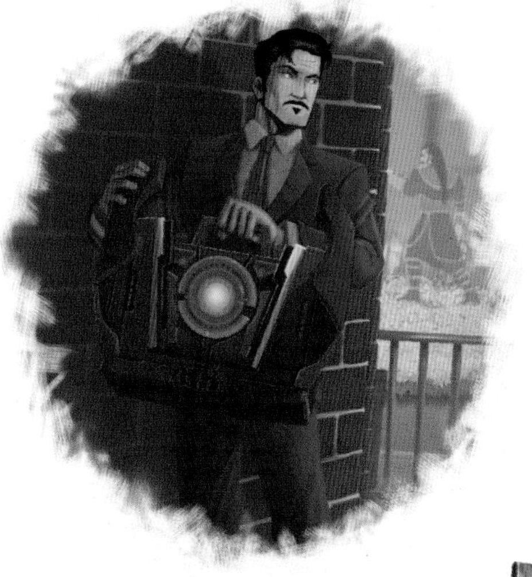

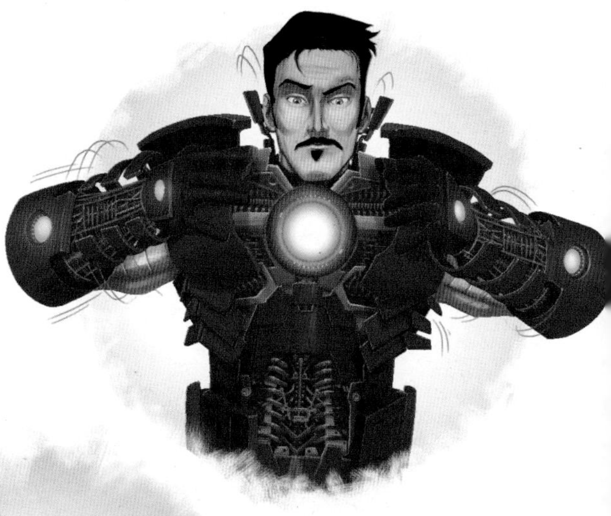

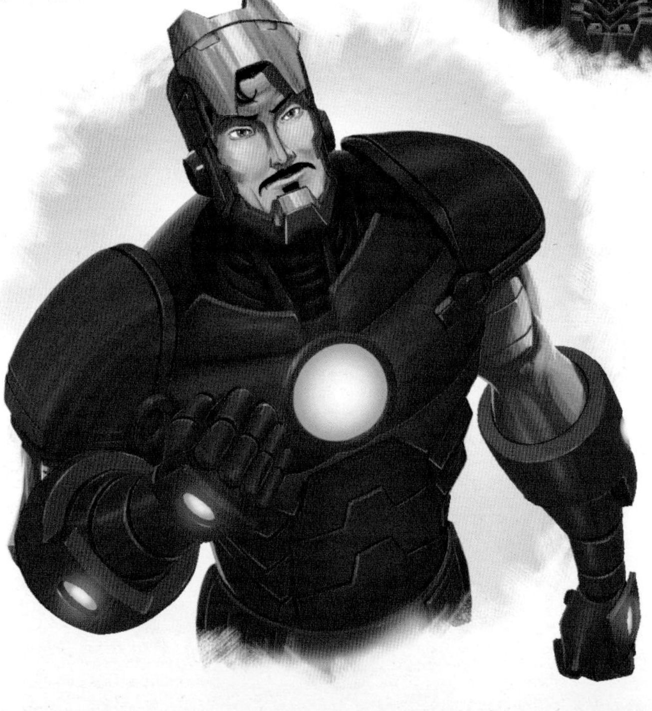

Armored up, Iron Man flies into action!

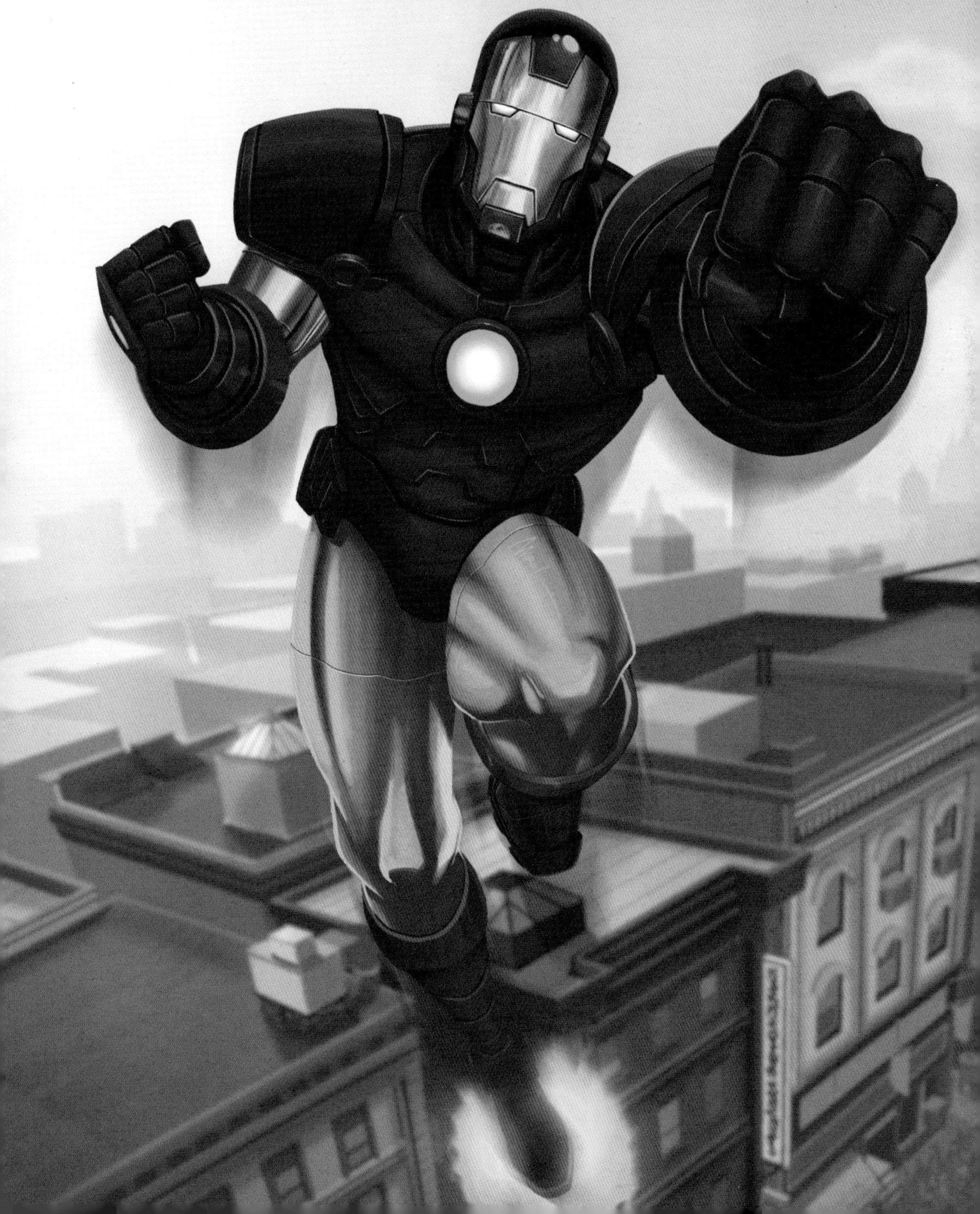

"Stop right there!" Iron Man commands.

The sinister Mandarin looks up to see who would dare challenge him.

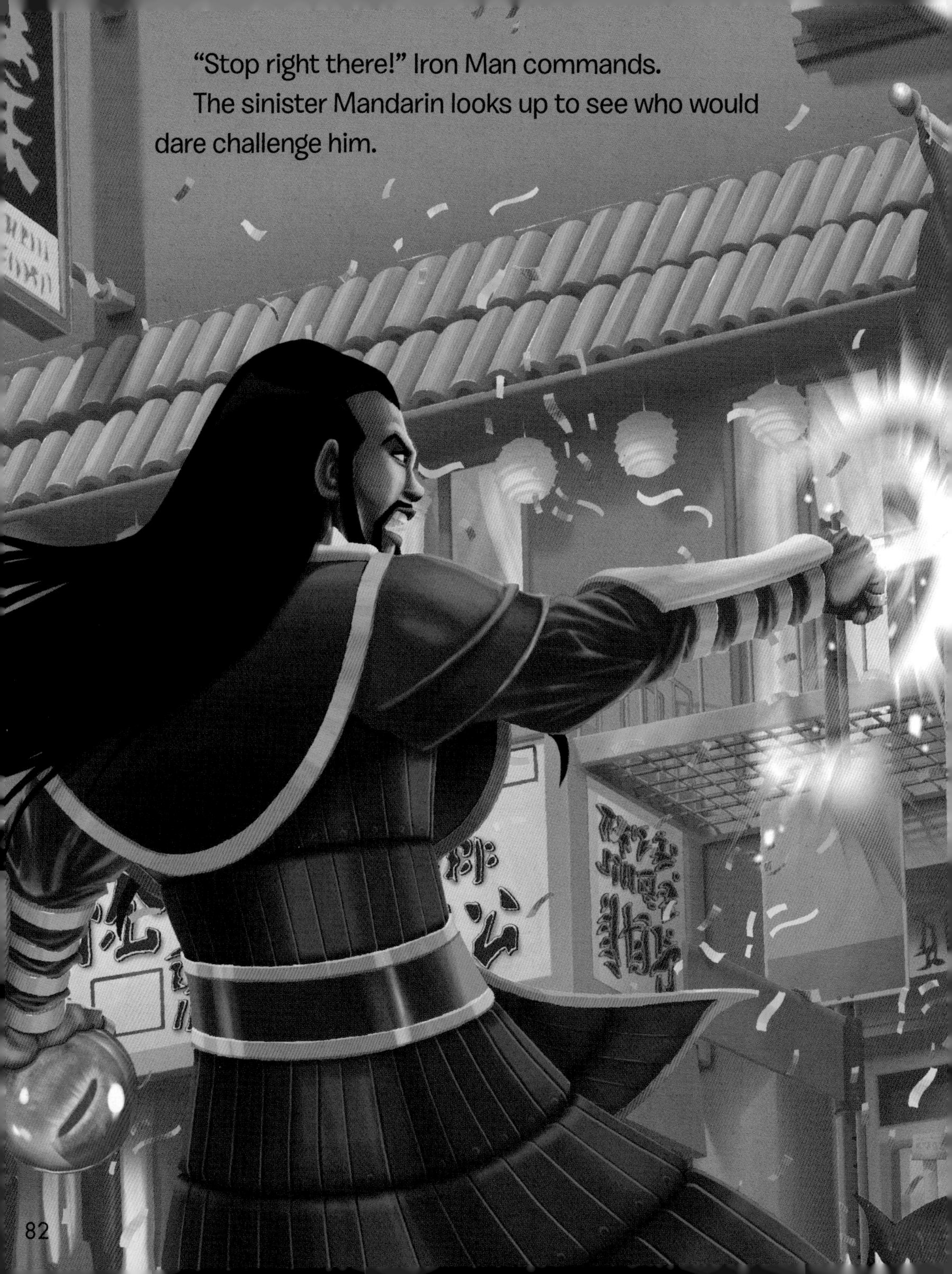

"Iron Man!" the Mandarin growls as he grabs the gem. He fires a beam of energy at the hero, but Iron Man's armor deflects the blast.

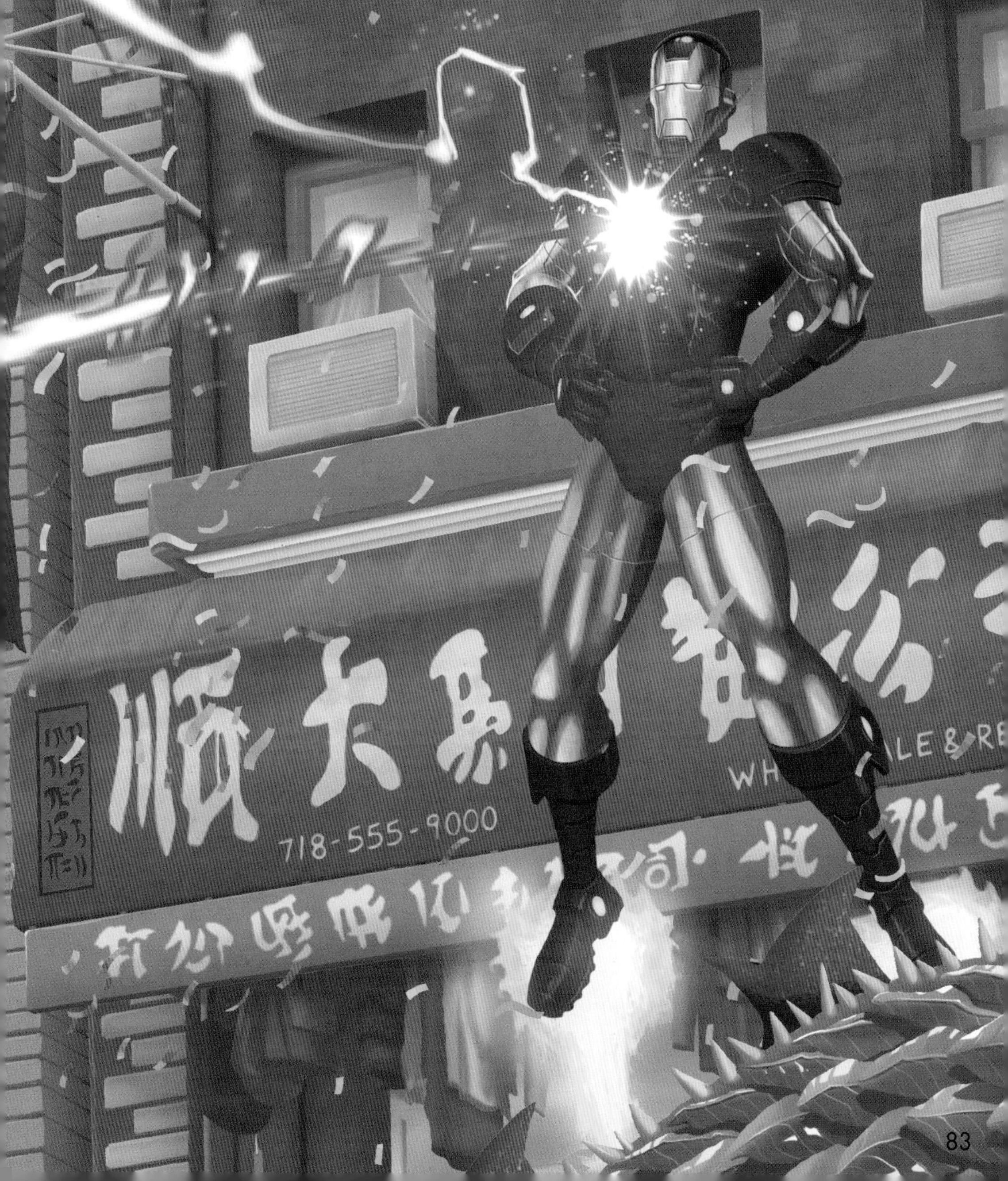
718-555-9000

"Your armor cannot withstand the might of my rings for long," the Mandarin boasts. "Each one is more than a match for you!"

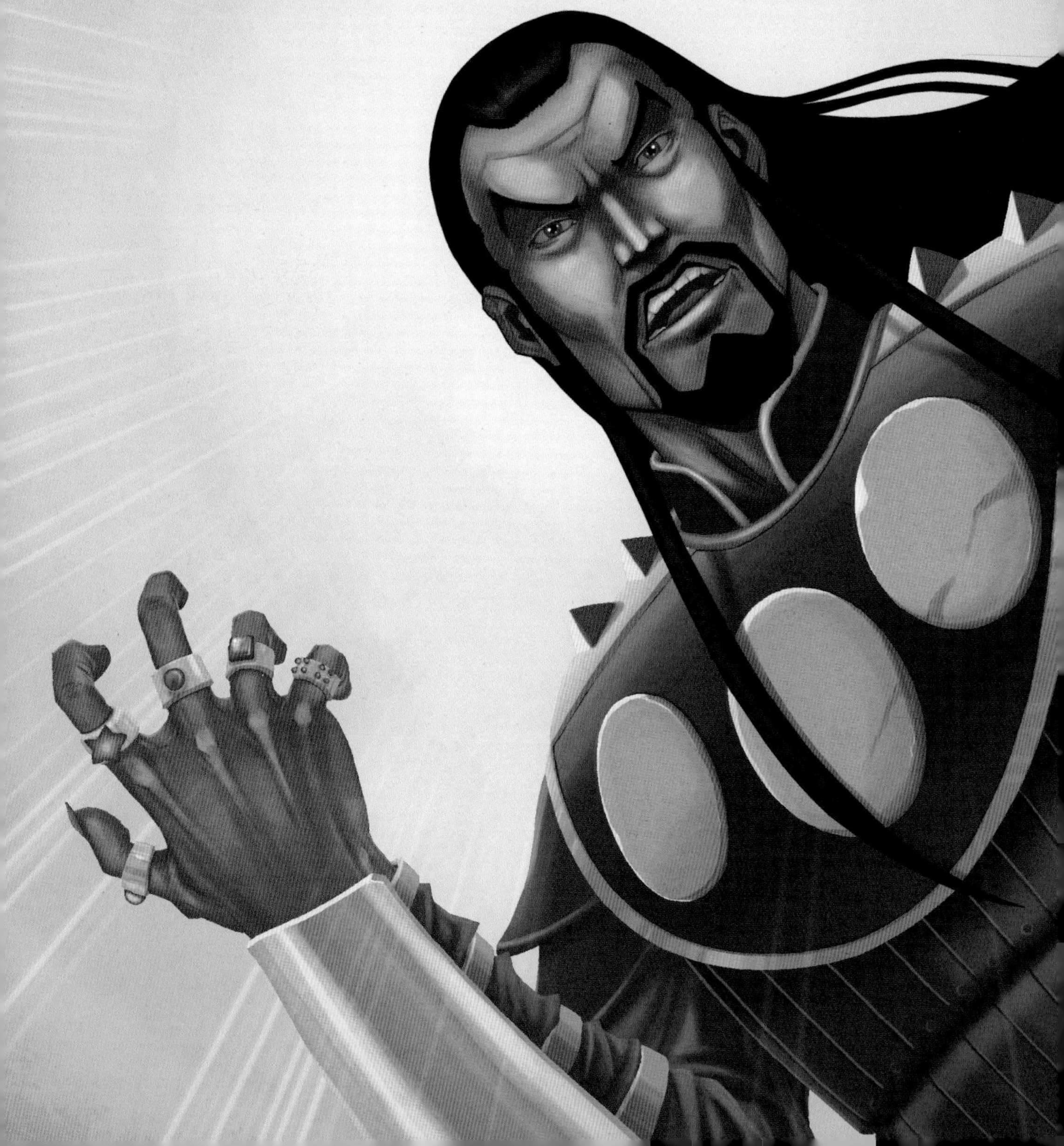

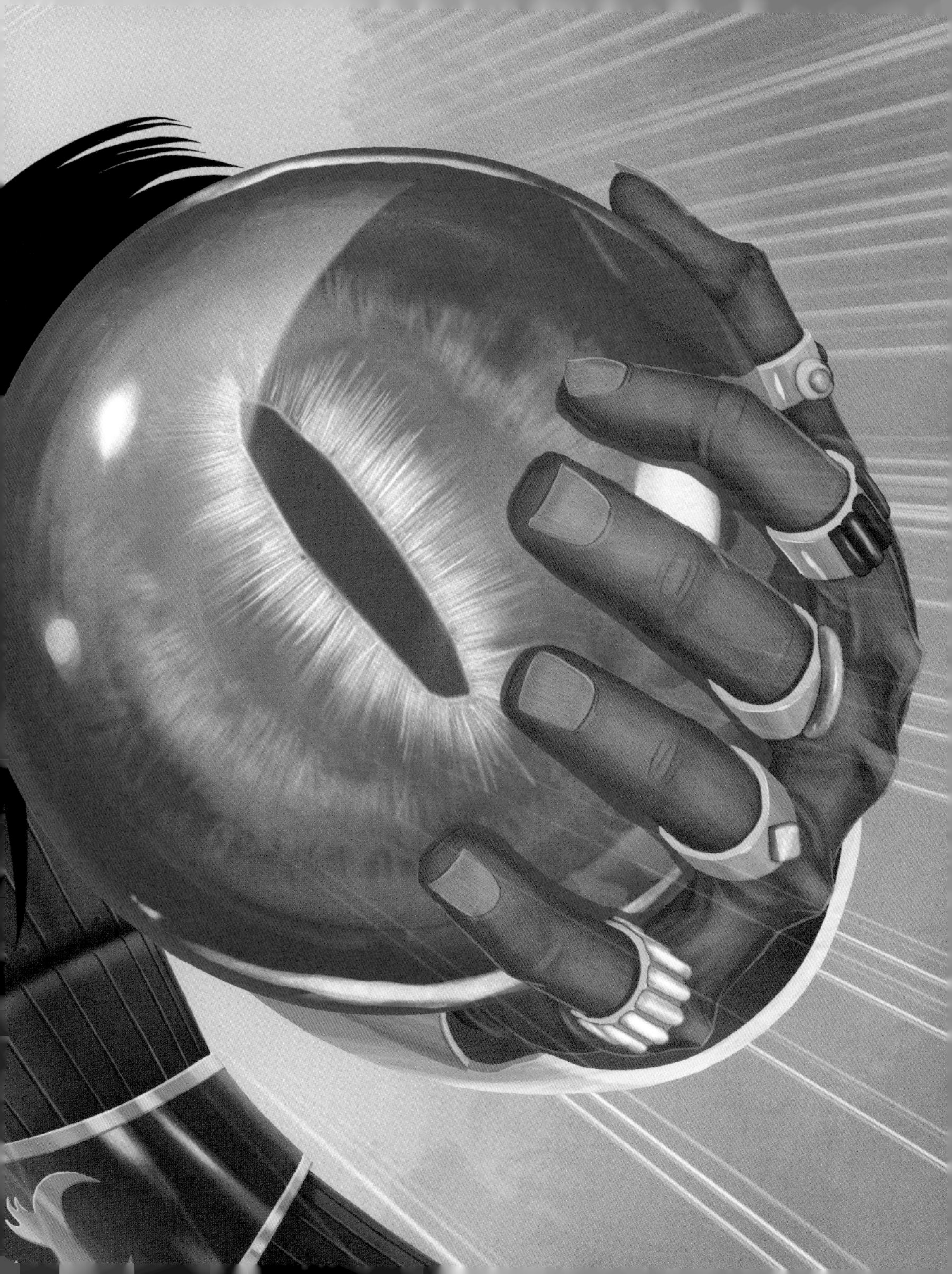

The Mandarin uses his Vortex ring to create a twisting tornado. It sends Iron Man spinning around and around.

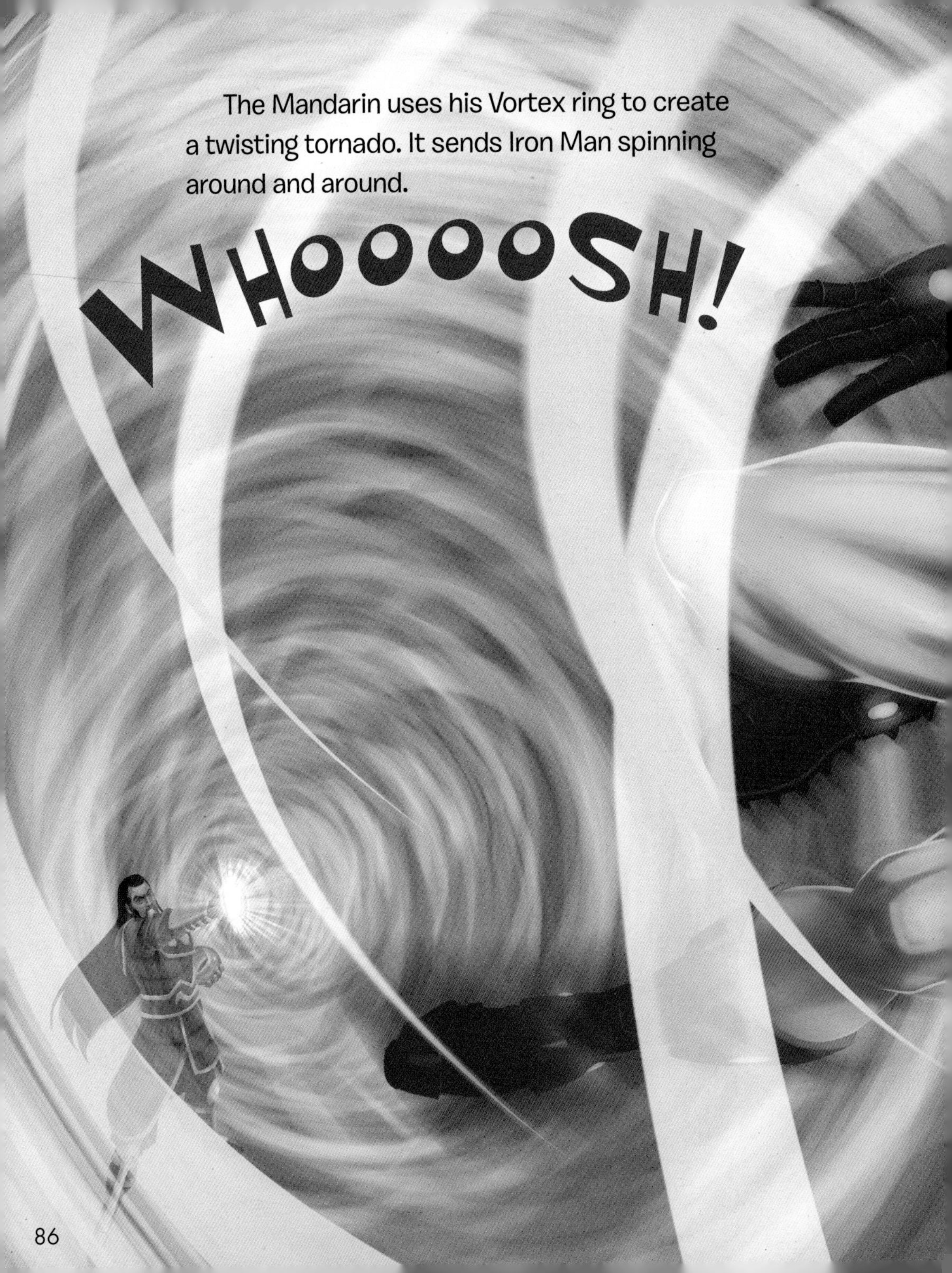
WHOOOOSH!

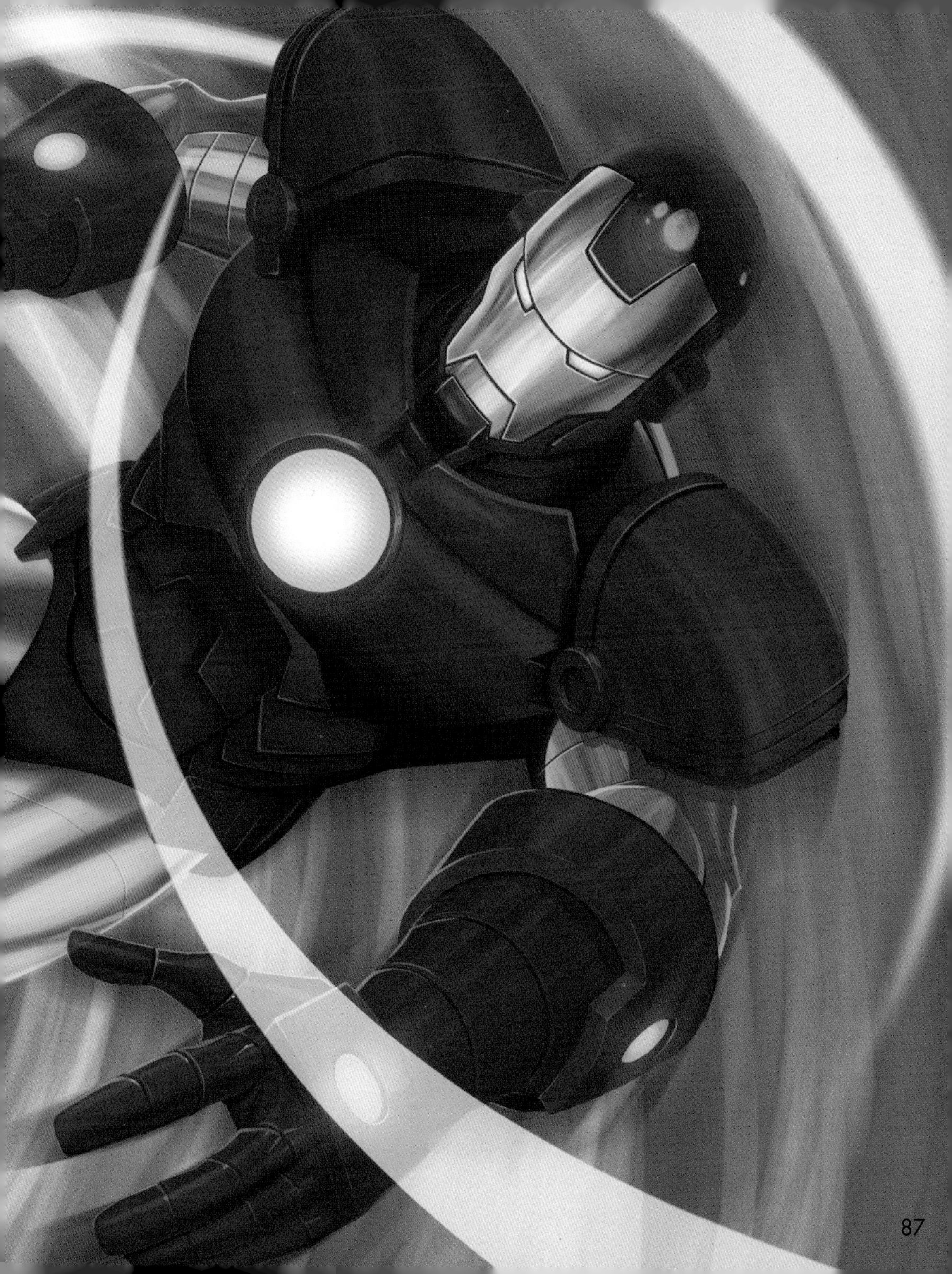

"Is that all you've got?" Iron Man says.

The Mandarin laughs triumphantly. Electricity crackles from his Electro-Blast ring.

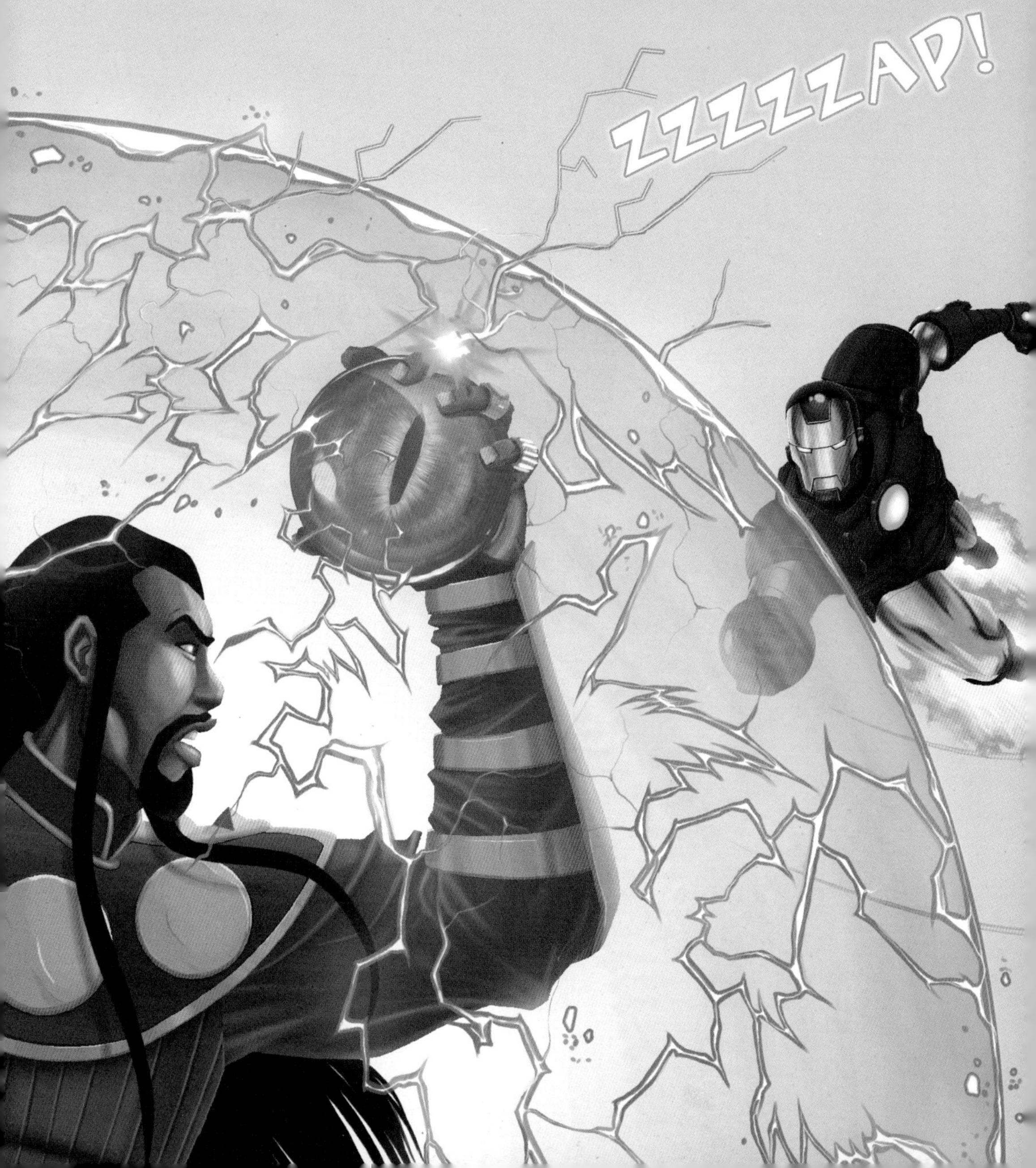
ZZZZZAP!

Iron Man scoops up a handful of fireworks and tosses them into the air. The Mandarin's electricity ignites the fireworks.

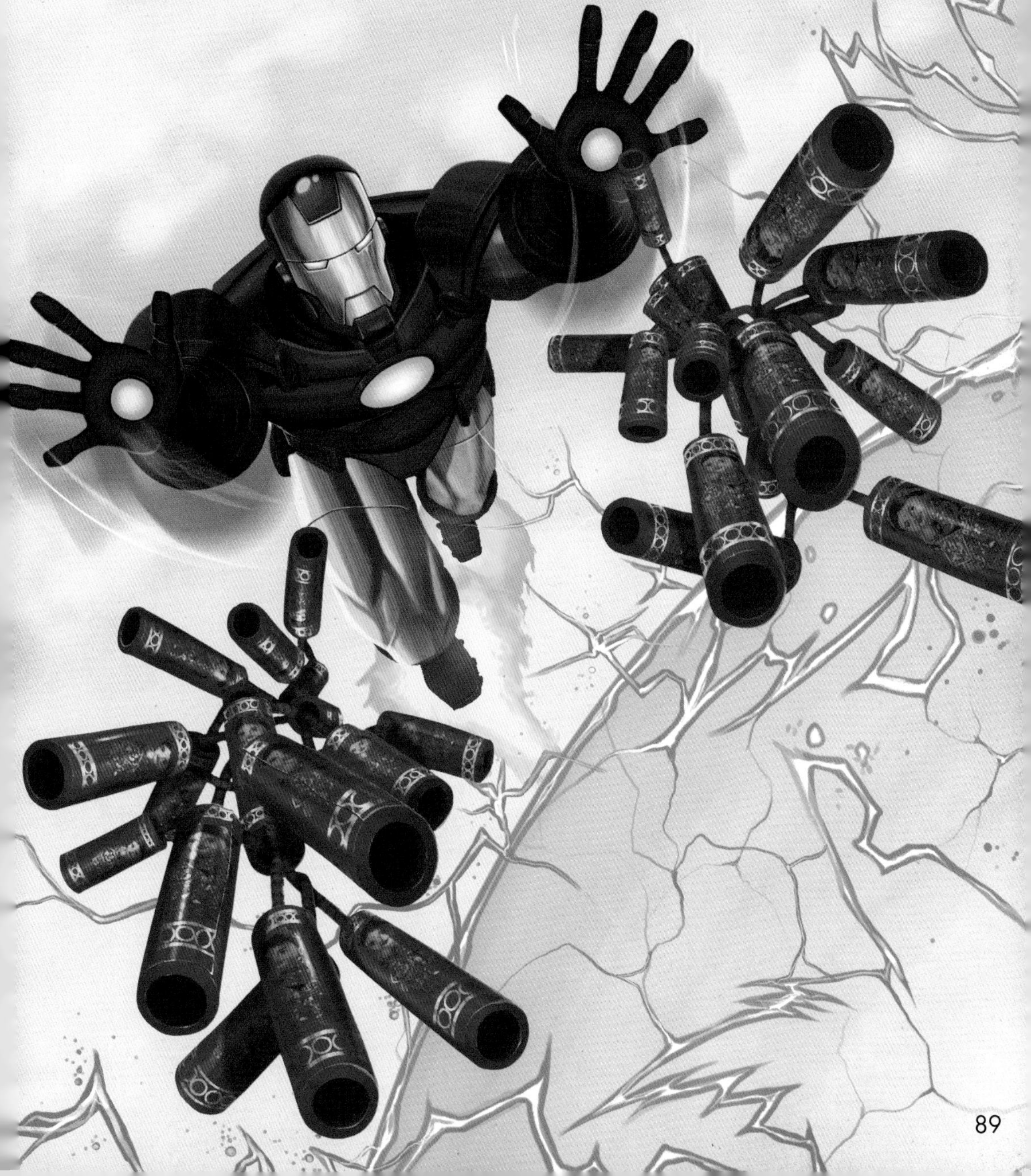

"Arrrghh!" the Mandarin cries out as the fireworks go off and light up the sky.

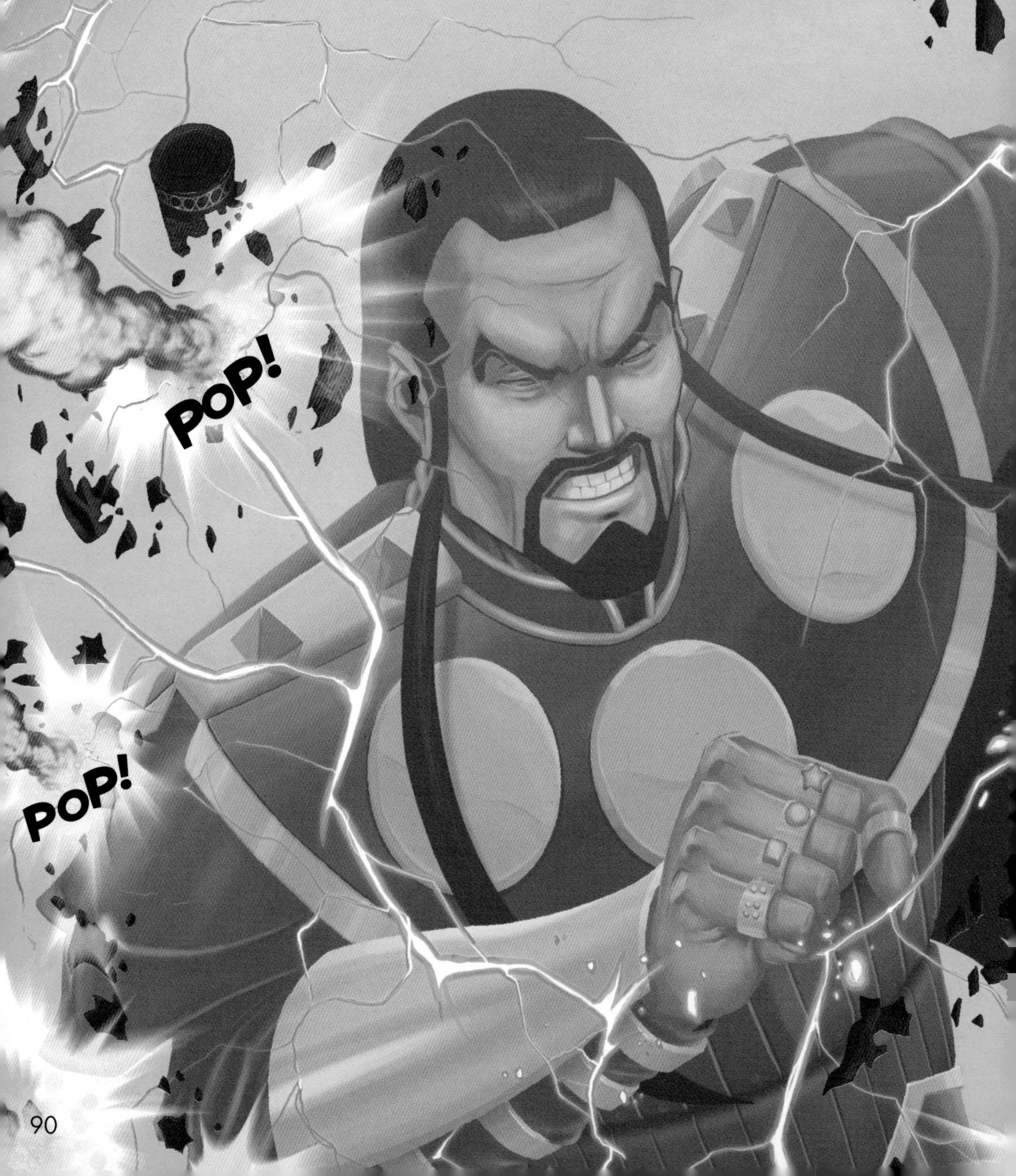
POP!
POP!

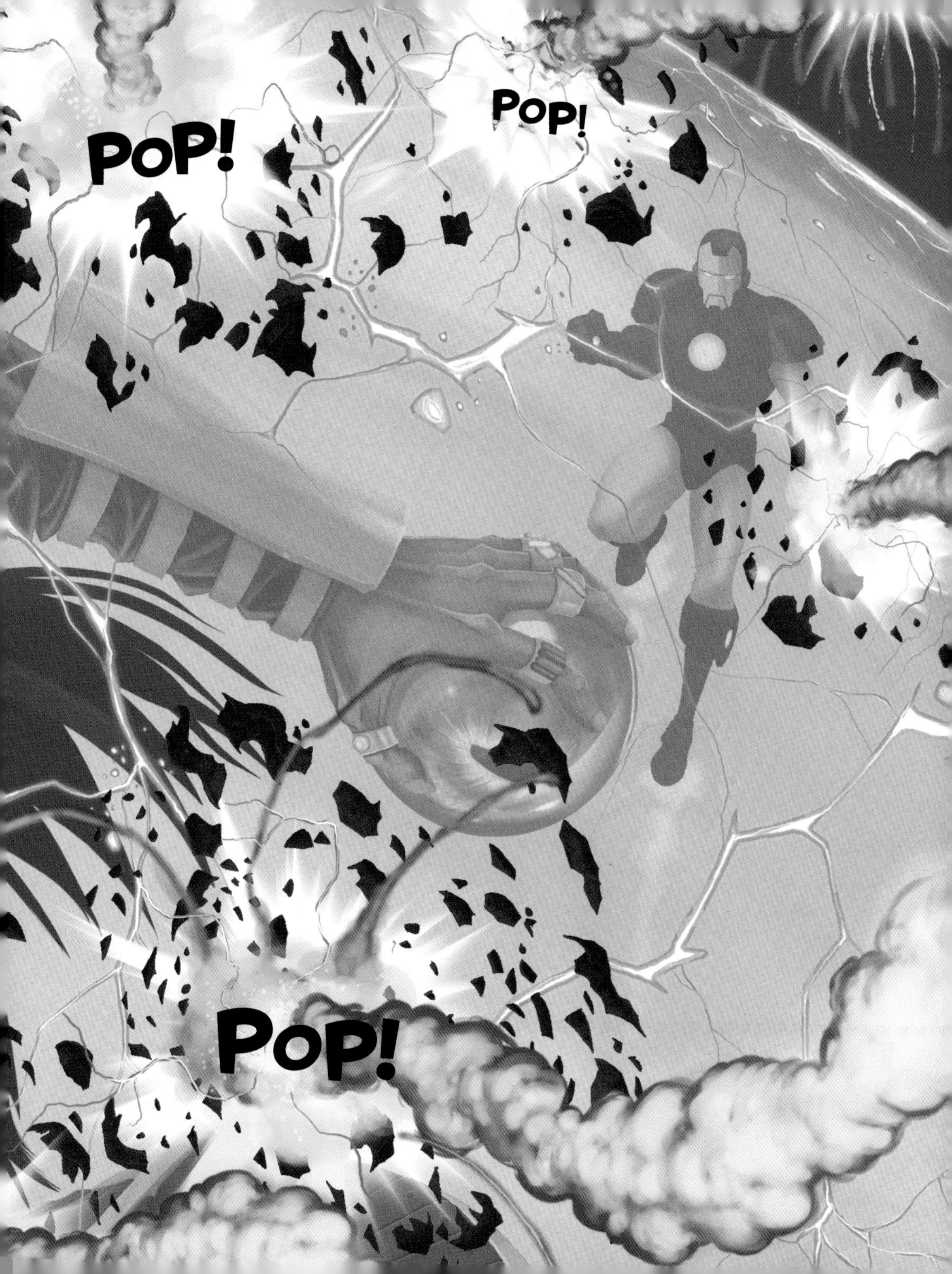
POP!
POP!
POP!

“Now it’s time to wrap things up,” Iron Man says, grabbing one of the long parade dragons.

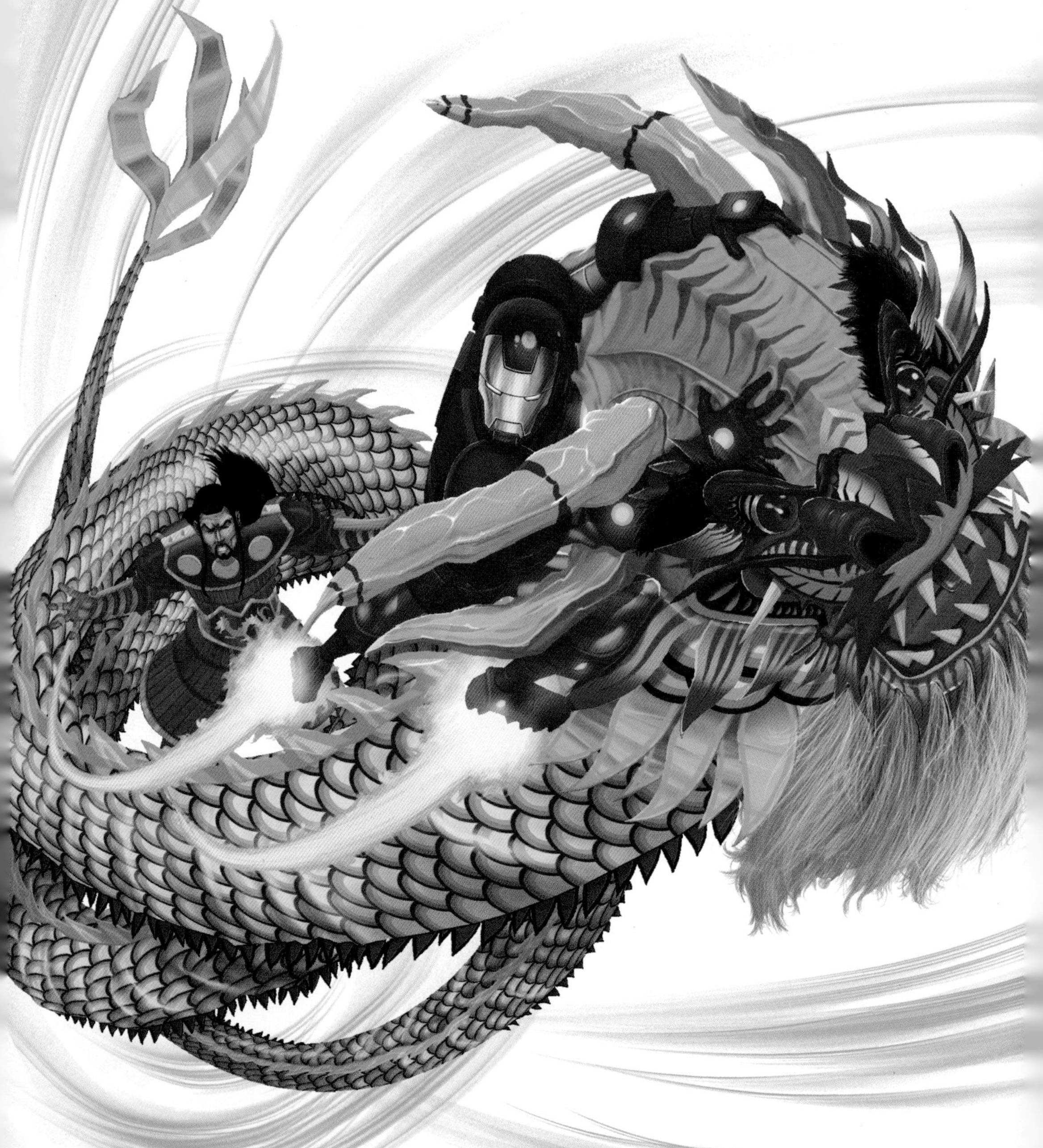

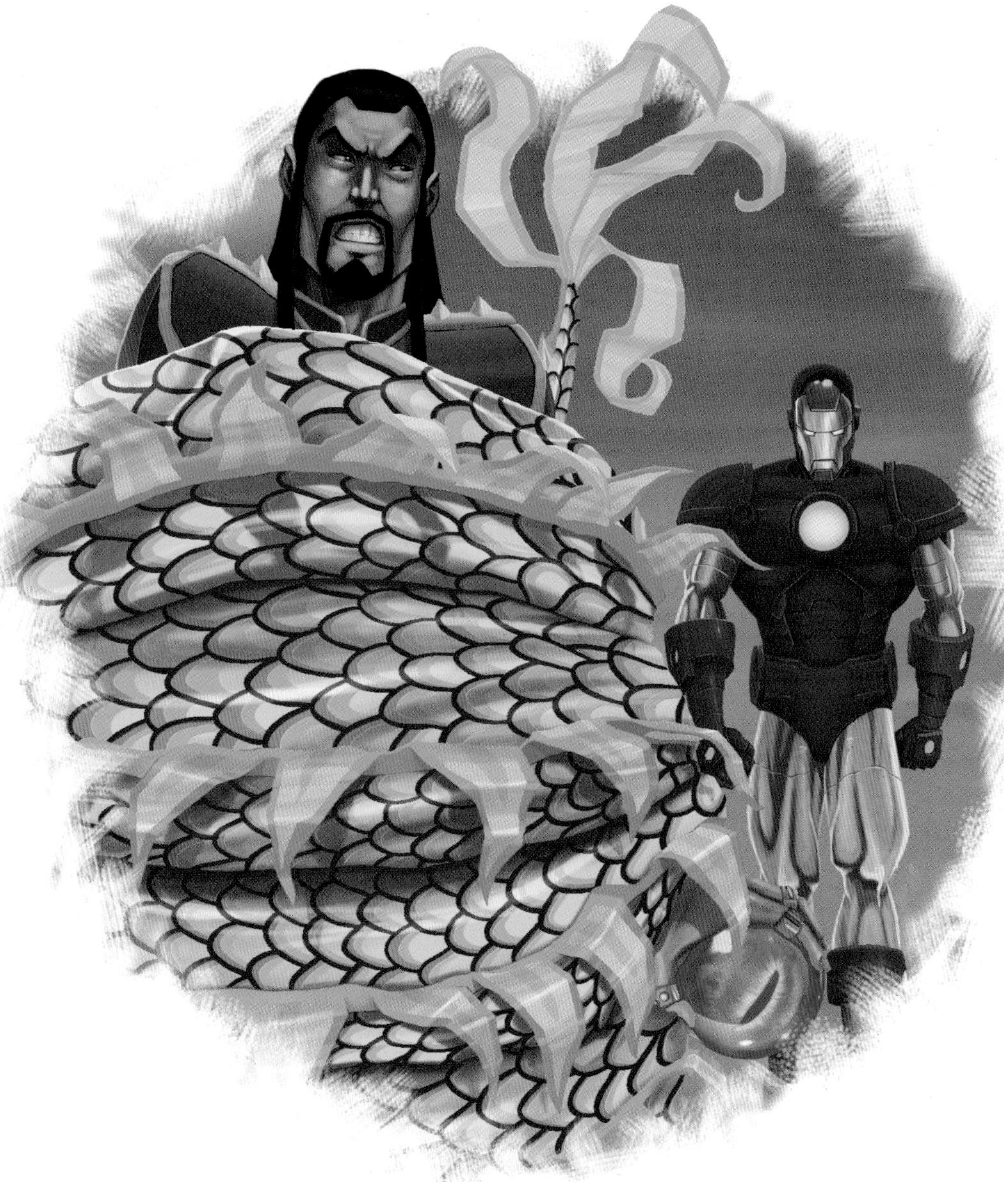

Iron Man ties the Mandarin up tight. The villain can't use his rings.

“The Eye of the Dragon is for everyone to enjoy,” Iron Man tells the Mandarin. “It’s not just for you.”

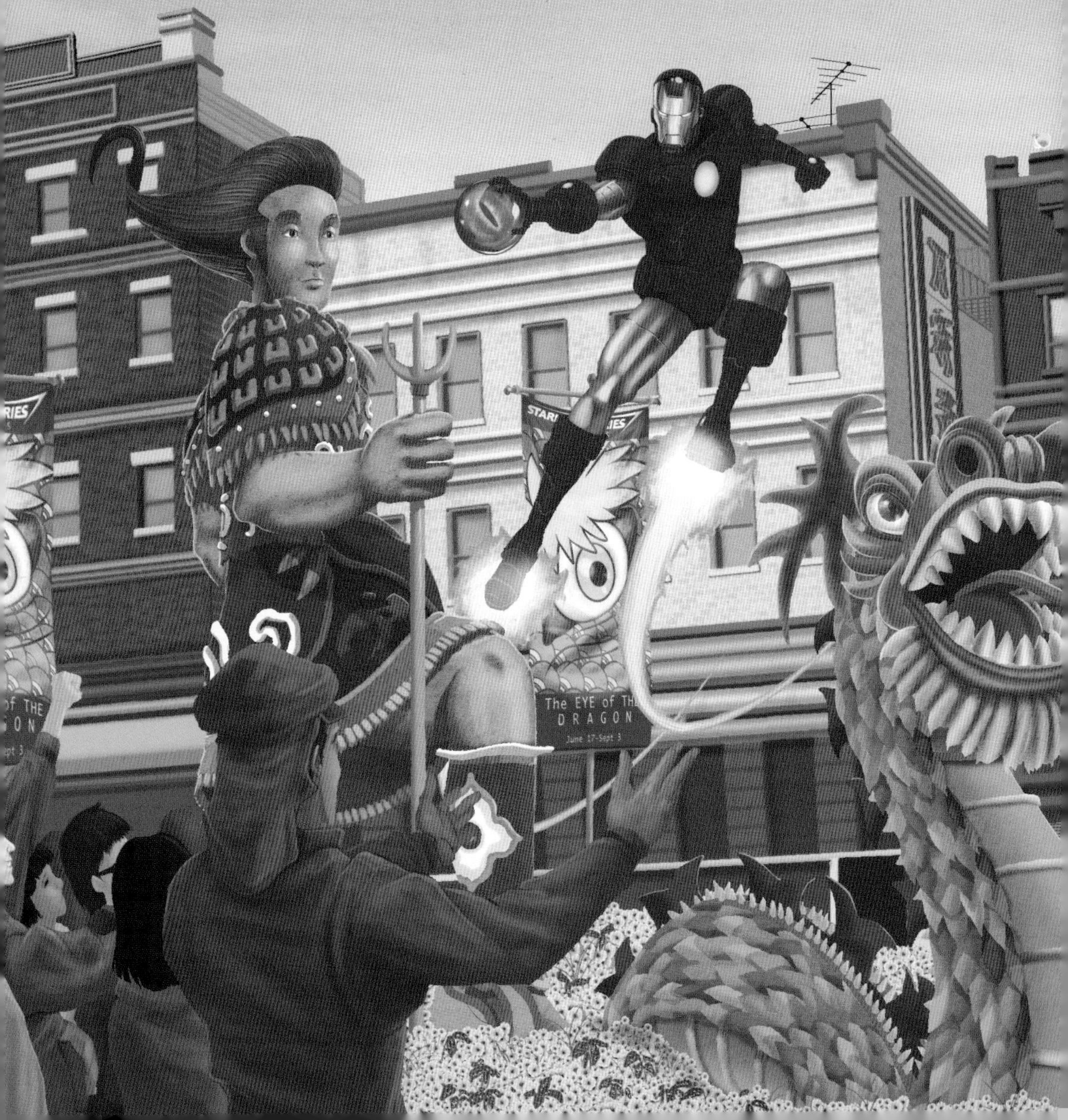
The EYE of
DRAGON
June 17-Sept 3

"Take him away," Iron Man says to the authorities. "We've got a parade to finish!"

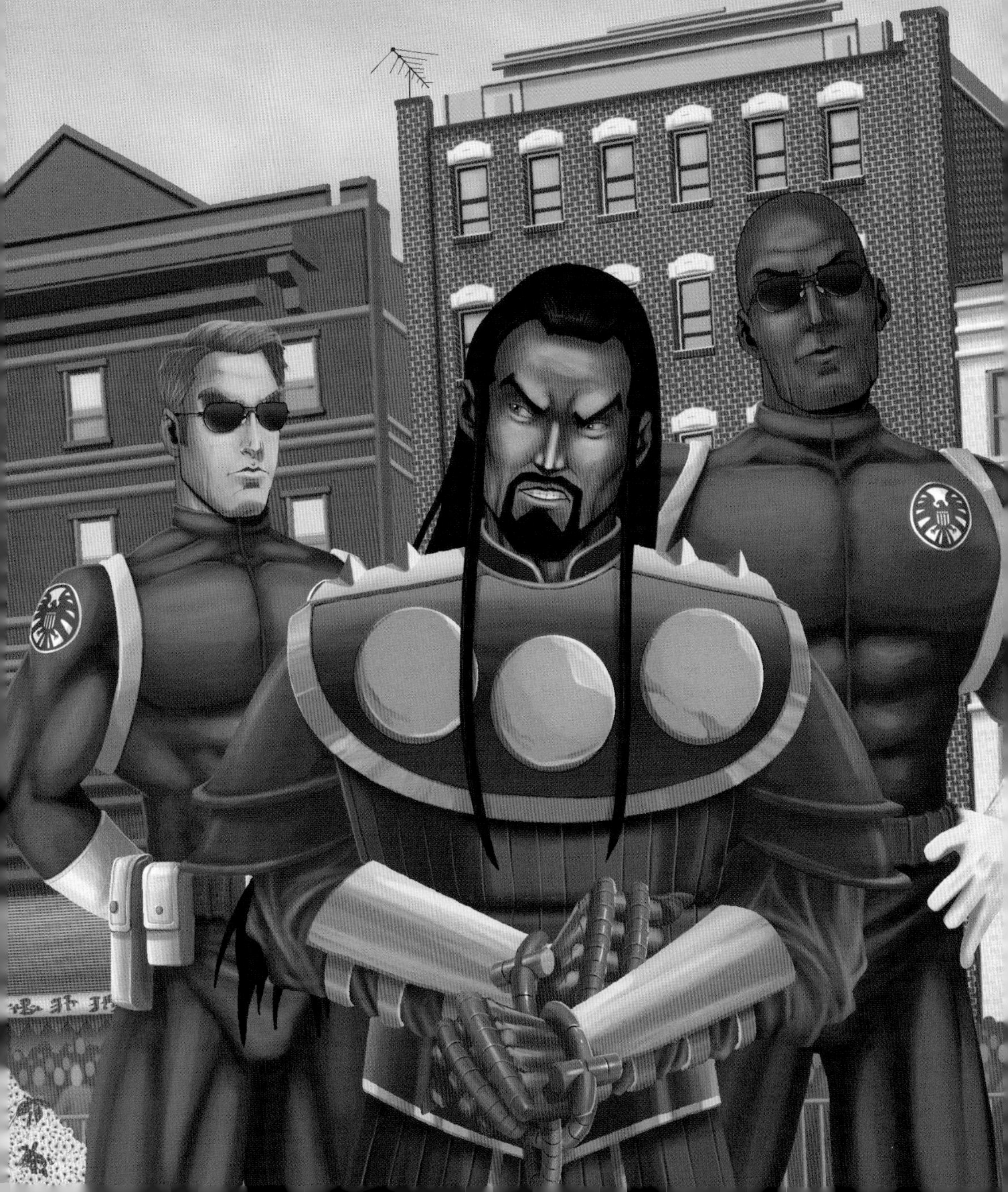

Iron Man fires his repulsor beams into the air, and they explode like fireworks. Everyone cheers.

GO, IRON MAN!

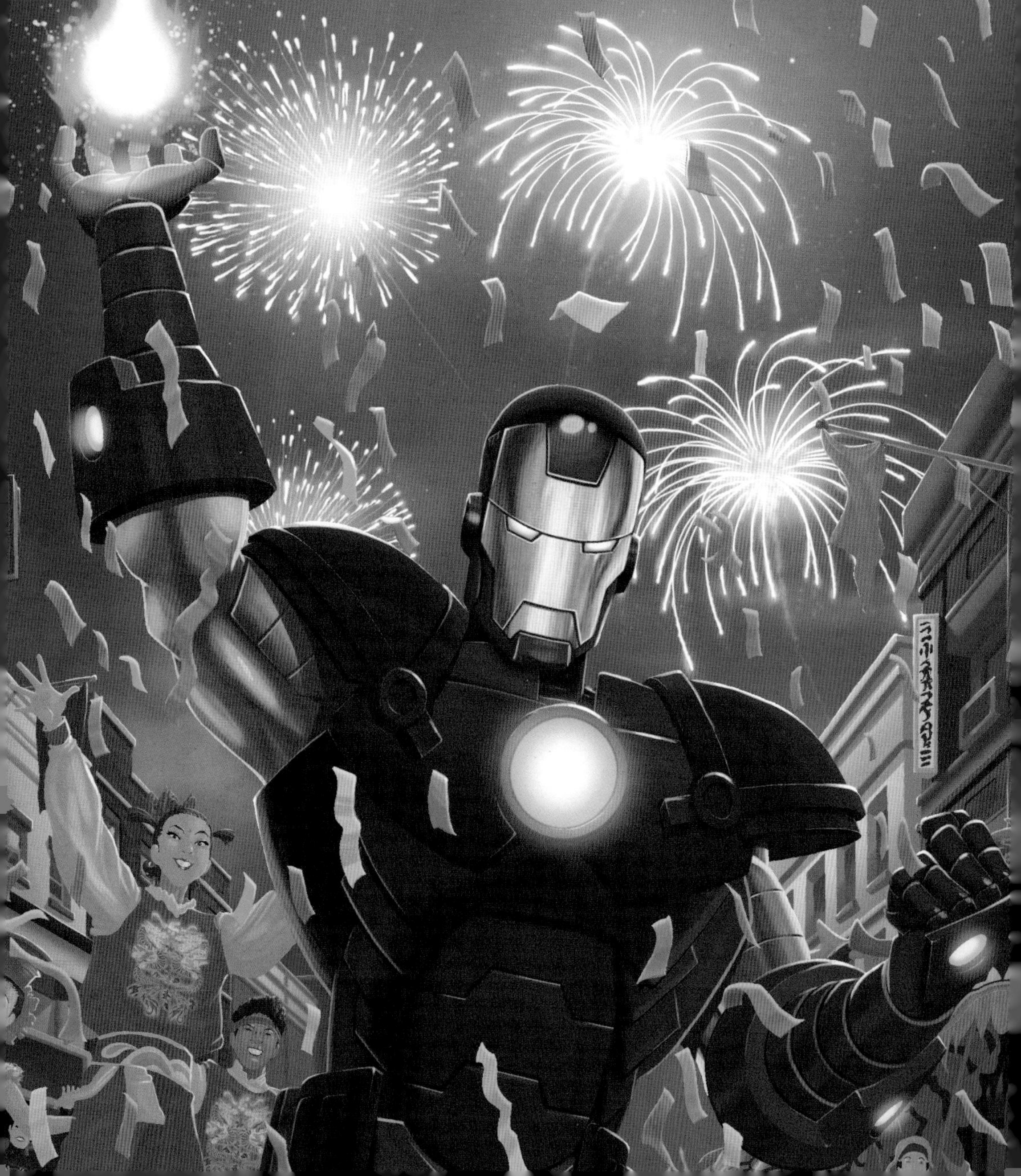

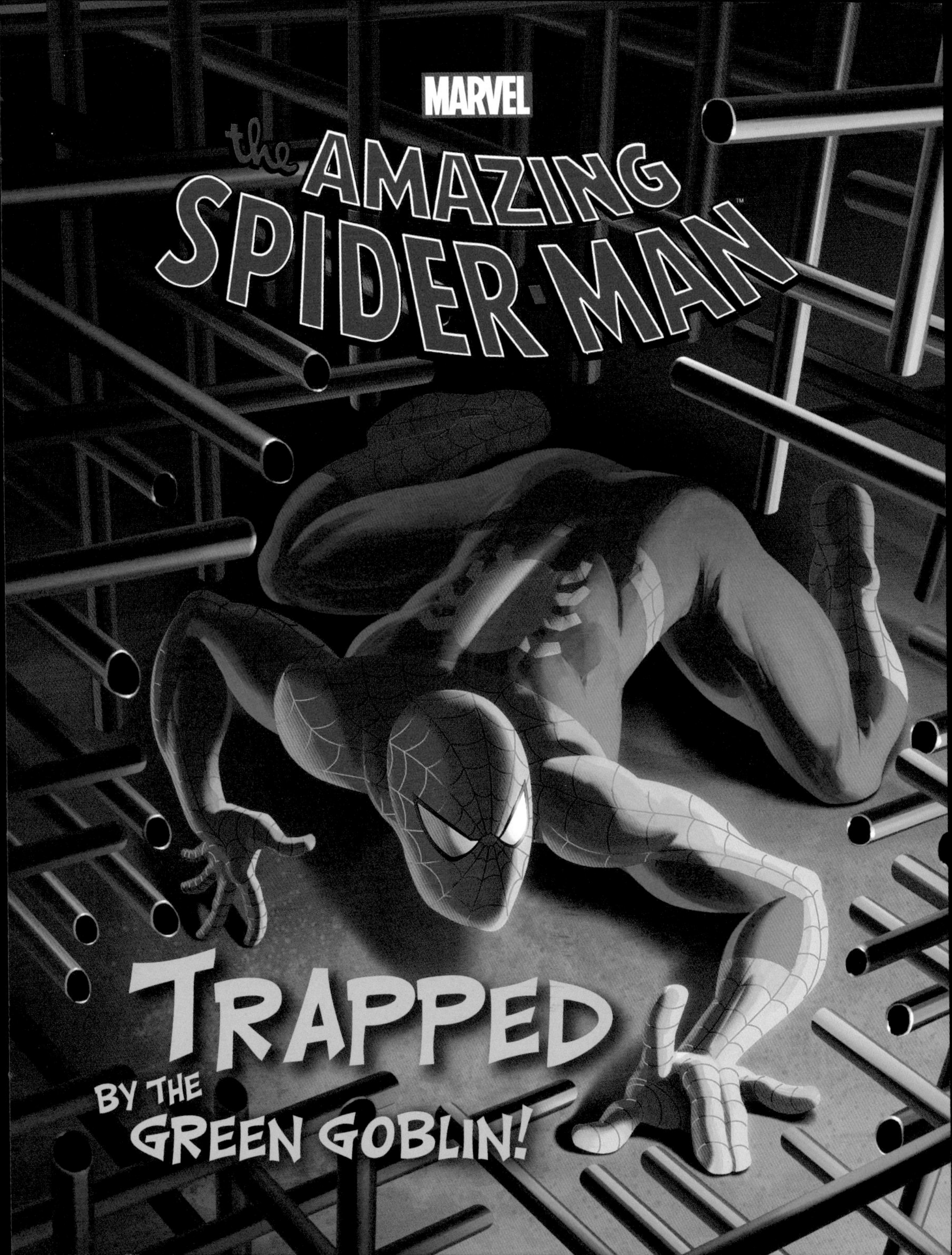
MARVEL
the AMAZING SPIDER-MAN™
TRAPPED
BY THE GREEN GOBLIN!

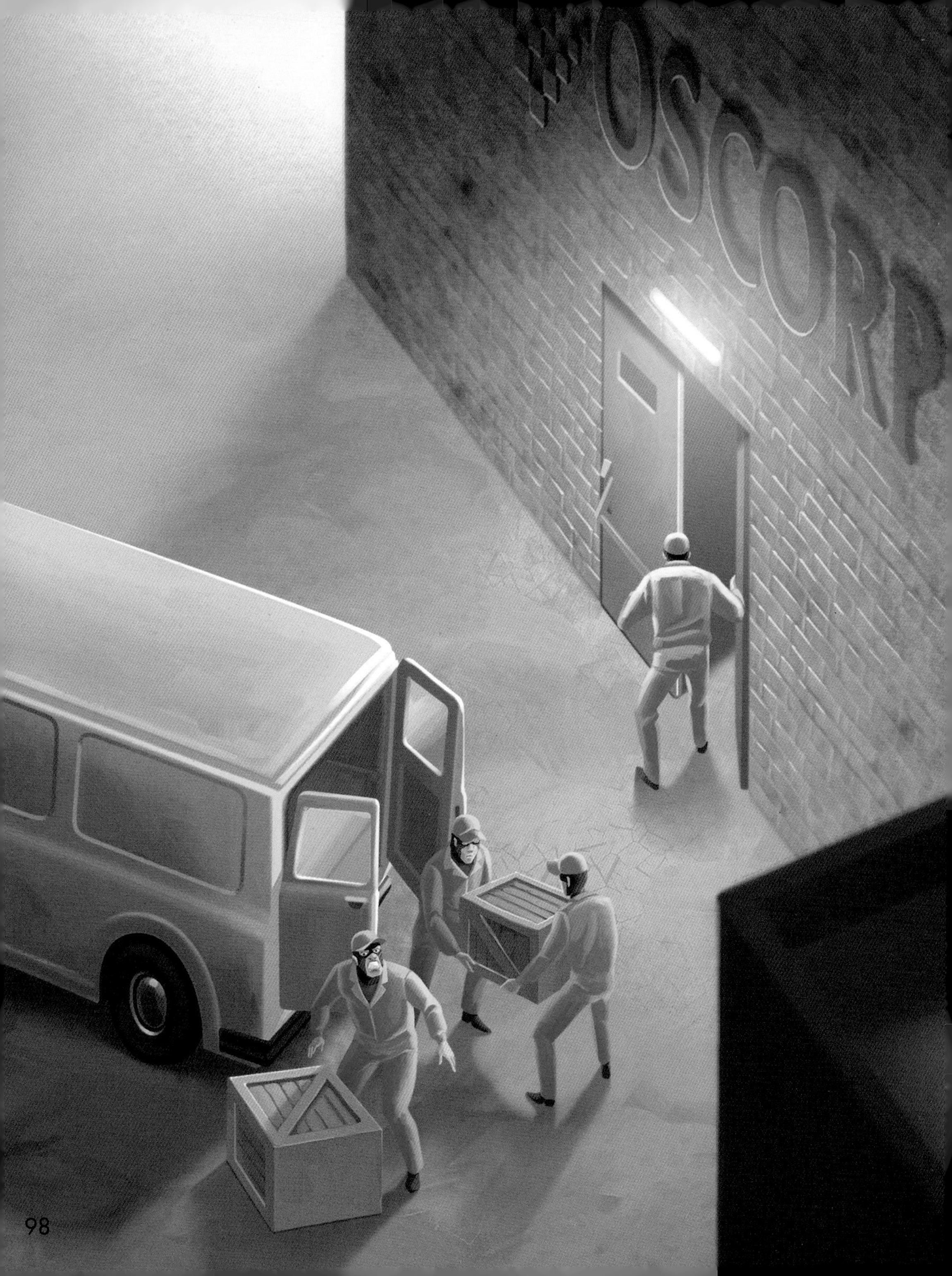
OSCORP

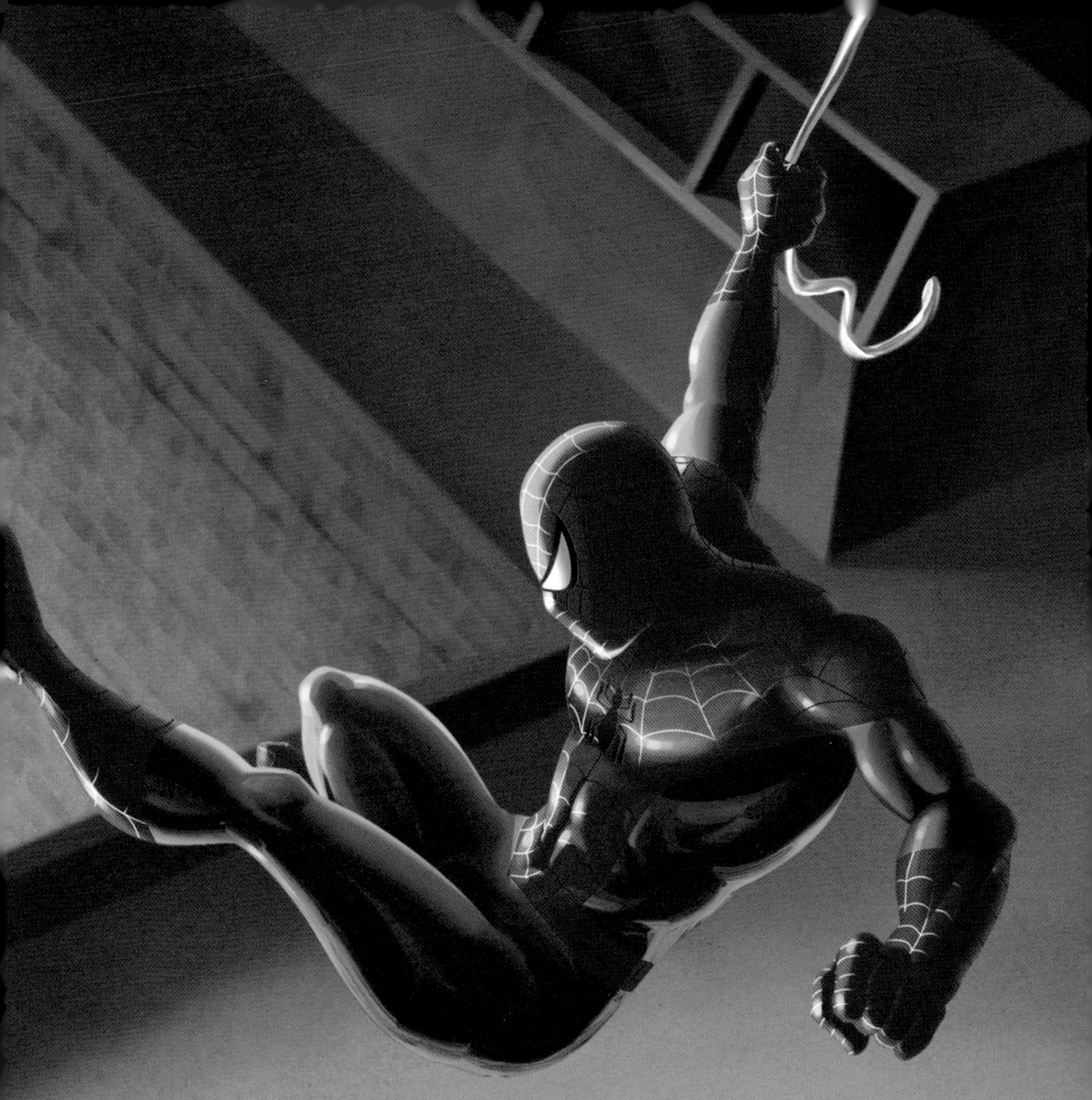

Late one night, the super hero **Spider-Man** saw some men robbing a warehouse.

"Isn't it a little late to be shopping?" Spider-Man asked as he swung down on them.

"Spider-Man! Let's get outta here!" yelled one of the men. He turned to run, but it was too late. Spider-Man used his **web-shooters** to stop the thief in his tracks!

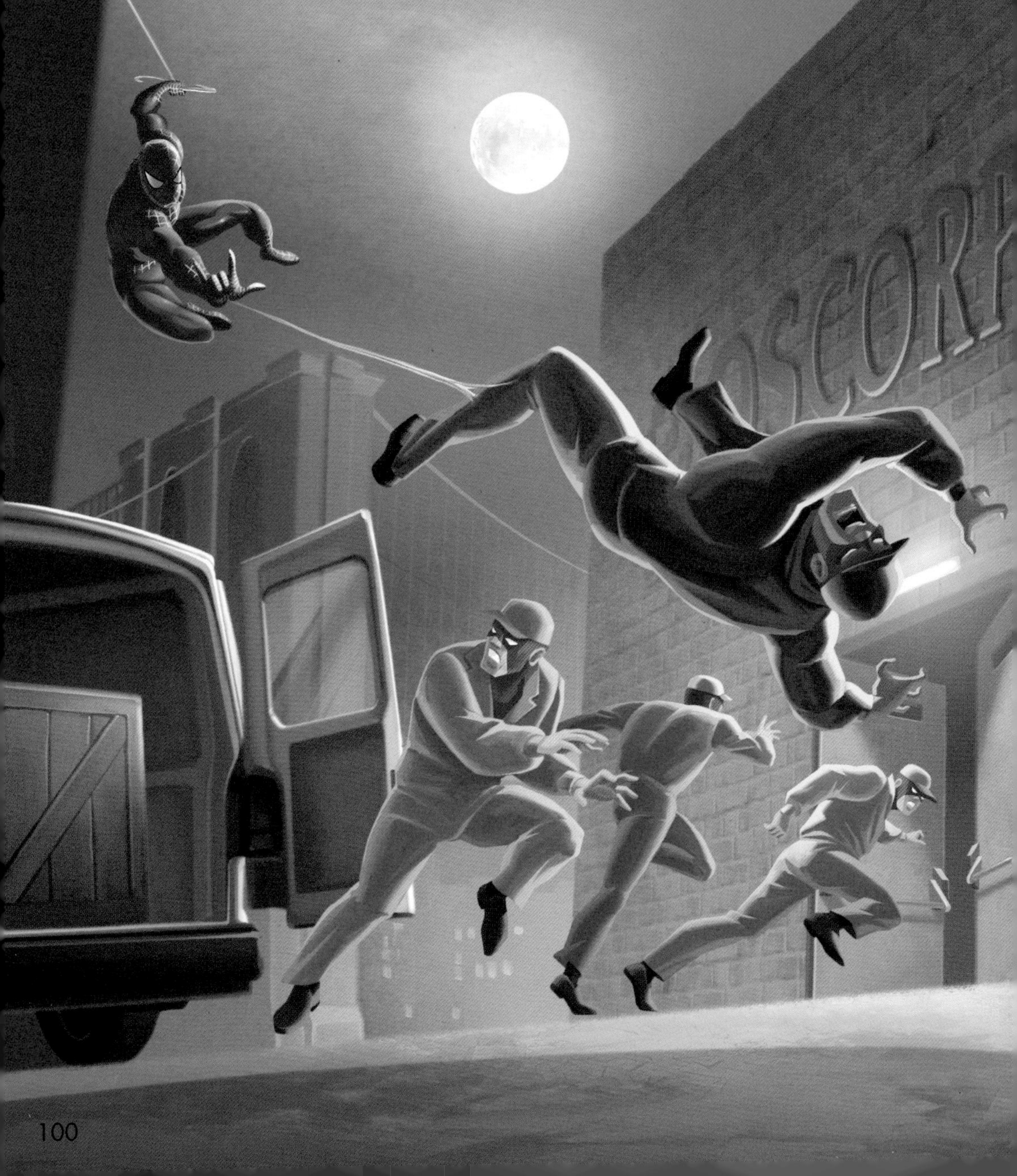

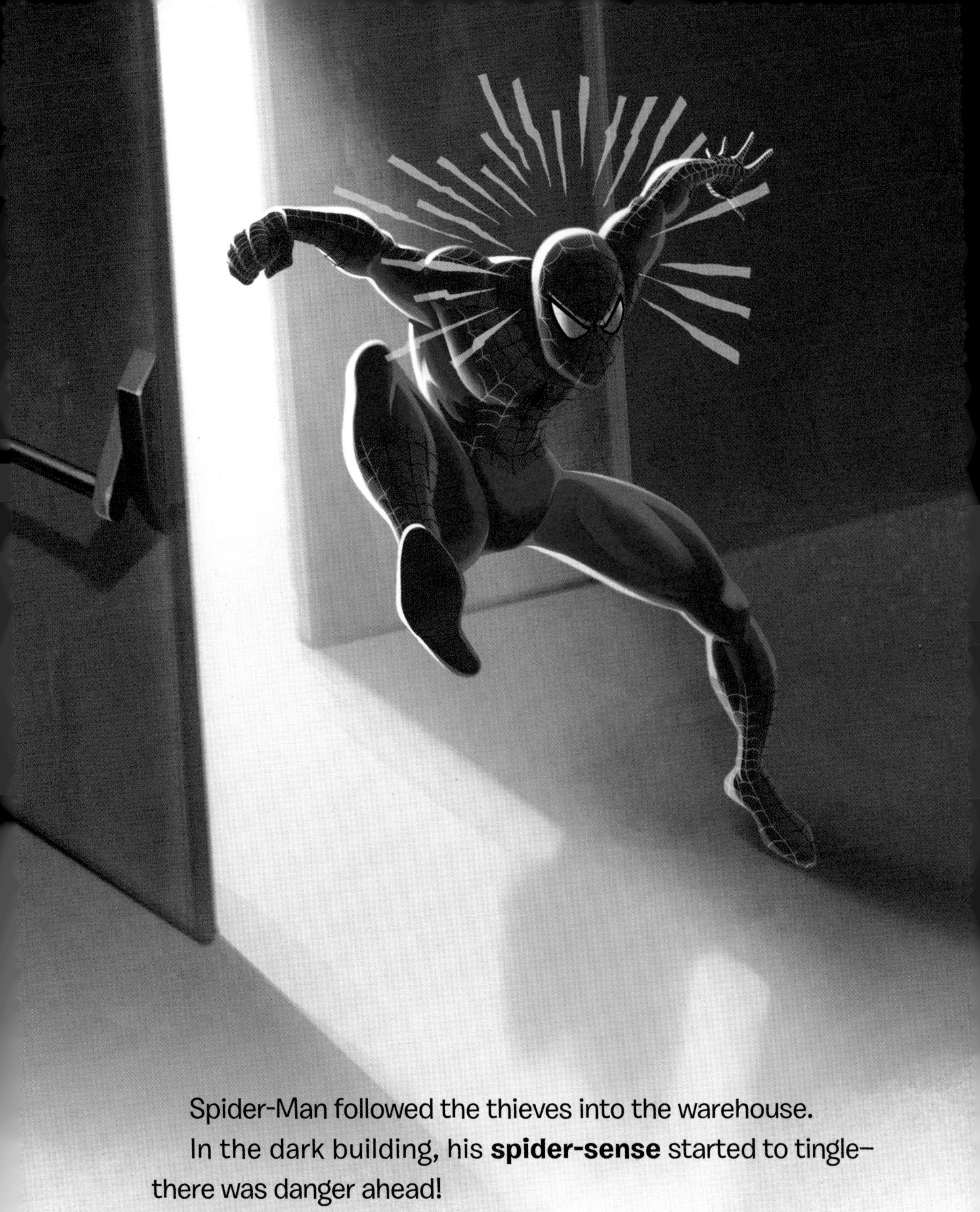

Spider-Man followed the thieves into the warehouse.

In the dark building, his **spider-sense** started to tingle—there was danger ahead!

Suddenly, the lights snapped on. It was a trap! The villain known as the **GREEN GOBLIN** laughed.

"All this for me?" Spider-Man joked. "And it's not even my birthday!"

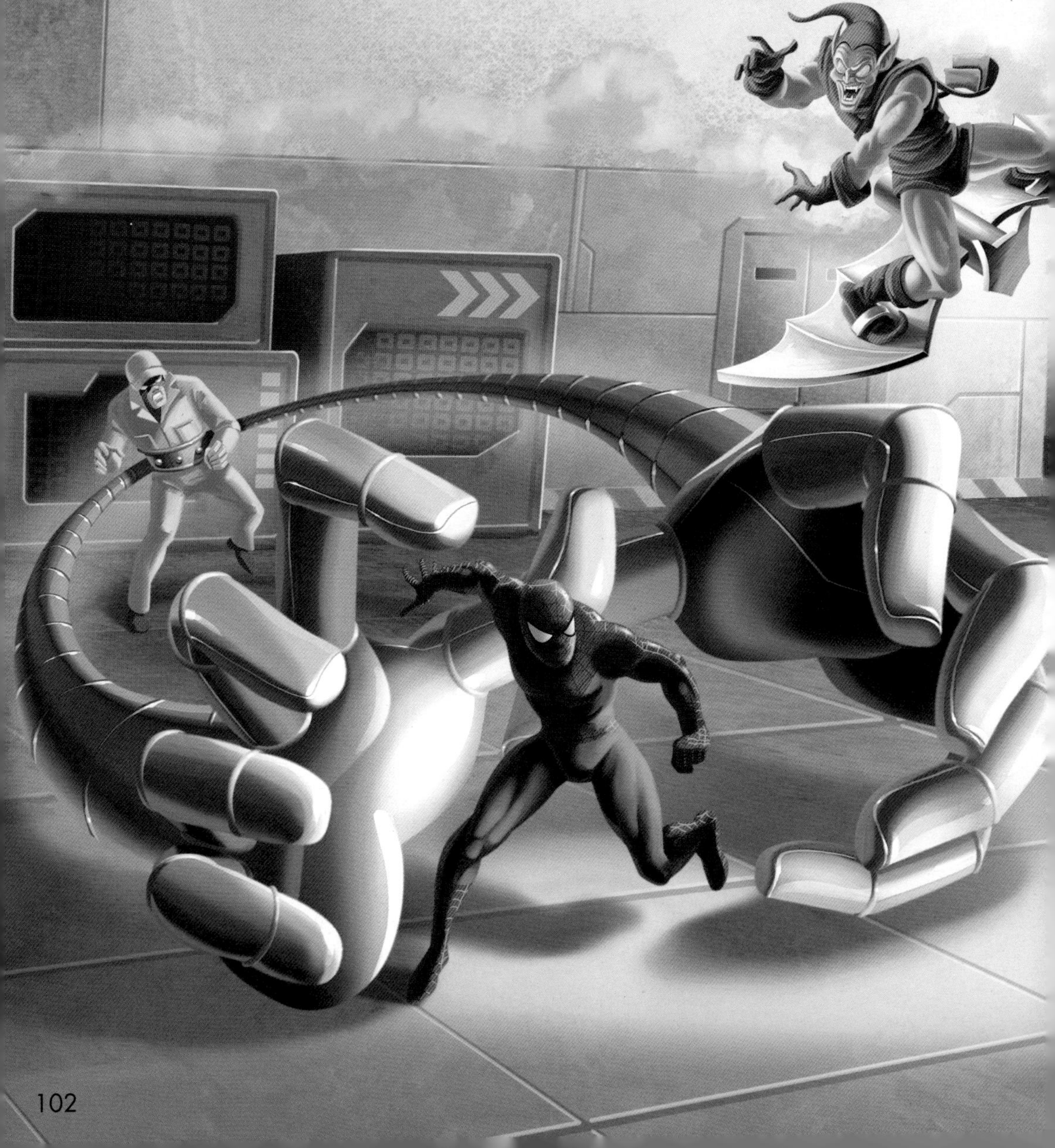

"I will make you wish you had never been born!" replied the Goblin. "Now crush him!"

One of the Goblin's thugs grabbed Spider-Man with his oversized mechanical hands and **SQUEEZED!**

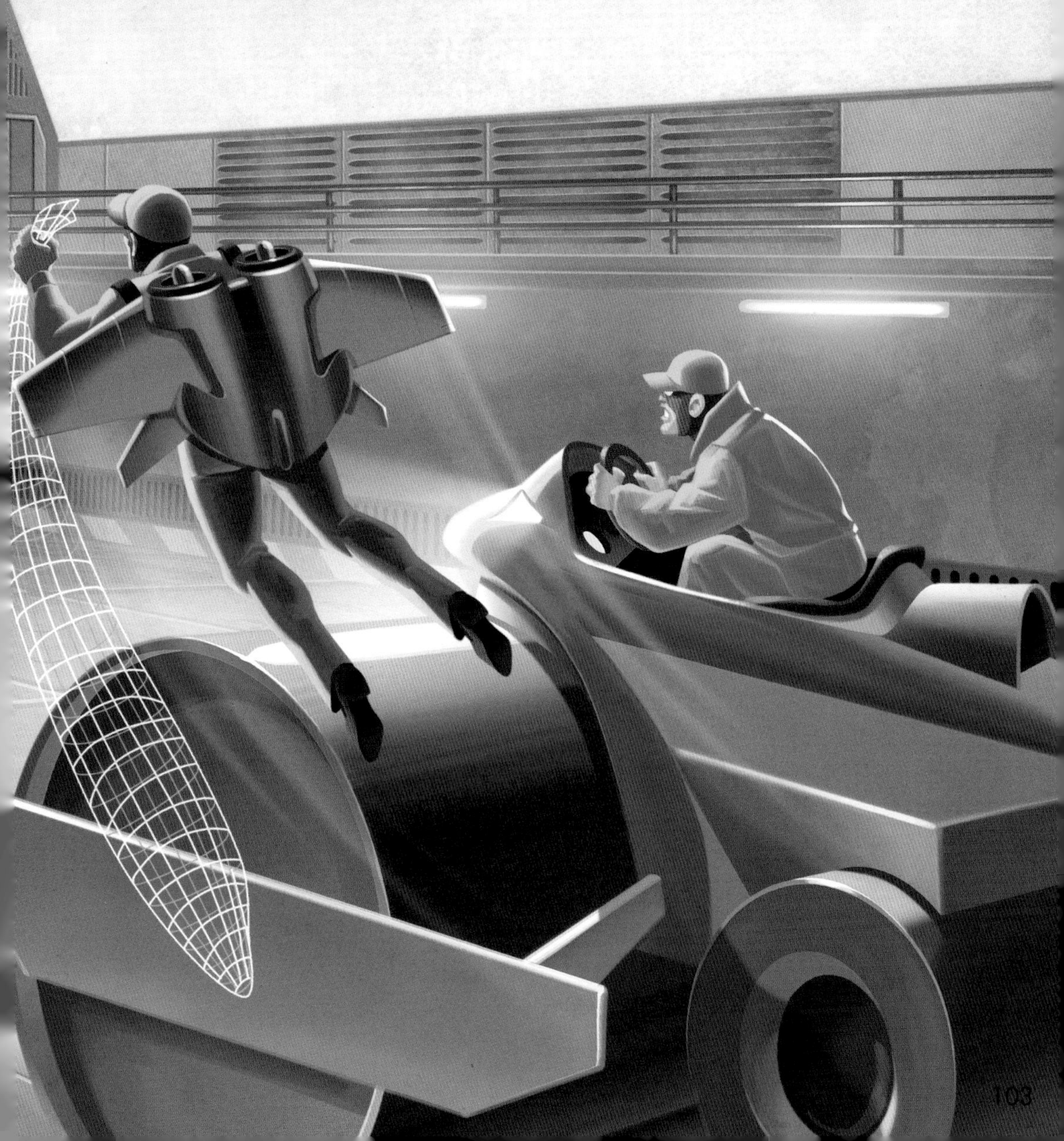

"Didn't your mother tell you to keep your hands to yourself?" Spider-Man said, bending the thug's mechanical arms out of shape.

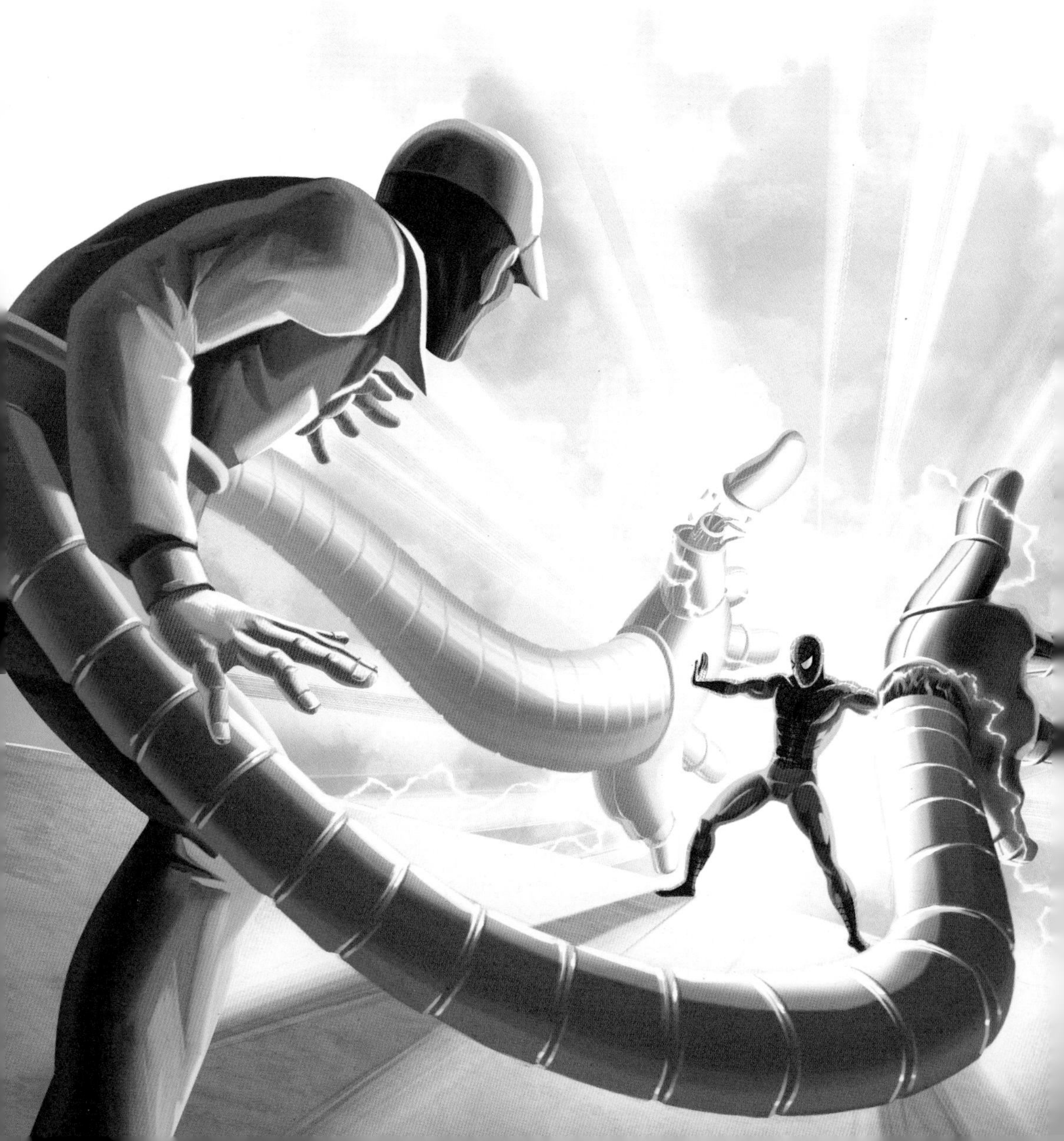

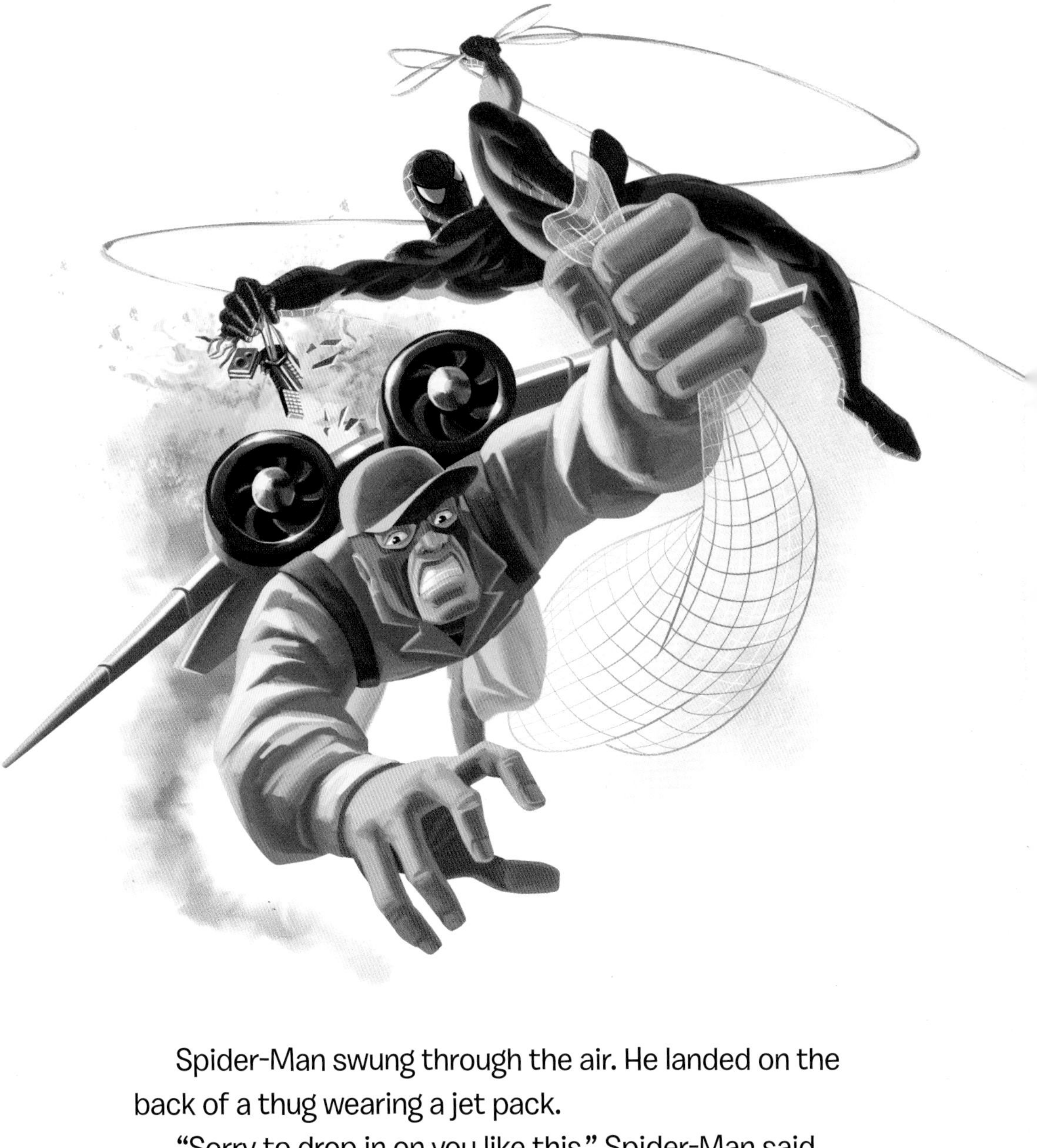

Spider-Man swung through the air. He landed on the back of a thug wearing a jet pack.

"Sorry to drop in on you like this," Spider-Man said, ripping out the jet pack's wires.

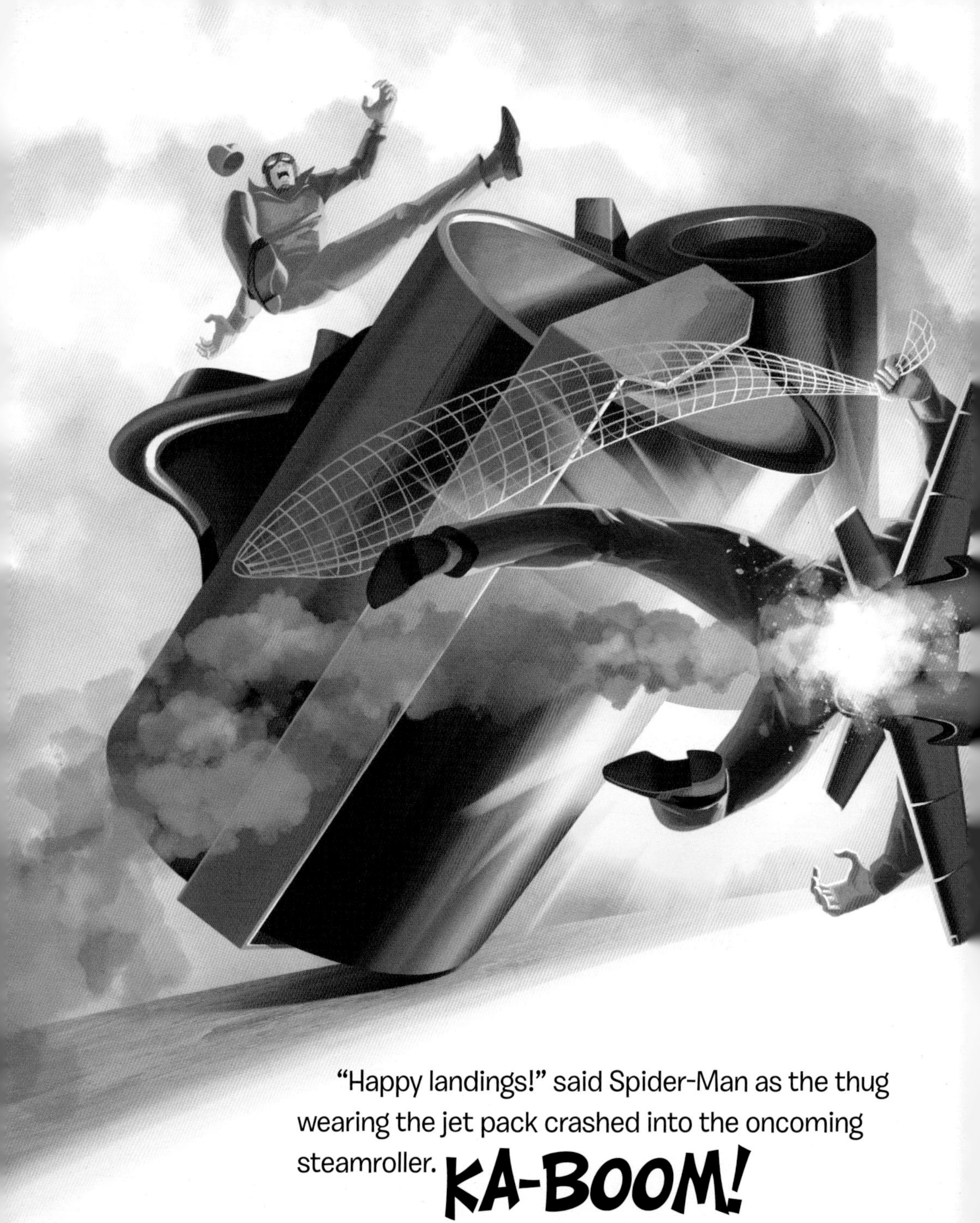

"Happy landings!" said Spider-Man as the thug wearing the jet pack crashed into the oncoming steamroller. **KA-BOOM!**

"Now it's just you and me, Goblin," said Spider-Man.

"Those fools failed to defeat you, but I won't," snarled the Green Goblin.

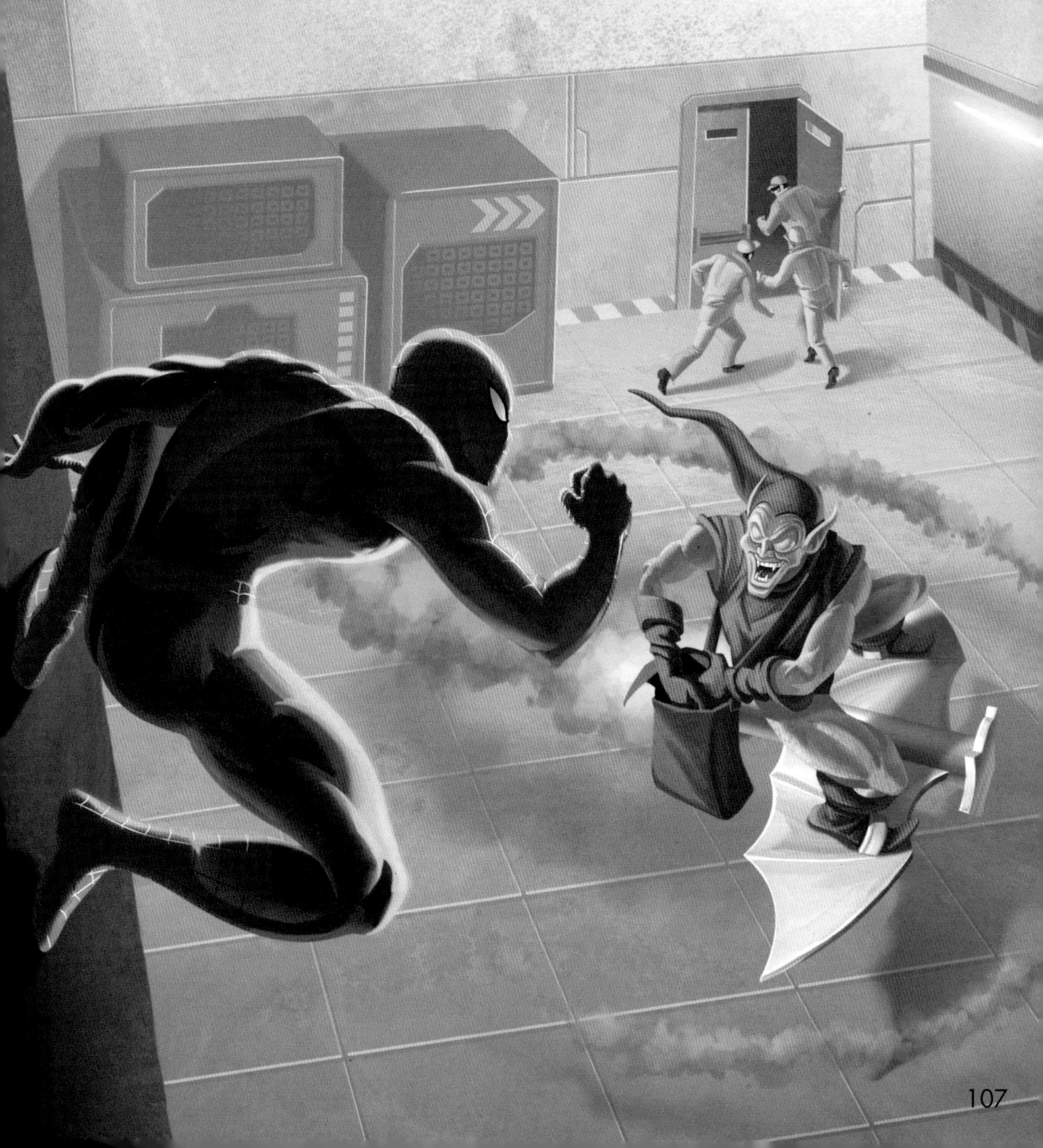

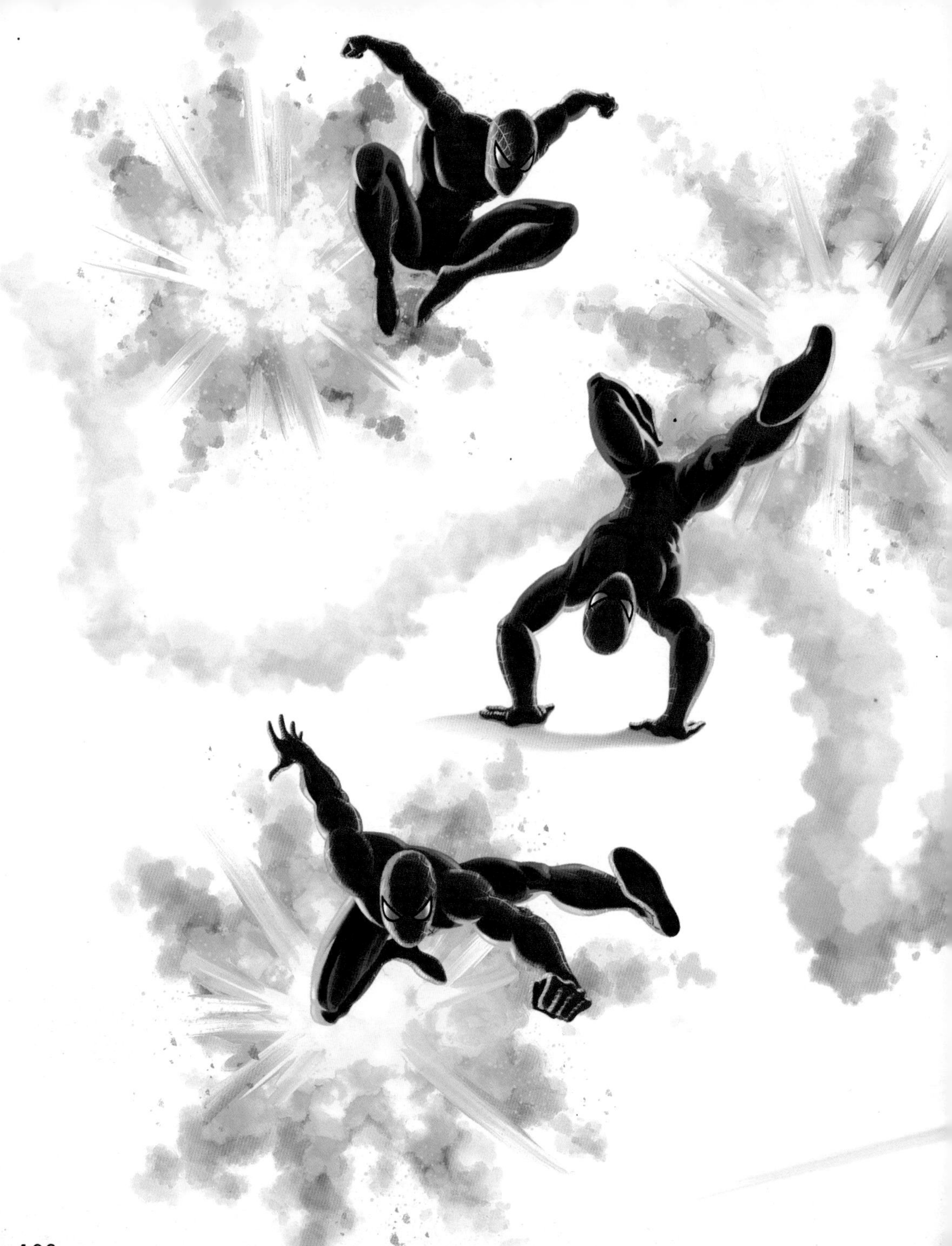

"Take this!" the Green Goblin yelled. He threw a handful of **pumpkin bombs** at Spider-Man.

The wall-crawler flipped out of harm's way as the bombs exploded around him.

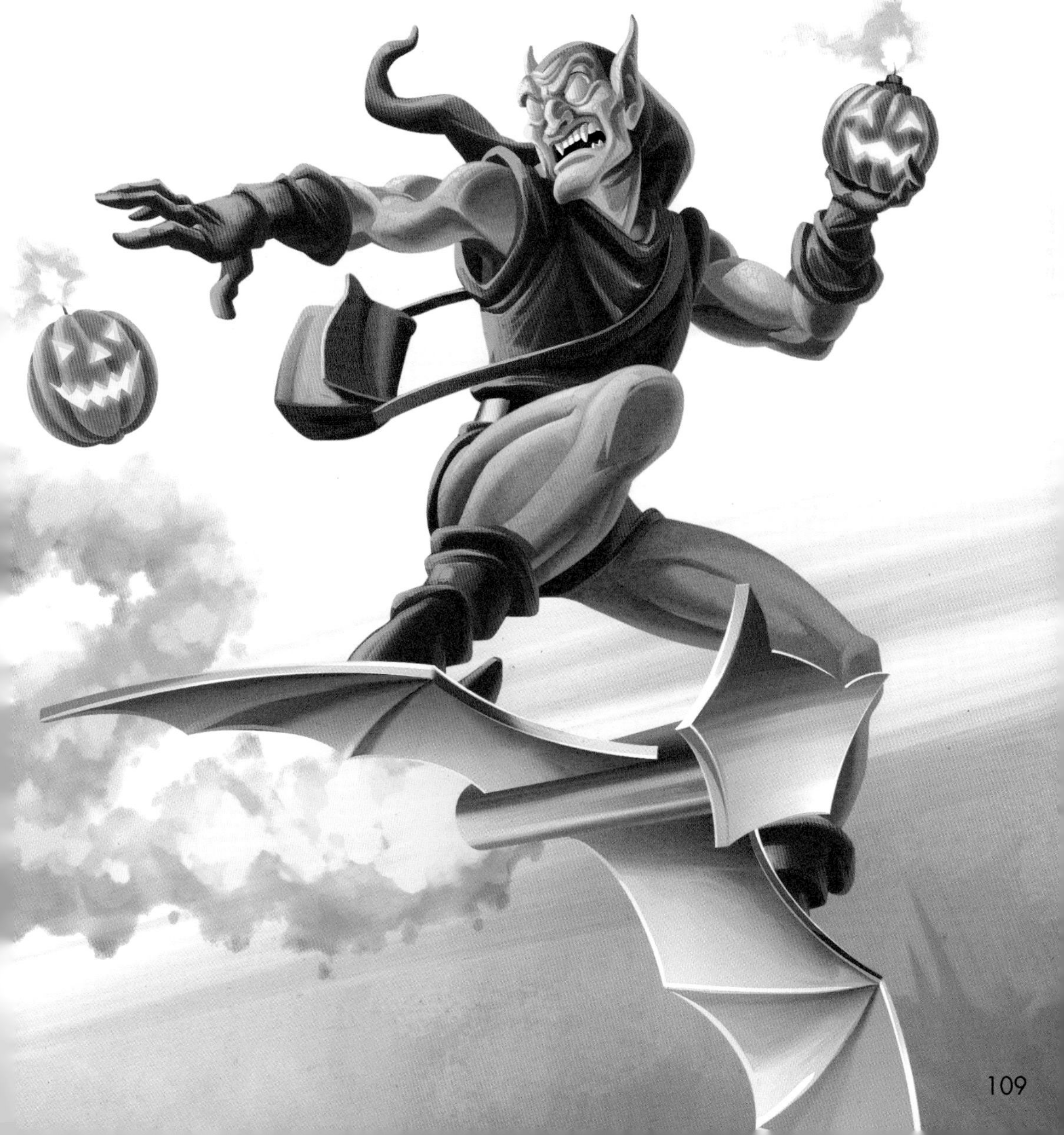

"Sorry, Goblin—you just don't blow me away!" said Spider-Man. But suddenly, the Green Goblin zapped him with a bolt of electricity!

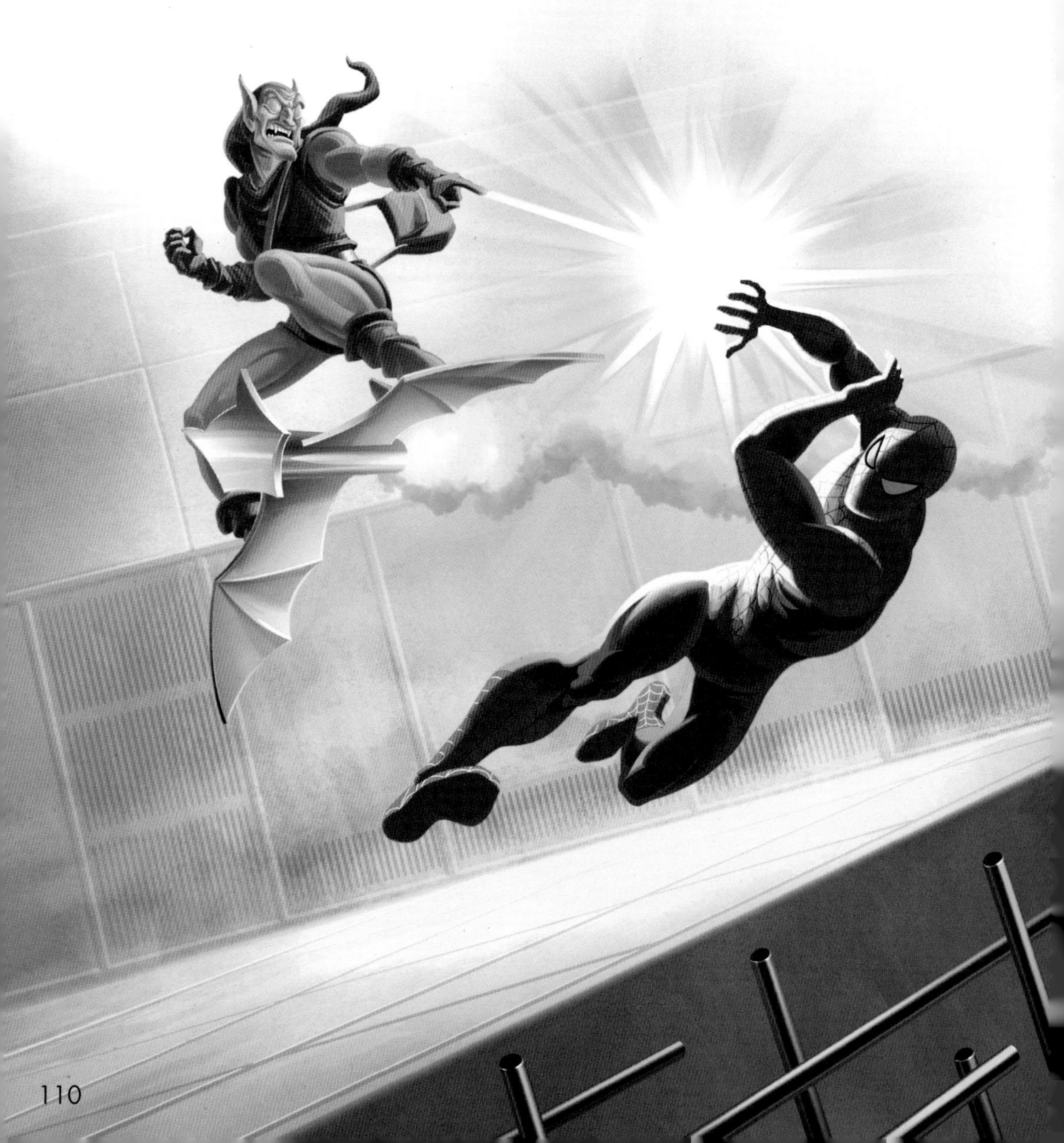

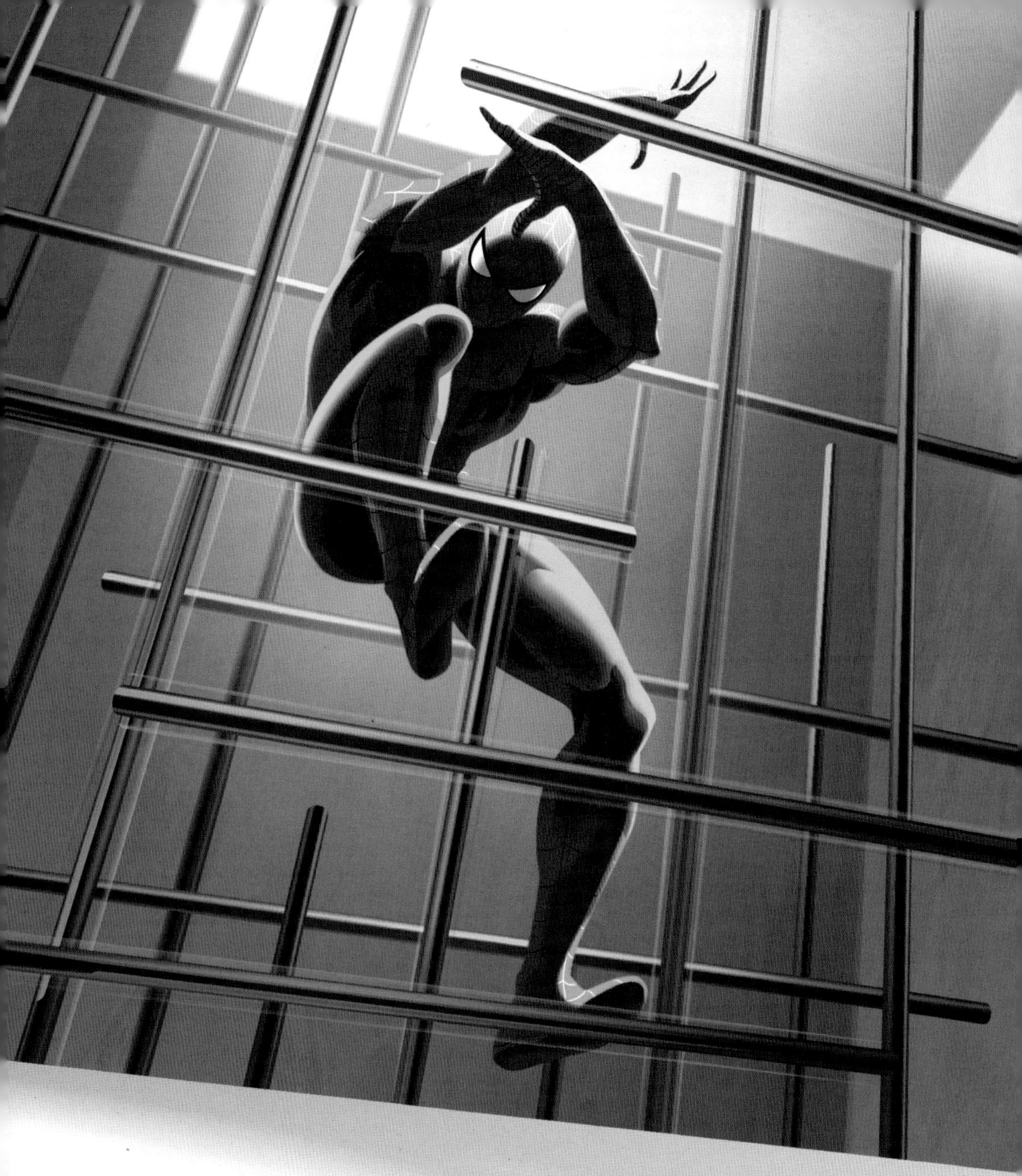

Spider-Man fell into a cage with fast-moving bars. He ducked and dodged the bars, but they were closing in. Soon, he'd be trapped!

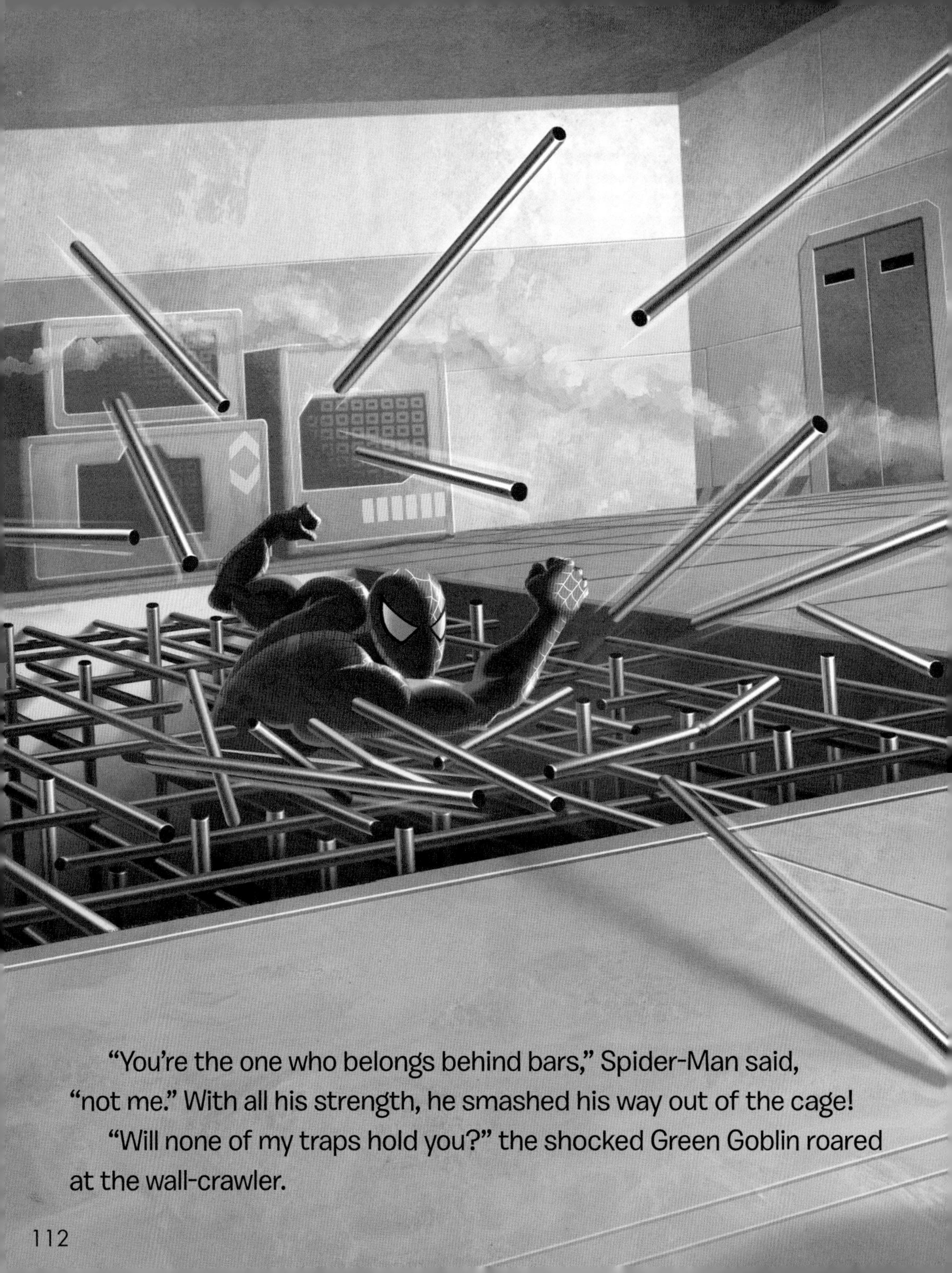

“You’re the one who belongs behind bars,” Spider-Man said, “not me.” With all his strength, he smashed his way out of the cage!

“Will none of my traps hold you?” the shocked Green Goblin roared at the wall-crawler.

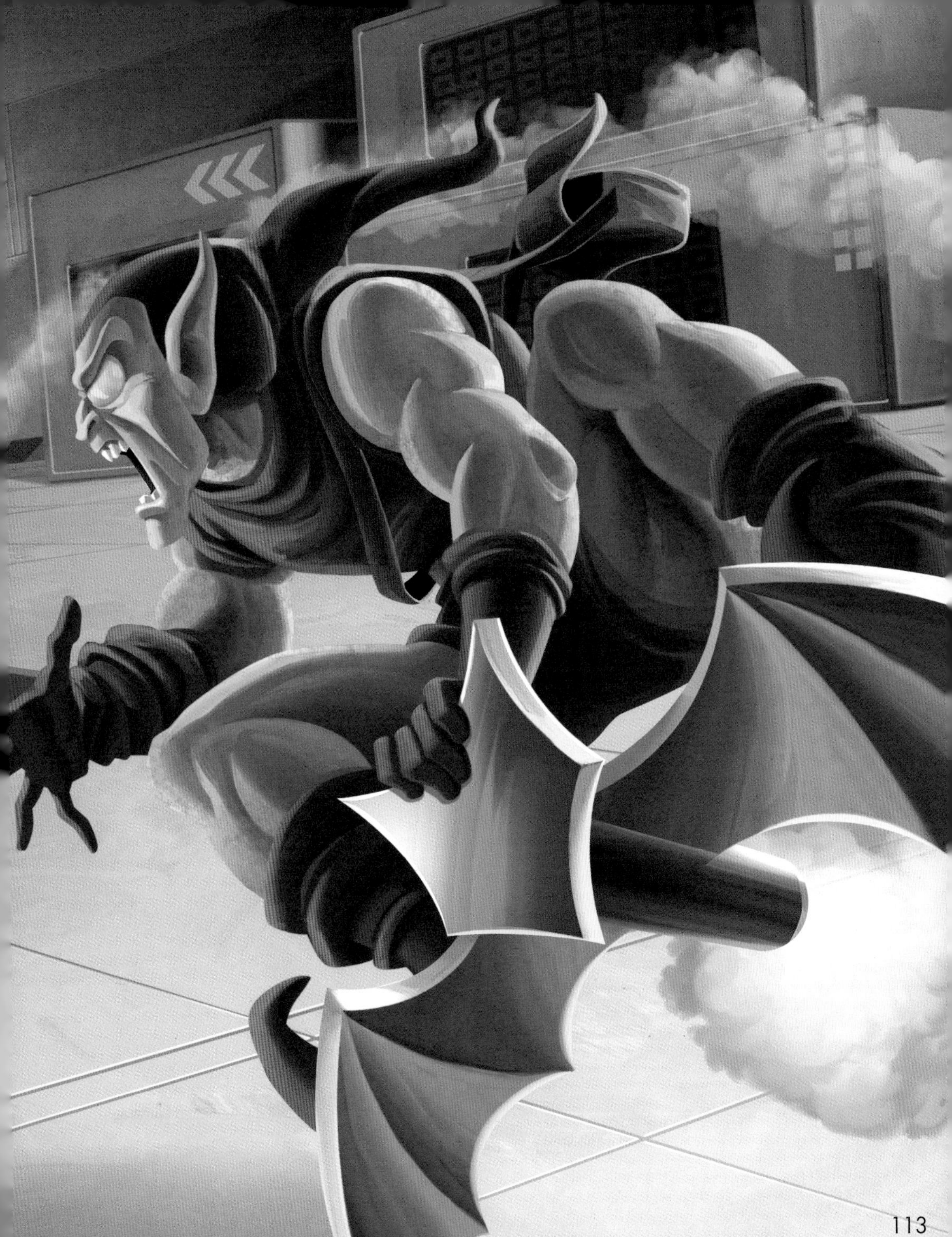

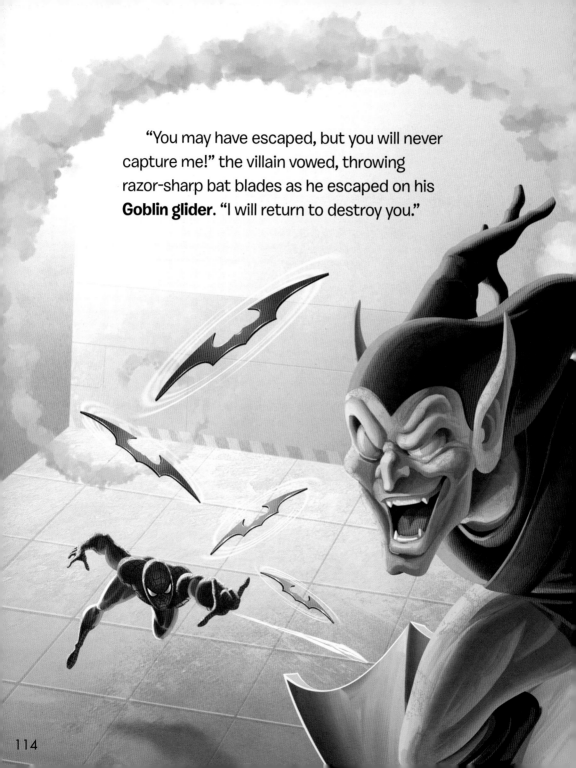

"You may have escaped, but you will never capture me!" the villain vowed, throwing razor-sharp bat blades as he escaped on his **Goblin glider**. "I will return to destroy you."

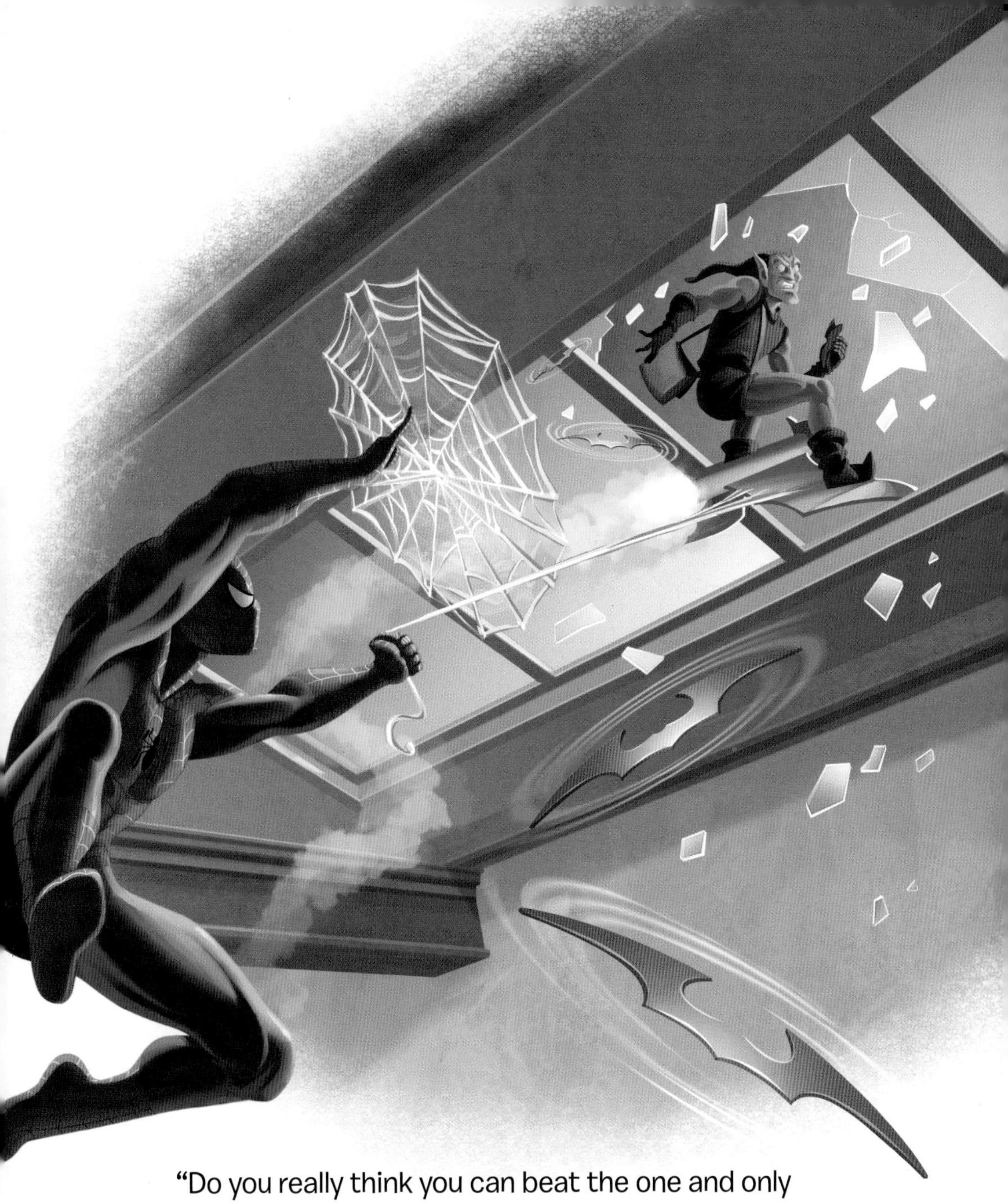

"Do you really think you can beat the one and only Spider-Man with a bunch of high-tech toys?" asked the super hero.

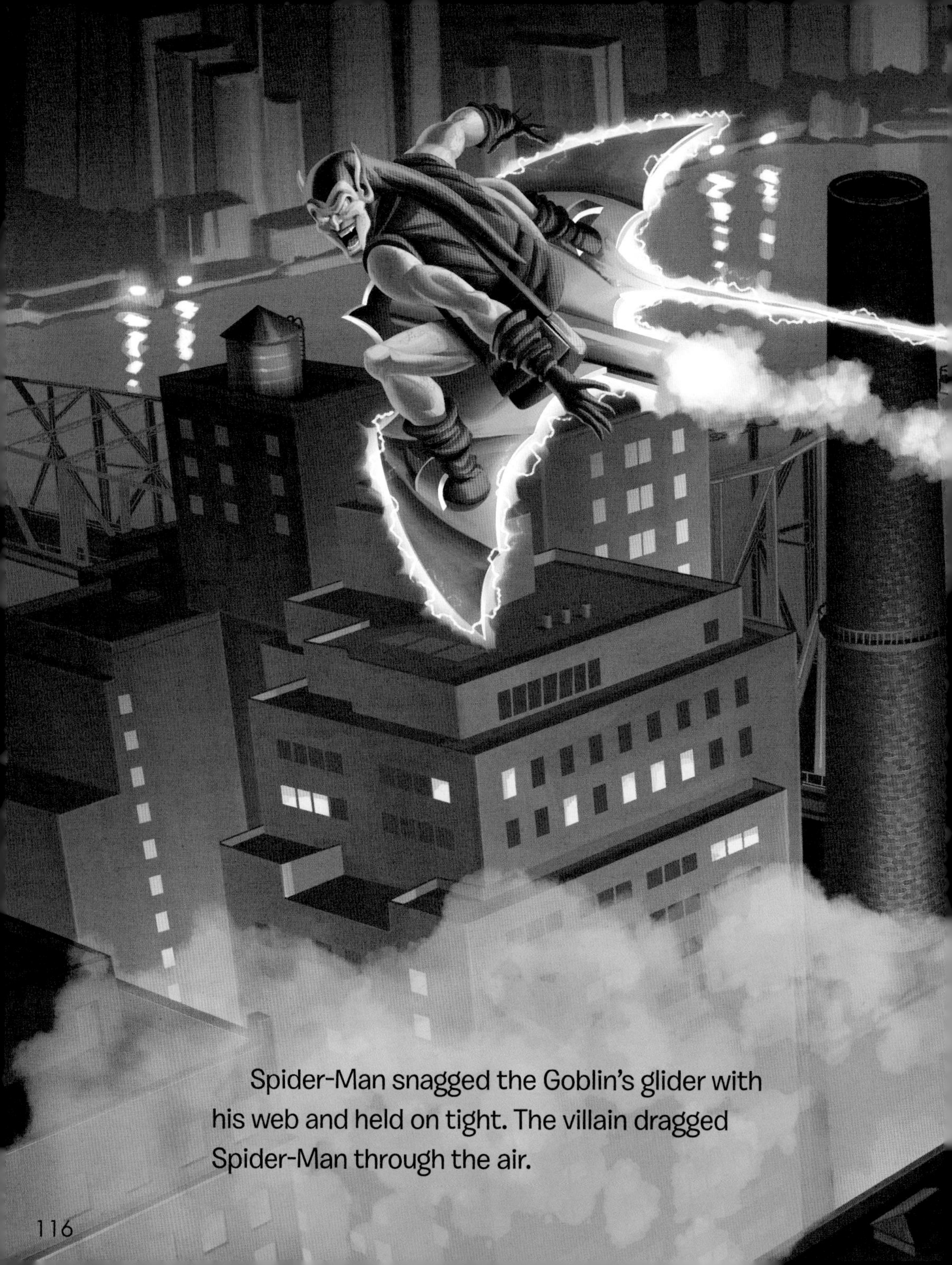

Spider-Man snagged the Goblin's glider with his web and held on tight. The villain dragged Spider-Man through the air.

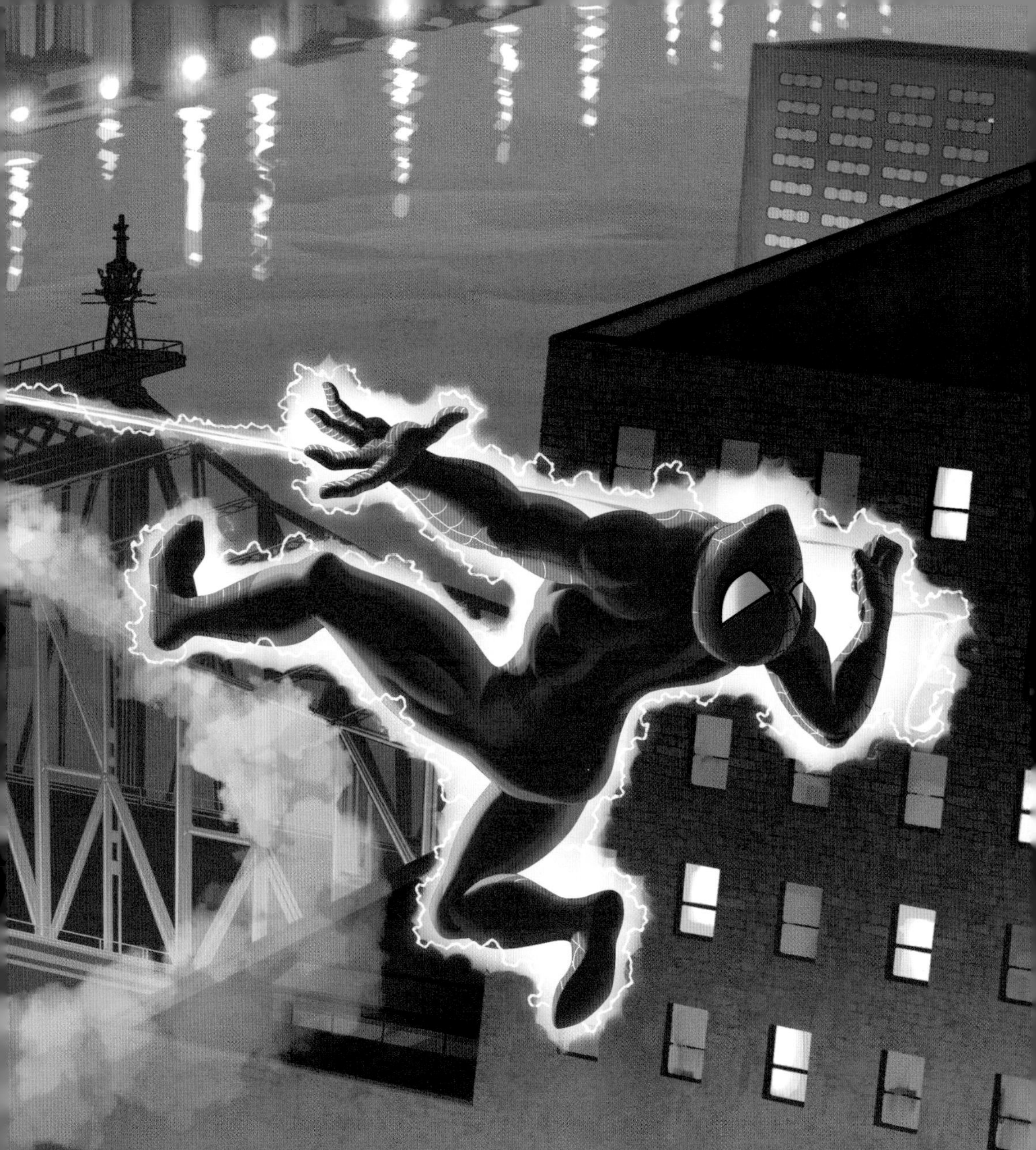

“Get off, you annoying insect!” yelled the Goblin.
He sent a bolt of electricity through the hero’s web.

The Green Goblin laughed and circled back to make sure the hero was done for. Suddenly, the web-slinger moved with incredible speed.

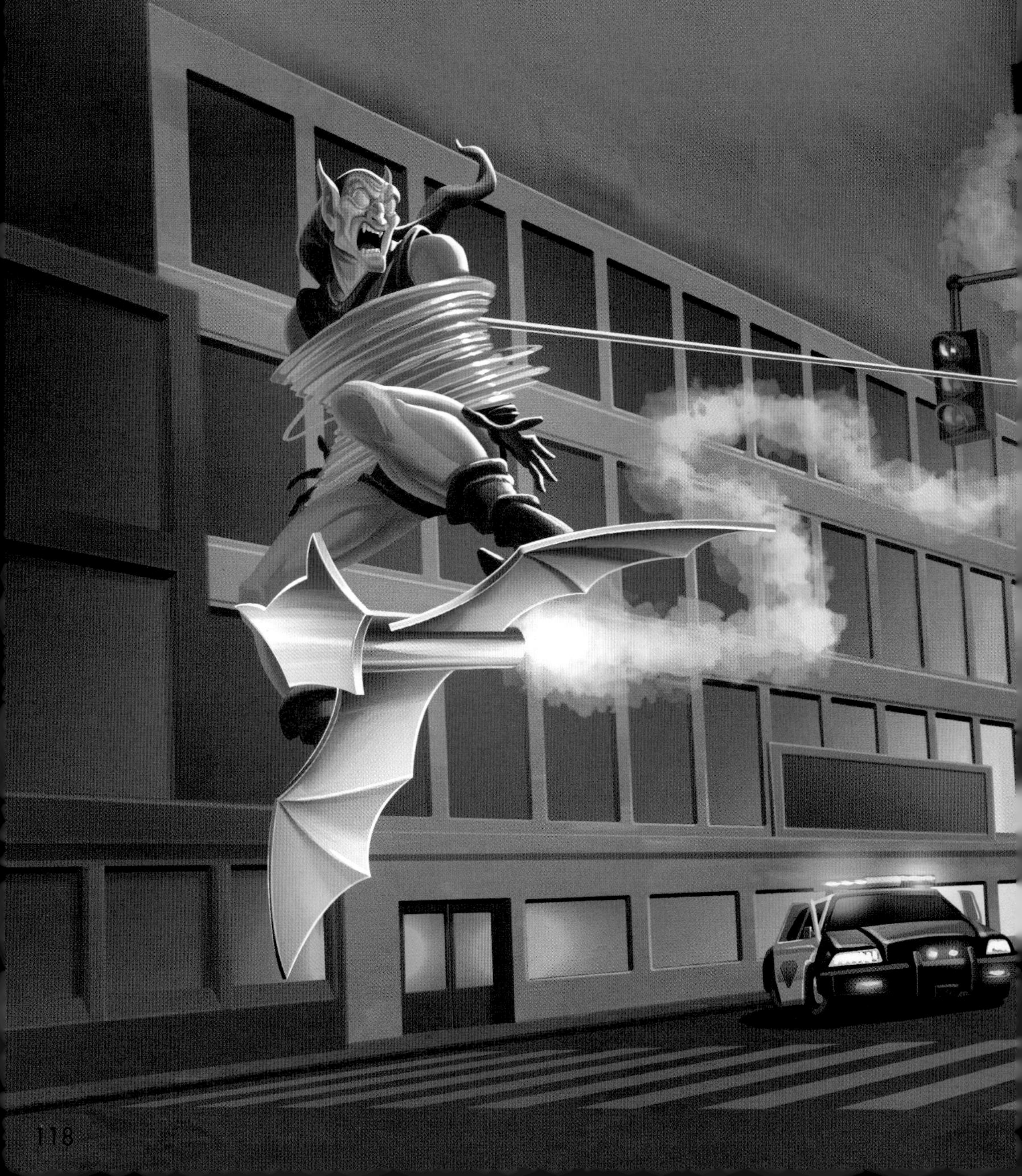

"I'm *shocked* you thought I would fall for that trick again." Spider-Man used his web-shooters to quickly wrap up the villain from head to toe.

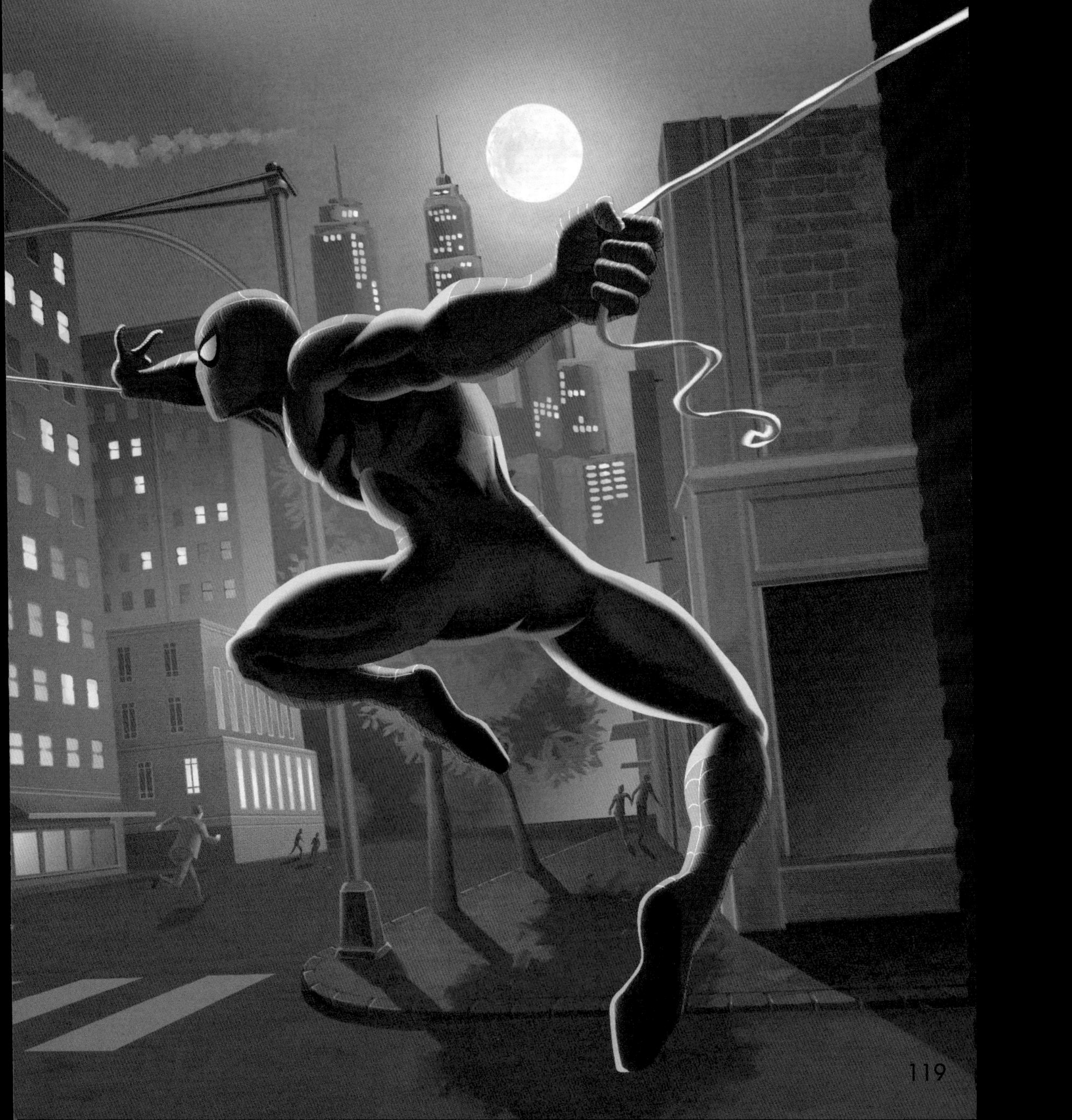

"There won't be any more tricks or treats for you," the hero told the villain, "unless there's Halloween in jail!"

Then your friendly neighborhood Spider-Man swung off in search of his next adventure.

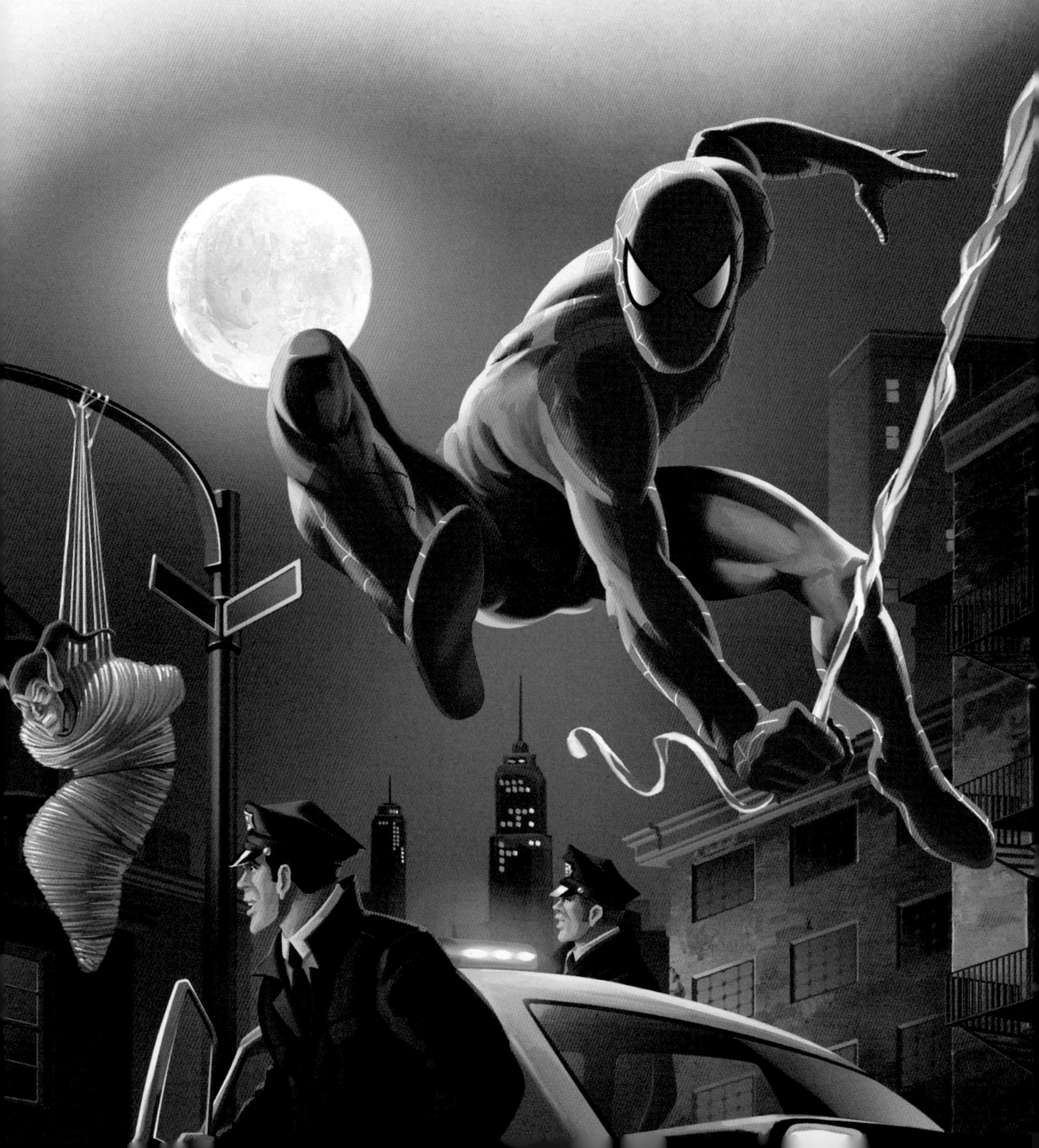

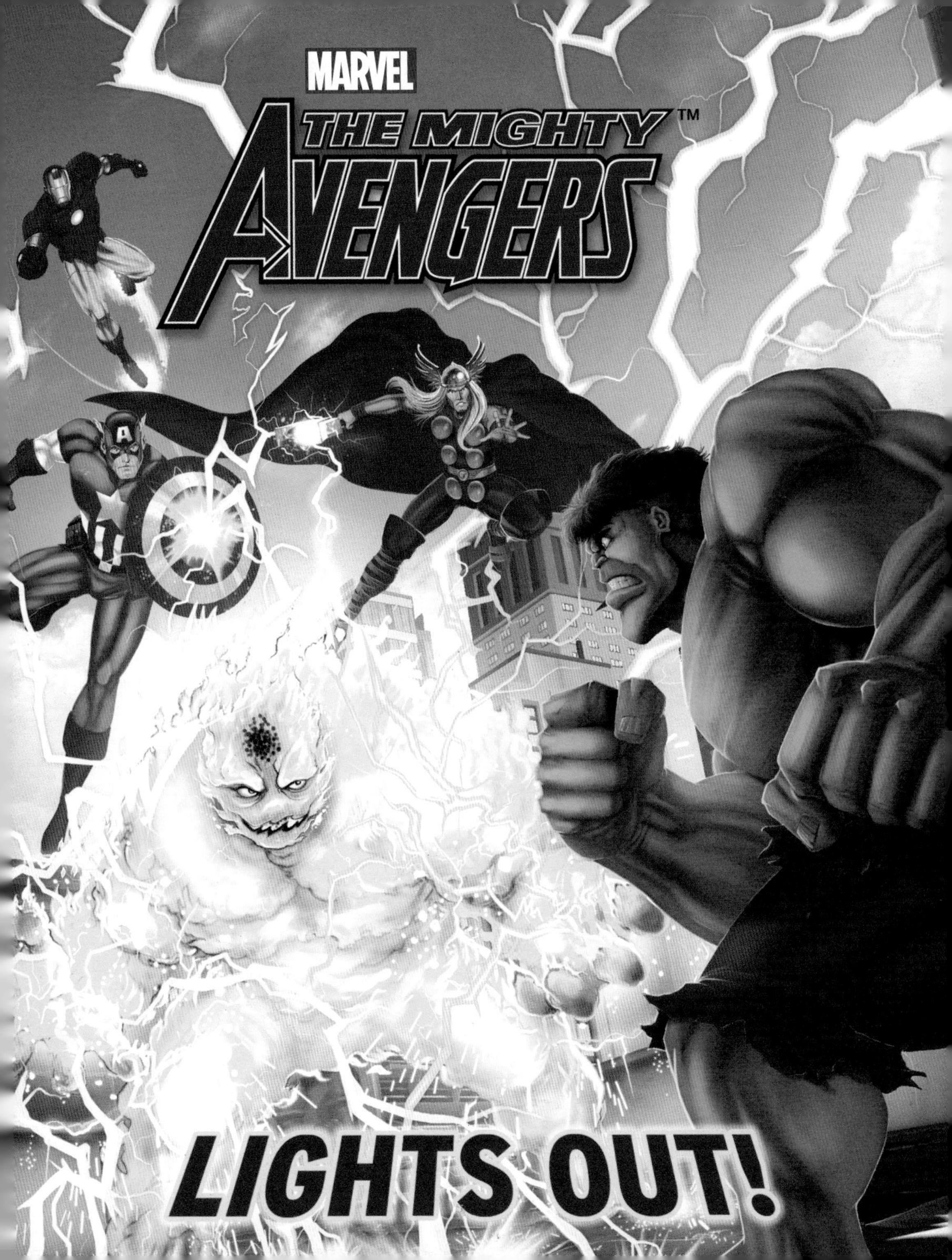
MARVEL
THE MIGHTY AVENGERS™
LIGHTS OUT!

Iron Man was the leader of the Avengers, a team of super heroes. He loved inventing new devices. His latest creation was a generator that would provide clean power for all of New York City.

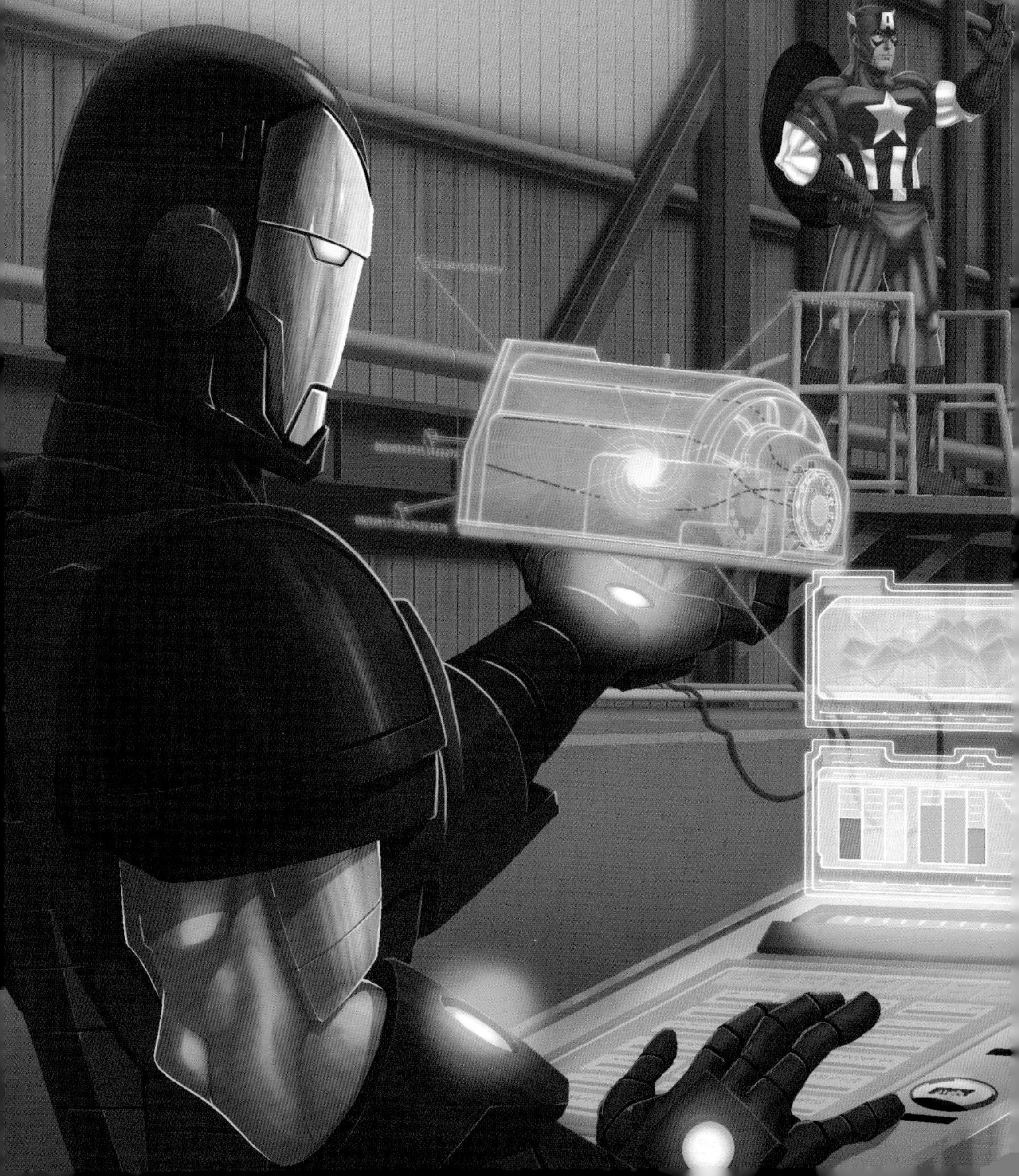

Captain America, Thor, and the Incredible Hulk were helping him install the new generator.

"Careful!" said Iron Man. "It has one hundred times the power of the old generator."

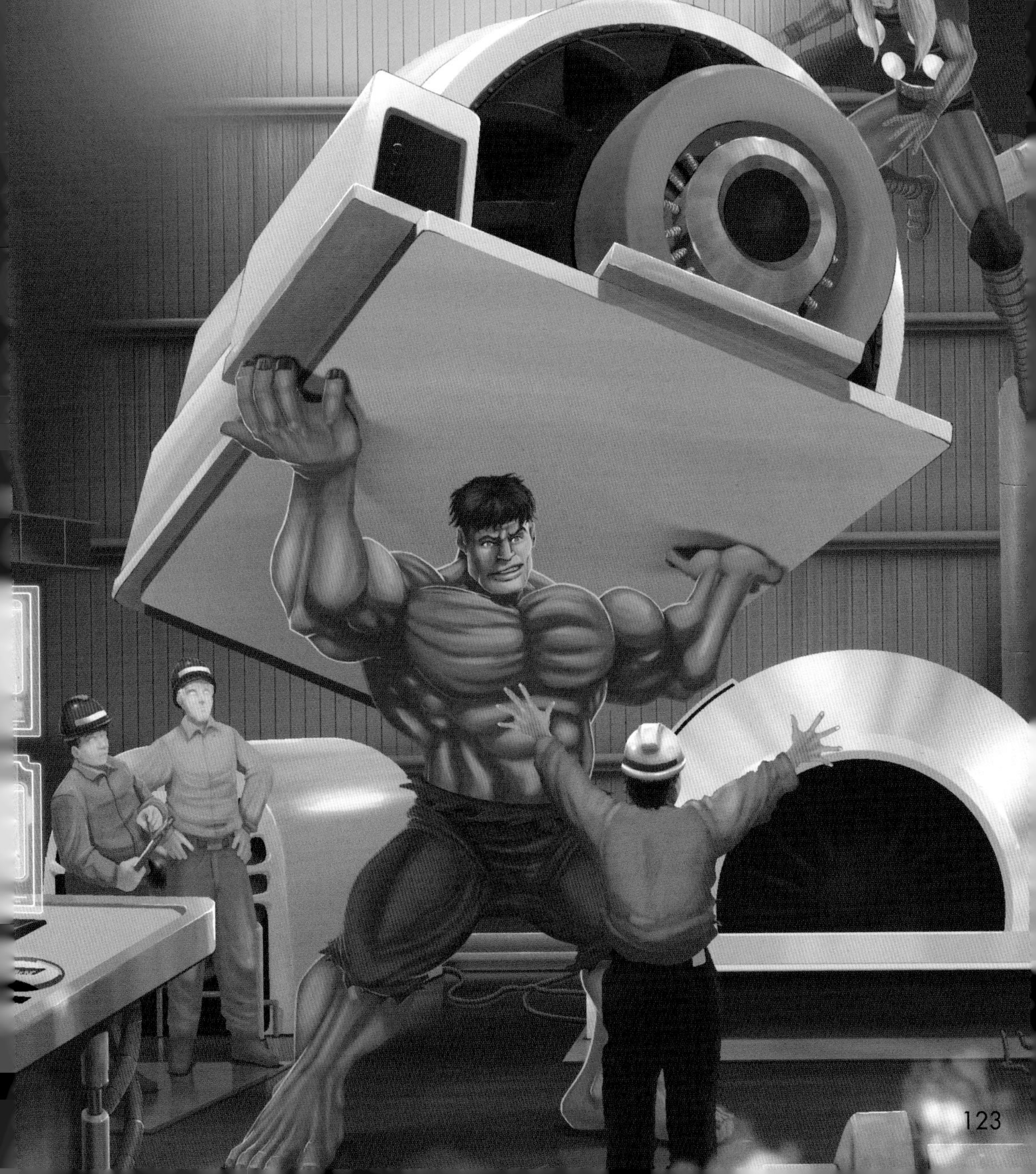

"Wait!" Iron Man shouted. "There are some strange energy readings coming from outside the generator's system!"

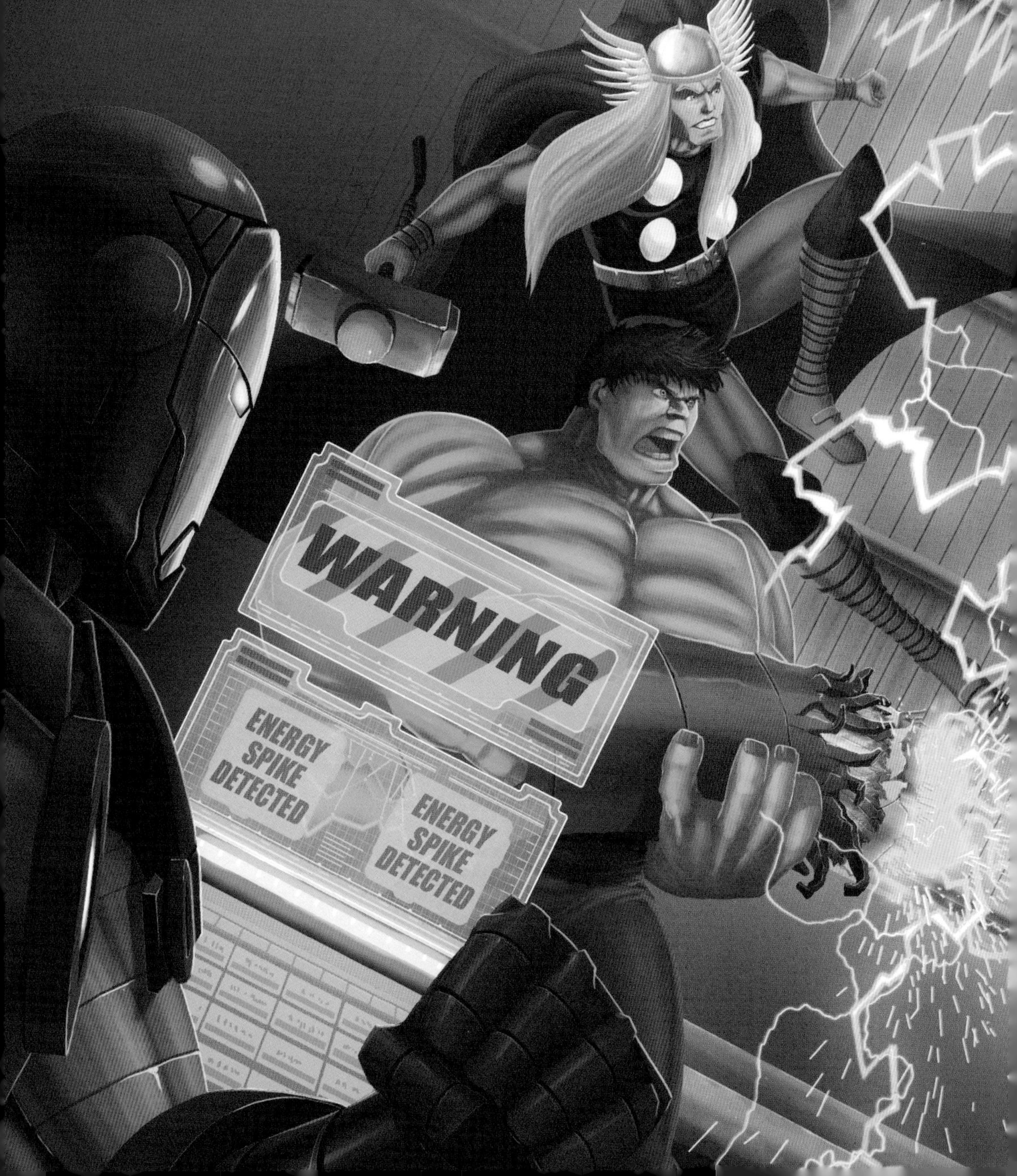
WARNING
ENERGY SPIKE DETECTED
ENERGY SPIKE DETECTED

But it was too late: **BOOM!** The generator exploded! The energy crackled and took on the form of a giant glowing monster.

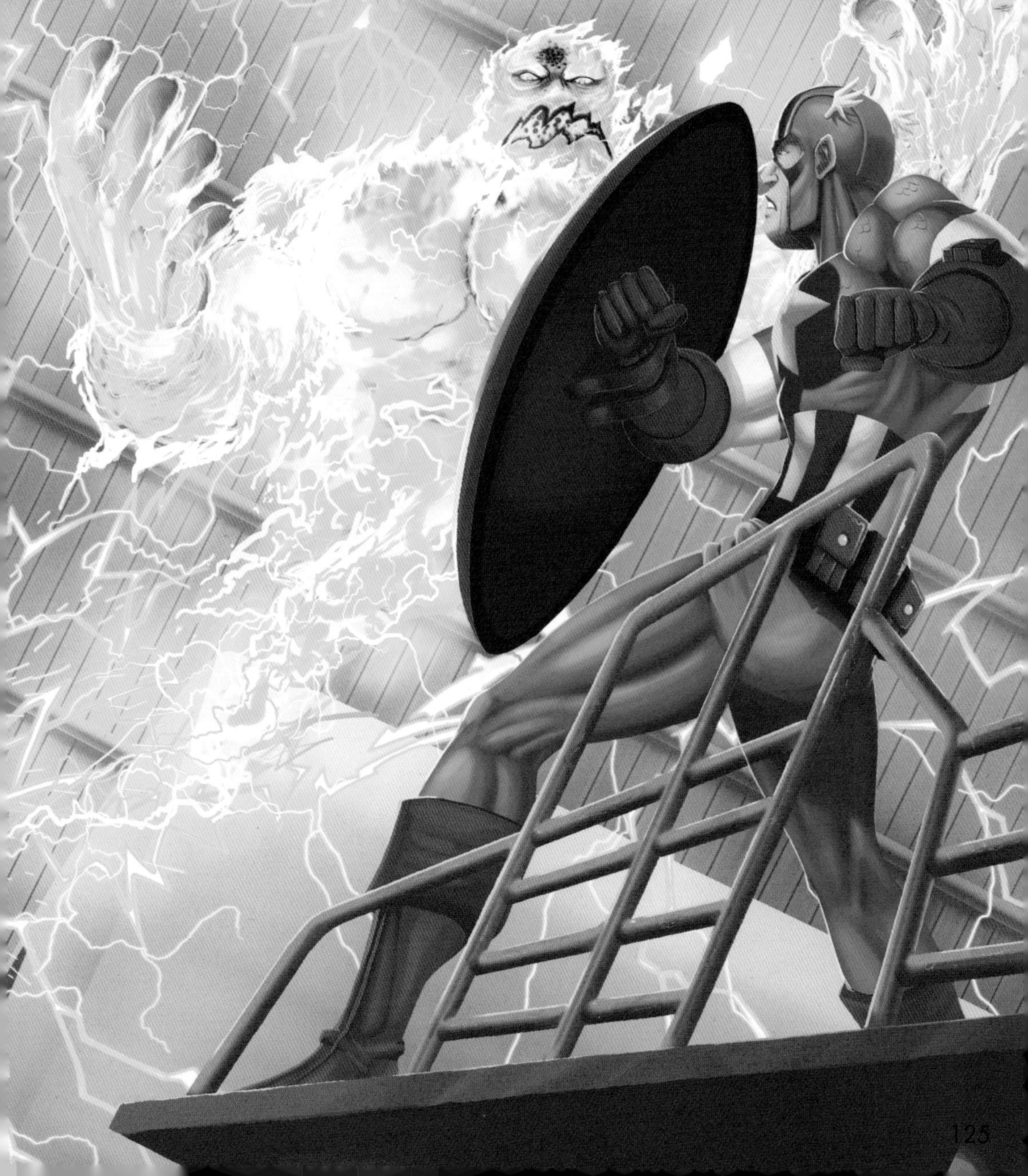

"Zzzax lives again!" the creature roared. "Zzzax hungers for more power!"

"Energy monster is Hulk's enemy," Hulk growled. "Hulk SMASH!"

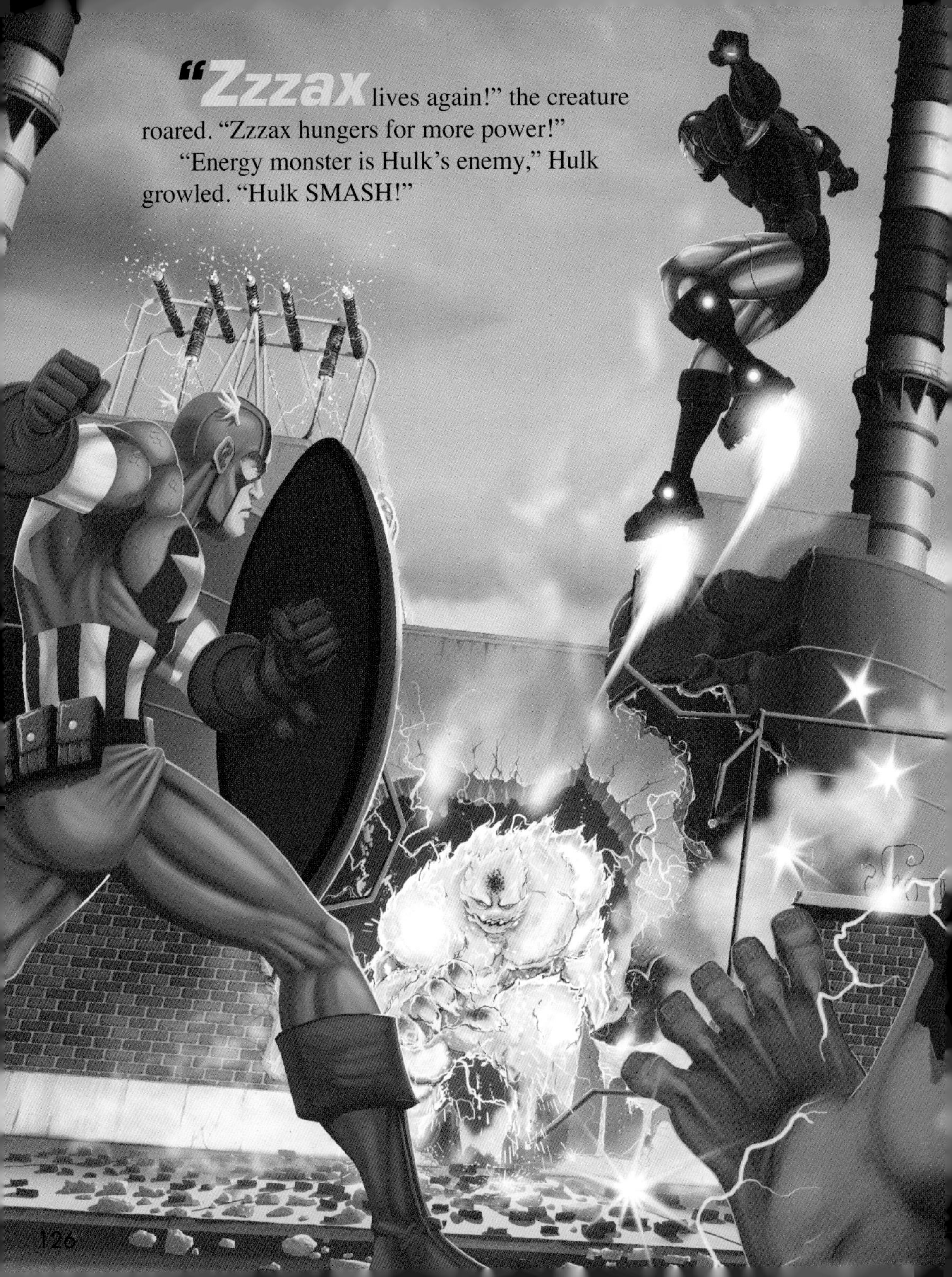

Zzzax unleashed an energy bolt that sent the green giant crashing through a wall.

"City has power!" Zzzax rumbled. He made his way toward the glowing lights of New York.

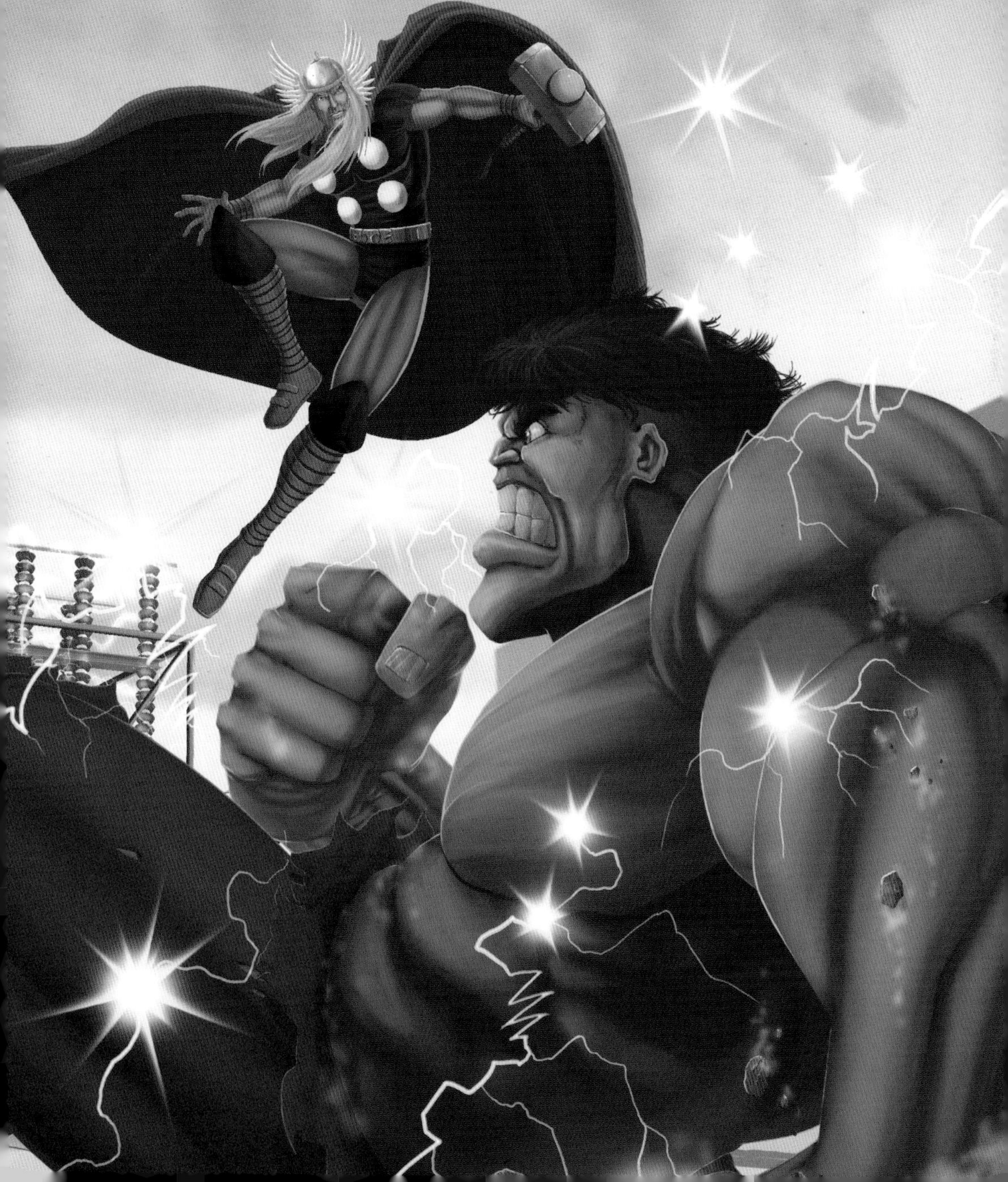

Zzzax stomped into the middle of Times Square. "Power will be mine!" he boomed. Zzzax grew bigger and stronger as he drained energy from the city!

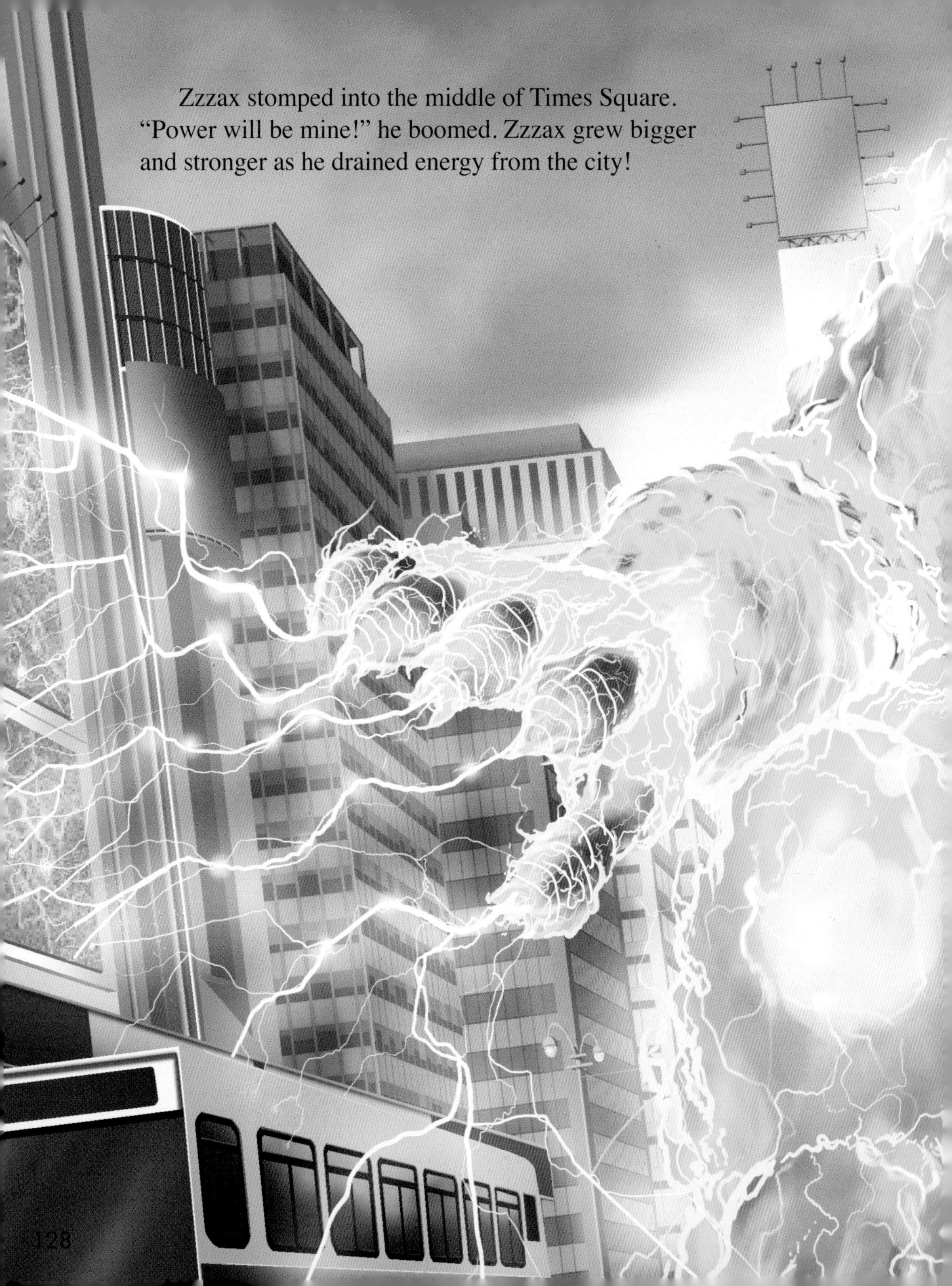

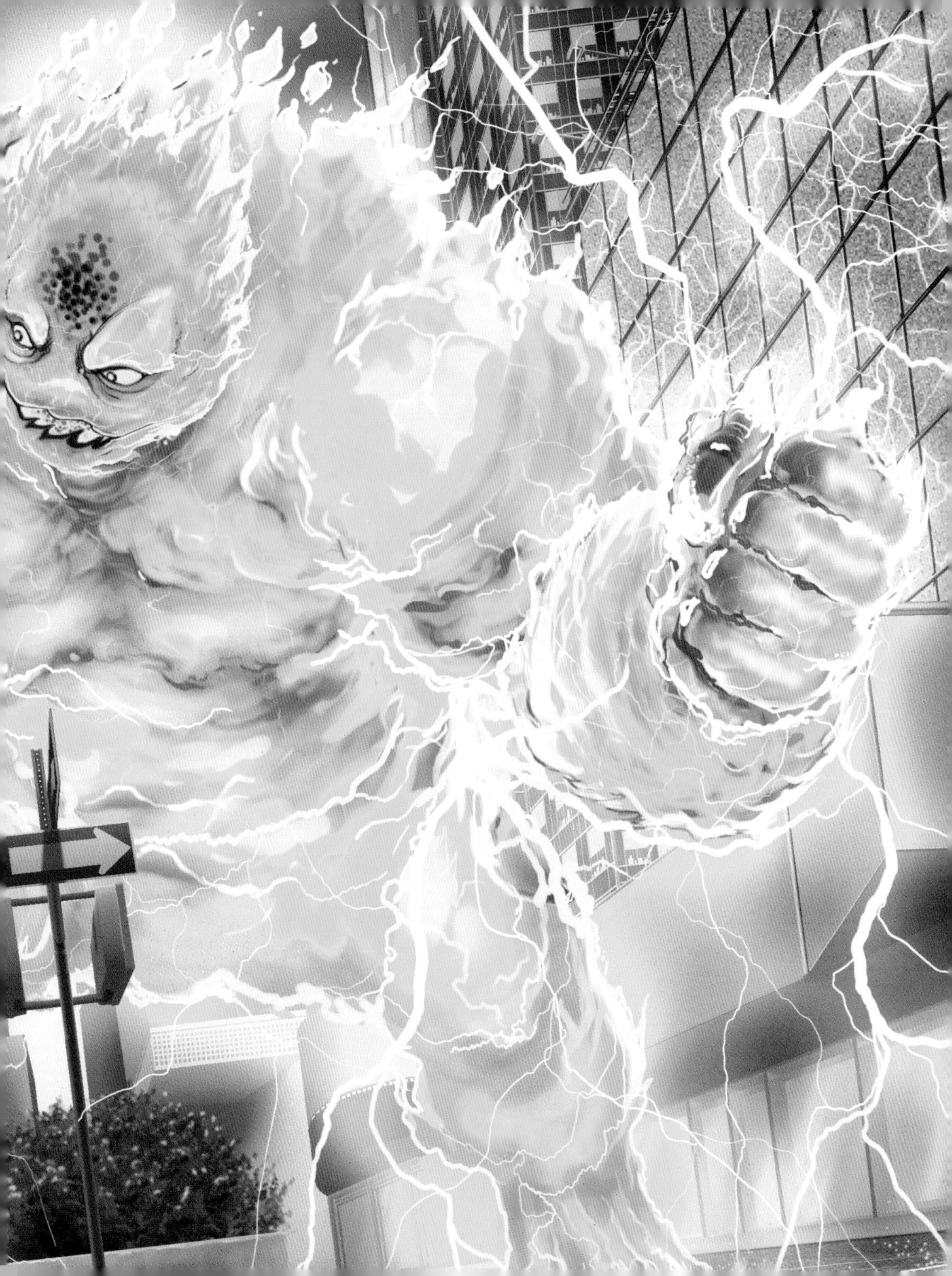

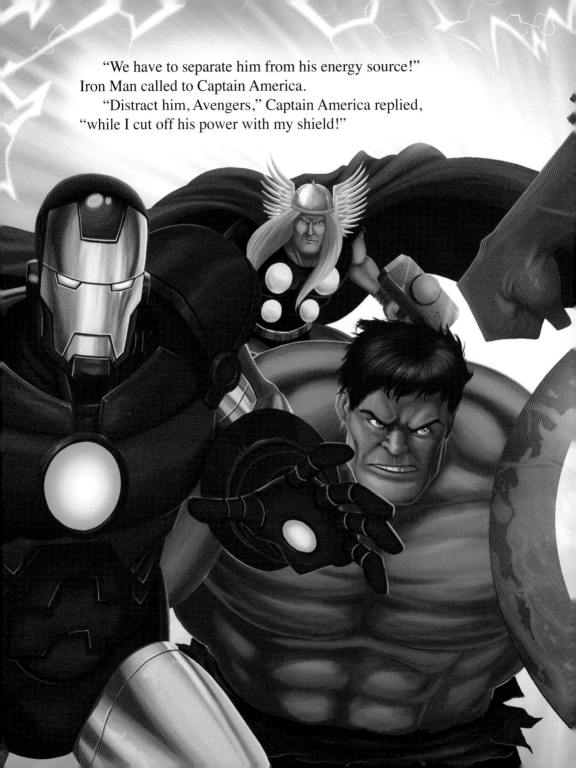

"We have to separate him from his energy source!"
Iron Man called to Captain America.

"Distract him, Avengers," Captain America replied,
"while I cut off his power with my shield!"

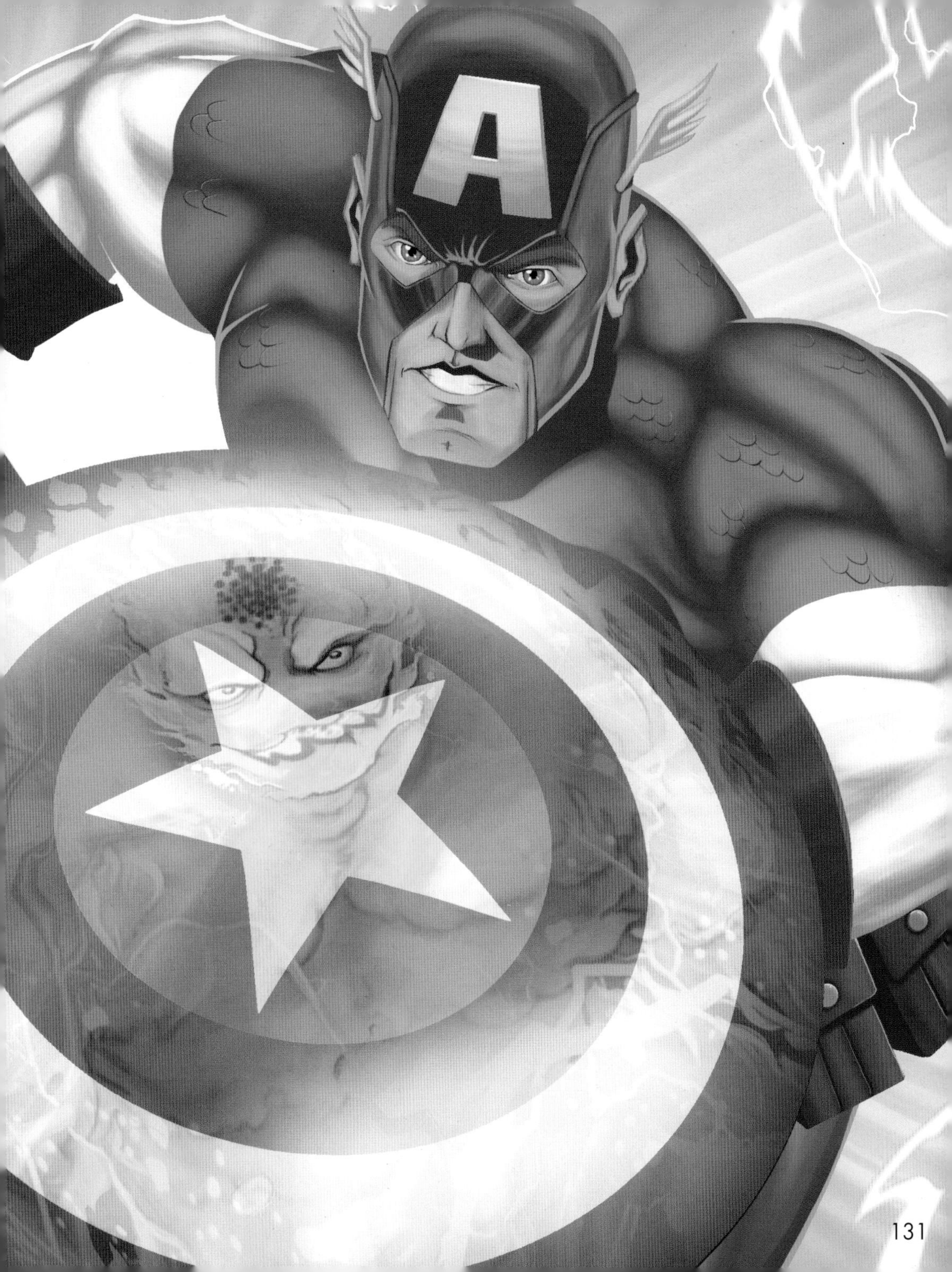

The Avengers attacked Zzzax. The monster swatted at them, but the heroes were too strong and too fast.

"Keep him busy, Avengers!" Iron Man shouted. "Now, Cap!"

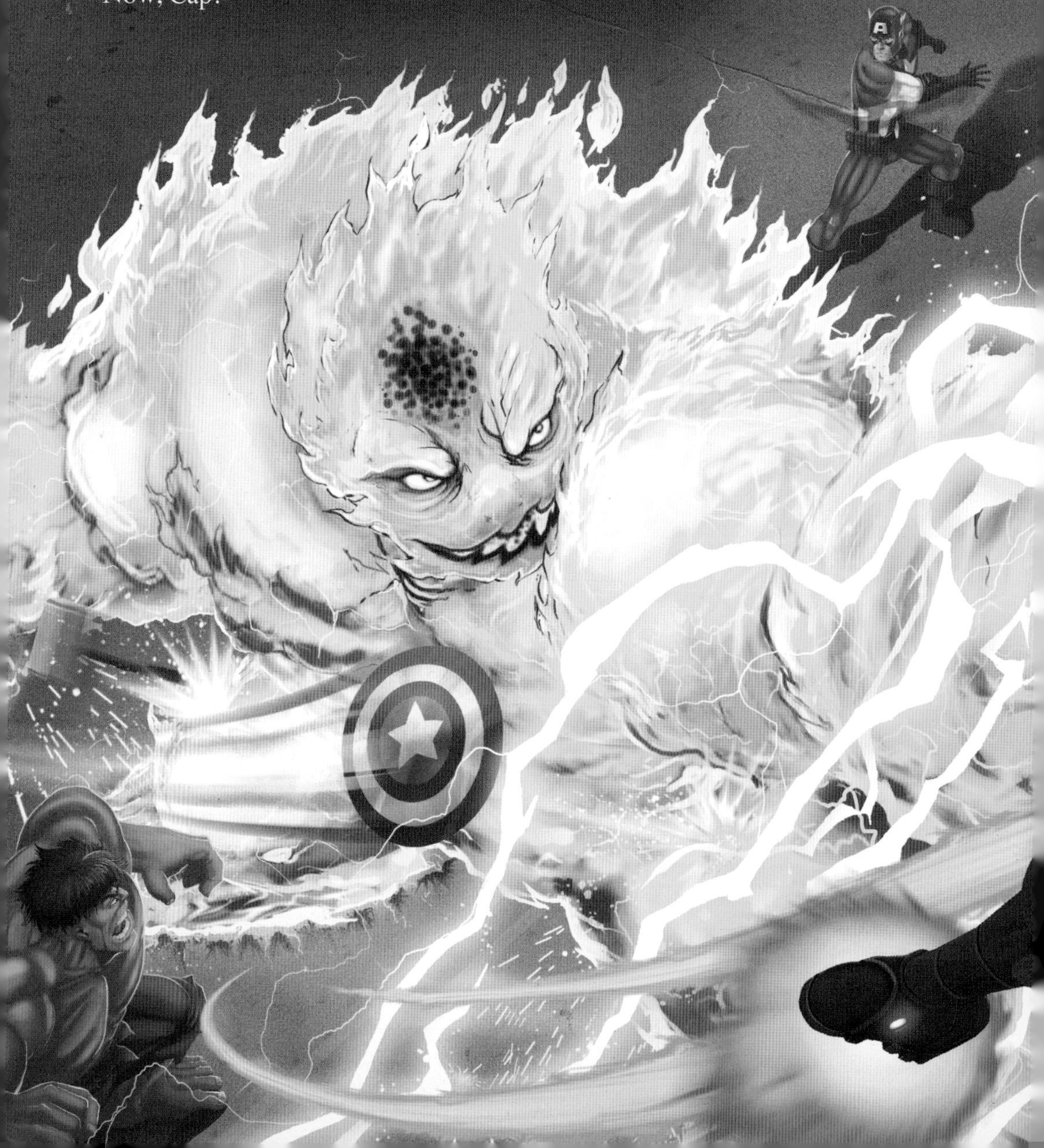

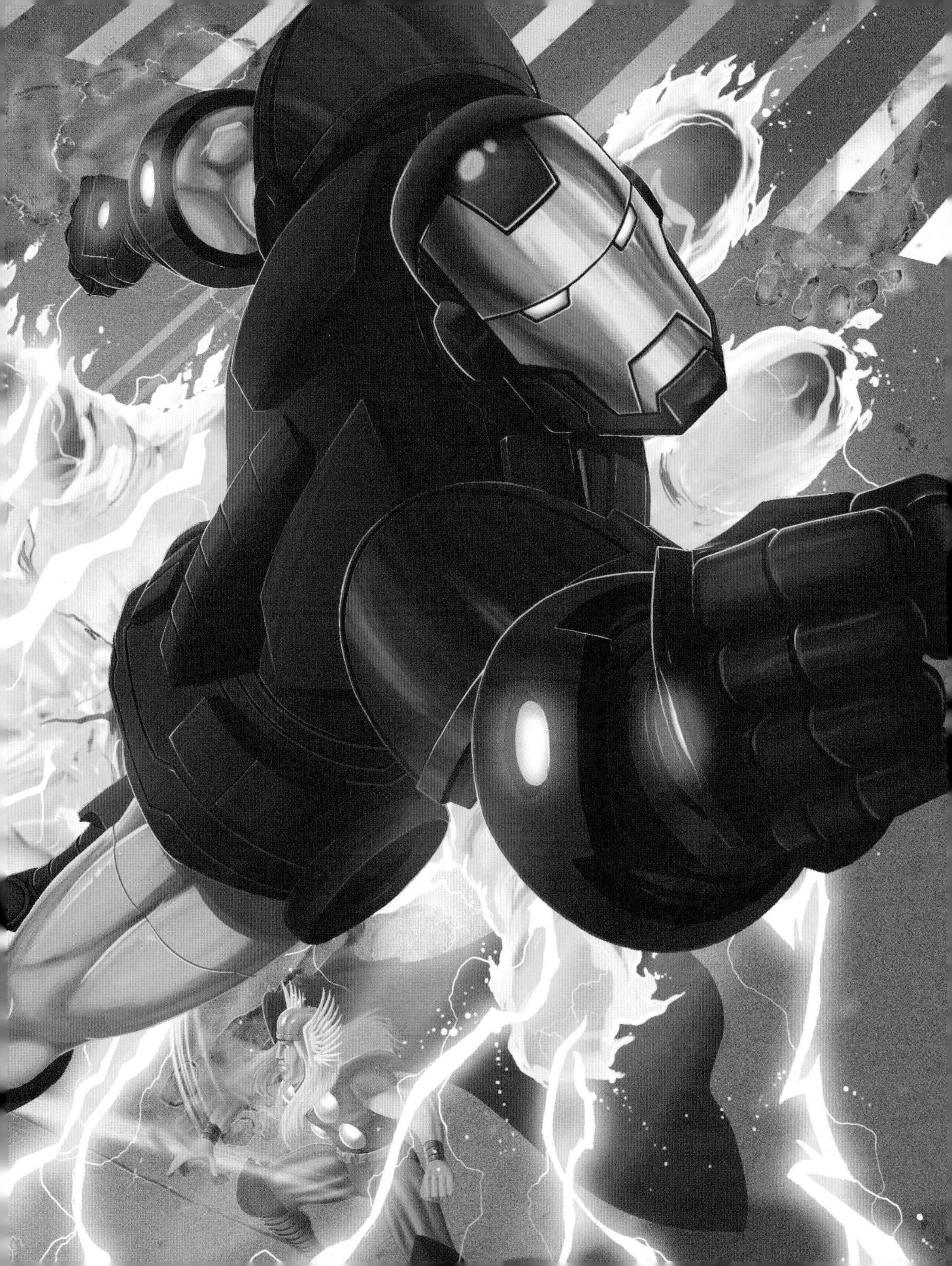

Captain America threw his mighty shield. It sliced through the arcs of electricity, interrupting the flow of power to the monster.

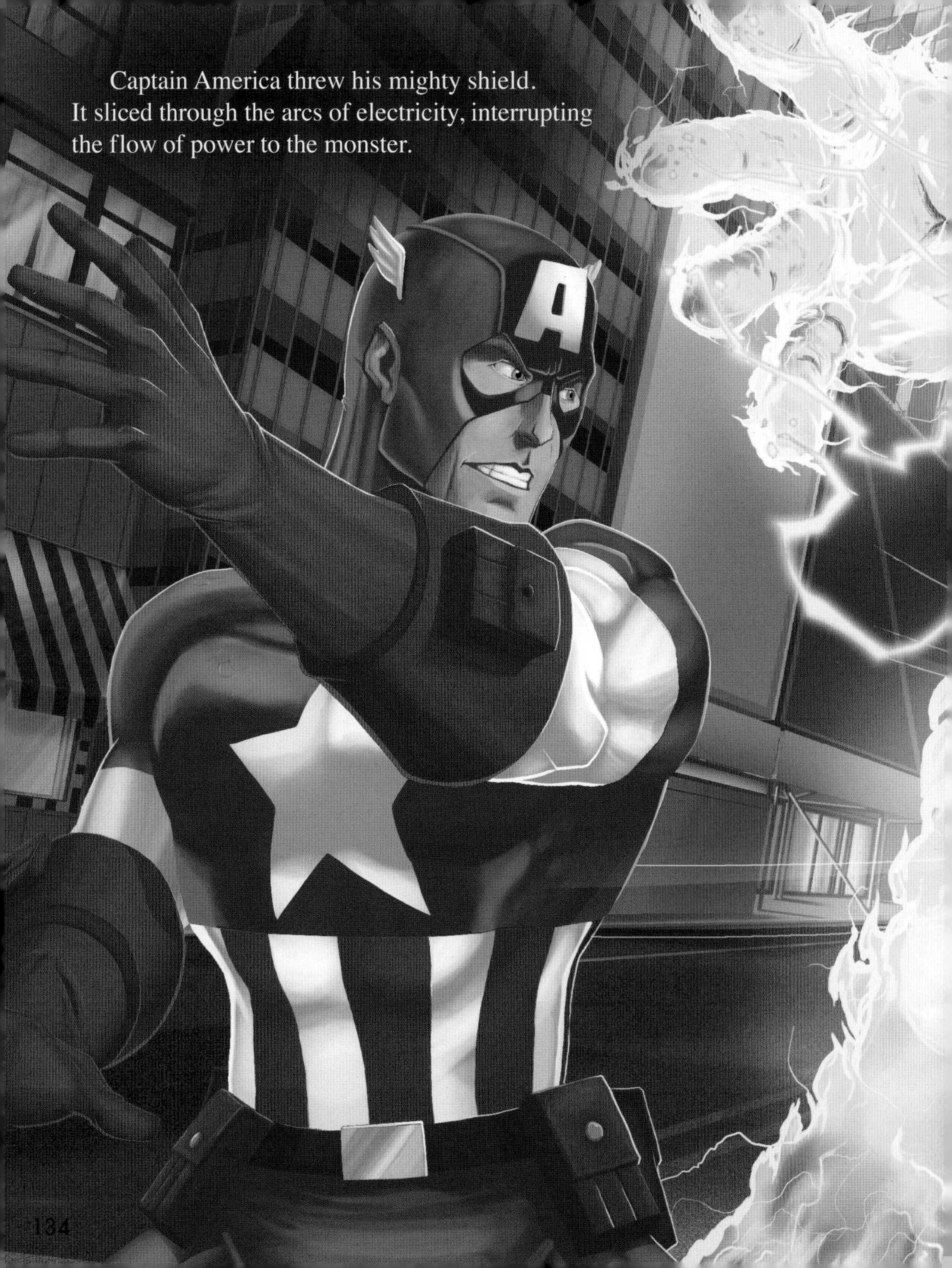

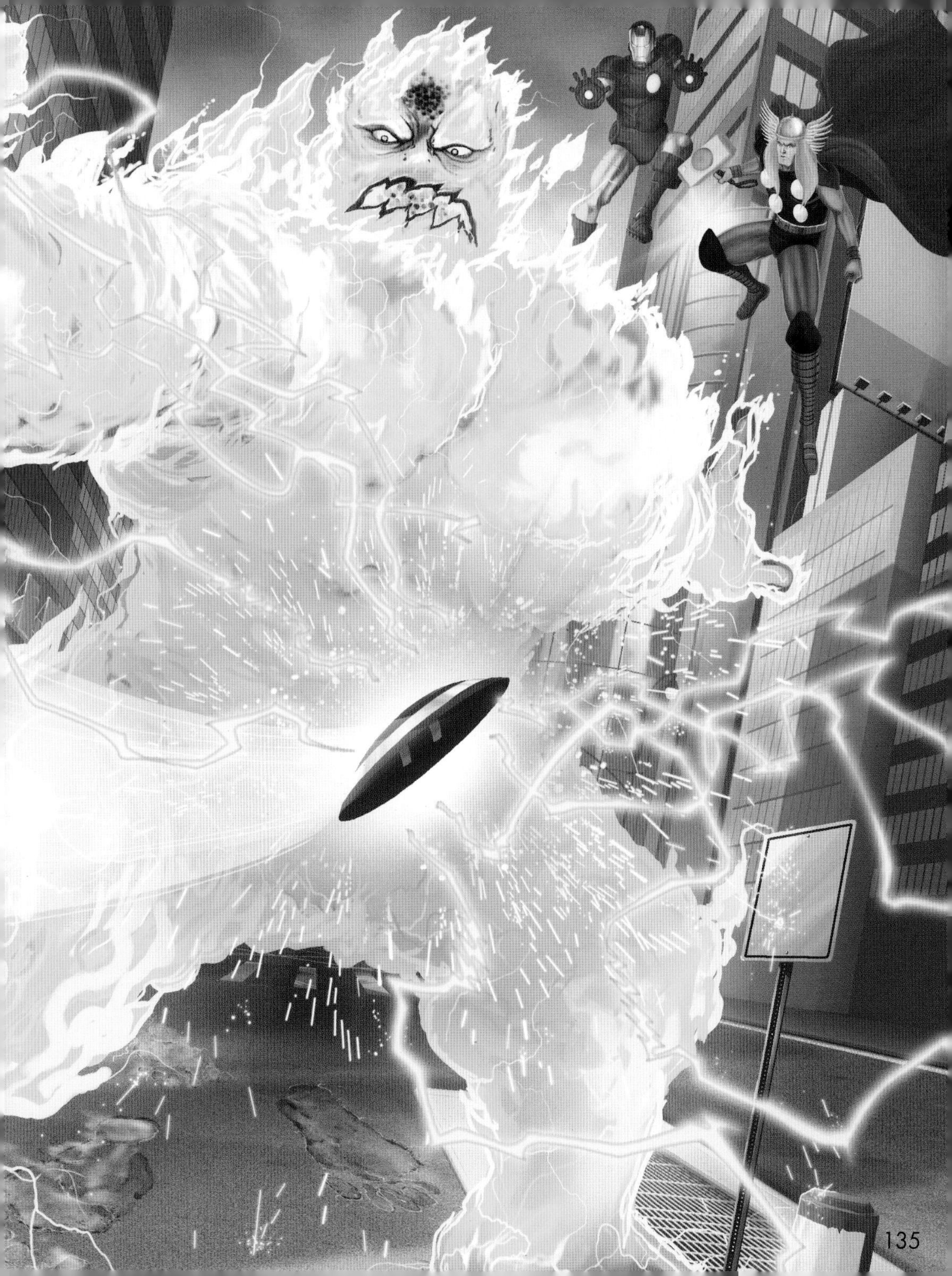

With his power cut off, Zzzax began to get smaller.

"Hulk stop Zzzax!" the green giant roared as he cracked open a nearby fire hydrant. "Hulk SPLASH!"

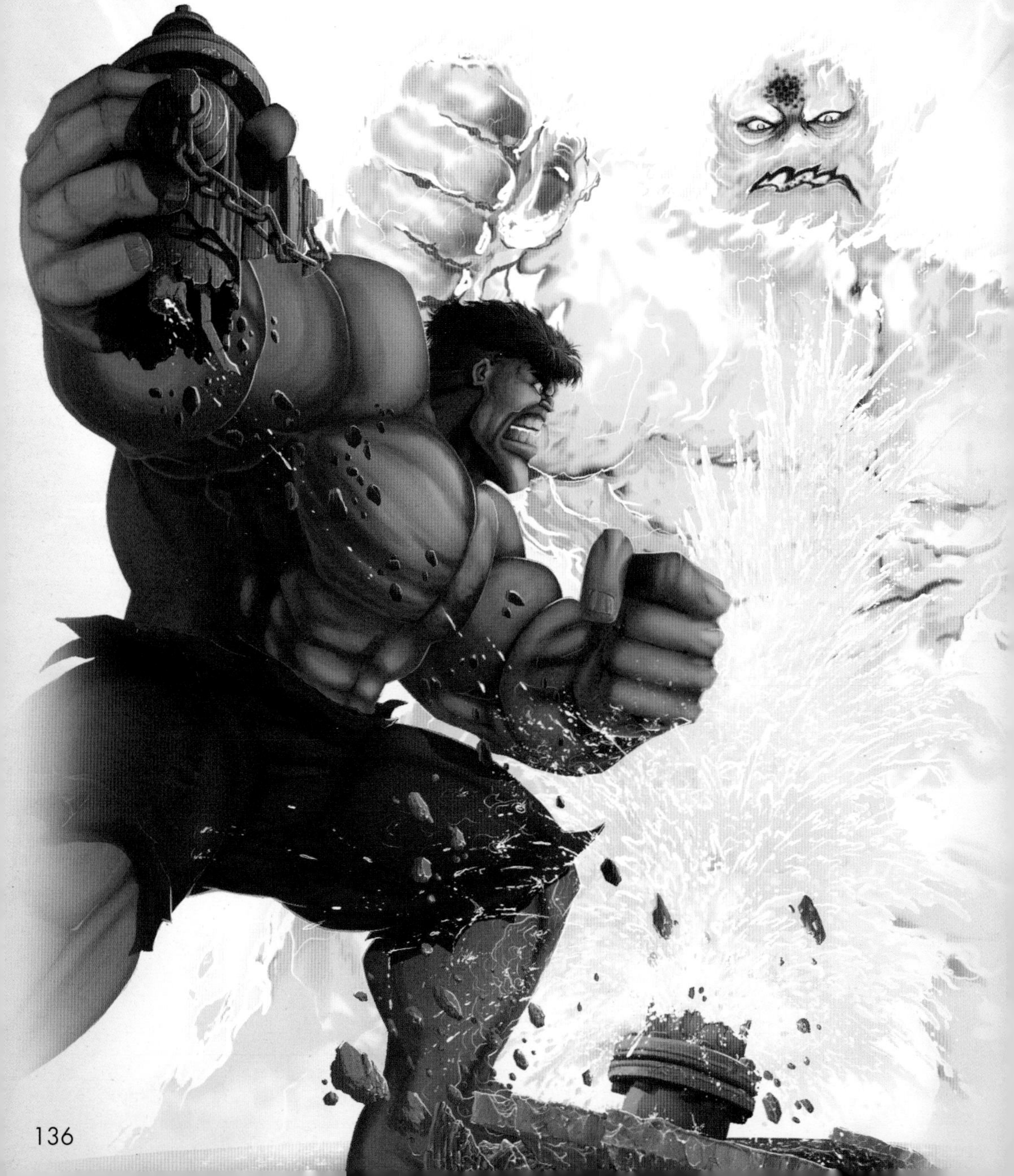

Water from the hydrant hit the monster, causing him to spark and short-circuit. Zzzax's energy began to drain away. "Zzzax is all washed up!" Captain America said.

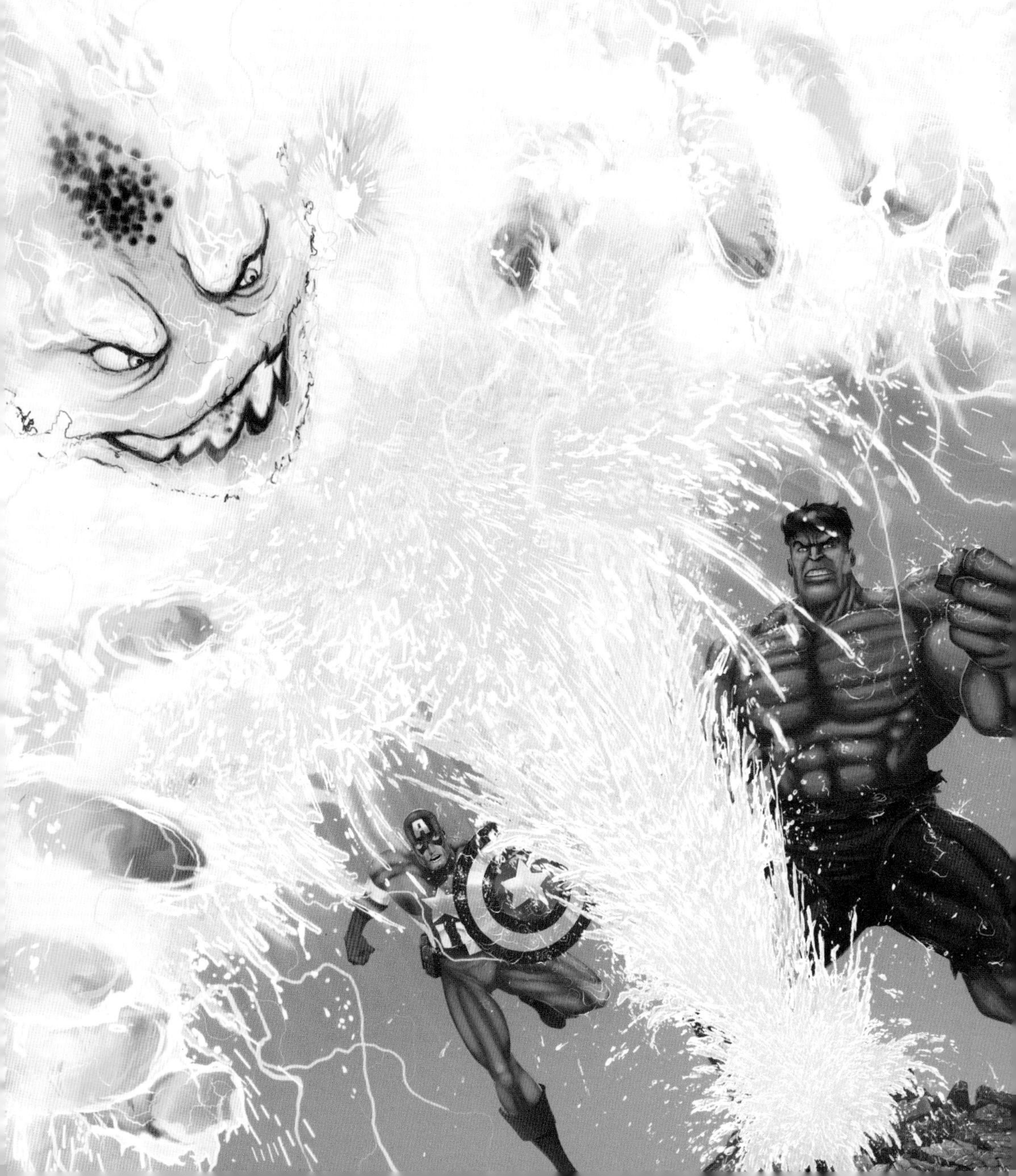

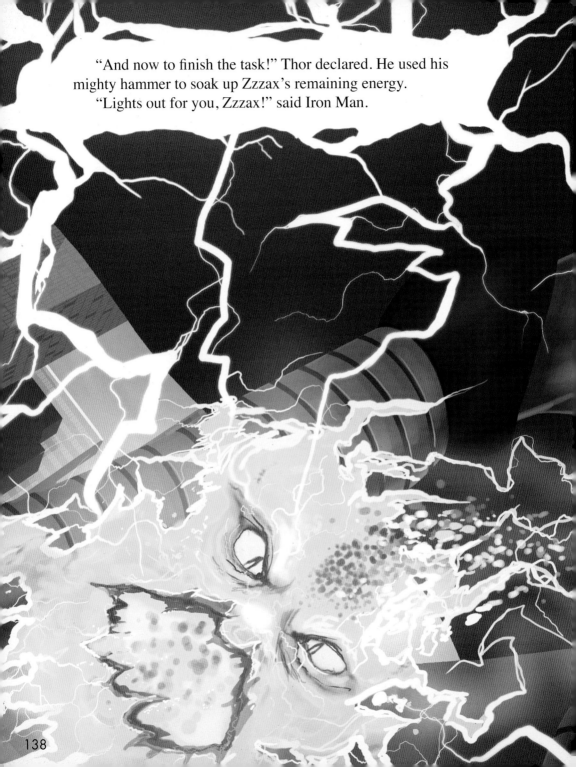

"And now to finish the task!" Thor declared. He used his mighty hammer to soak up Zzzax's remaining energy.

"Lights out for you, Zzzax!" said Iron Man.

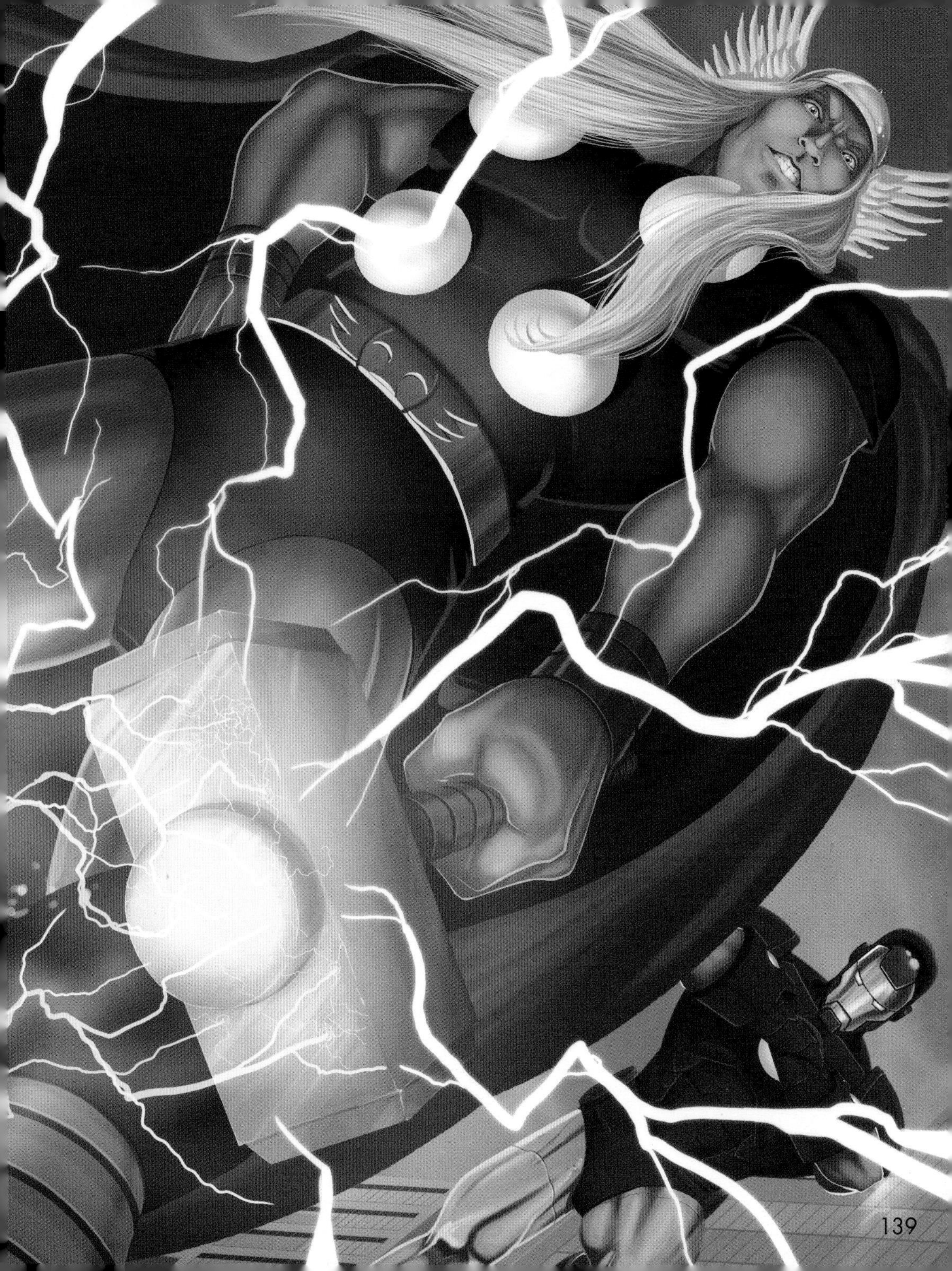

Then Thor held the hammer high above his head.

"Power, back from whence you came!" he thundered, releasing the energy. The city lit up once more!

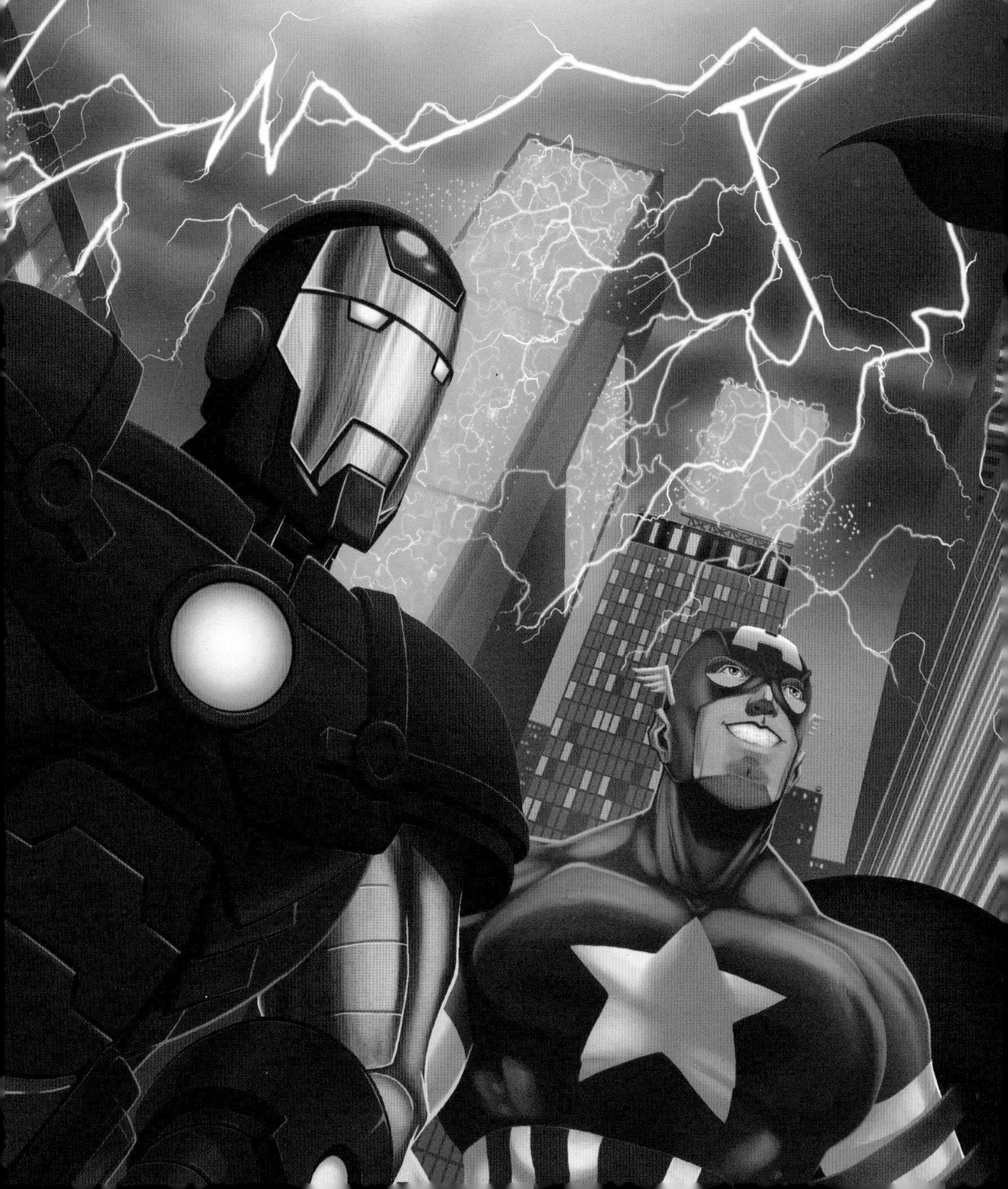

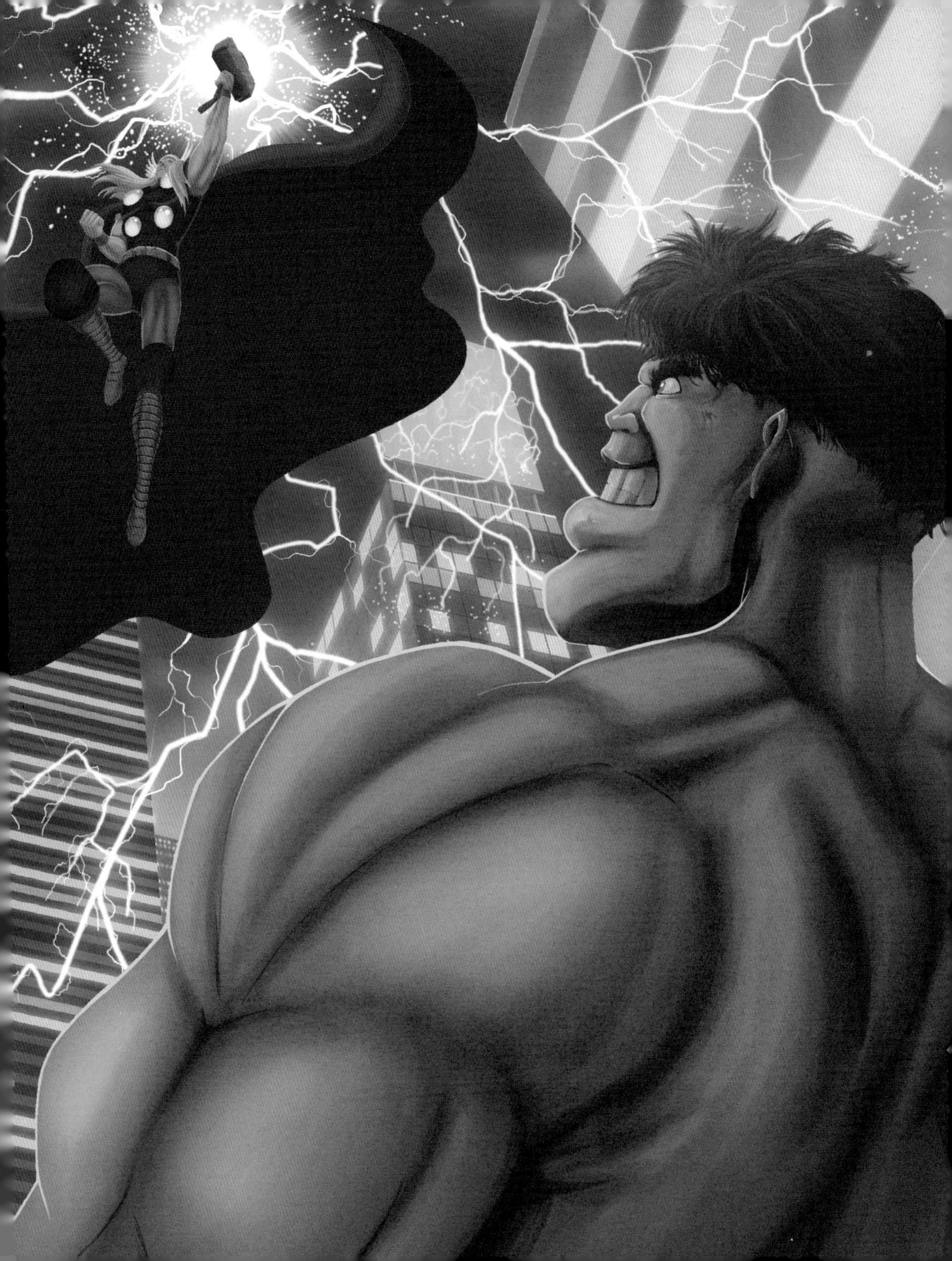

"The lights are on again in the city that never sleeps," said Captain America.

"Hulk like sleep," the green giant rumbled.

"Not now, Hulk. We've got a power plant to rebuild," Iron Man said. "Come on, Avengers."

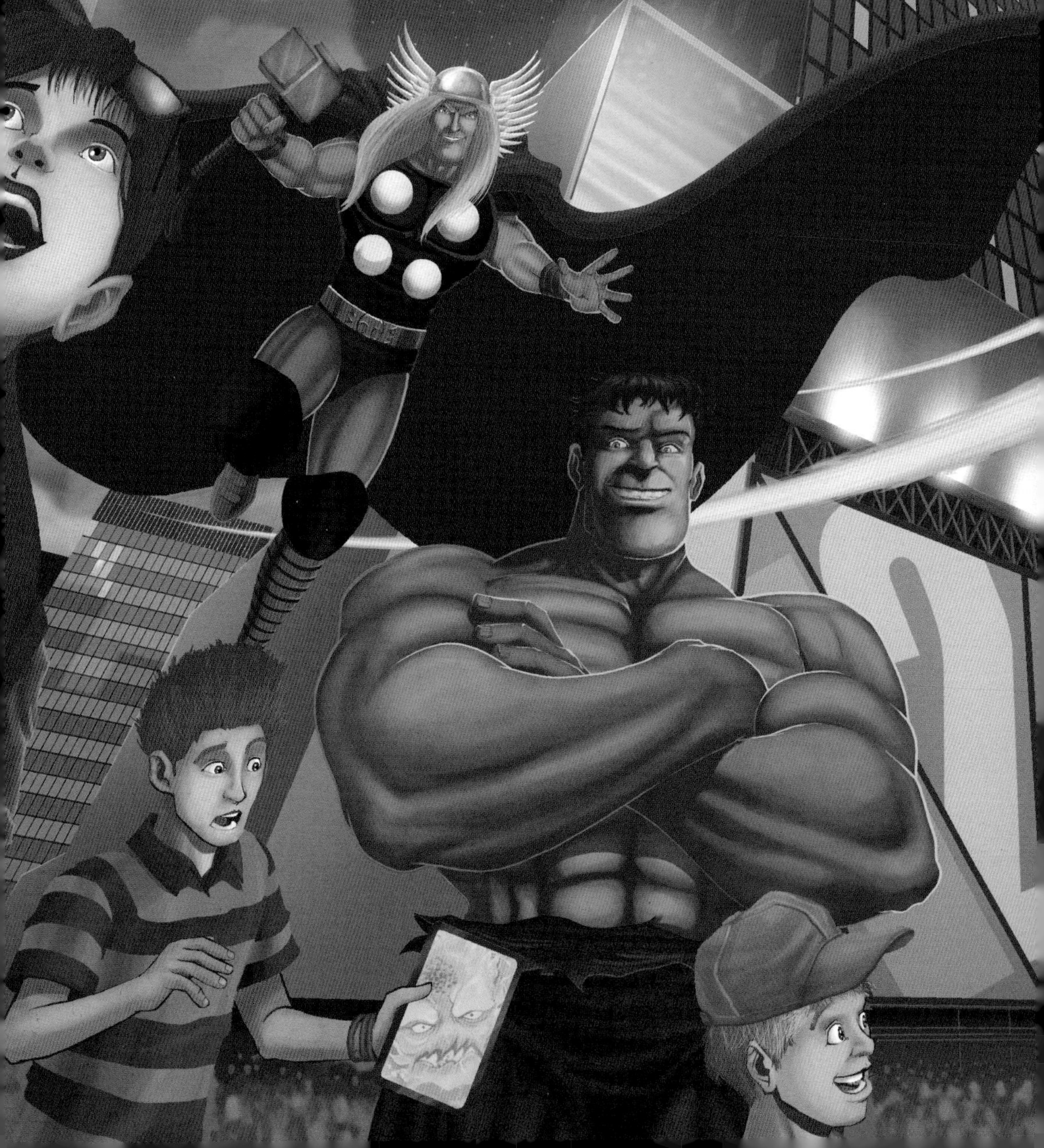

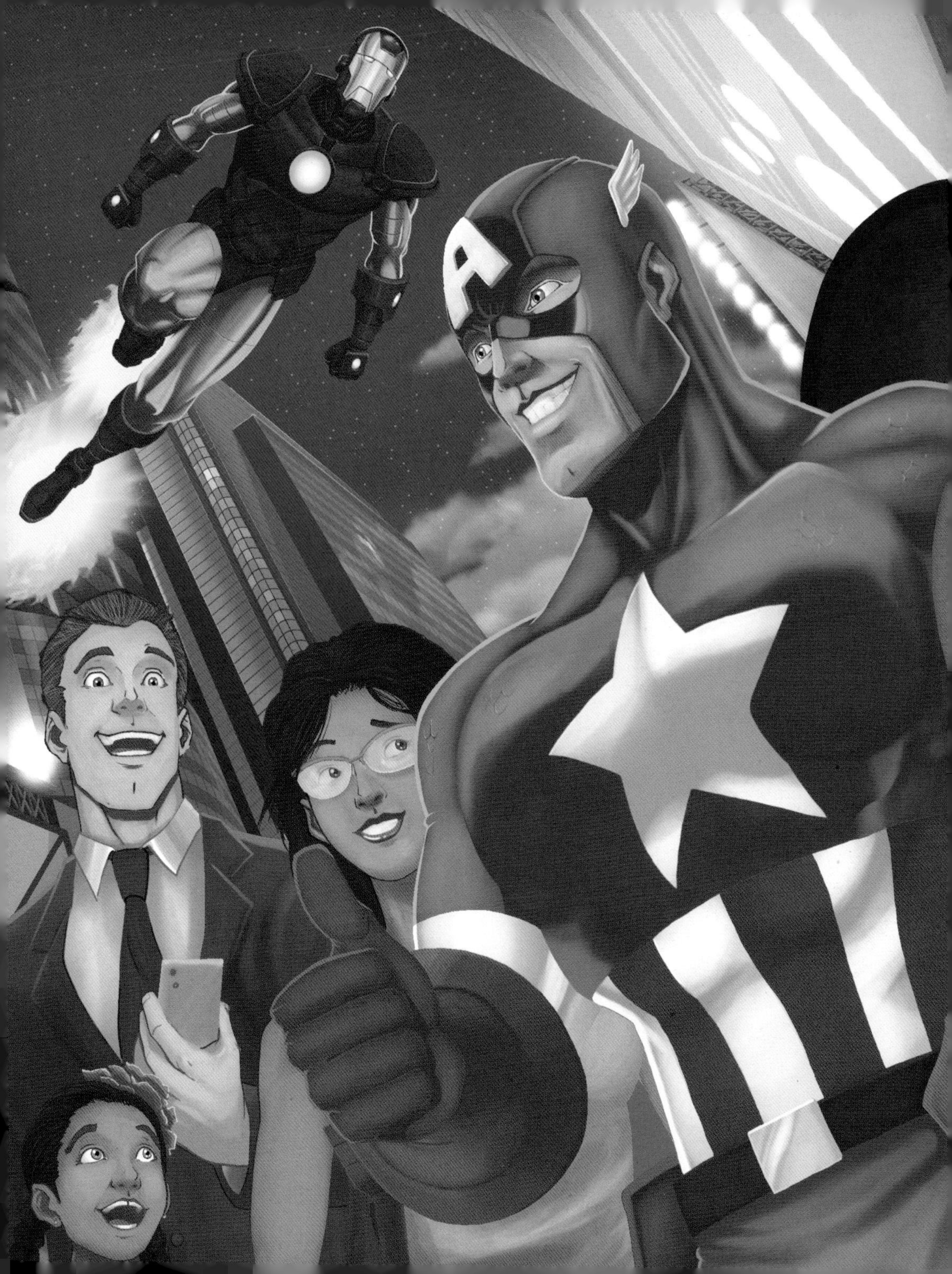

AVENGERS ASSEMBLE!

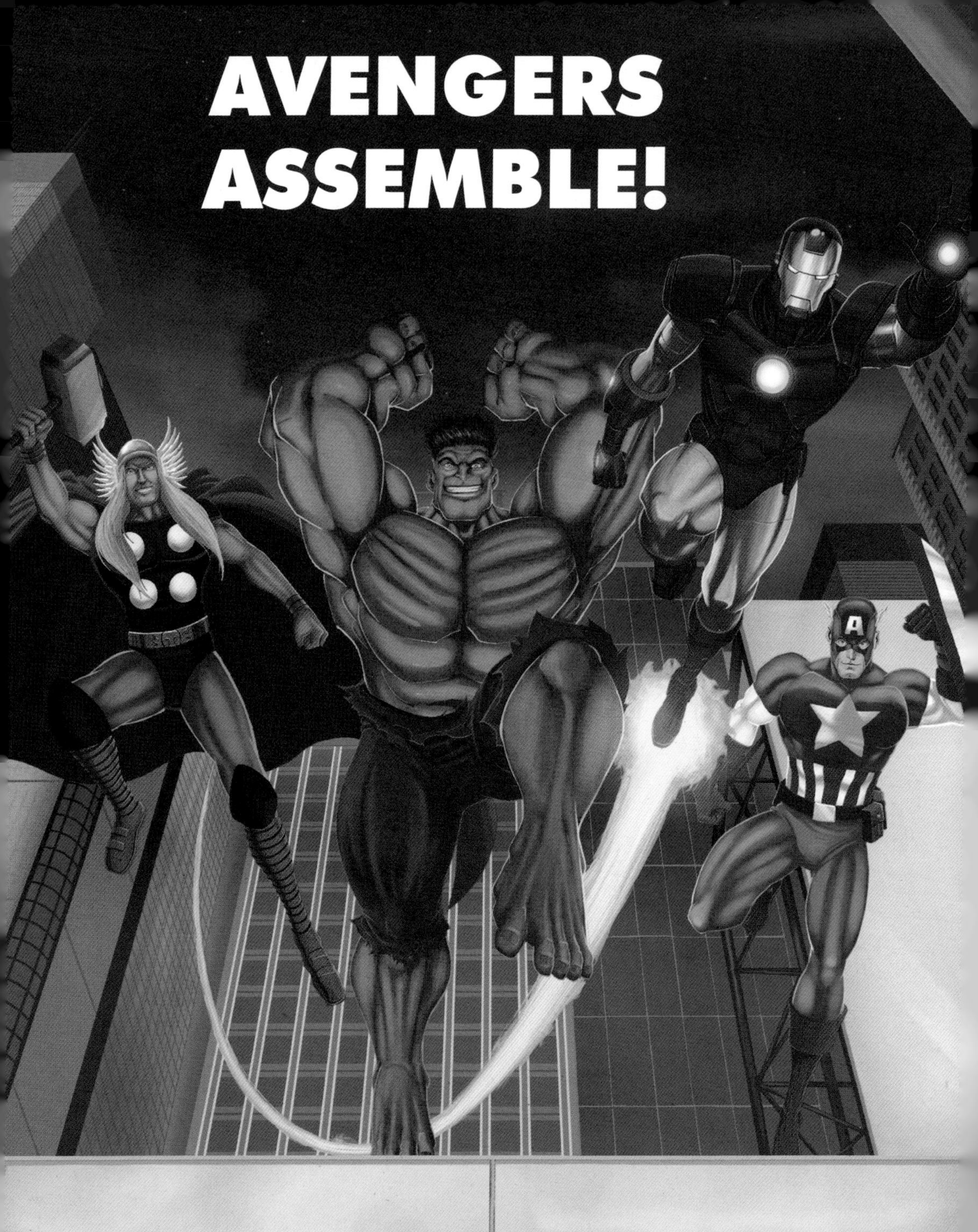

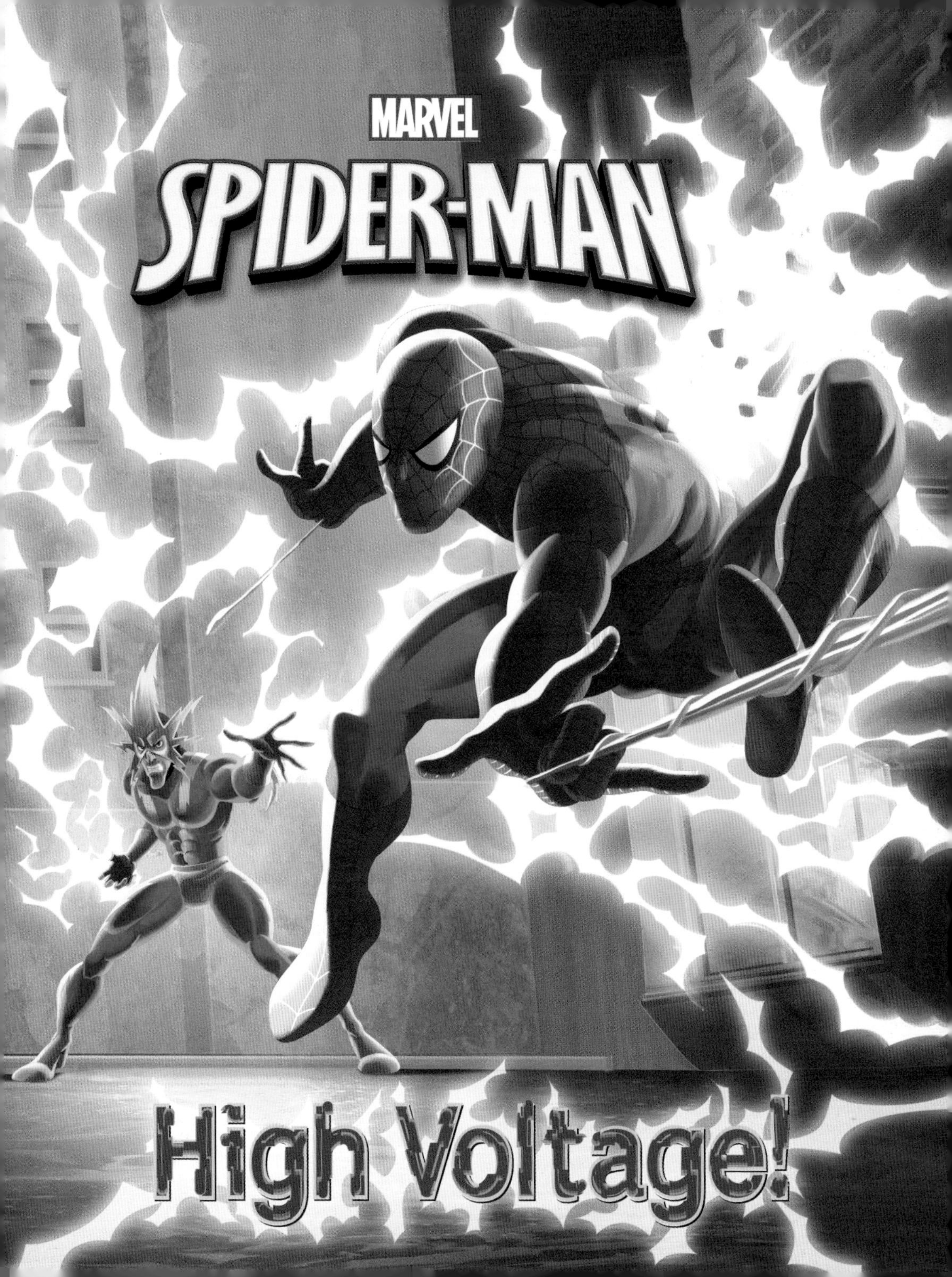
MARVEL
SPIDER-MAN
High Voltage!

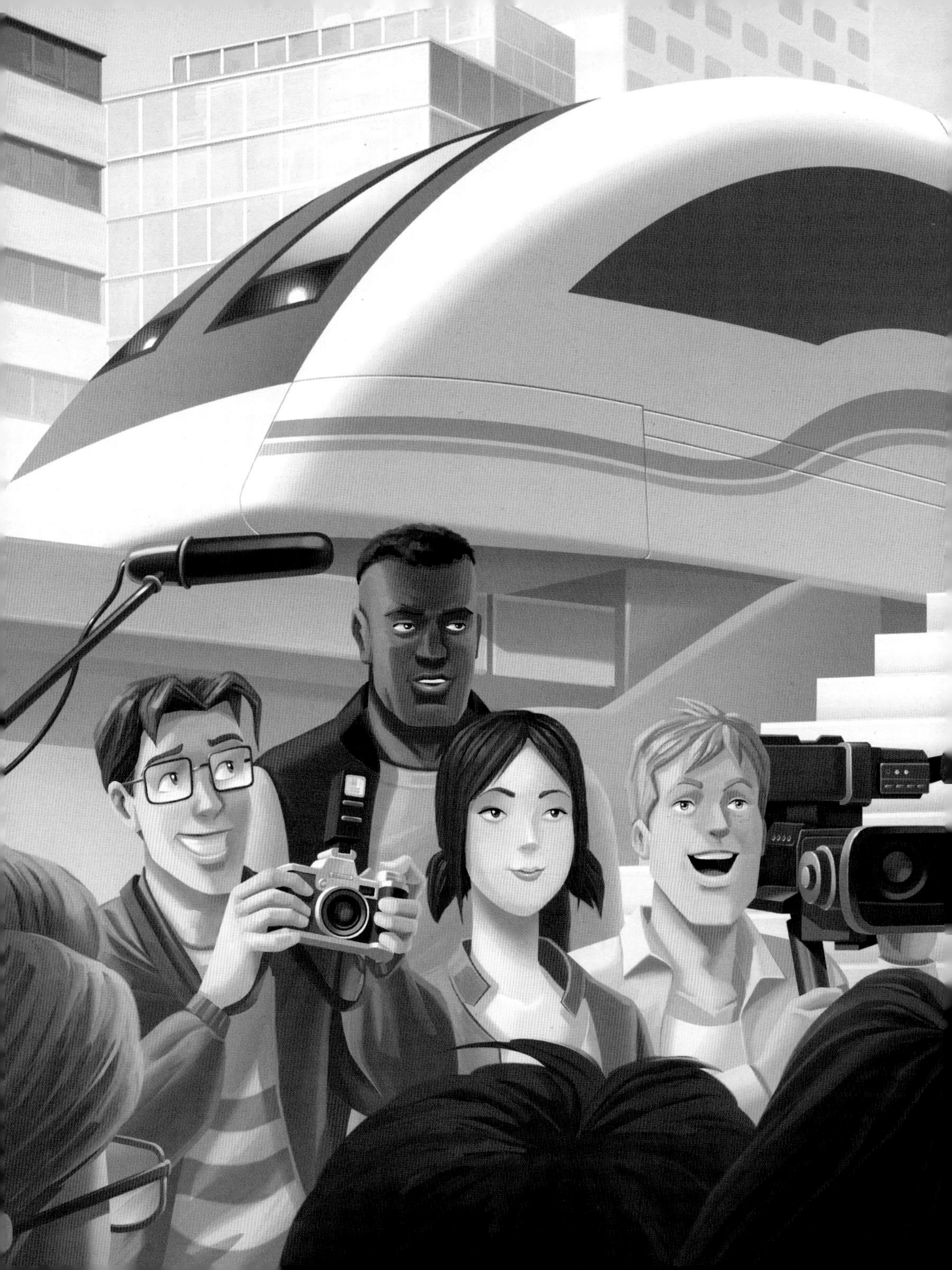

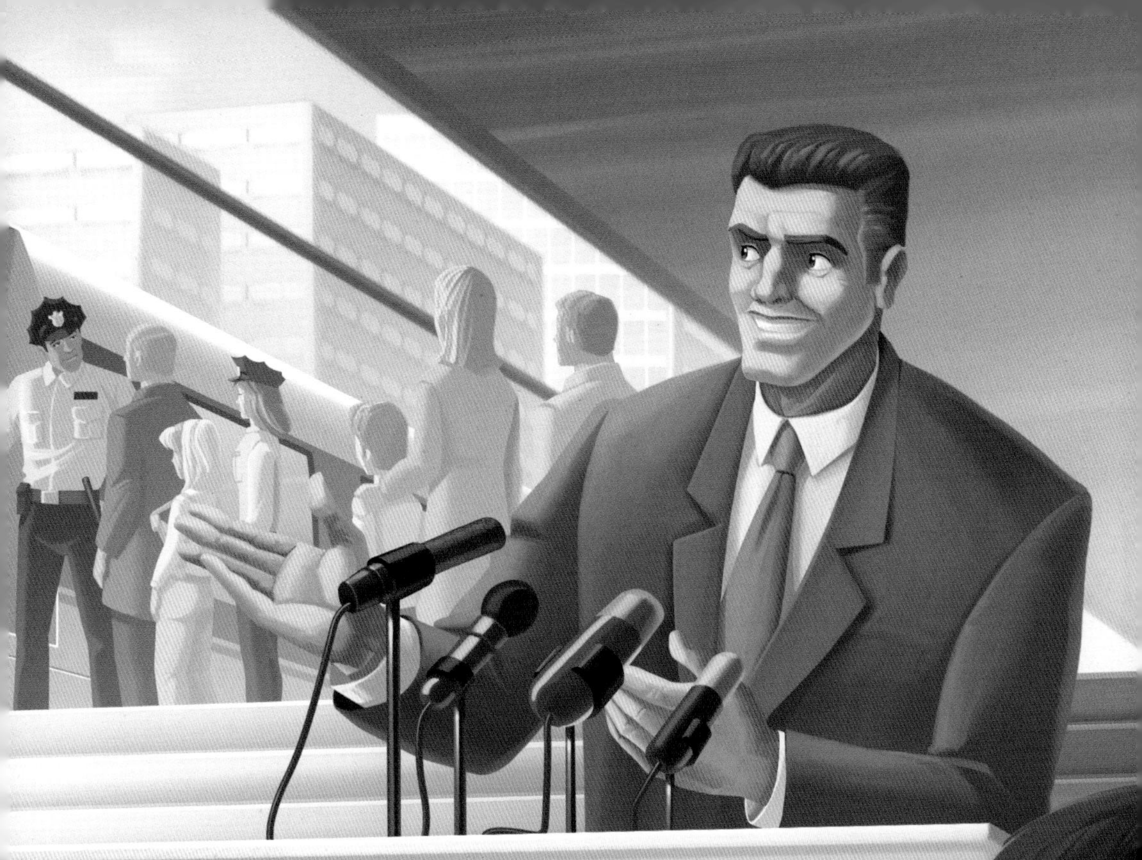

"Thank you all for coming out today to celebrate the first trip of our brand-new high-speed electric train," said the mayor.

Photographer Peter Parker was taking pictures for the *Daily Bugle* newspaper. No one would ever suspect that teenager Peter was also the hero known as the **AMAZING SPIDER-MAN!**

As Peter made his way through the crowd, his **spider-sense** suddenly started to tingle—there was danger nearby!

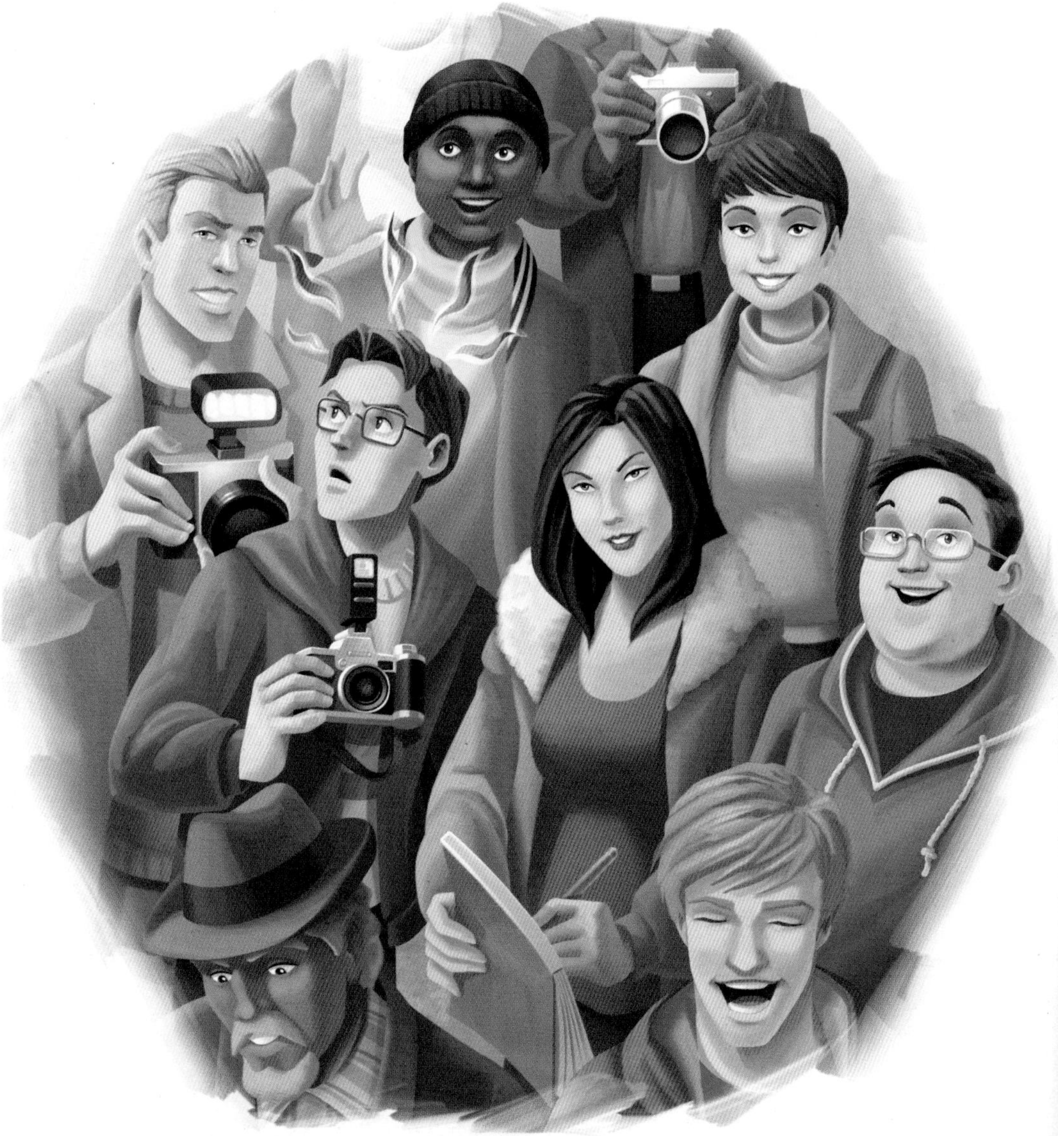

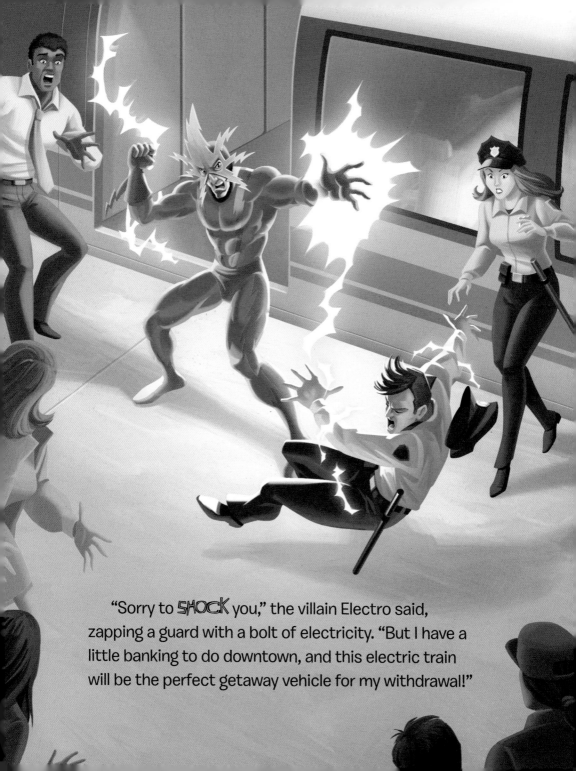

"Sorry to 𝕊ℍ𝕆ℂ𝕂 you," the villain Electro said, zapping a guard with a bolt of electricity. "But I have a little banking to do downtown, and this electric train will be the perfect getaway vehicle for my withdrawal!"

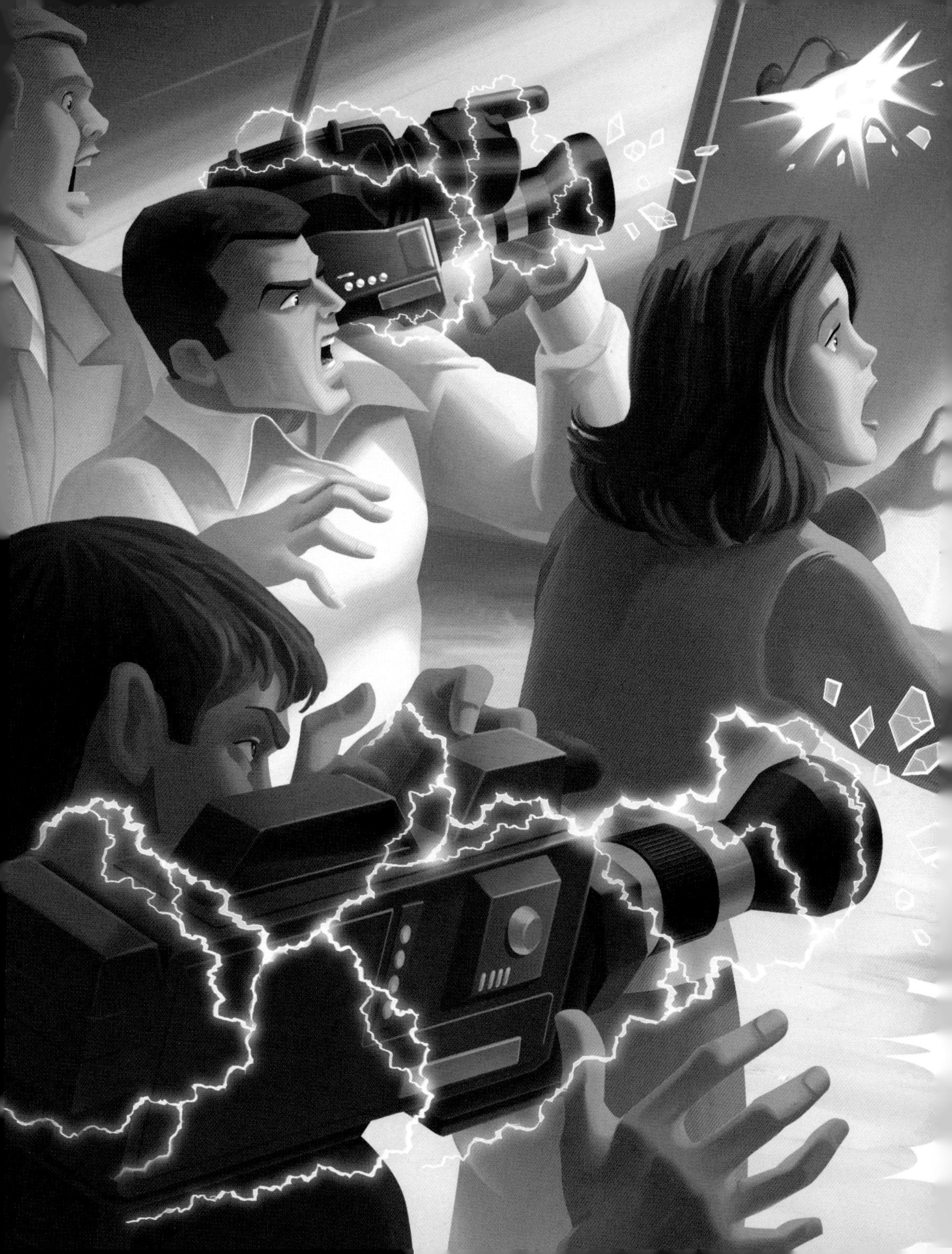

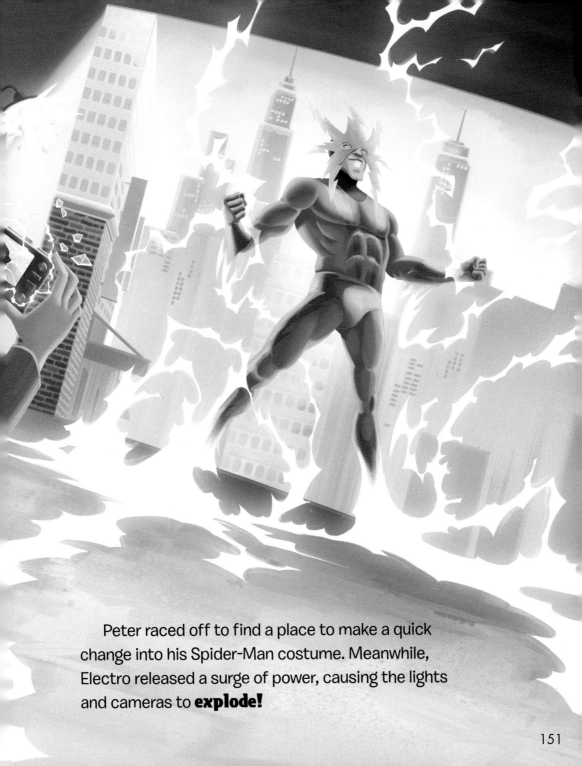

Peter raced off to find a place to make a quick change into his Spider-Man costume. Meanwhile, Electro released a surge of power, causing the lights and cameras to **explode!**

"All aboard the Electro Express!" announced the villain.

With a powerful SPARK from his hands, Electro started the electric train to make his escape. Little did he know, Spider-Man was in pursuit!

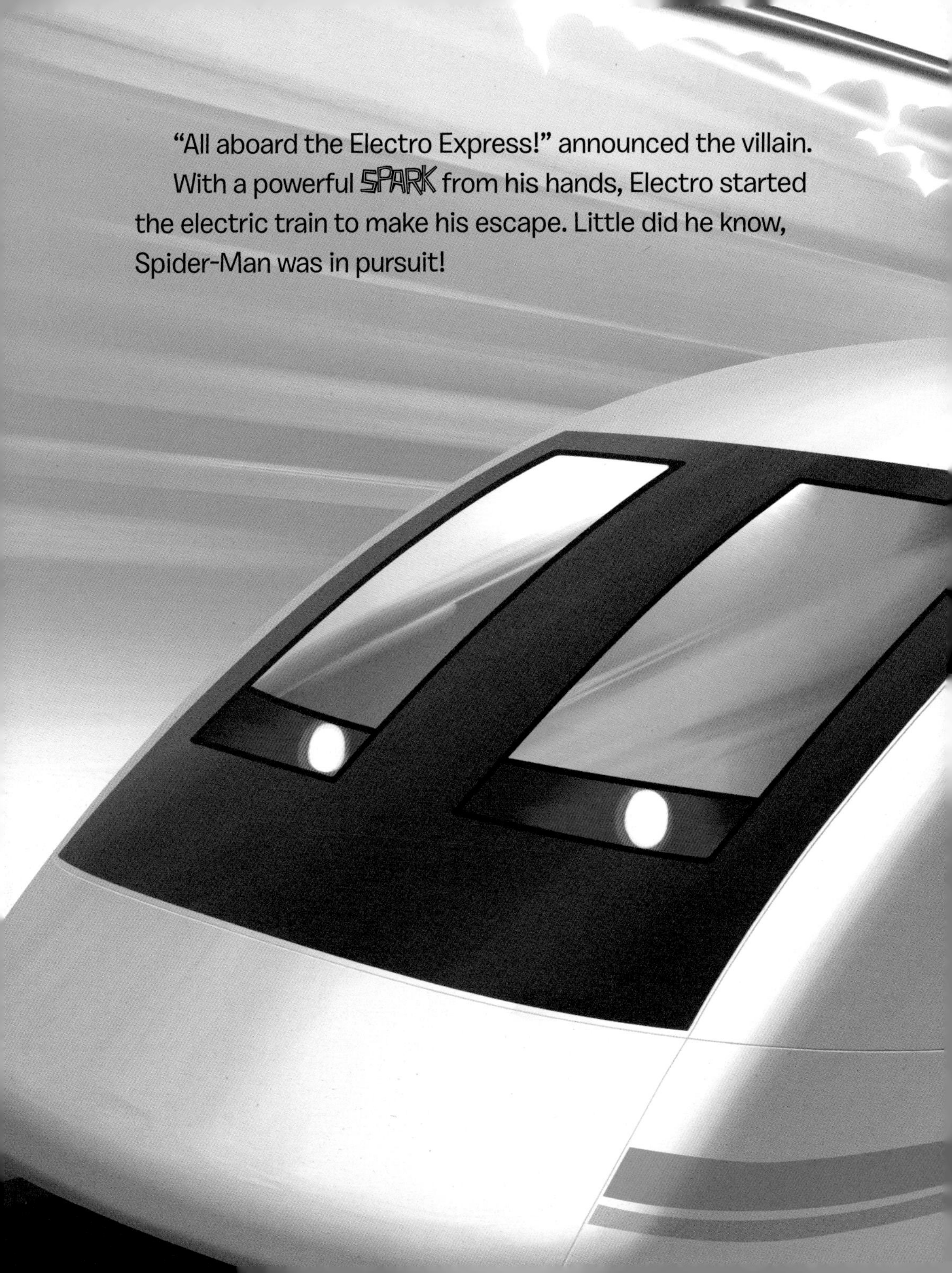

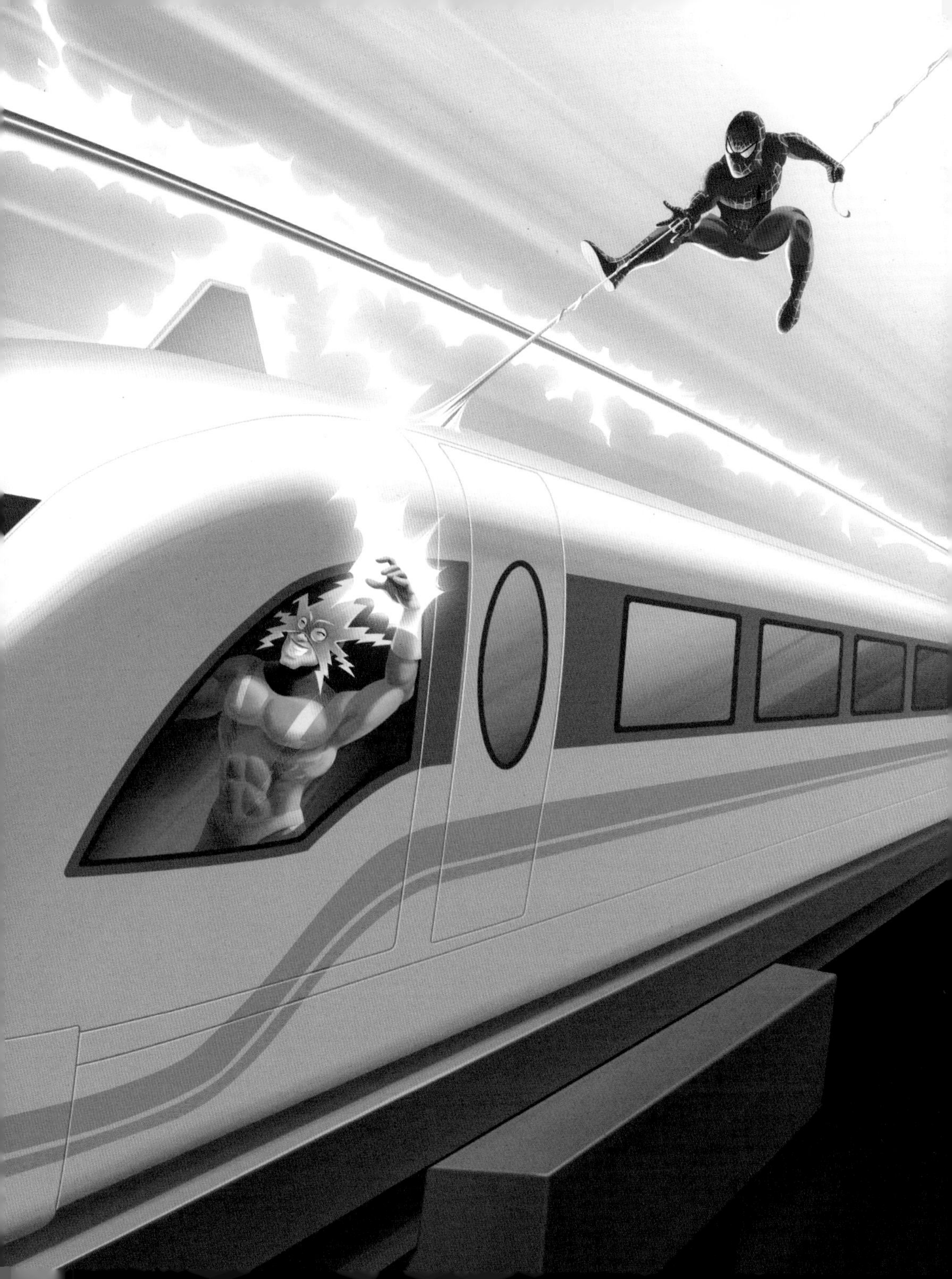

"I hope you weren't going to leave without saying goodbye to your friendly neighborhood Spider-Man!" joked the **web-slinger**. With a mighty kick, he sent Electro flying!

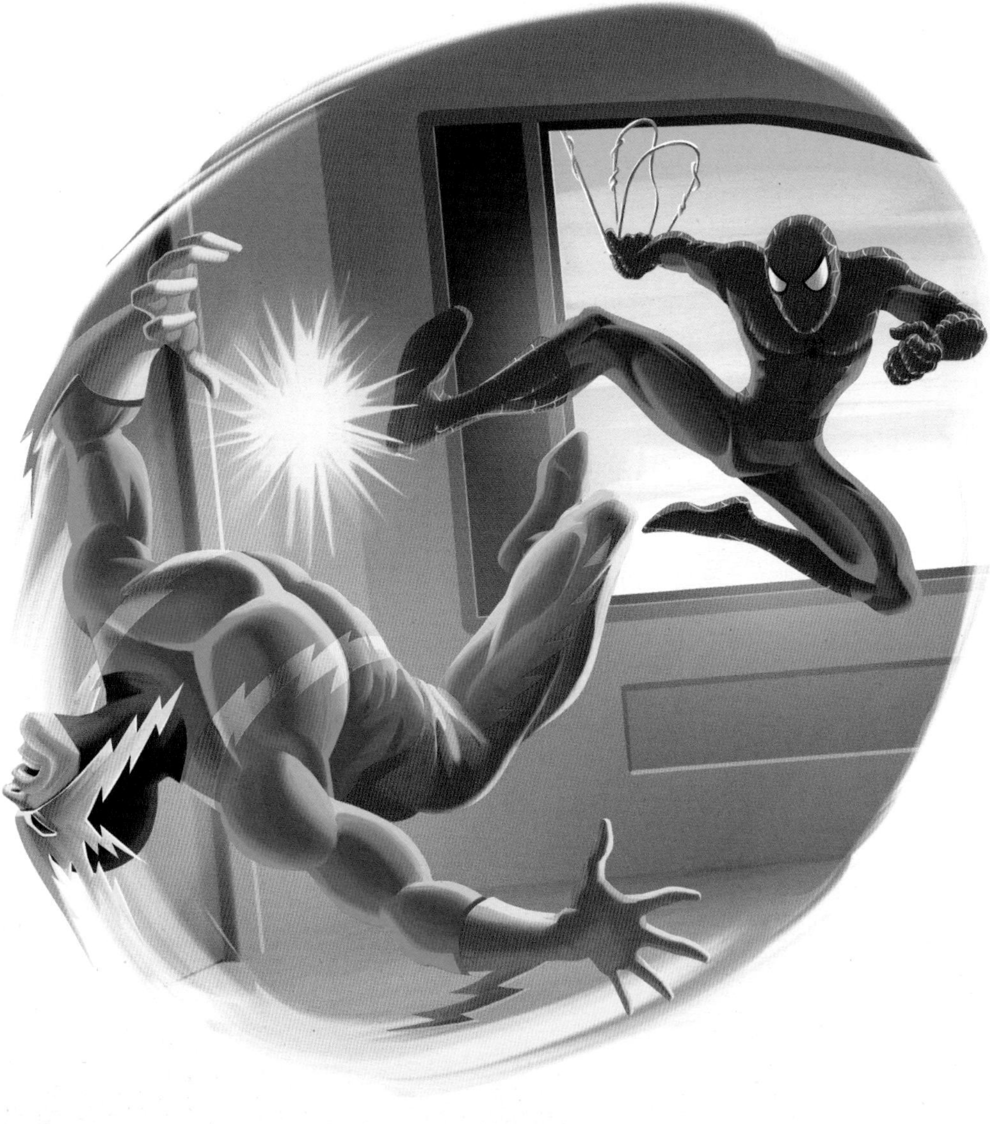

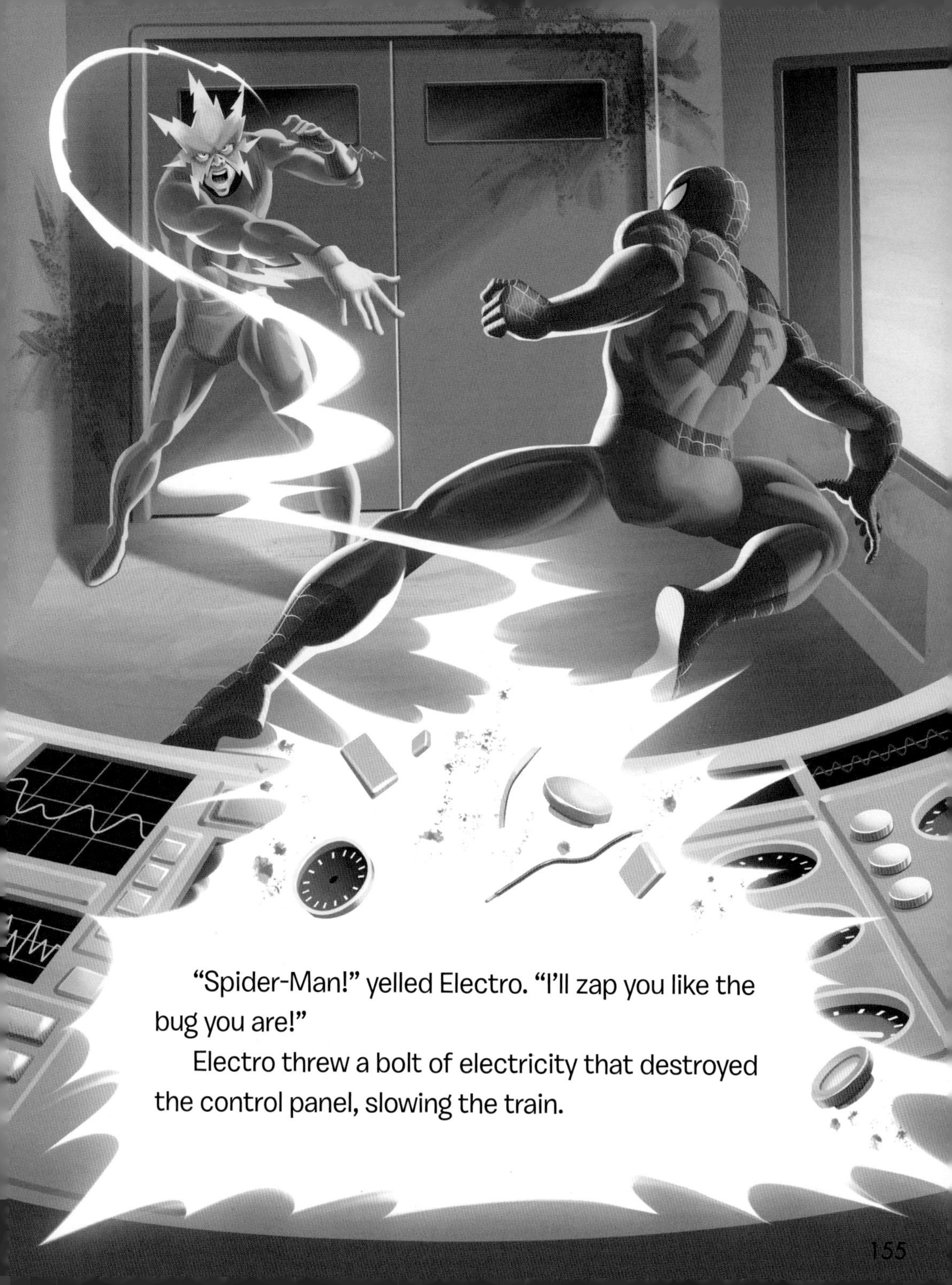

"Spider-Man!" yelled Electro. "I'll zap you like the bug you are!"

Electro threw a bolt of electricity that destroyed the control panel, slowing the train.

"Guess this is my stop!" said Spider-Man. The web-slinger dashed deeper into the dark train tunnel. He wanted to make sure no one was around to get hurt by the **super-charged** bad guy.

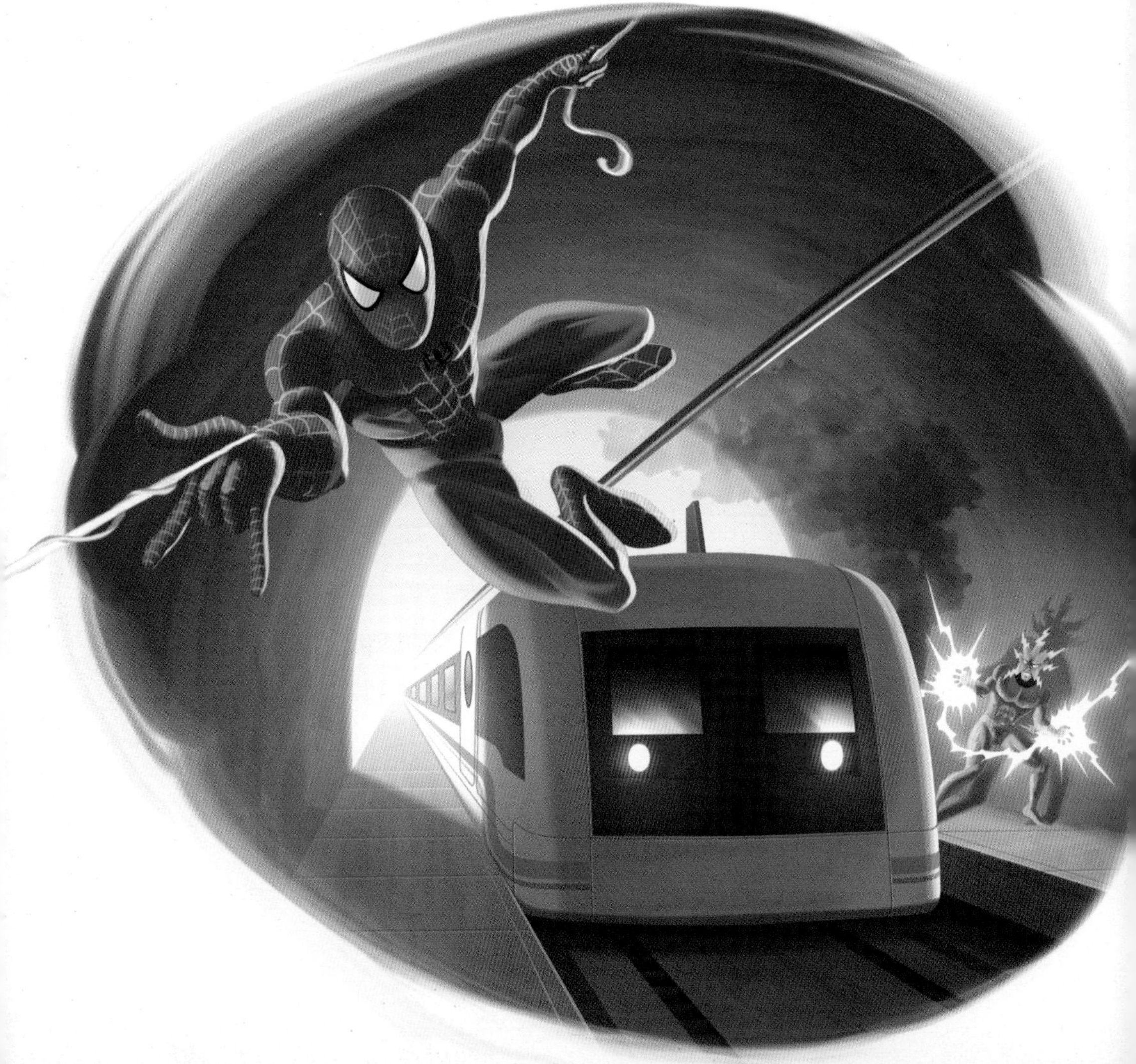

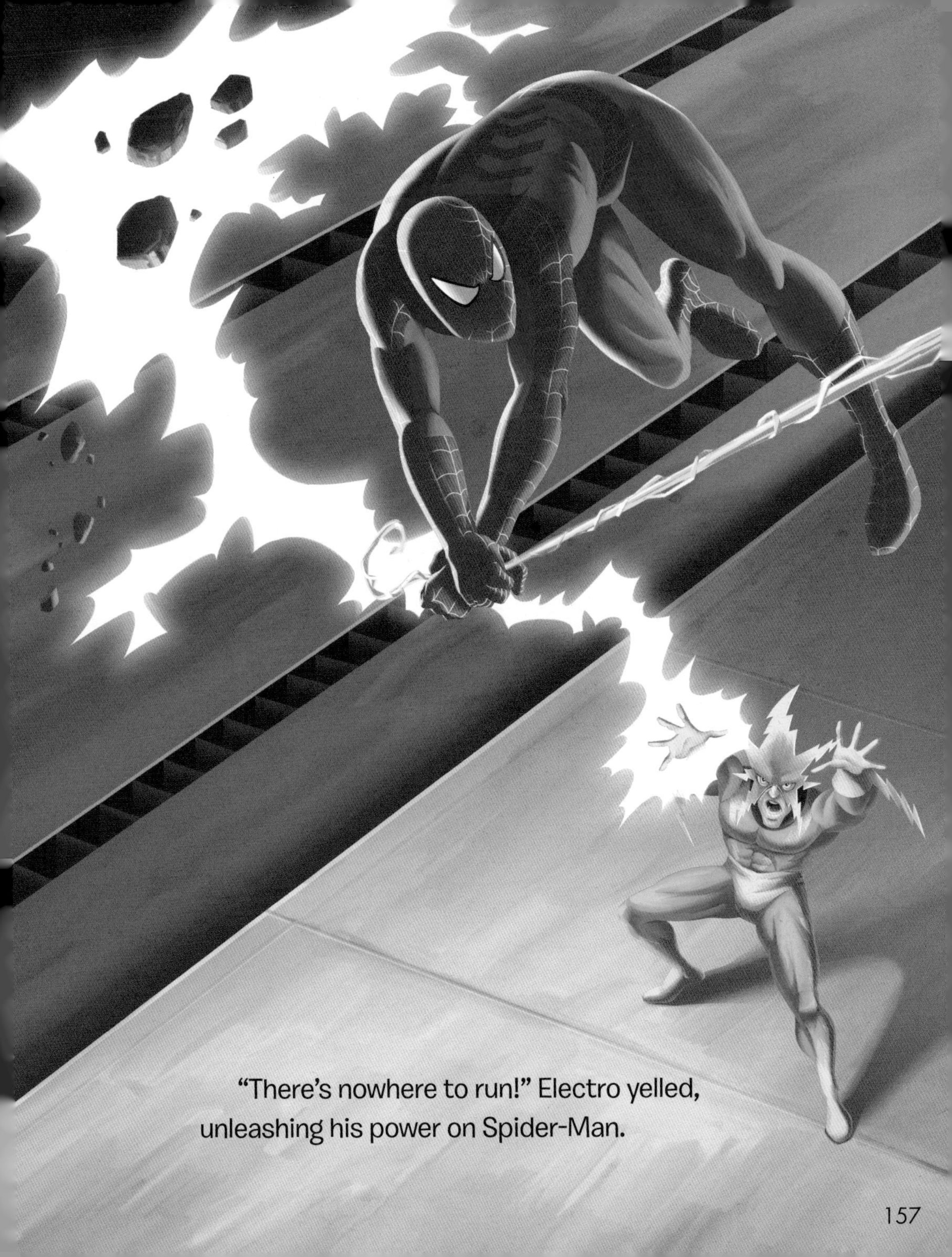

"There's nowhere to run!" Electro yelled, unleashing his power on Spider-Man.

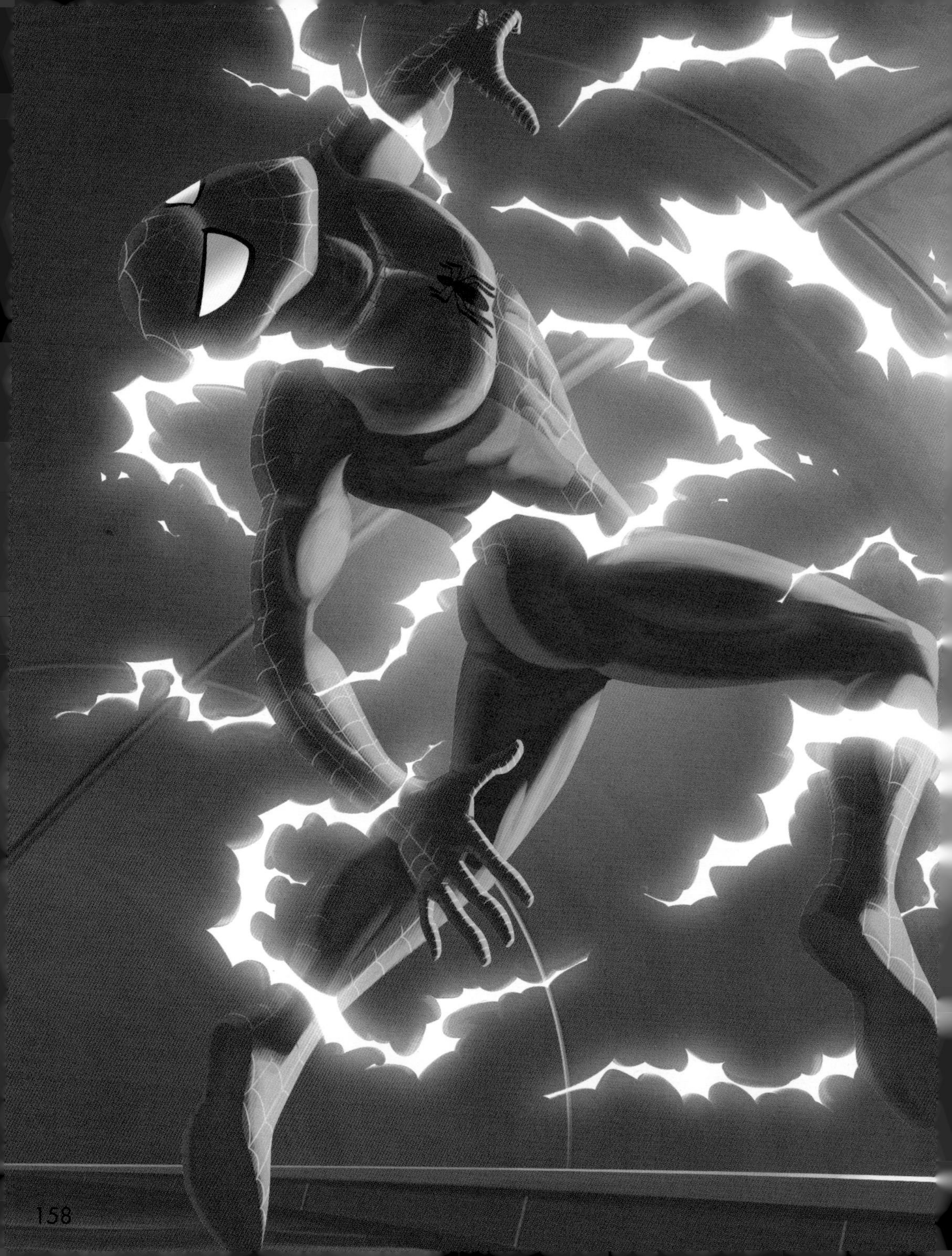

Electro hit Spider-Man with a burst of electricity. "Now let's see if lightning can strike twice," he snarled, getting ready to zap the wall-crawler again.

"I need a plan," Spidey thought as he struggled to stay on his feet.

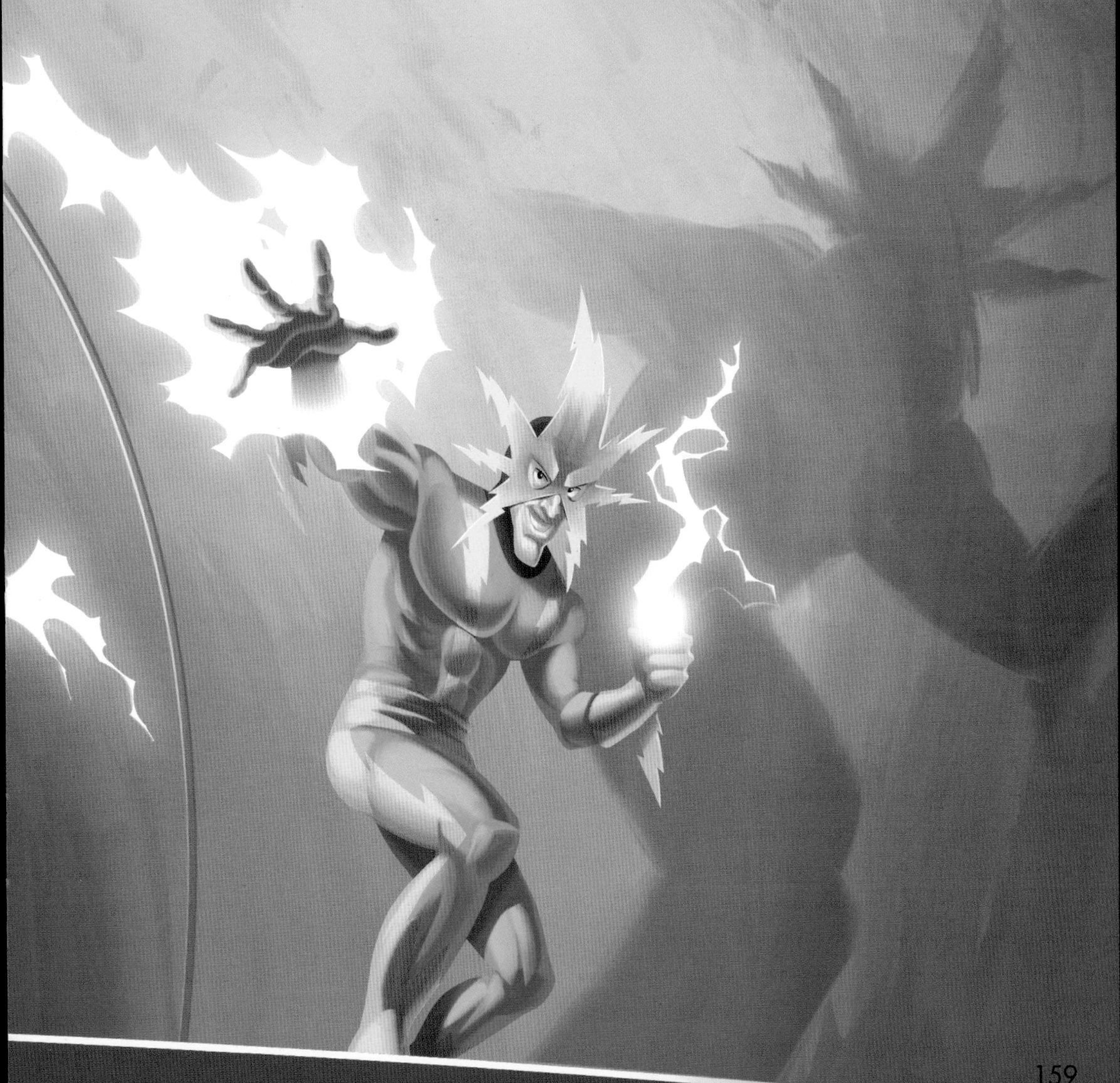

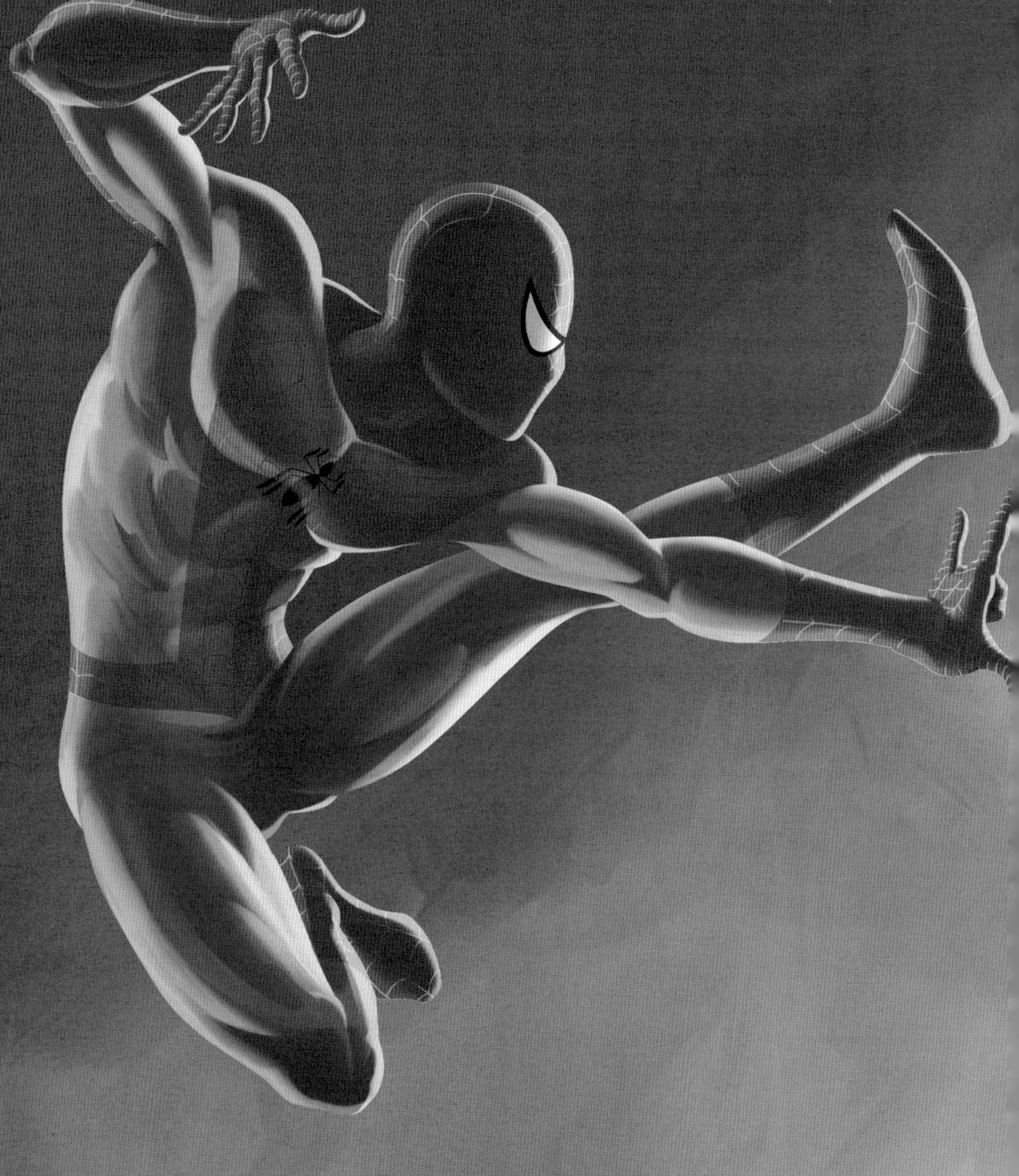

"I think it's time for **lights-out** and a nap!" Spidey joked. Using his web-shooters, Spider-Man covered Electro's eyes with webbing so thick that the villain couldn't see!

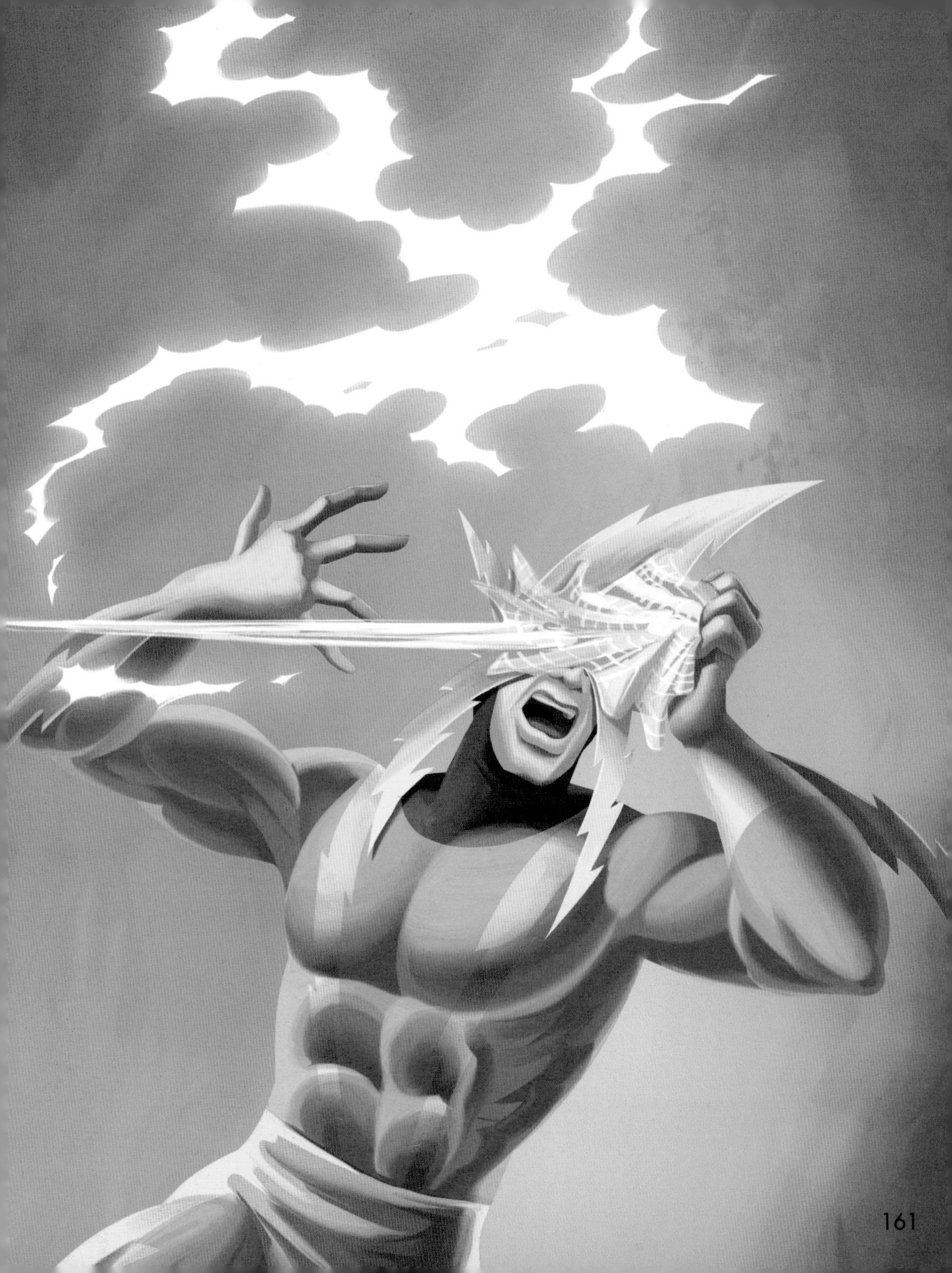

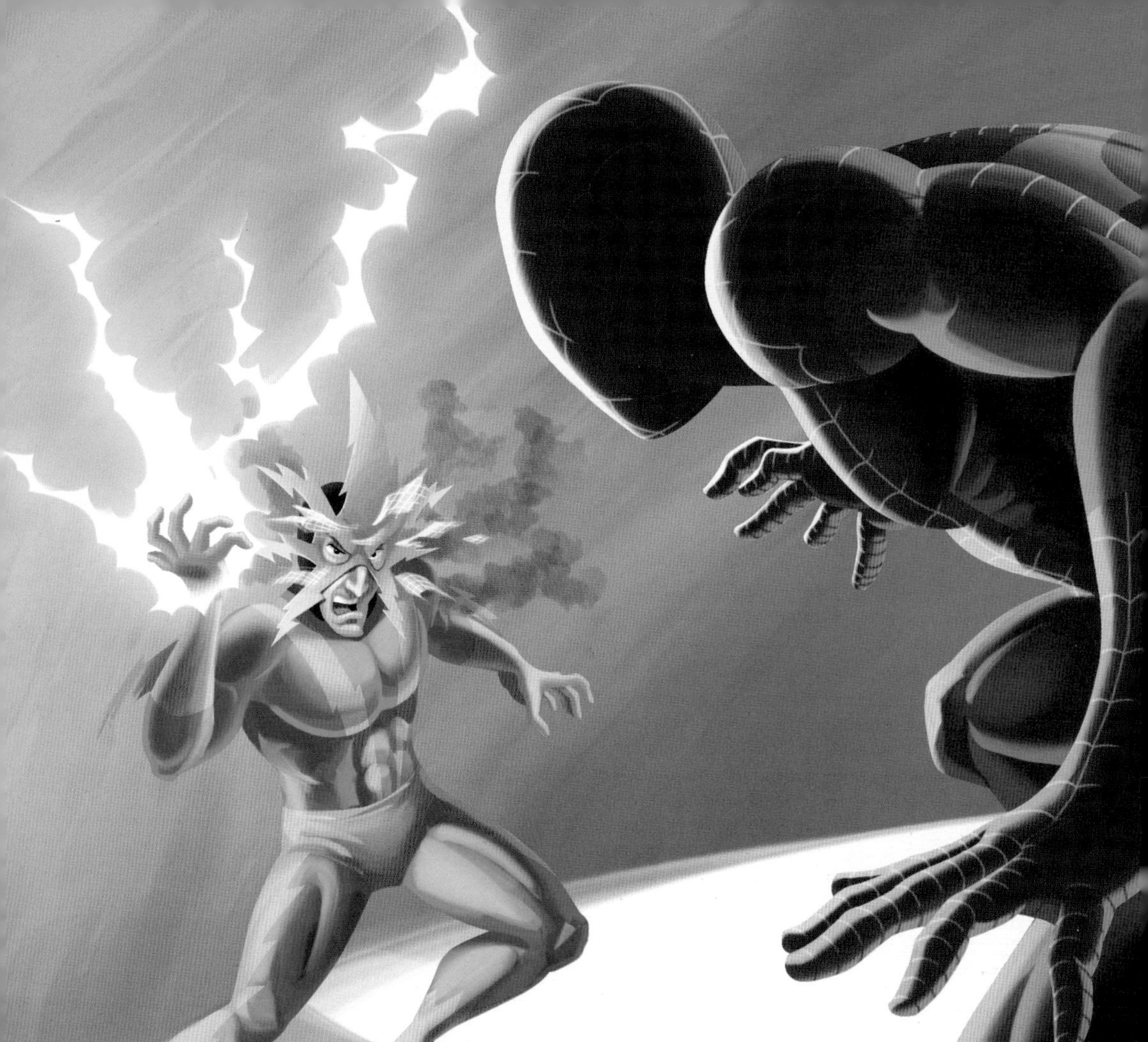

"This web of yours won't stop me for long!" the villain growled. "My electric powers can **burn** through anything!"

The angry villain chased Spider-Man out of the tunnel and into a darkened building.

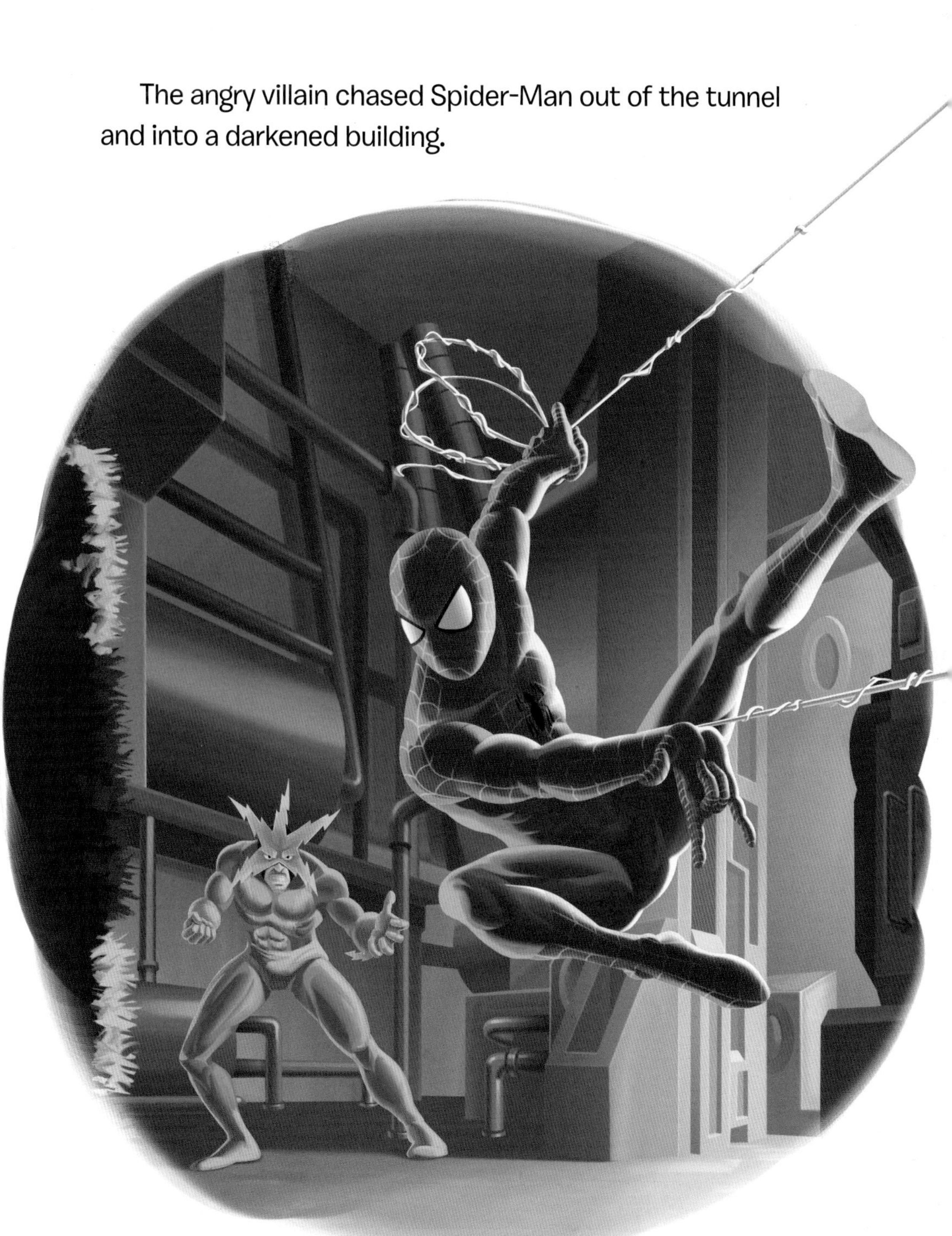

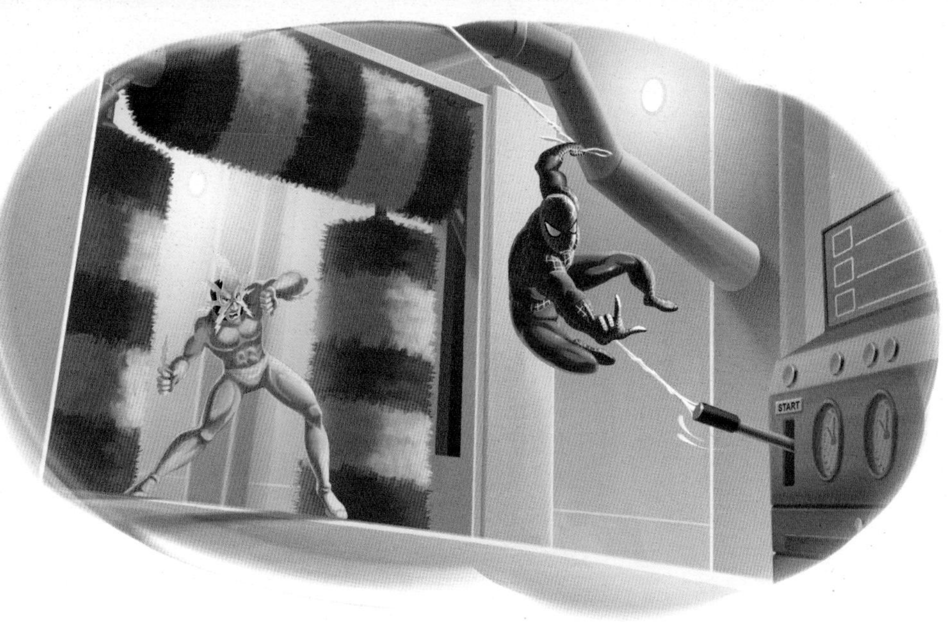
START

"I think it's time for you to cool off!" said Spider-Man. With the pull of a lever, lights turned on and machines whirred to life.

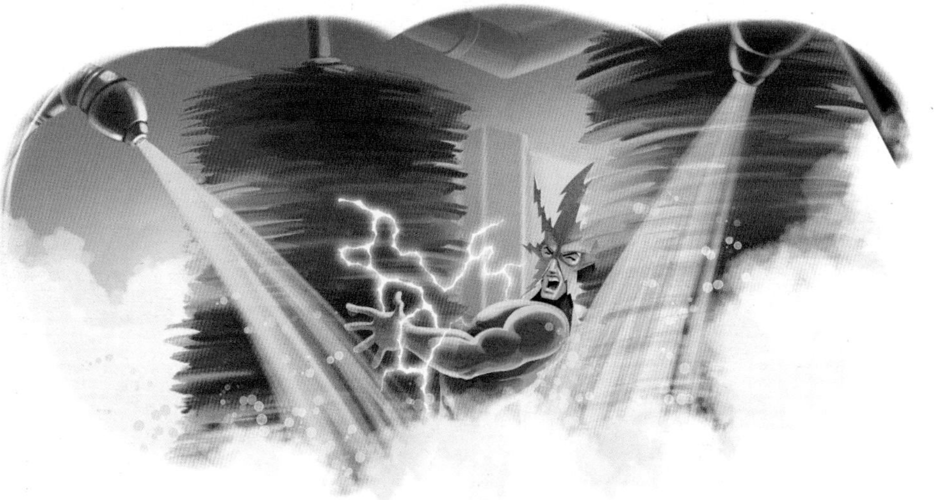

"Nooo!" screamed Electro. Two huge spinning car-wash brushes popped out and spun Electro around like a top. Then two spray nozzles covered him with soap and water!

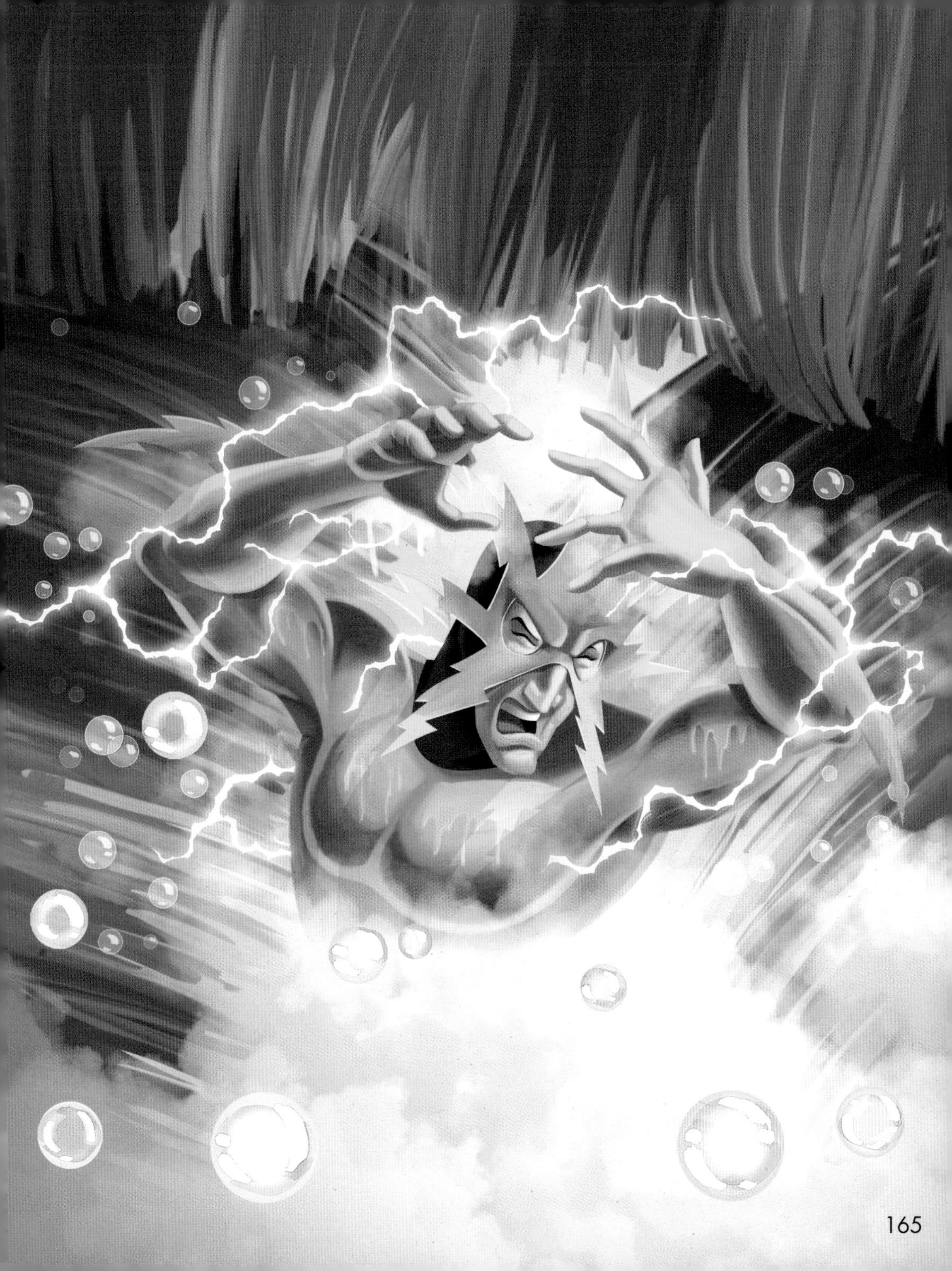

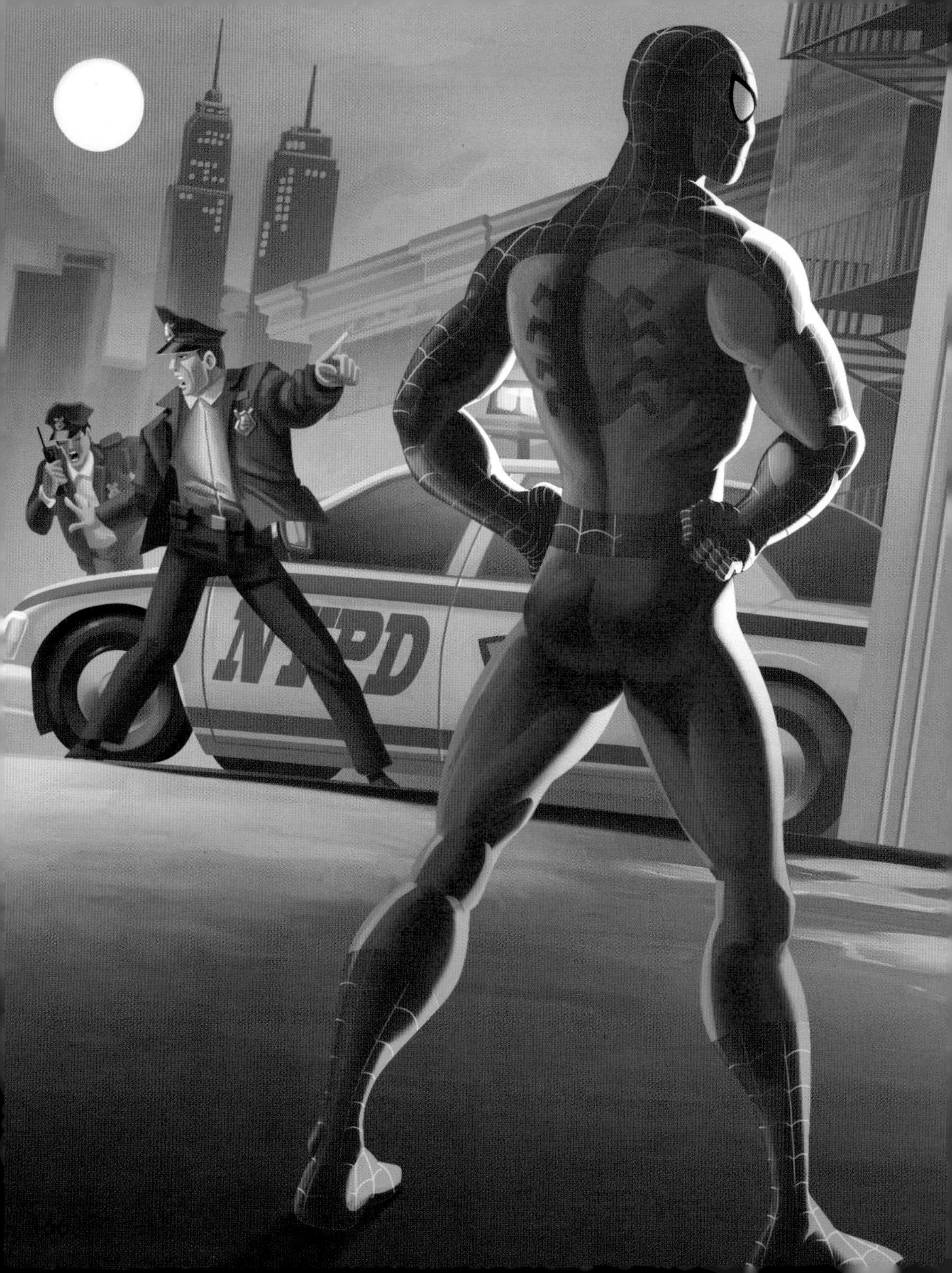
NYPD

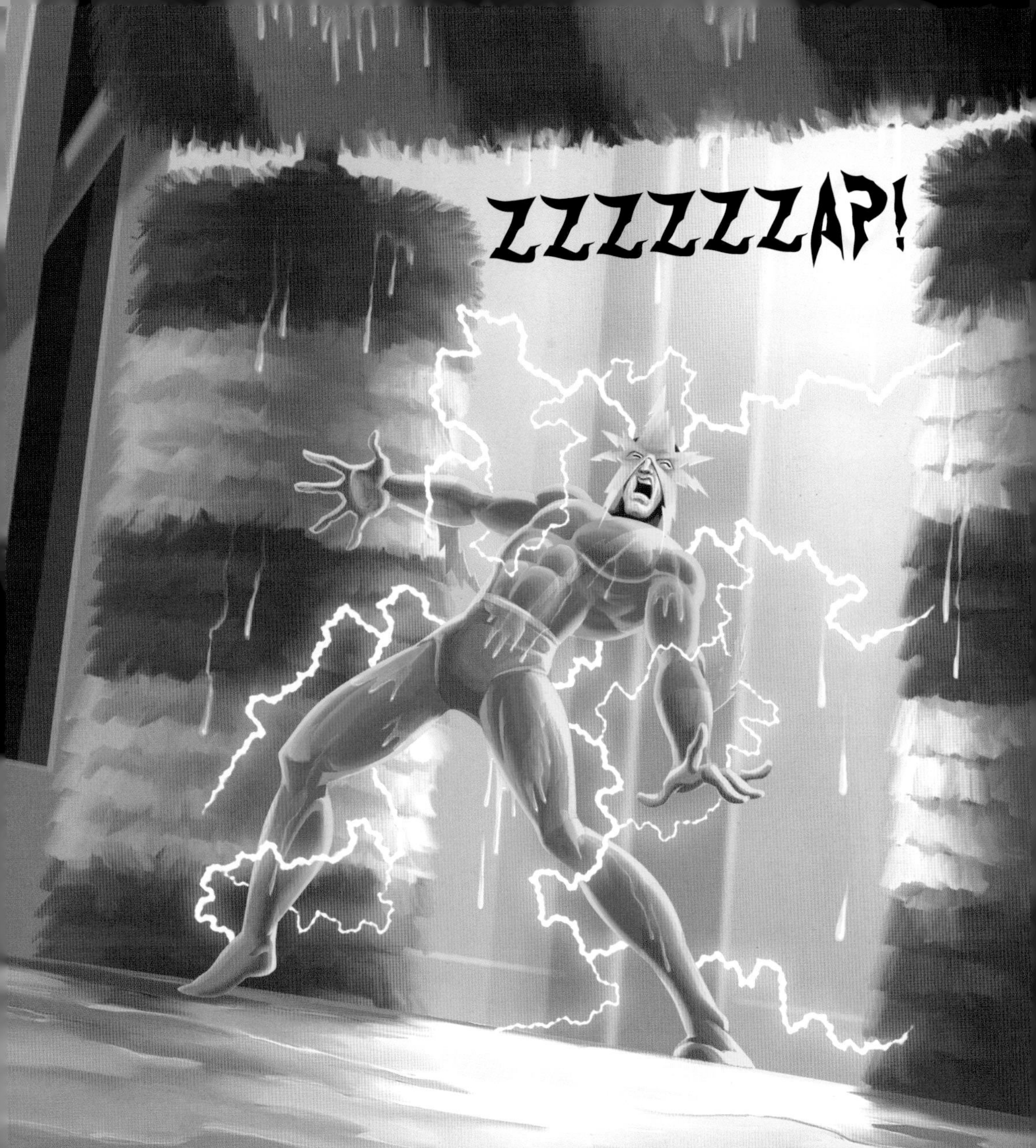
ZZZZZZZAP!

The water caused Electro to spark and short-circuit.

"Everyone knows water and electricity don't mix," said Spidey. "He's all yours, Officers."

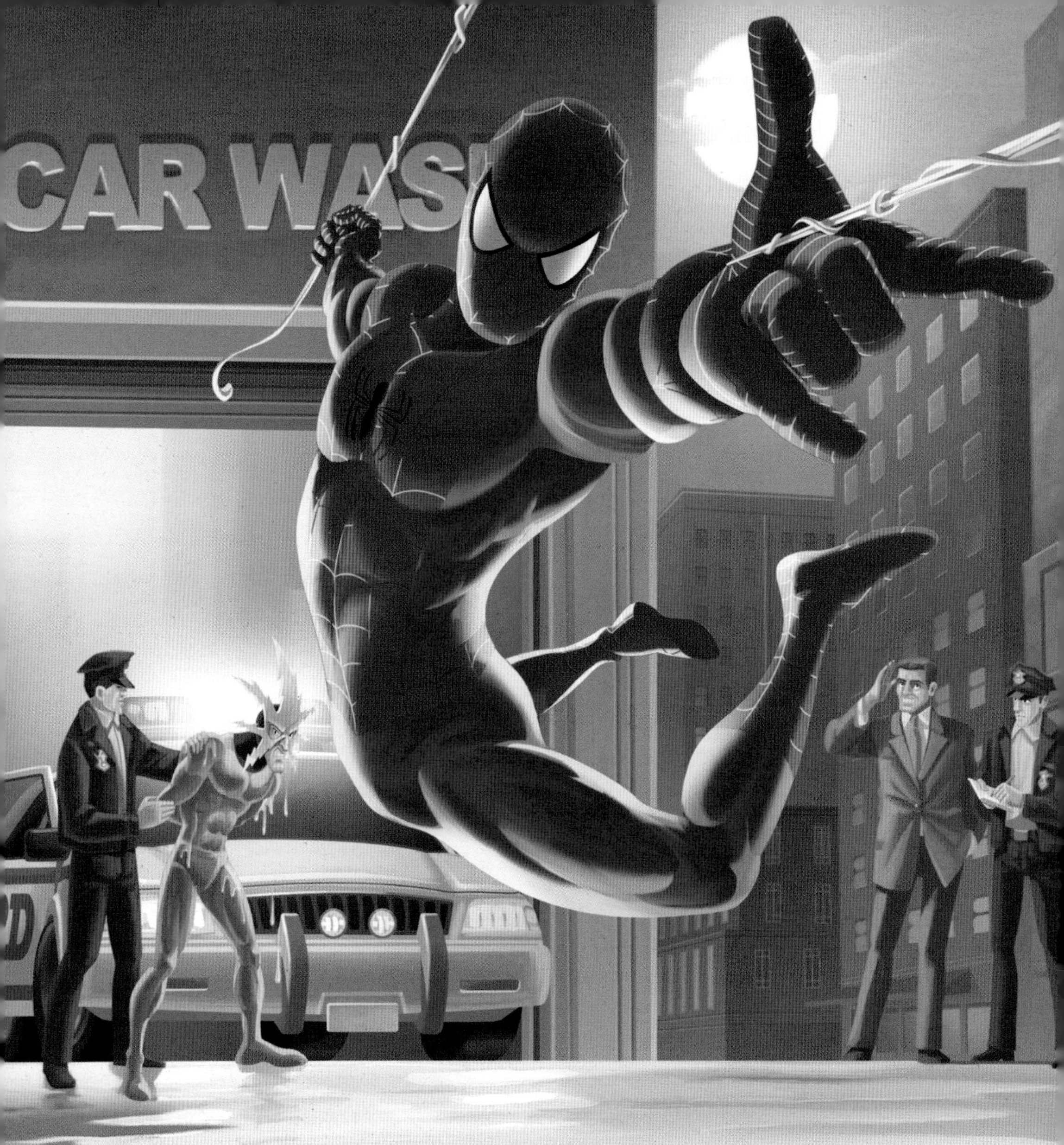
CAR WAS

"I'm always happy to help clean up this town!" the web-slinger said, swinging away as the police took Electro off to jail.

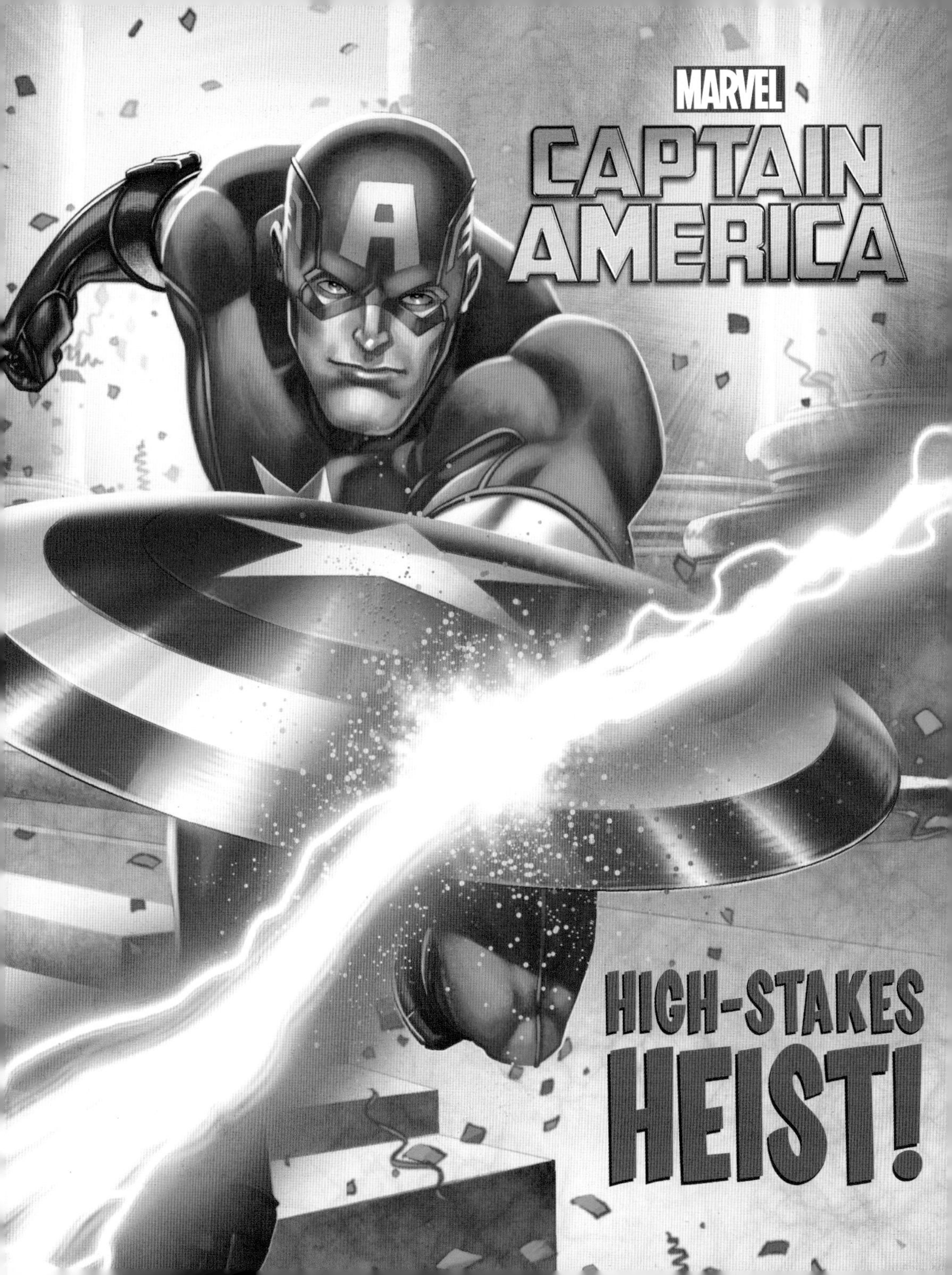
MARVEL
CAPTAIN AMERICA
HIGH-STAKES HEIST!

Early one morning, the super hero Captain America and his sidekick, Bucky Barnes, were on patrol at the US Mint in Washington, DC.

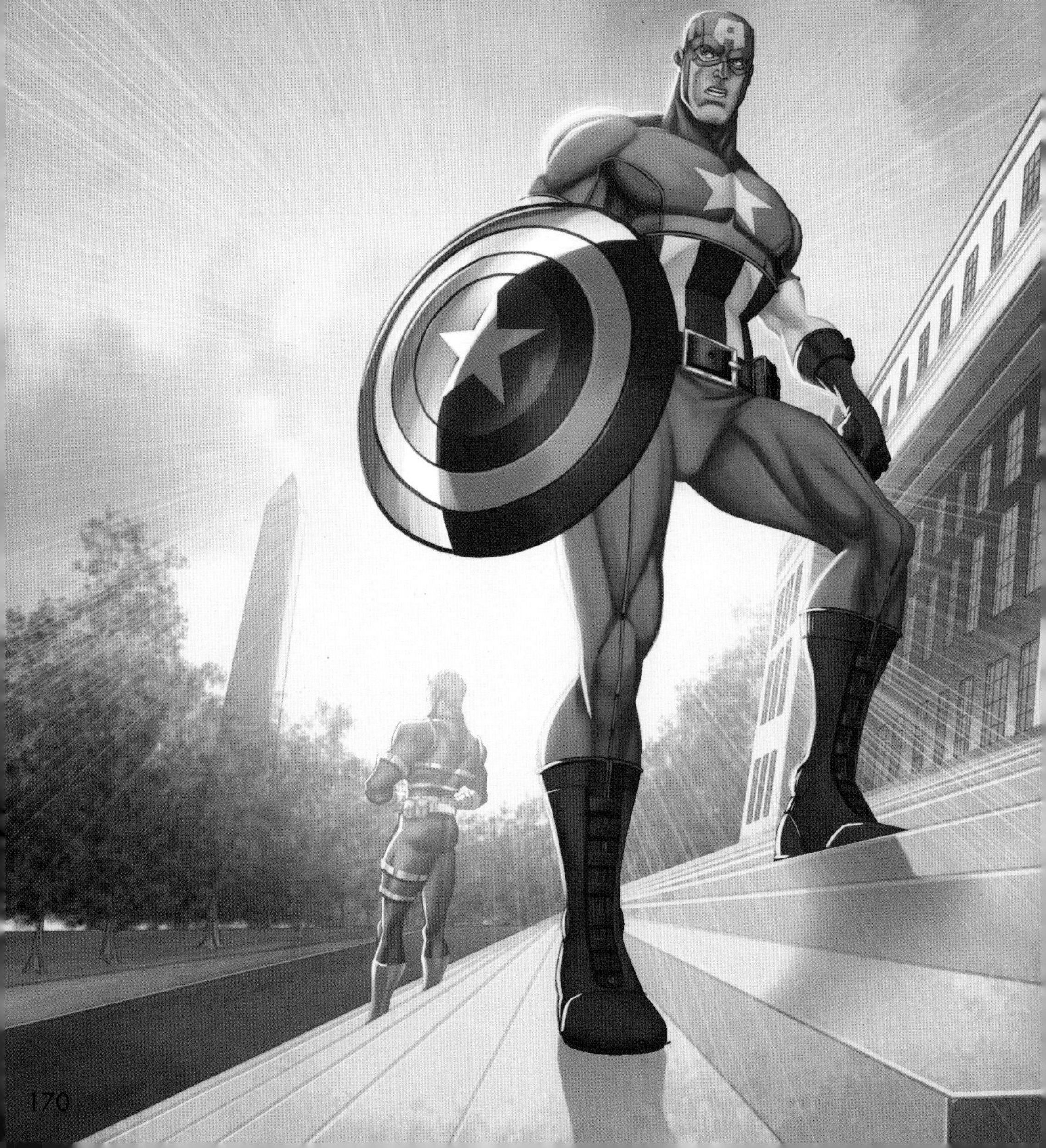

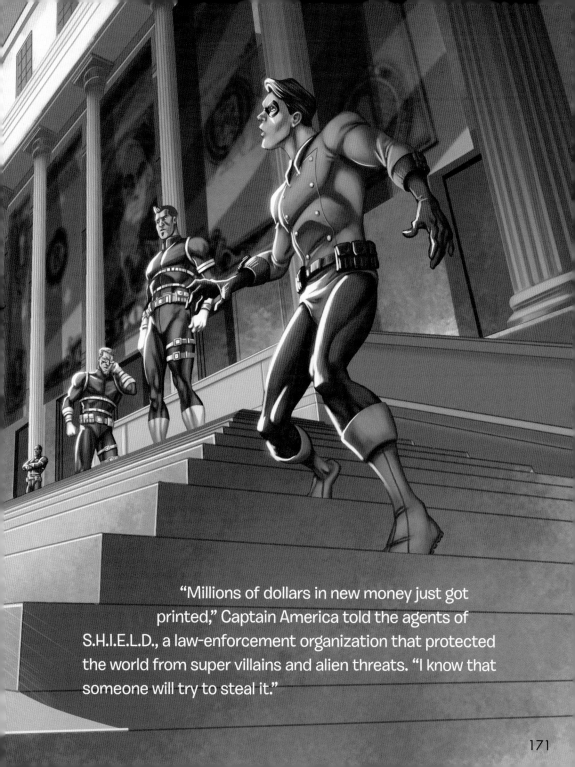

"Millions of dollars in new money just got printed," Captain America told the agents of S.H.I.E.L.D., a law-enforcement organization that protected the world from super villains and alien threats. "I know that someone will try to steal it."

Suddenly, energy blasts erupted from the sky!
Moving swiftly, Captain America used his
indestructible shield to protect Bucky.
"Quick! Get behind me," Captain
America shouted.

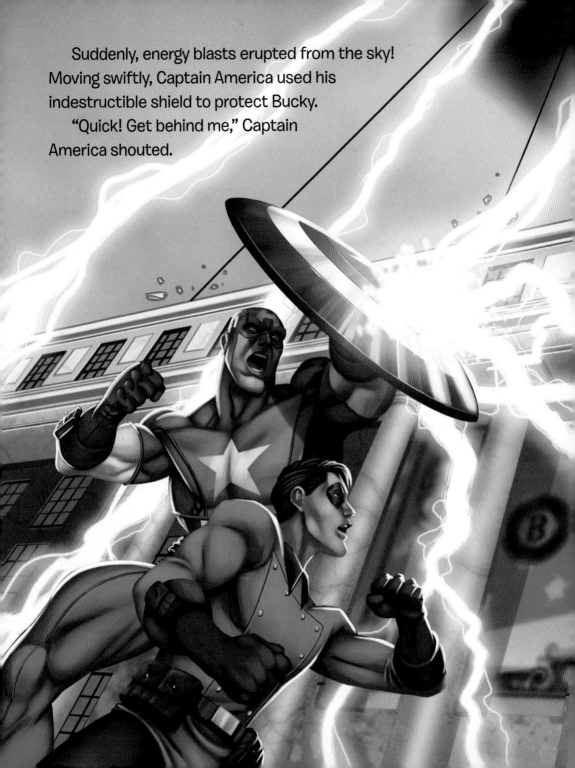

"Cap, I saw something on the roof," Bucky said.

"Let's go," Captain America replied.

The heroes dashed into action.

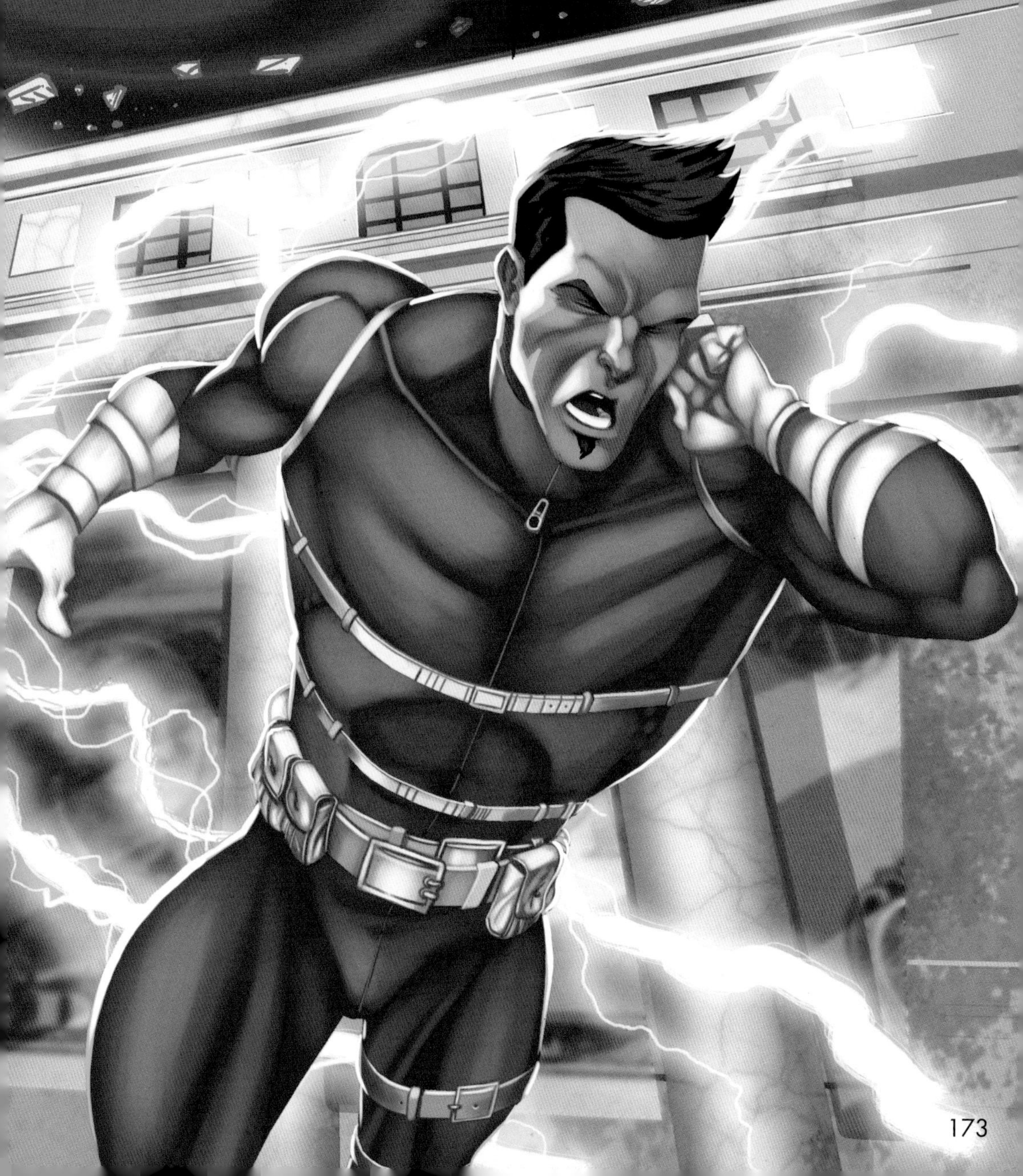

“The doors are locked from the inside,” said Bucky.

“Follow me!” Captain America shouted as he began to climb the building.

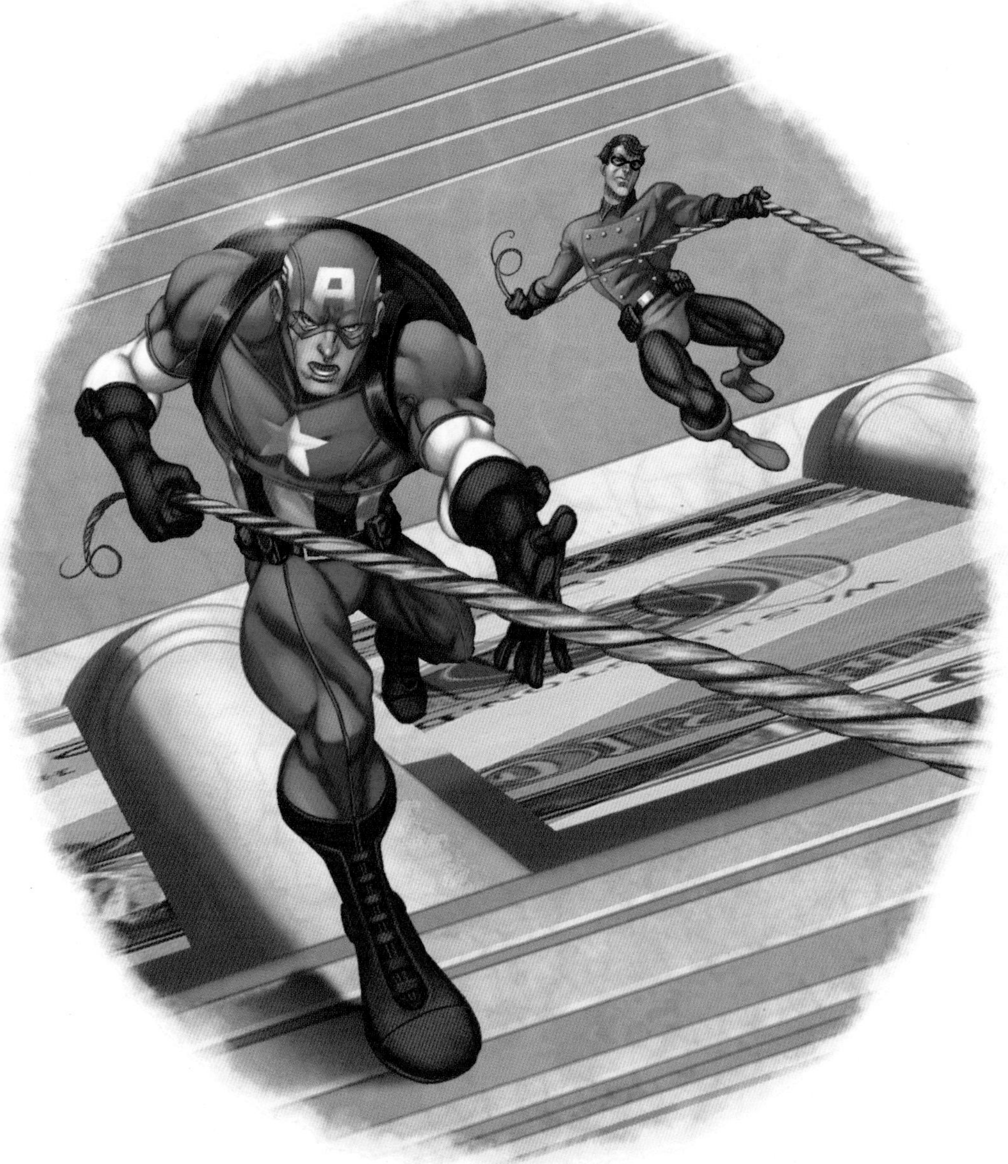

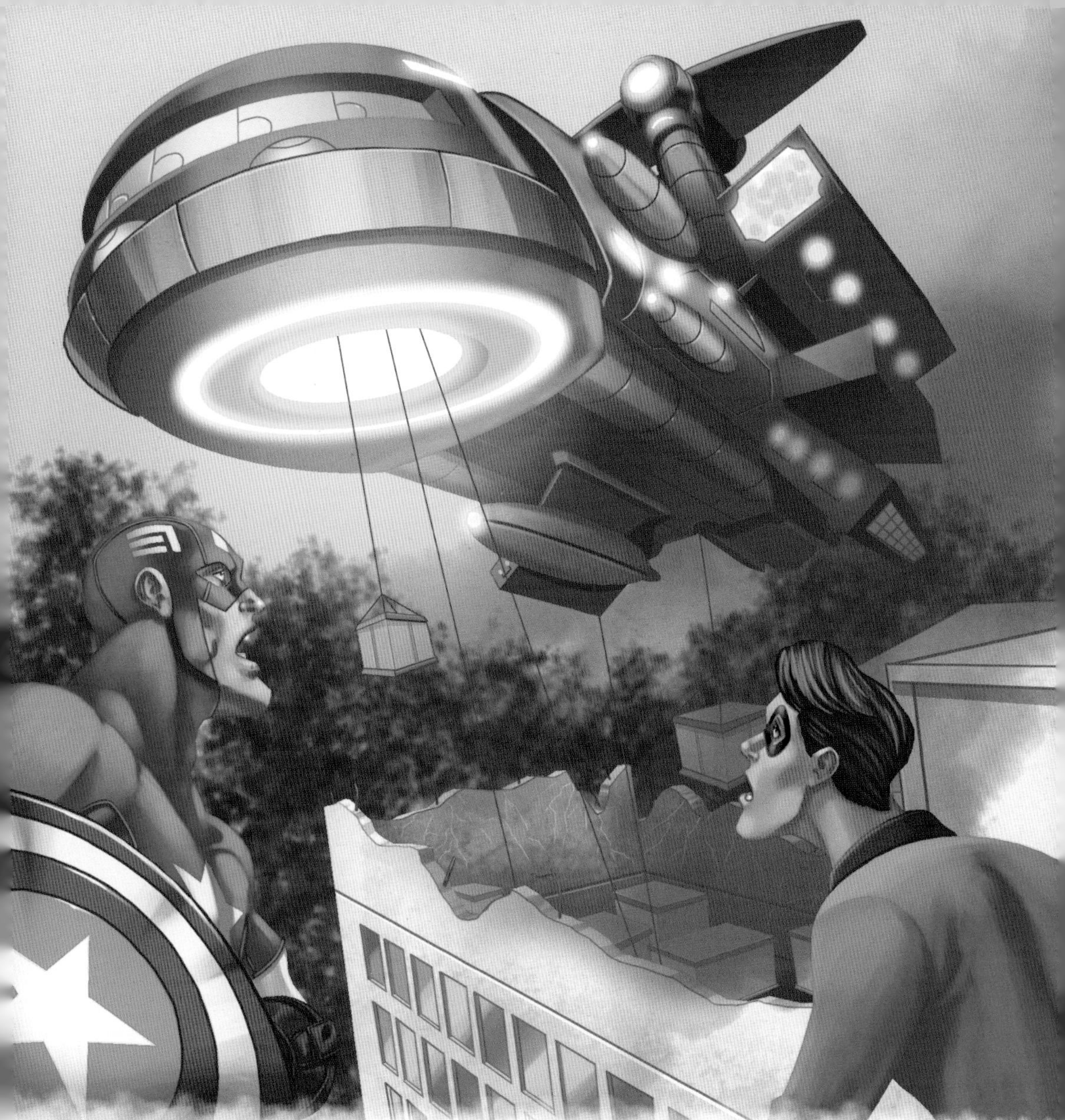

"They tore off the roof!" Bucky exclaimed.

"Somebody really wants those new bills," Captain America said. "Let's find out who it is—and stop them!"

"Get every last dollar," a robotic villain barked at his monster-men. "I will use these riches in my plans to take over the world!"

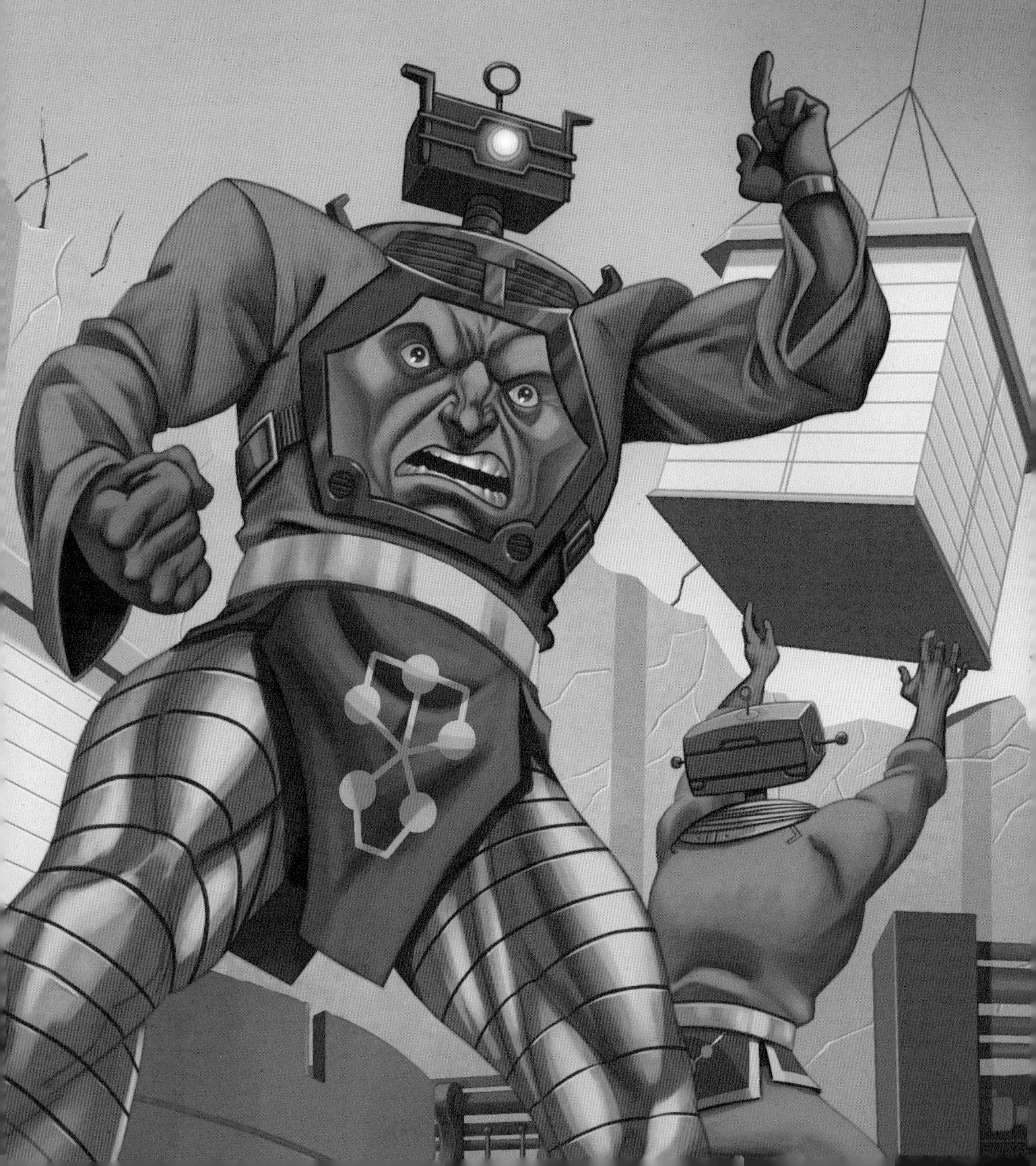

"You're going to have to put your money where your mouth is, ARNIM ZOLA!" Captain America shouted. "Because the buck stops here!"

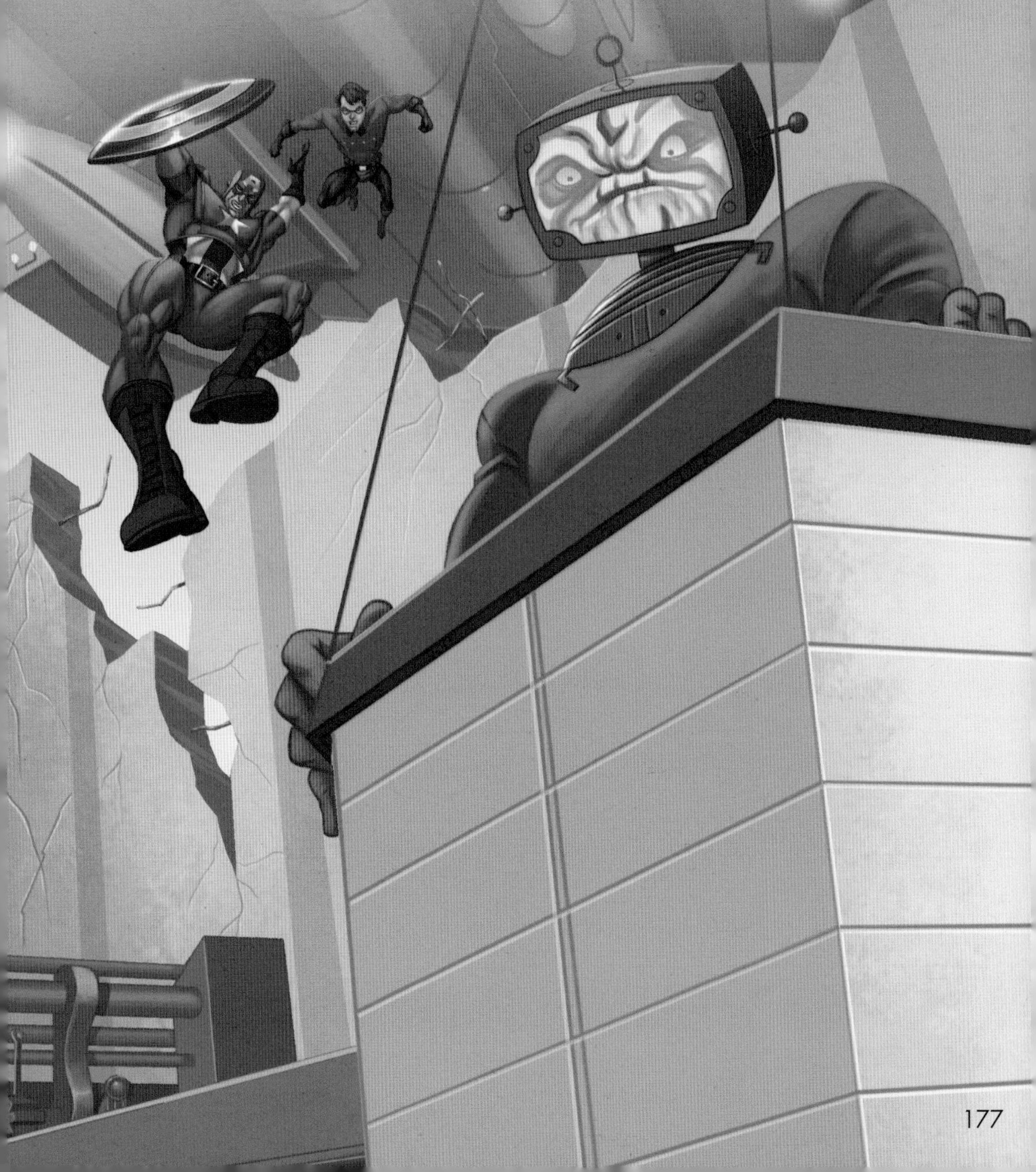

"You're a day late and a dollar short, Captain—my monster-men are more than a match for you," Arnim Zola replied. "Get them!"

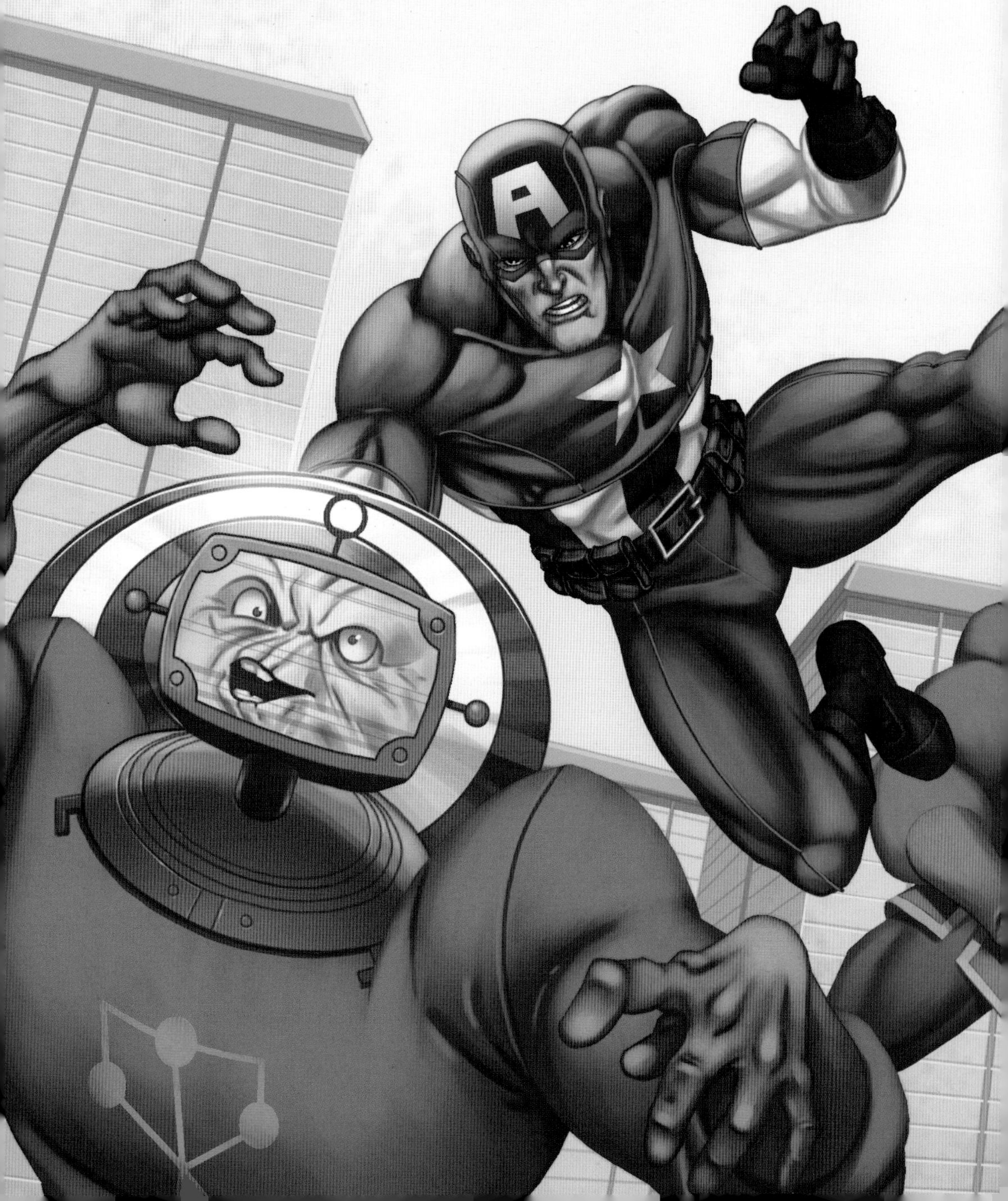

The monster-men lumbered forward.

"I hope this fight doesn't cost us an arm and a leg," Bucky joked.

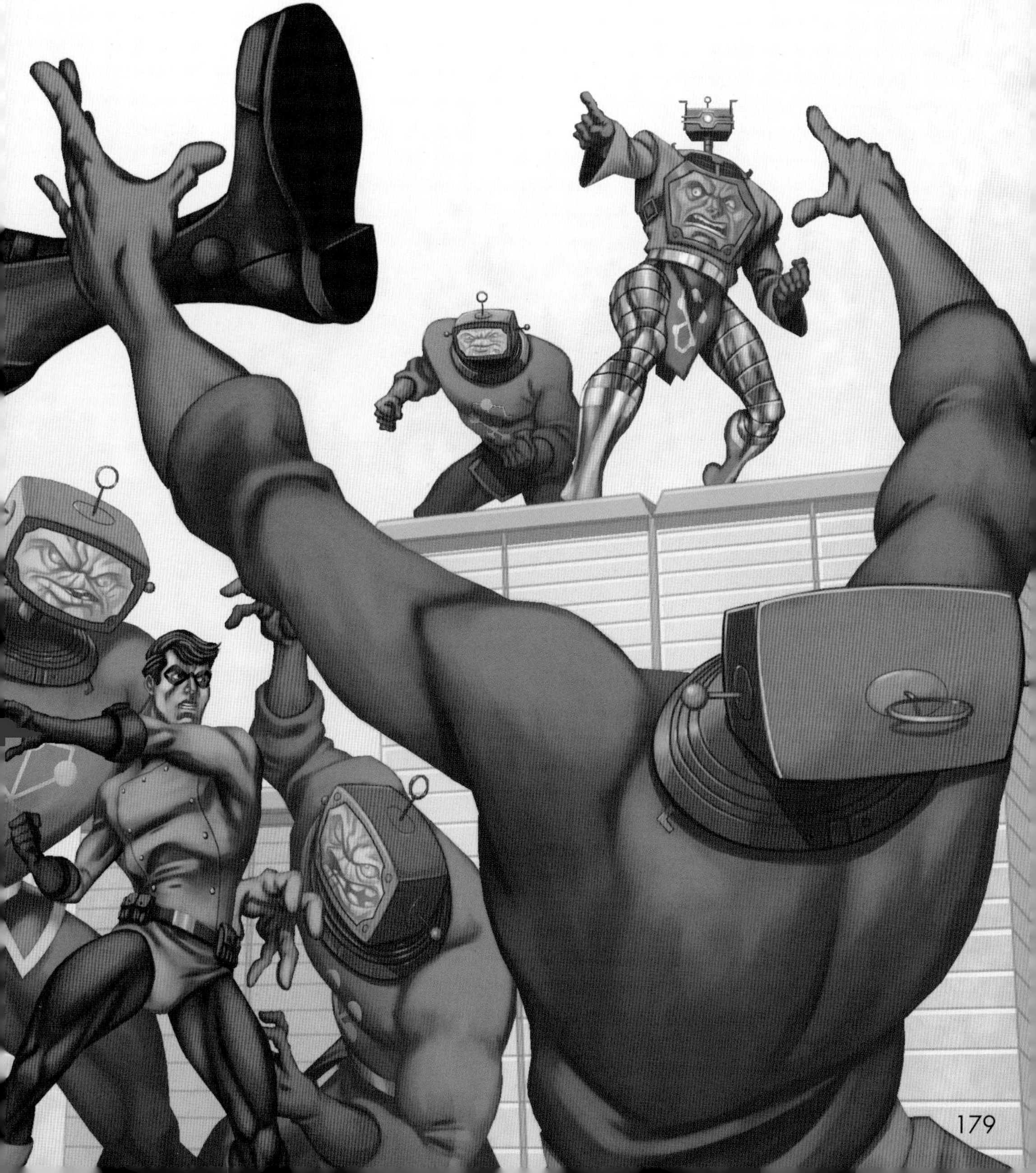

The monster-men were no match for Captain America and Bucky. Arnim Zola's creatures were strong, but the heroes were too fast and too skilled at fighting.

"Time to pay the piper, Zola!" Captain America said, stopping the last monster-man with his shield.

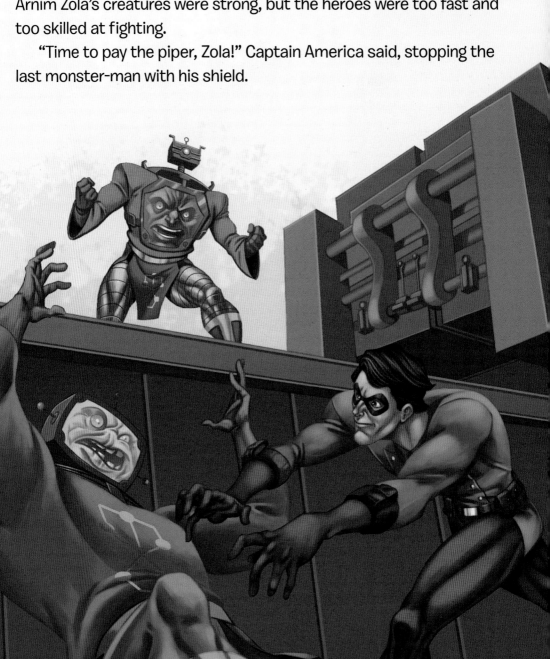

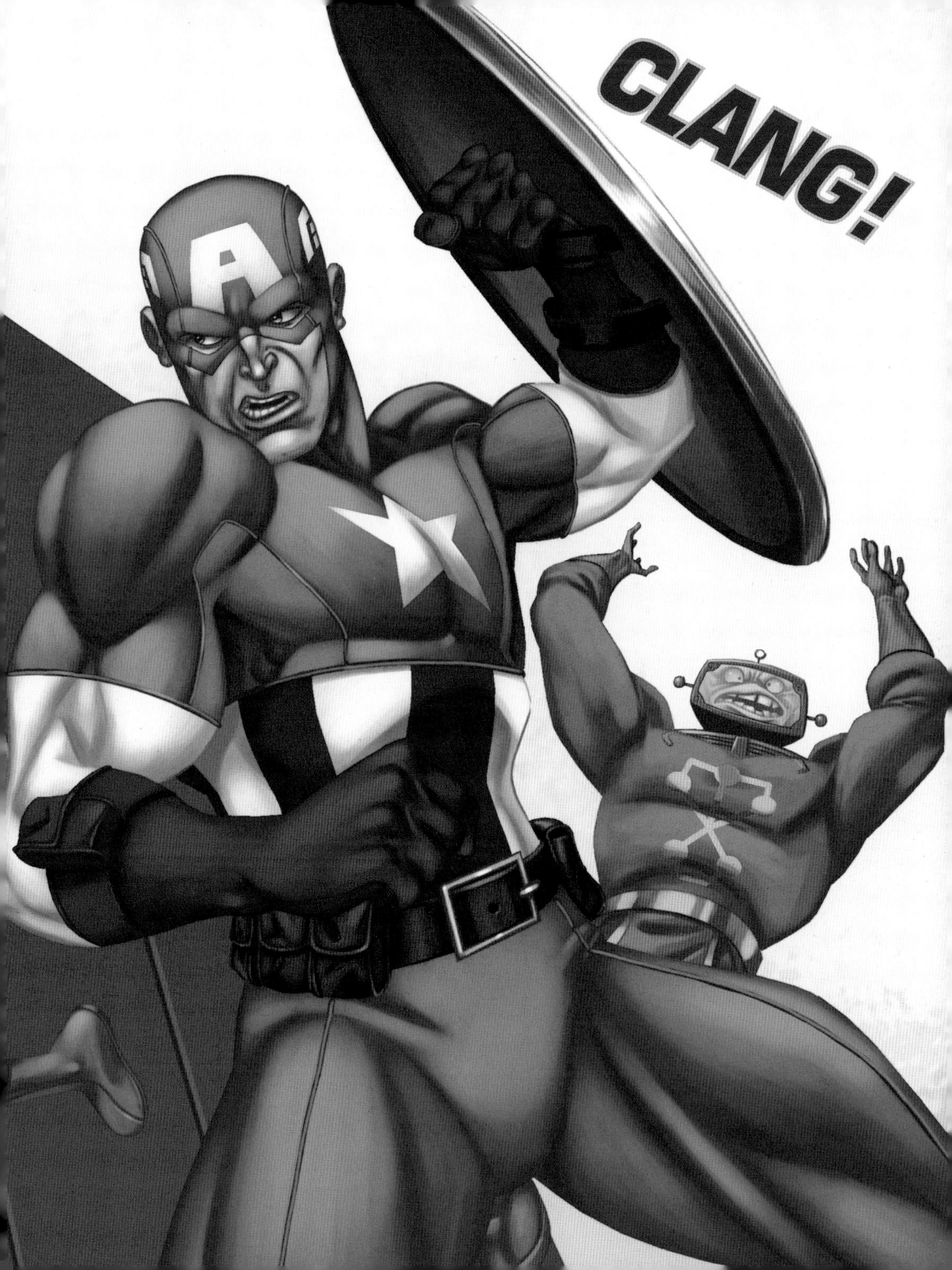
CLANG!

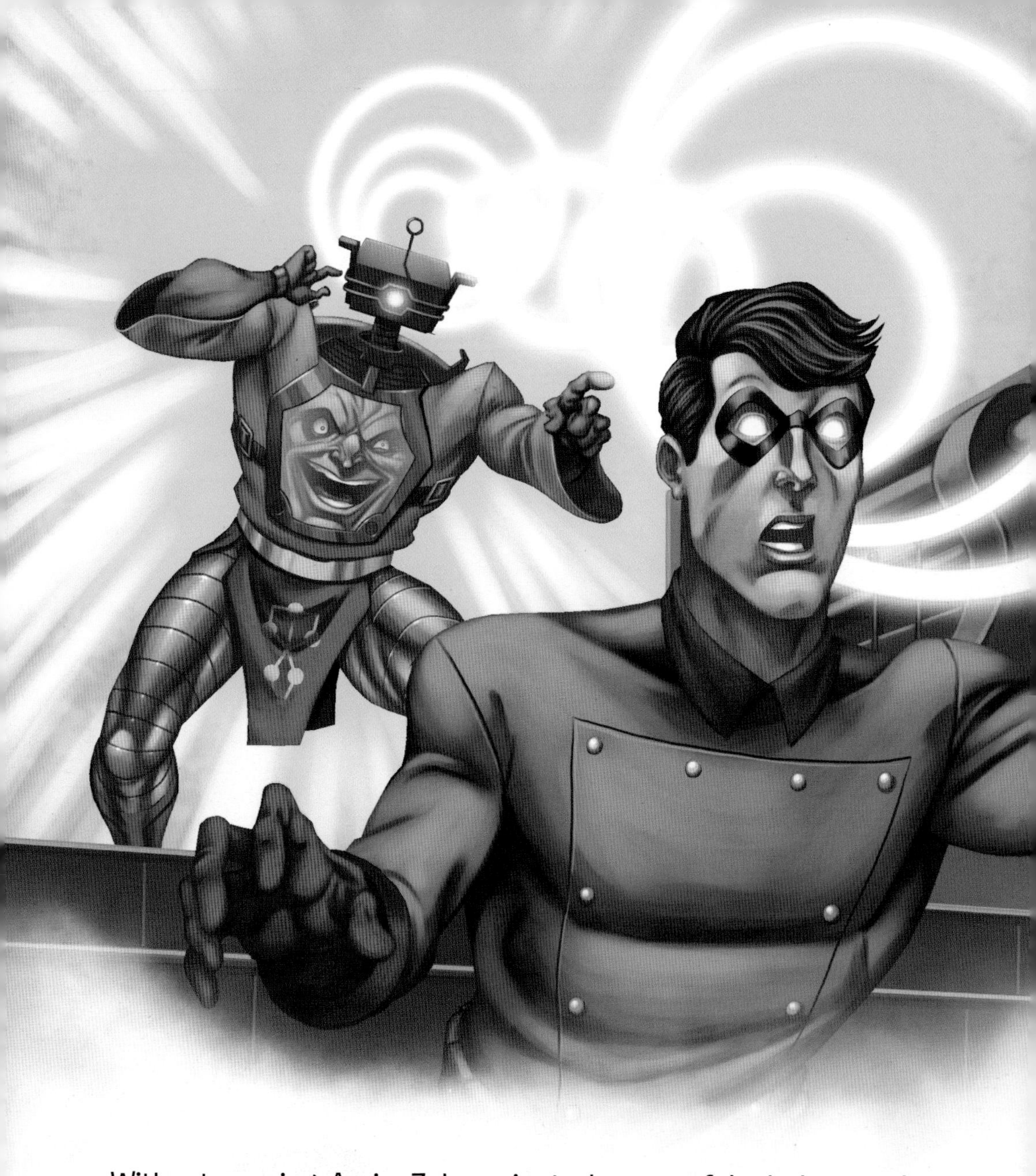

Without warning, Arnim Zola projected a powerful mind-control beam at Bucky. "There's one person you can't defeat," the villain said, laughing. "I will make your best friend your worst foe!"

The young hero's eyes turned white, and he began moving like a zombie toward Captain America!

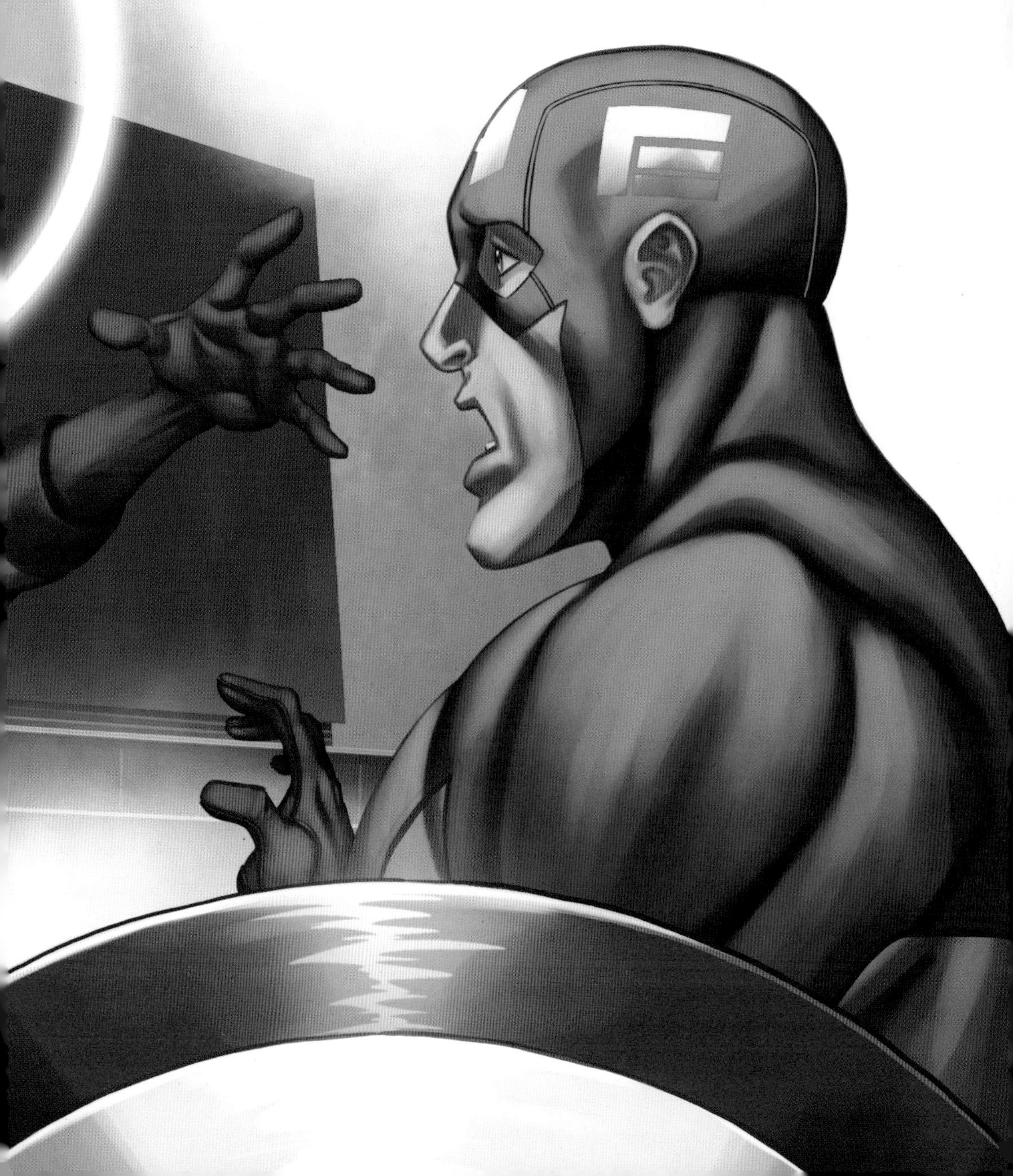

Bucky grabbed Captain America in a vise-like grip.

"Bucky, it's me, Cap!" the hero pleaded. He didn't want to hurt his friend. "We have to stop Zola!"

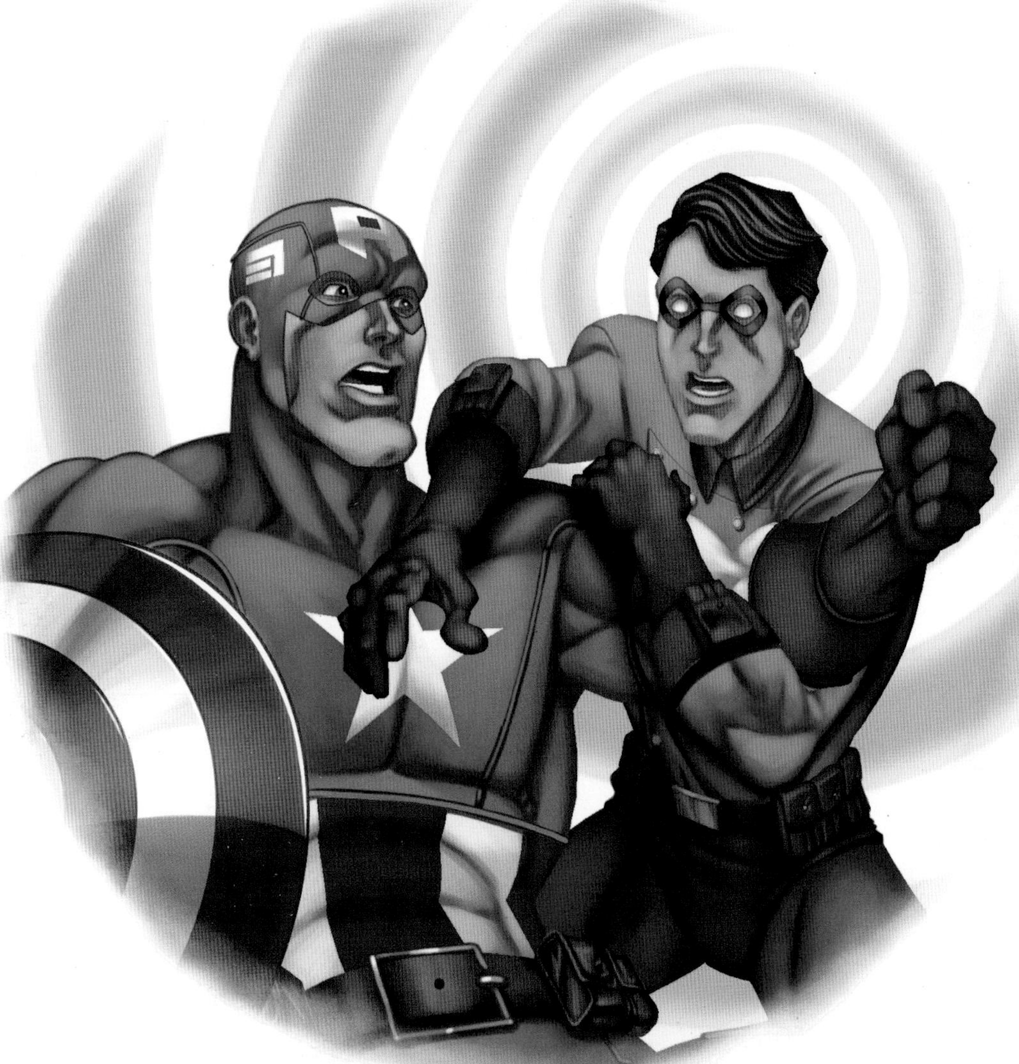

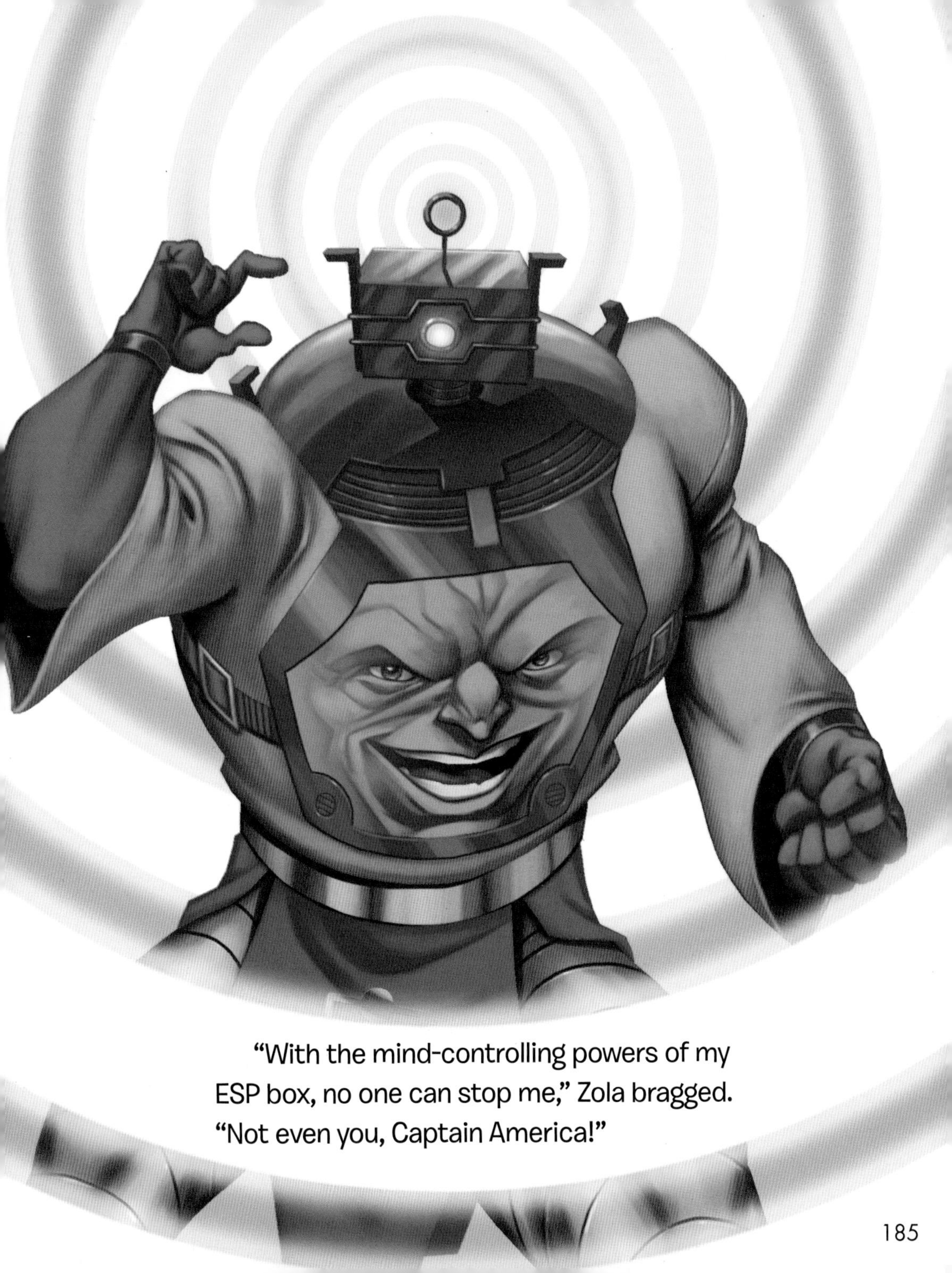

“With the mind-controlling powers of my ESP box, no one can stop me,” Zola bragged. “Not even you, Captain America!”

"Enough of your mind games!" Captain America shouted. He threw his shield. It hit Zola's ESP box, shattering the device.

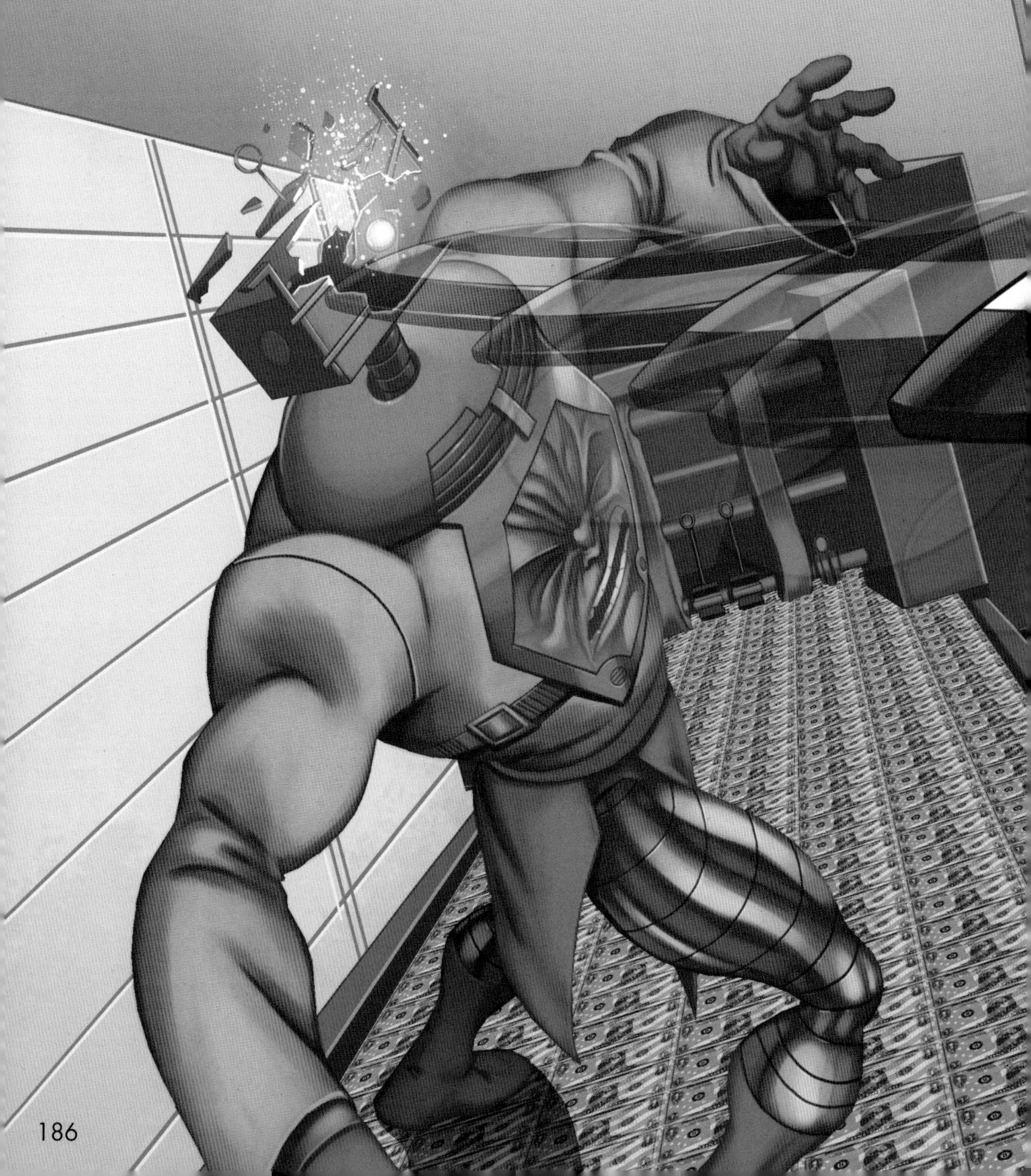

Captain America's shield bounced off the villain and hit the printing press's controls. The machine roared to life!

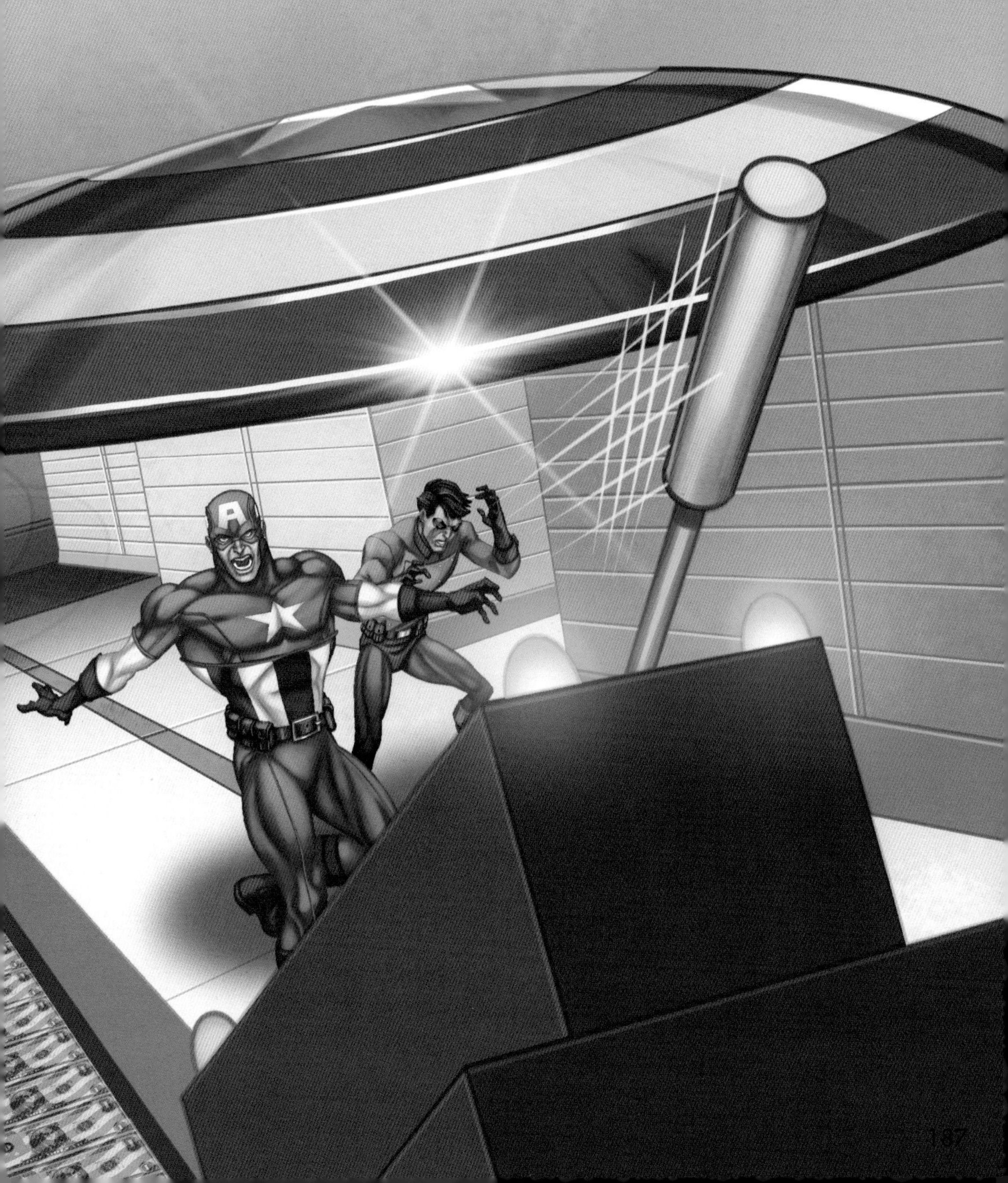

Arnim Zola's feet flew out from under him—

THUMP!

—and he was sucked into the printing press!

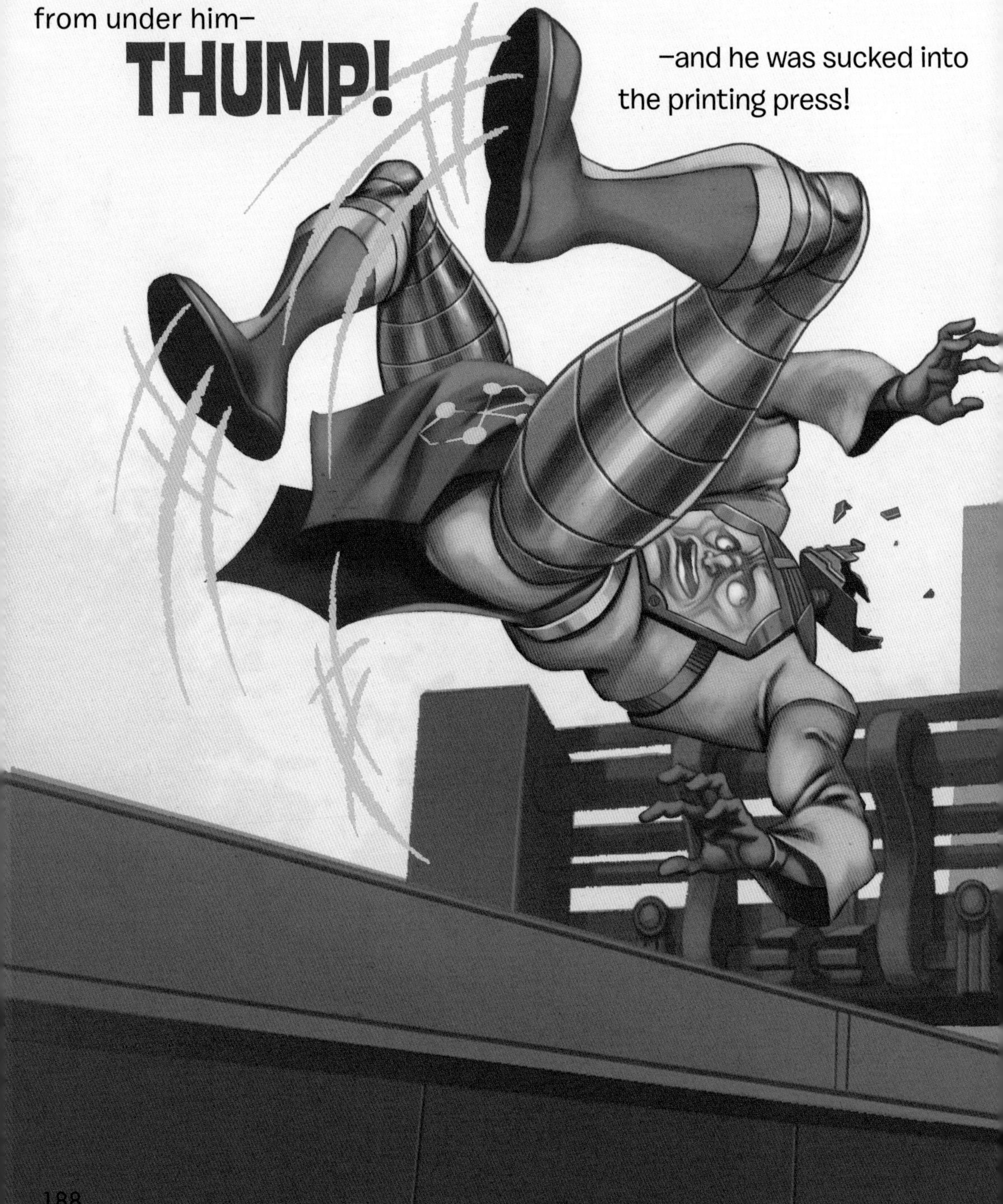

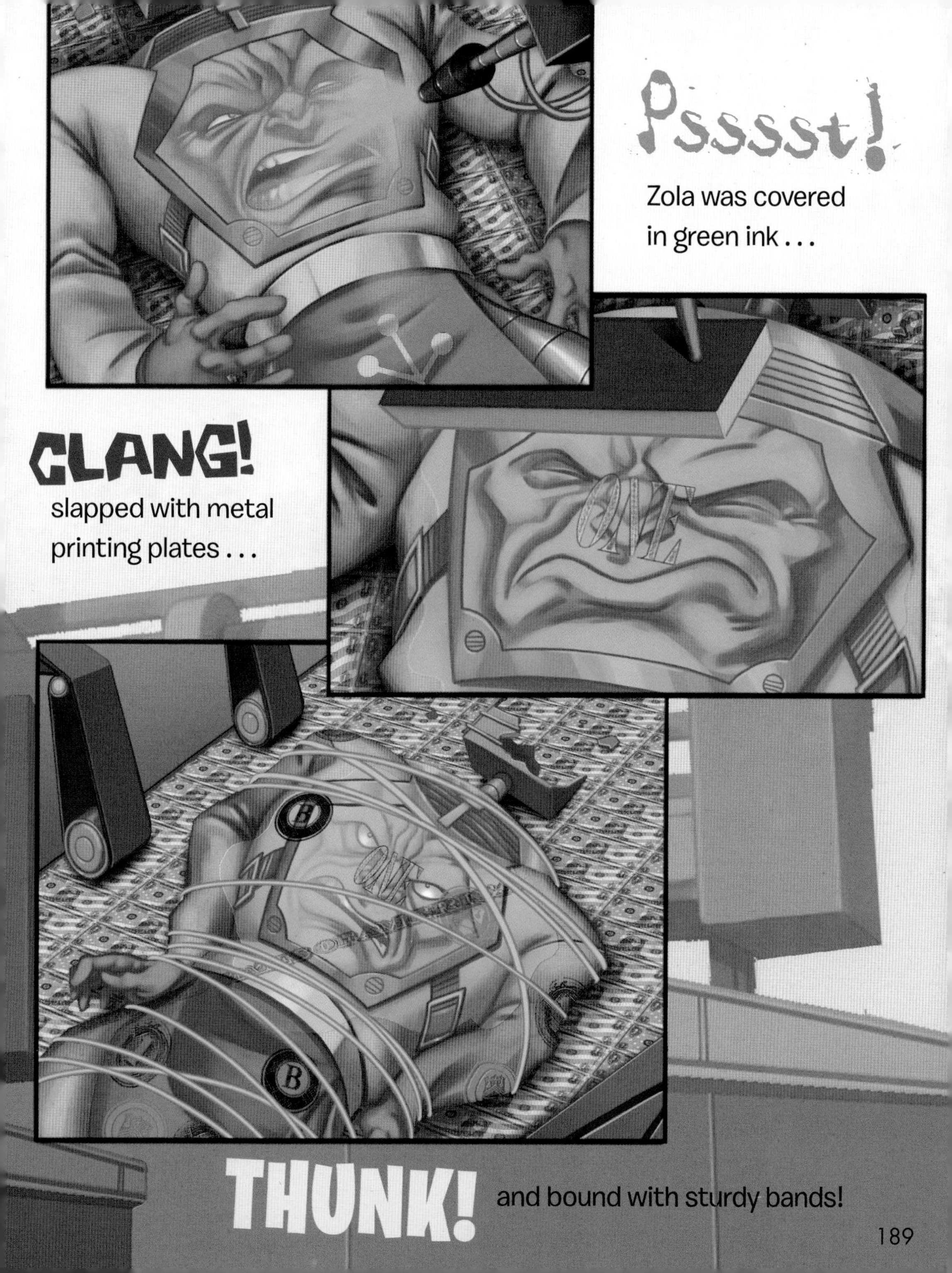
Psssst!
Zola was covered in green ink . . .
CLANG!
slapped with metal printing plates . . .
THUNK!
and bound with sturdy bands!

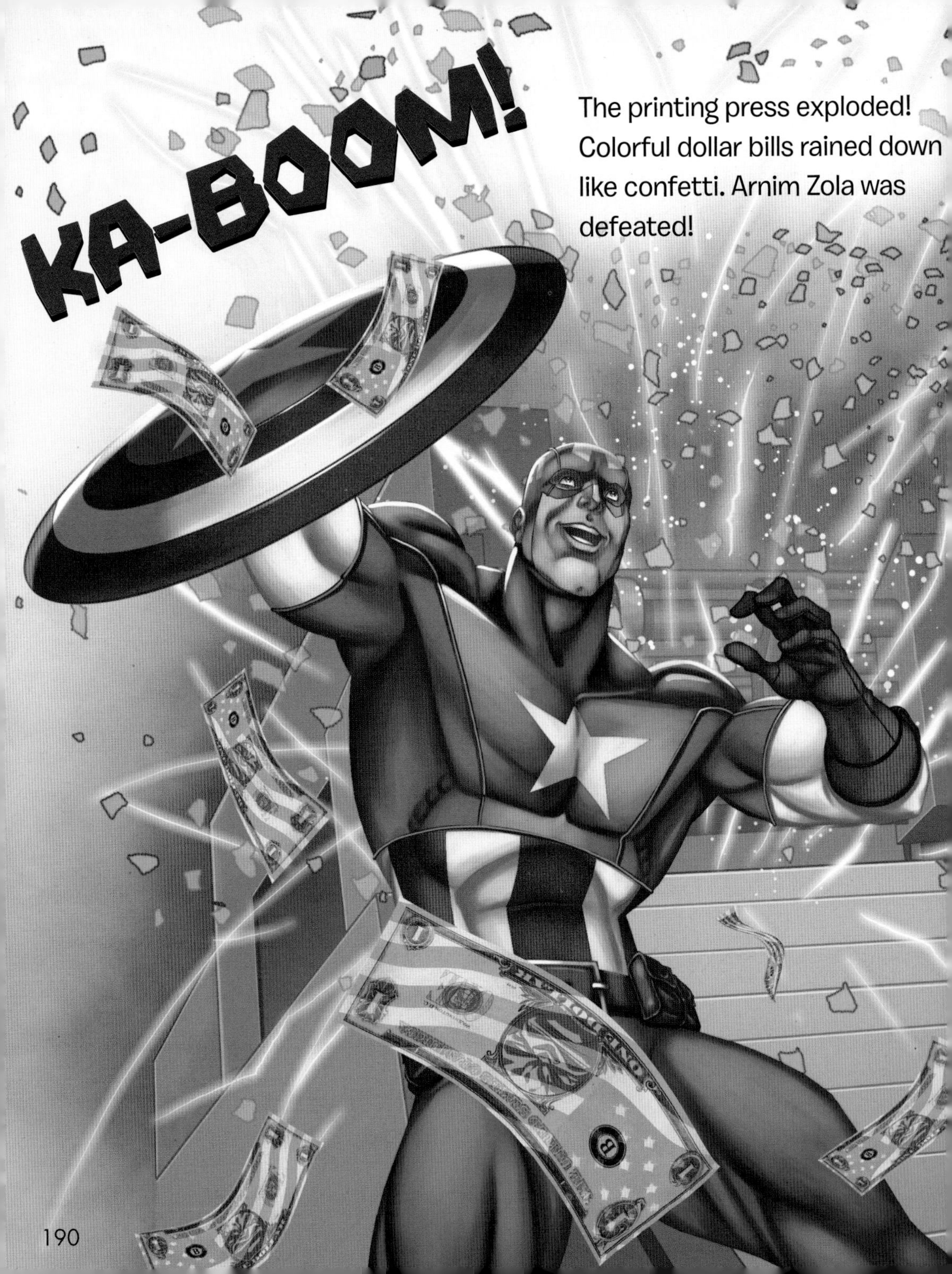
KA-BOOM!

The printing press exploded! Colorful dollar bills rained down like confetti. Arnim Zola was defeated!

Bucky unlocked the front door for the S.H.I.E.L.D. agents. Captain America handed the super villain over to them.

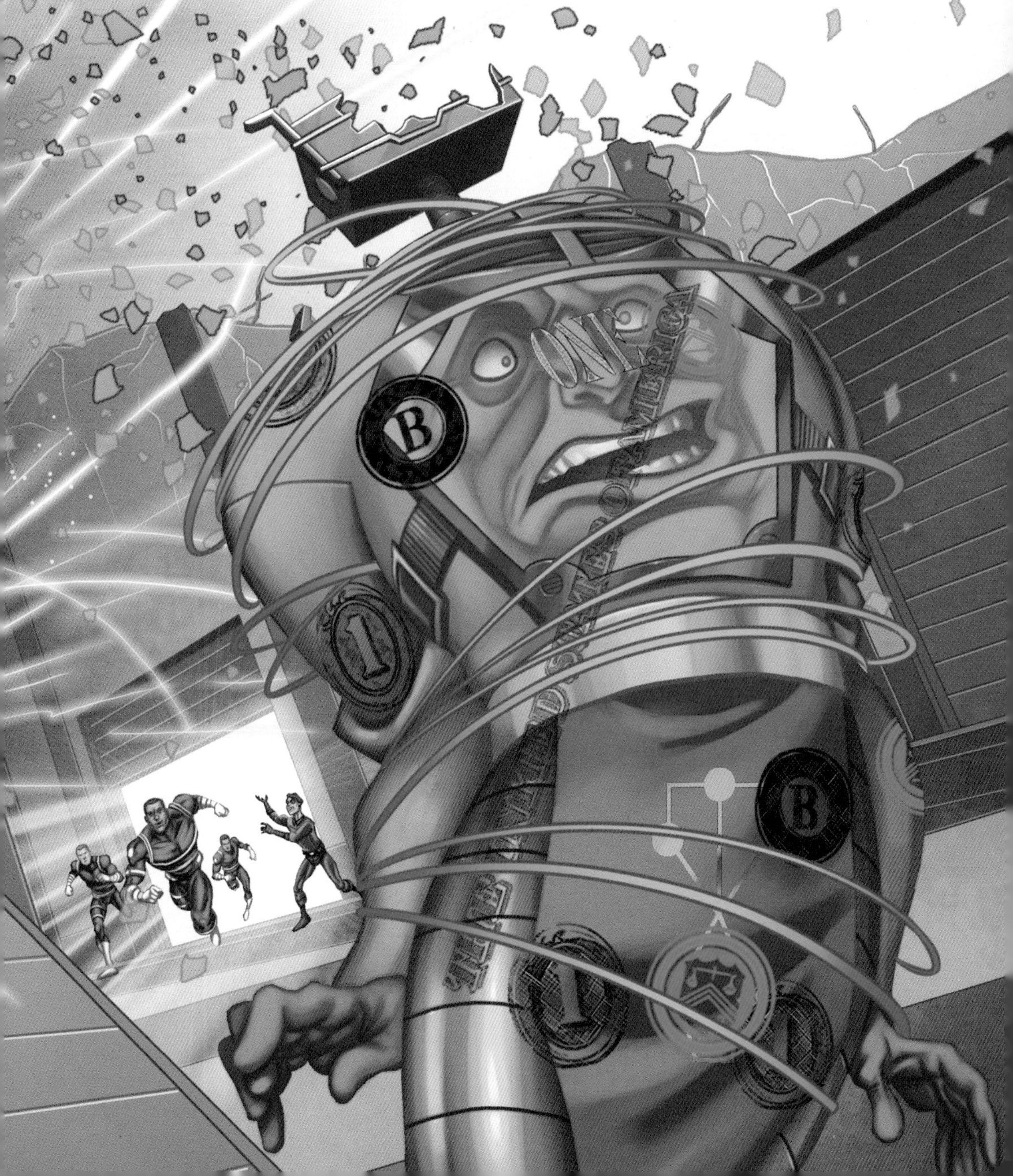

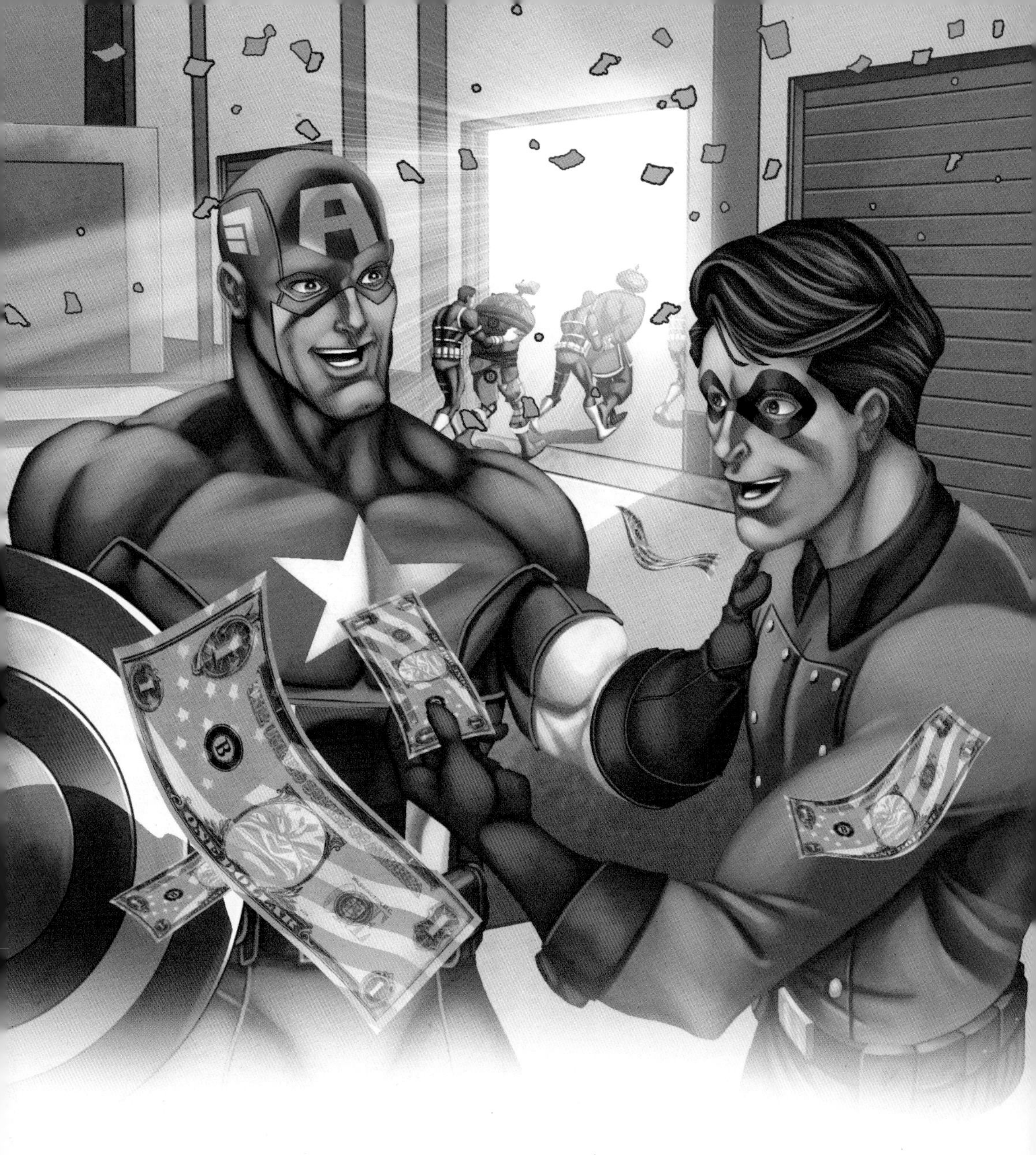

"Looks like Arnim Zola learned that crime doesn't pay," Captain America said as Bucky held up a dollar bill printed with Zola's face. "Now he's going to **spend** his time in jail."

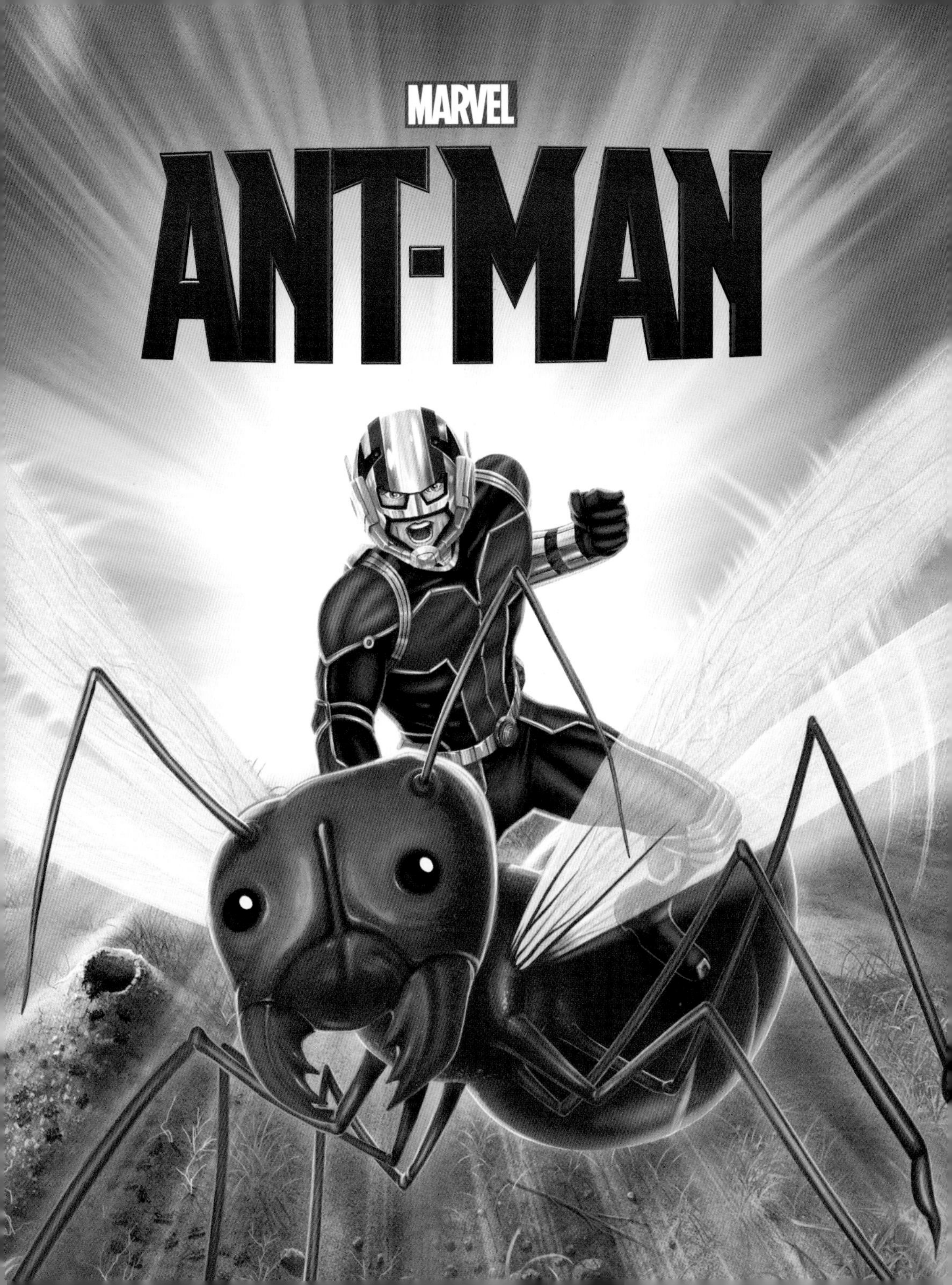
MARVEL
ANT-MAN

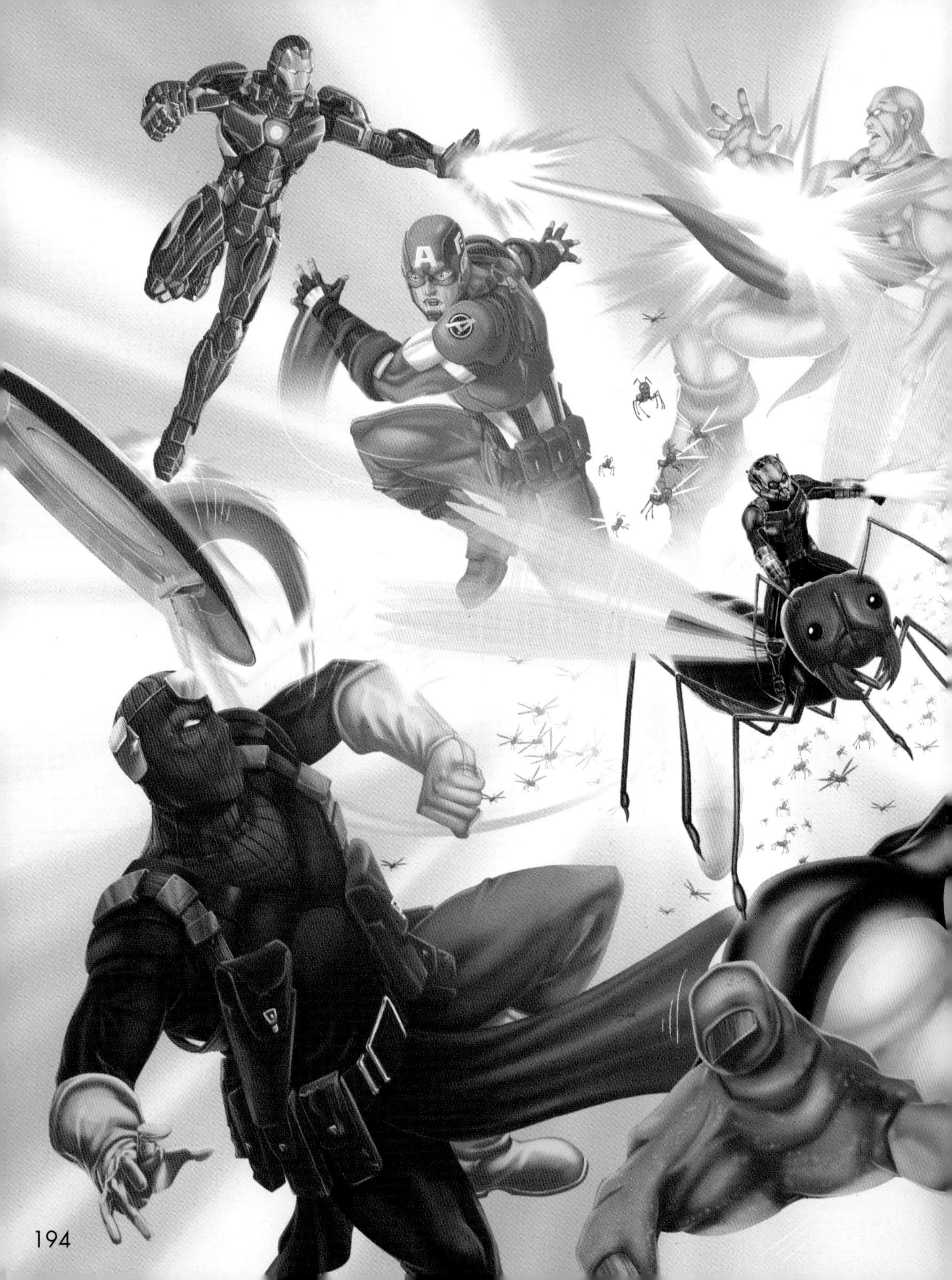

ANT-MAN is the tiniest member of the superhero team known as the **AVENGERS**. But don't let his size fool you—Ant-Man packs a powerful punch!

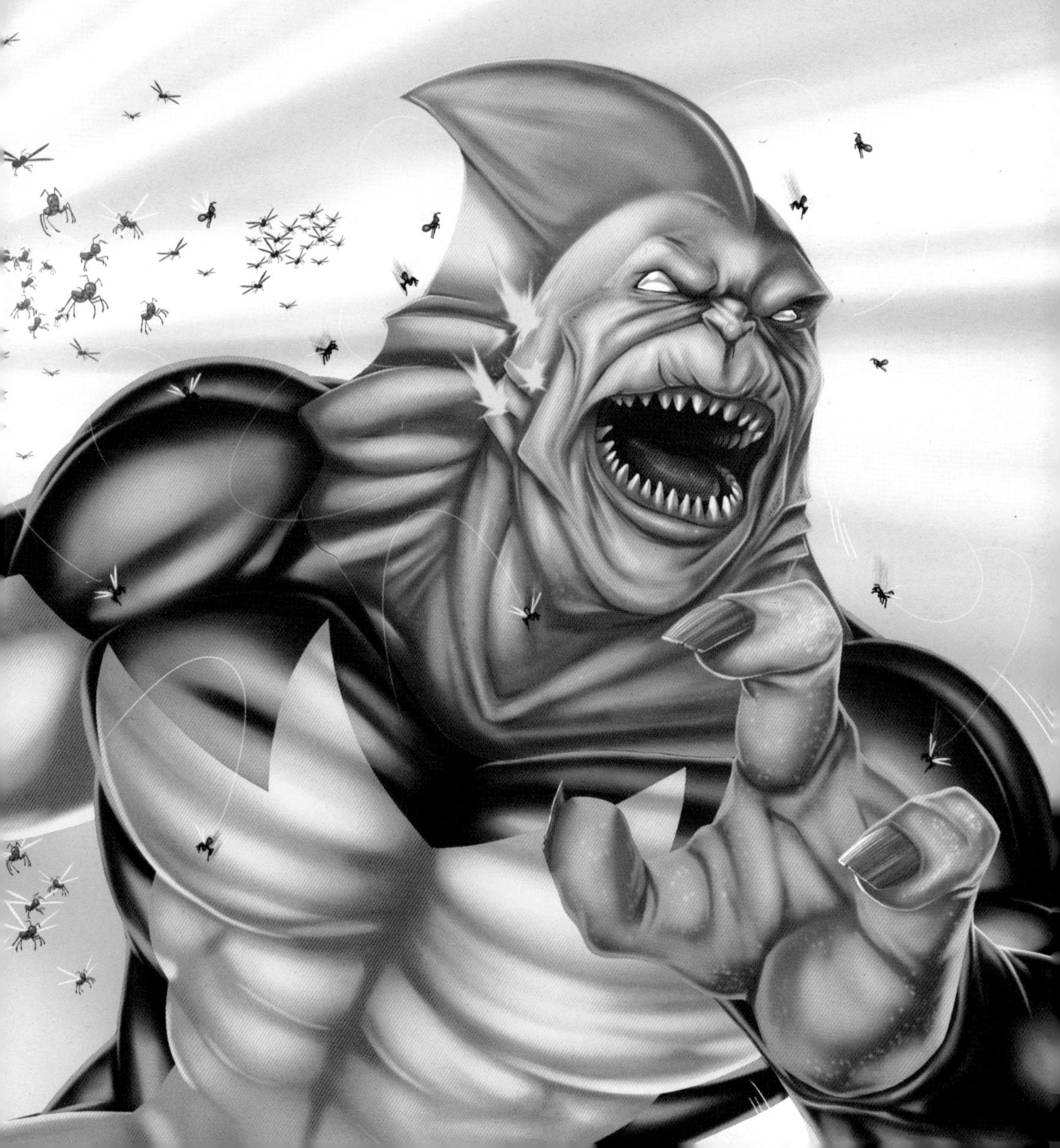

Ant-Man's real name is Scott Lang. He was once a thief, but he had a good heart.

A scientist named Dr. Hank Pym saw the potential in the young man. He gave Lang the chance to become a hero.

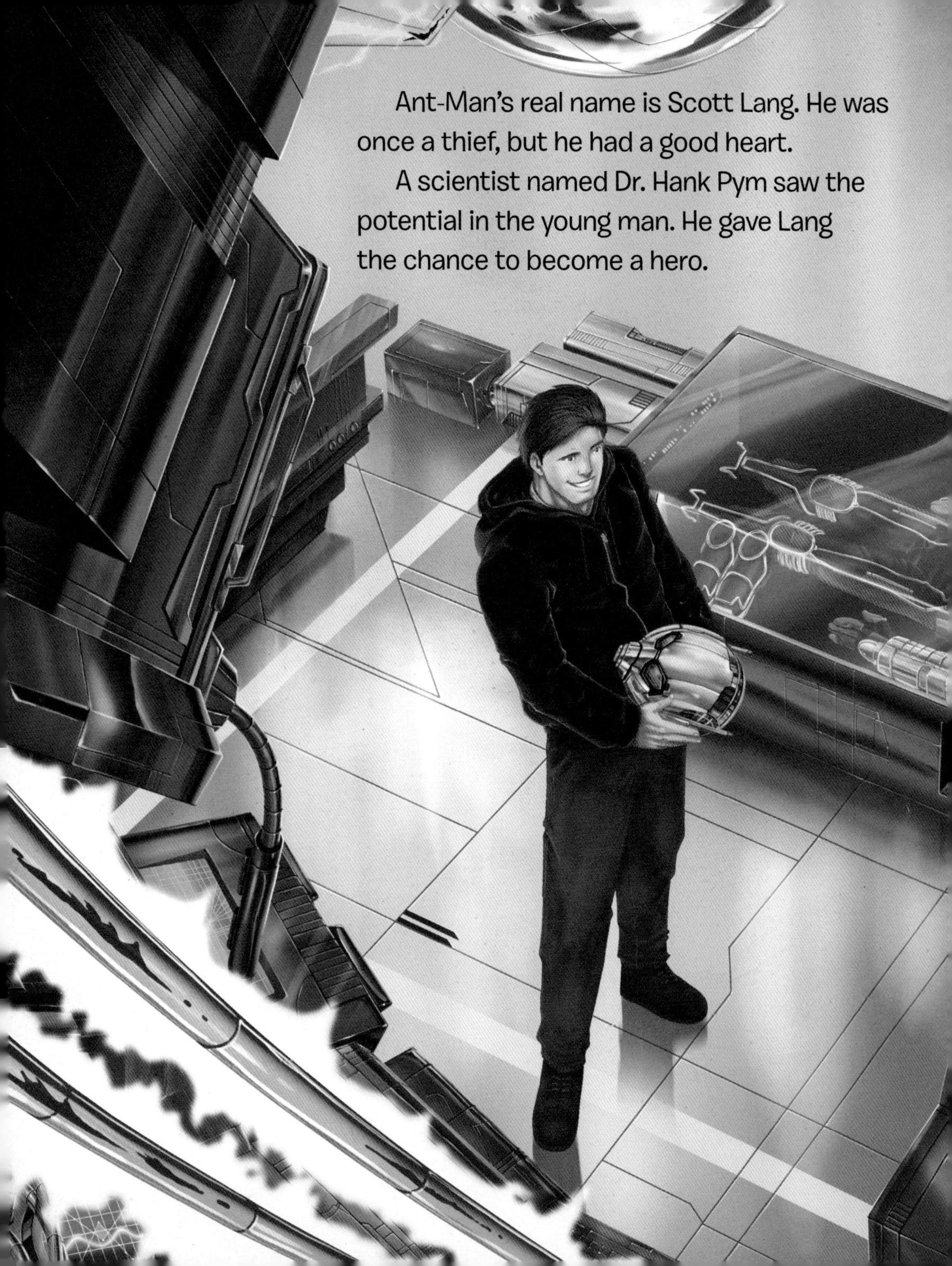

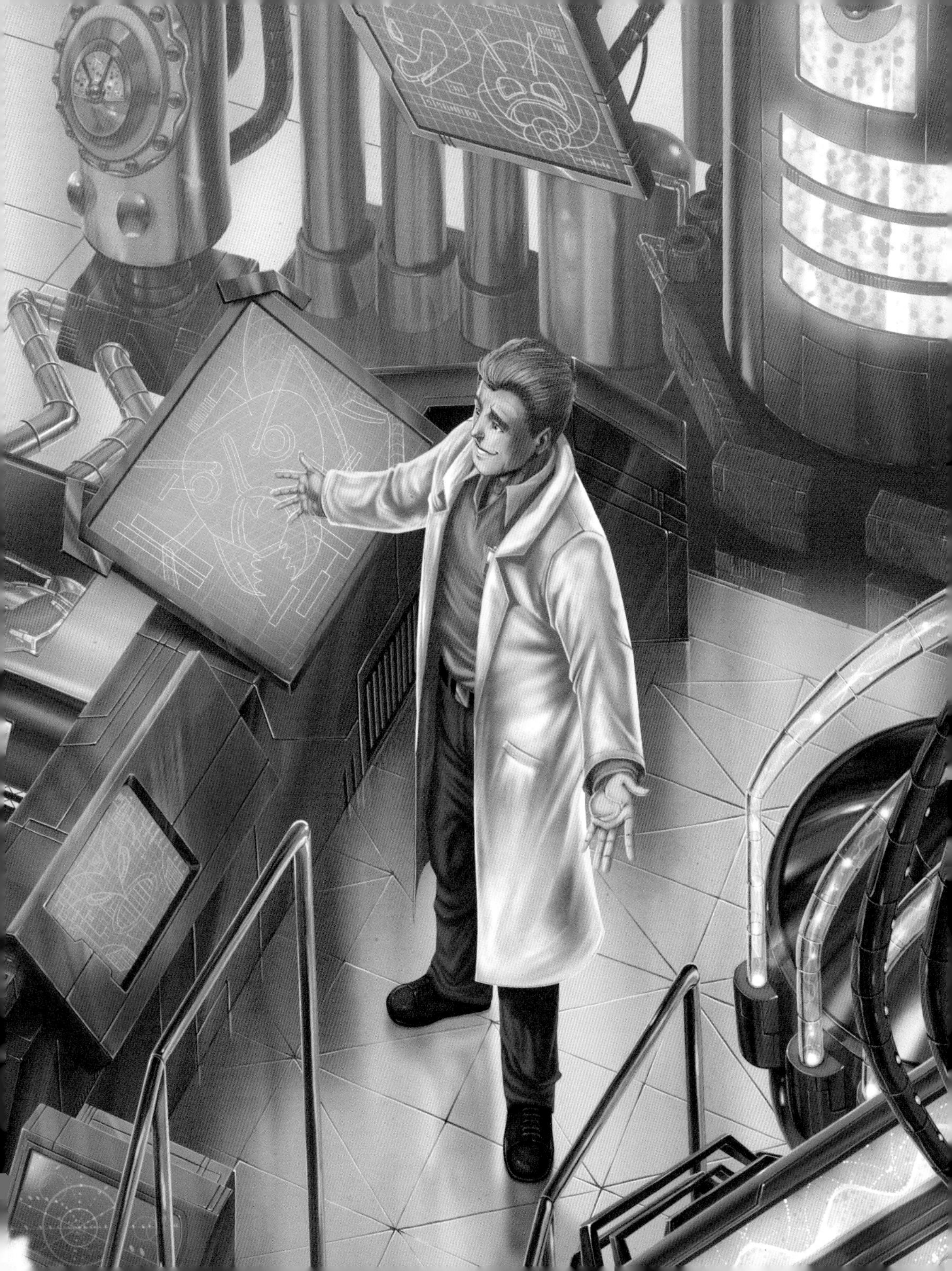

Whenever he is exposed to Dr. Pym's amazing Pym Particles, Scott Lang shrinks to only half an inch tall!

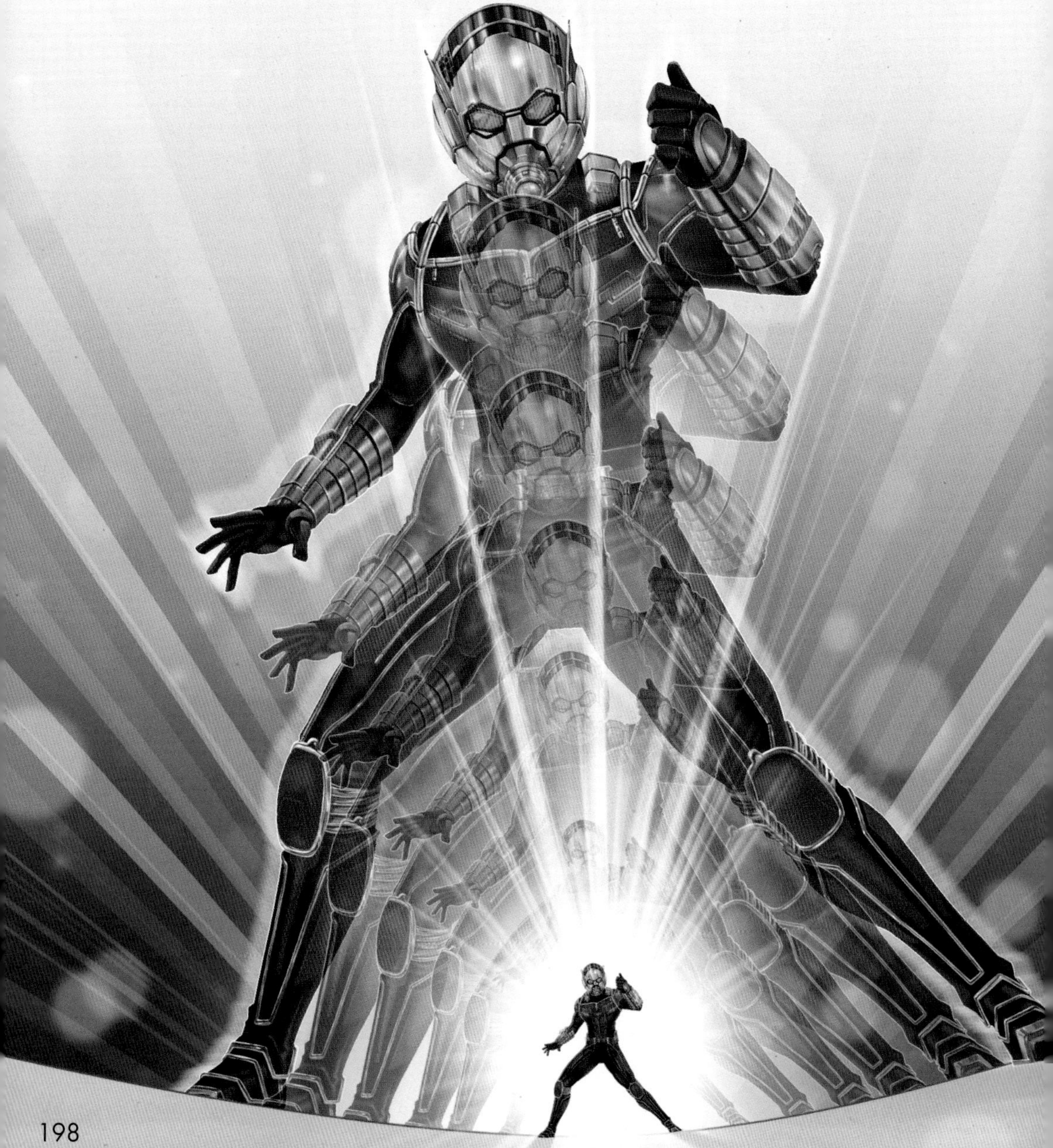

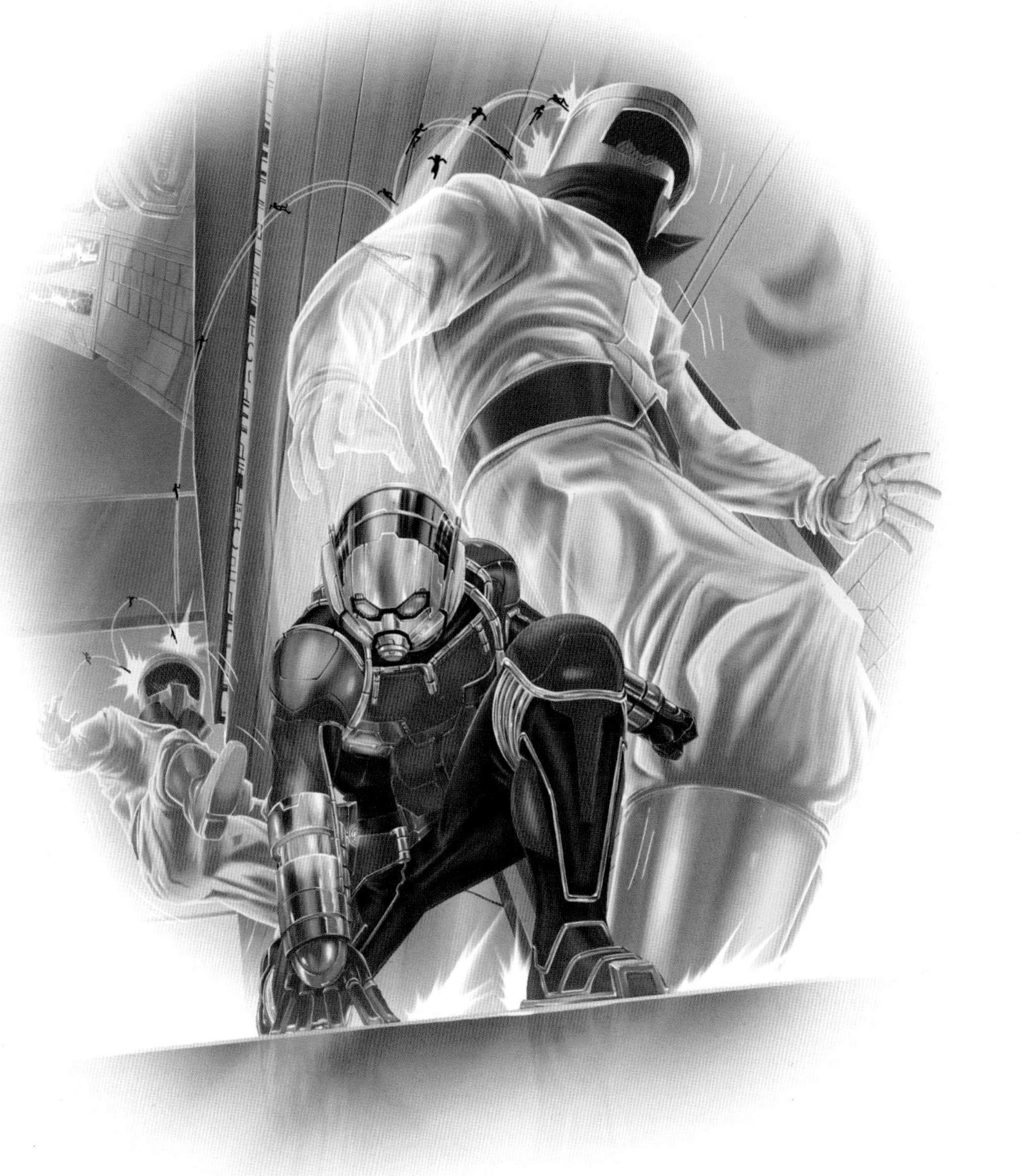

Using the special helmet, wrist blasters, and super-suit created by Dr. Pym, Lang goes into action as the ***ASTONISHING ANT-MAN***. There's no secret lair this tiny hero can't sneak into.

Even when he is small, Ant-Man has the strength of a full-grown man.

That can be quite a surprise for the bad guys!

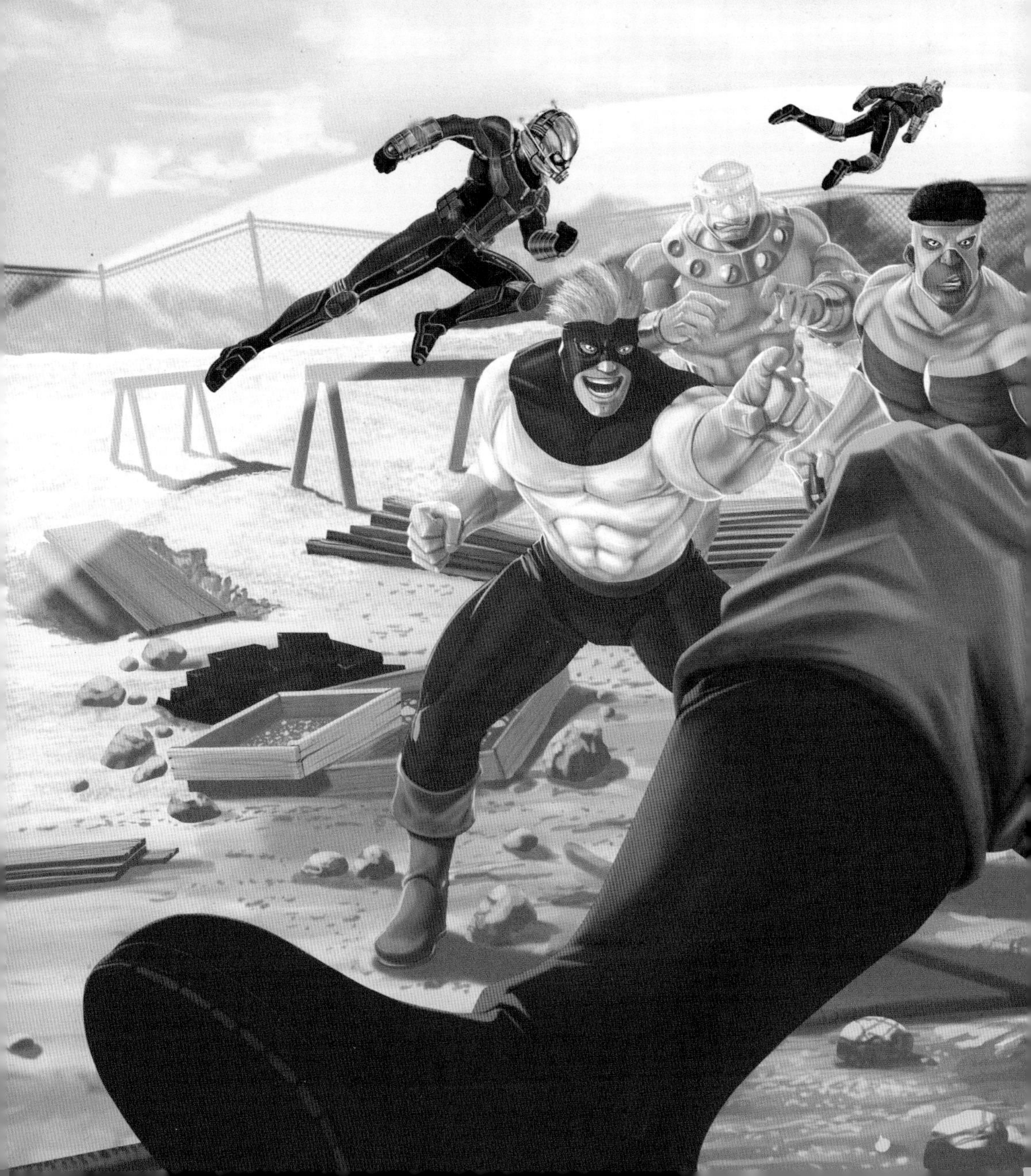

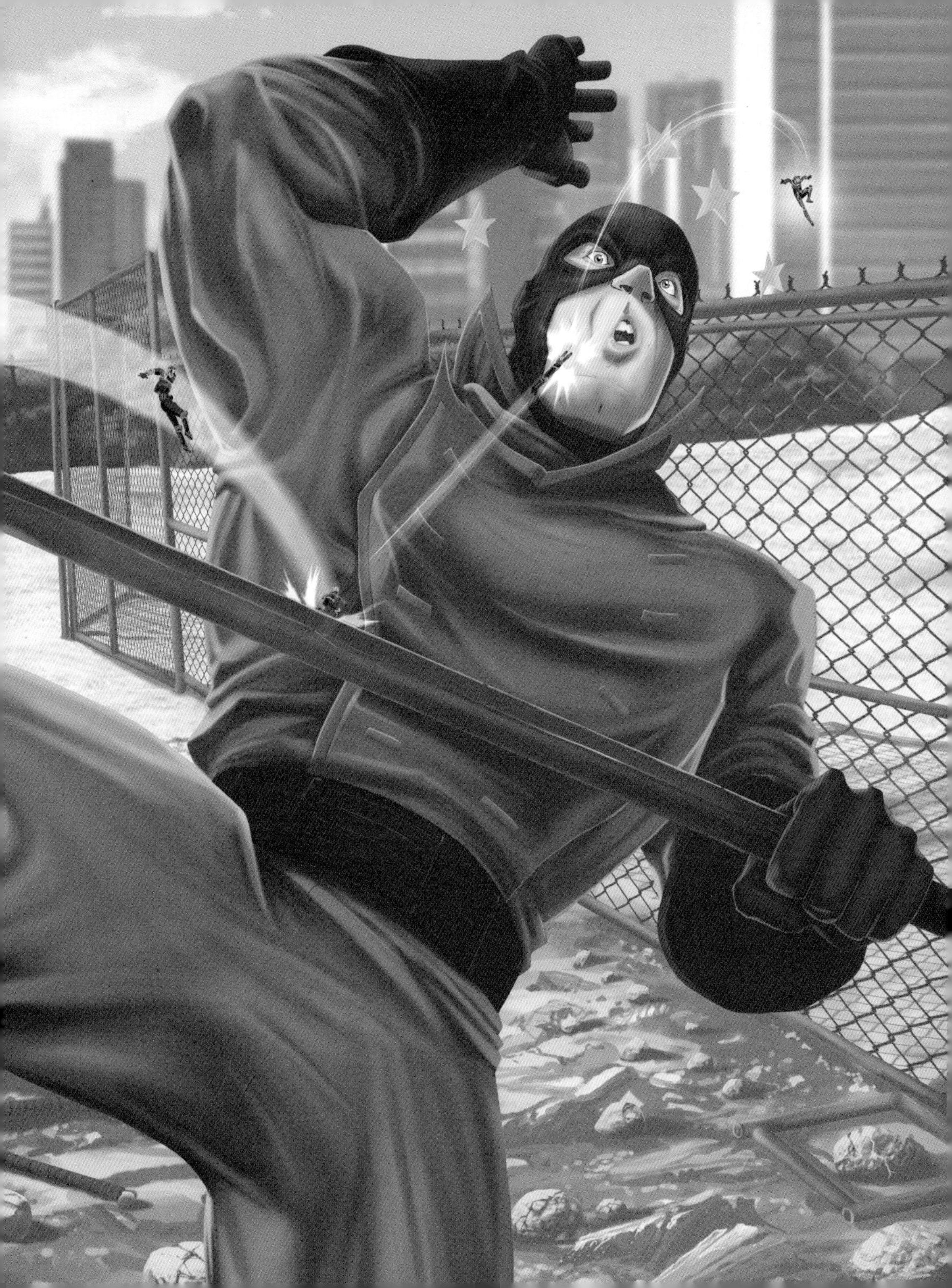

"Feel my sting!" Ant-Man shouts. He uses his wrist blasters to deliver powerful shocks.

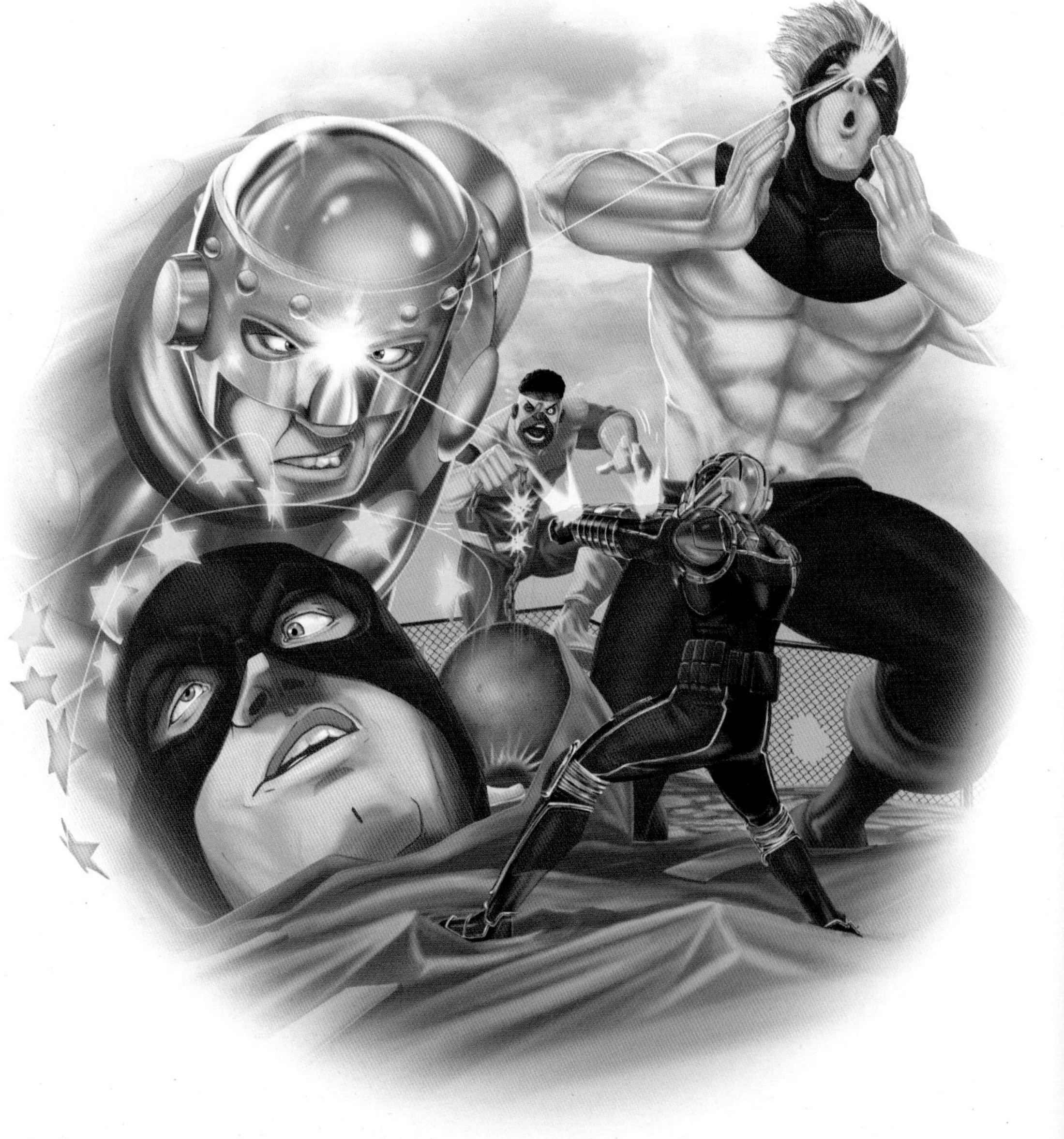

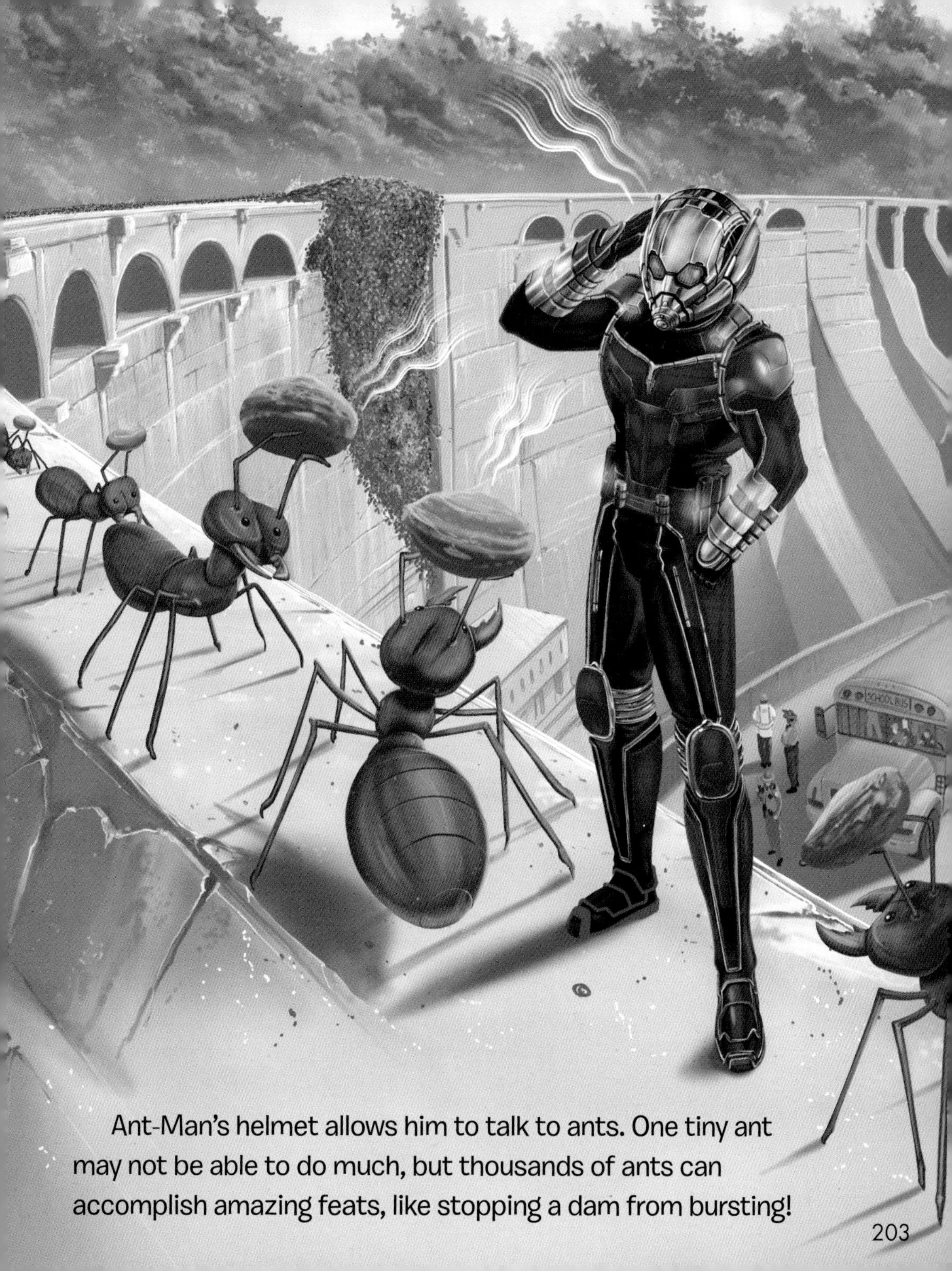

Ant-Man's helmet allows him to talk to ants. One tiny ant may not be able to do much, but thousands of ants can accomplish amazing feats, like stopping a dam from bursting!

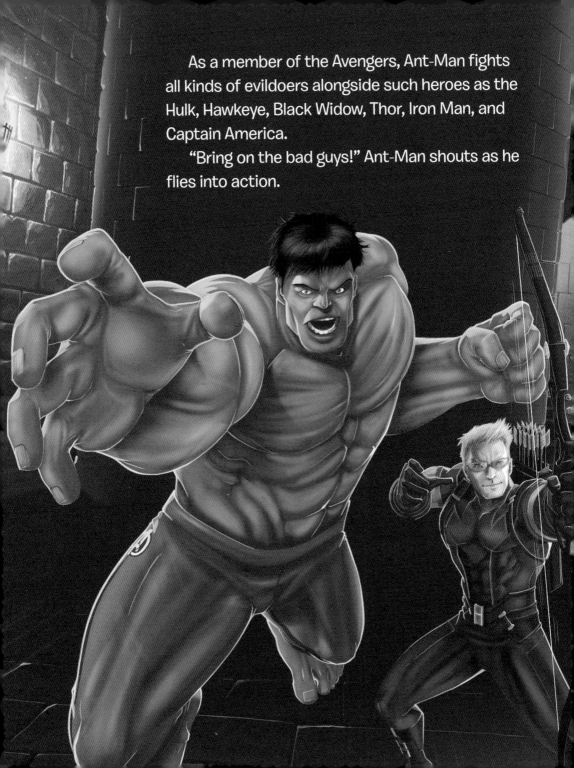

As a member of the Avengers, Ant-Man fights all kinds of evildoers alongside such heroes as the Hulk, Hawkeye, Black Widow, Thor, Iron Man, and Captain America.

"Bring on the bad guys!" Ant-Man shouts as he flies into action.

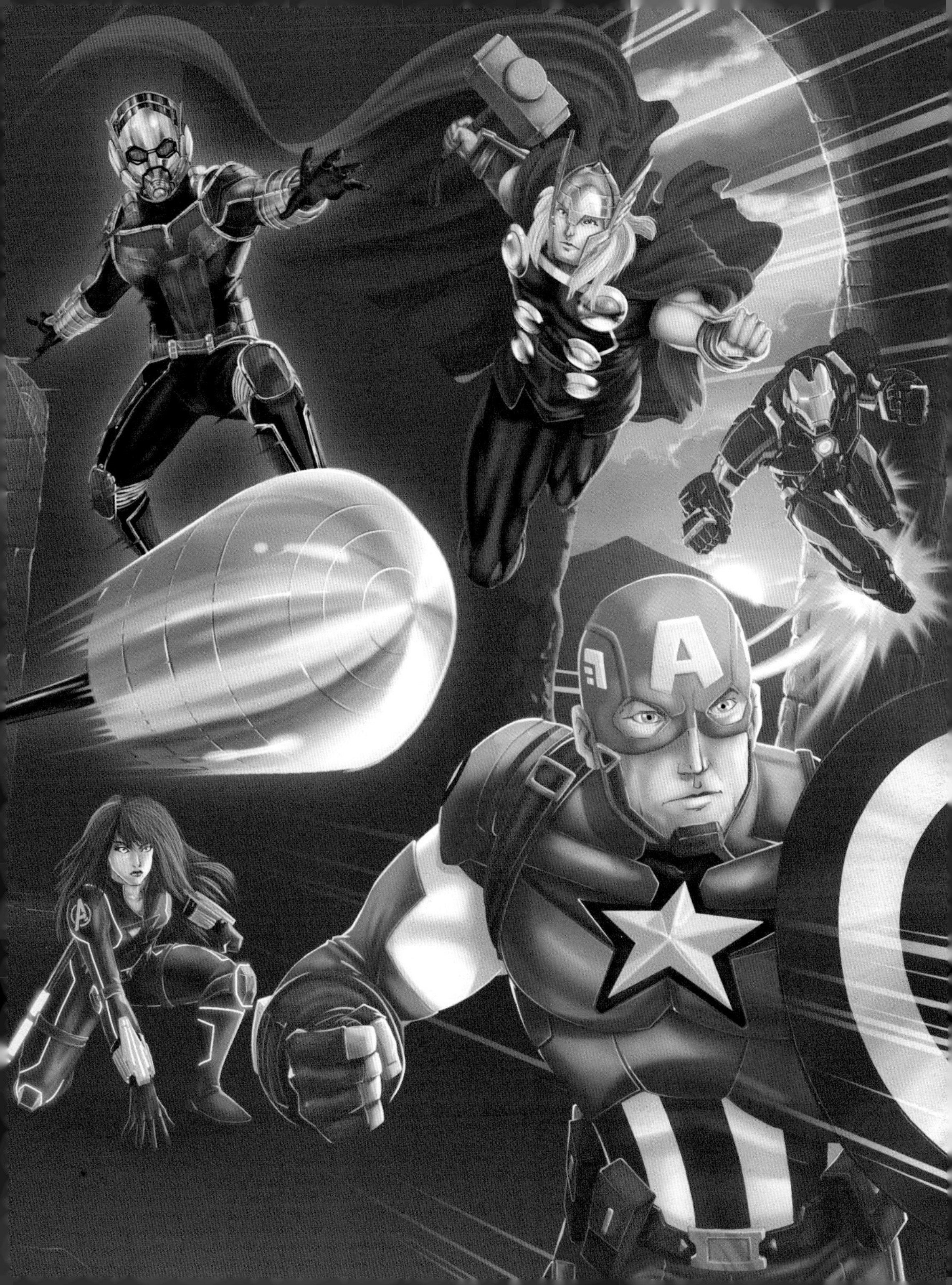

ULTRON is an almost indestructible robot created by Dr. Pym to help mankind. The robot went bad, and now it wants to destroy the world.

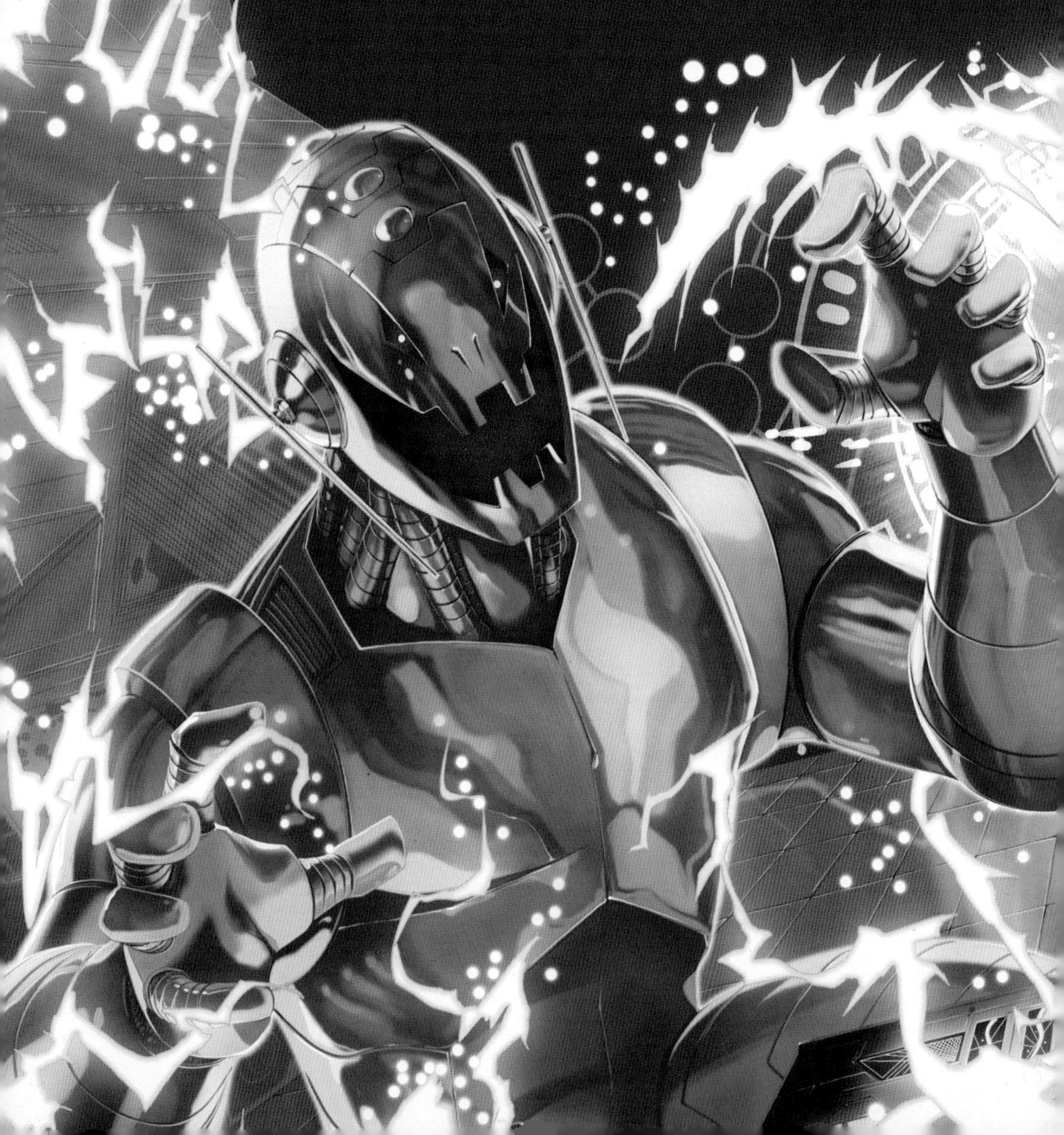

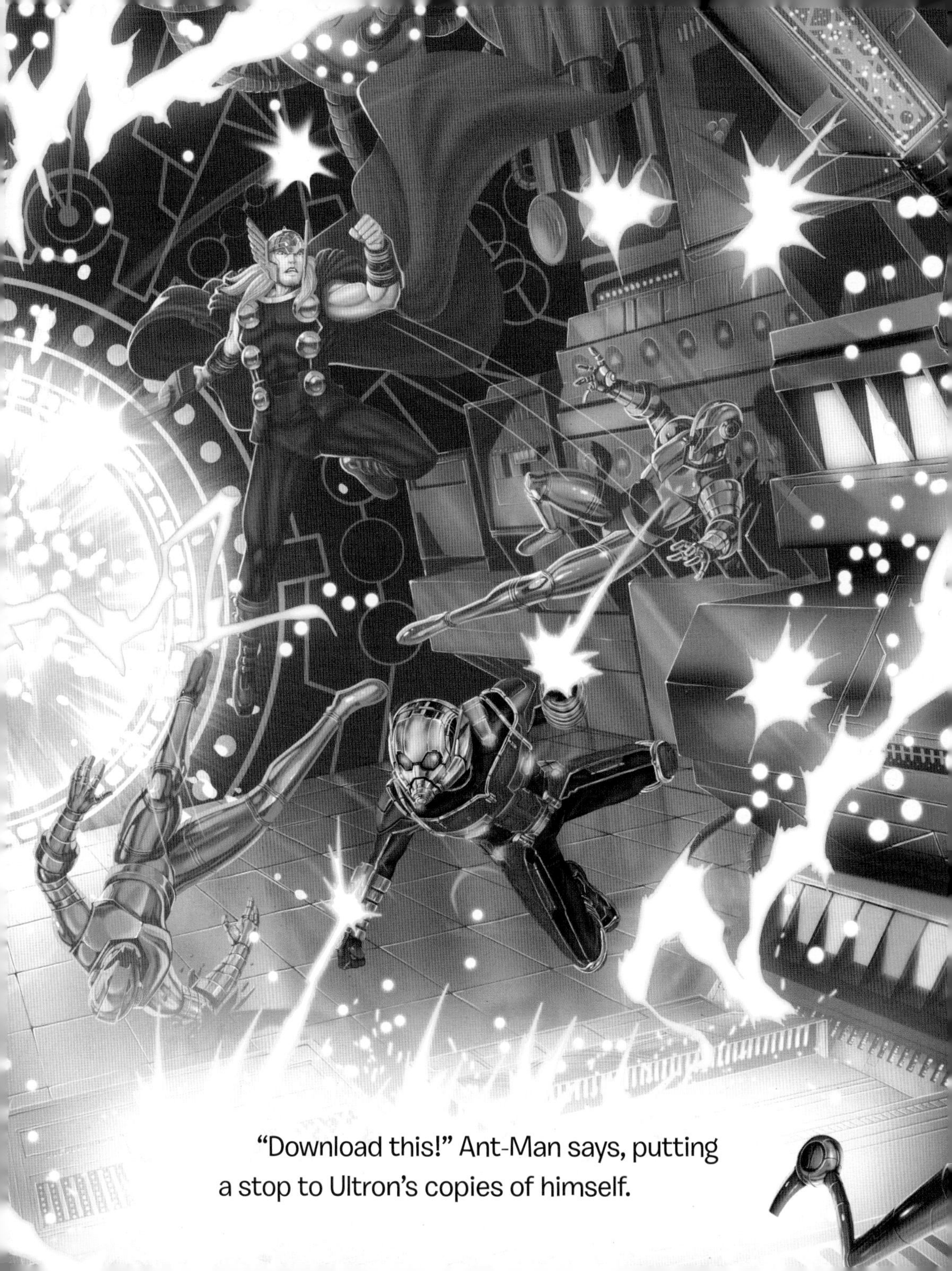

"Download this!" Ant-Man says, putting a stop to Ultron's copies of himself.

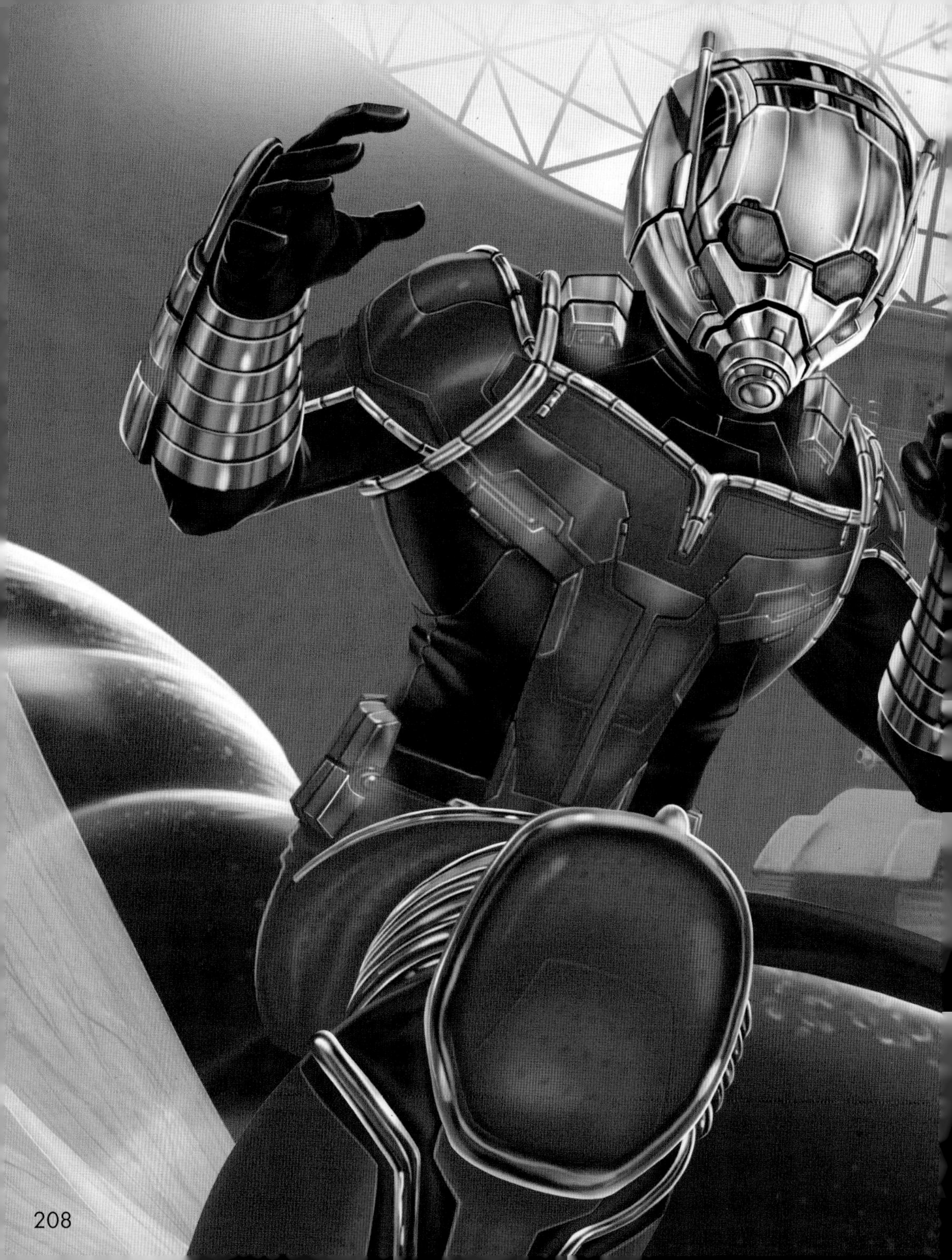

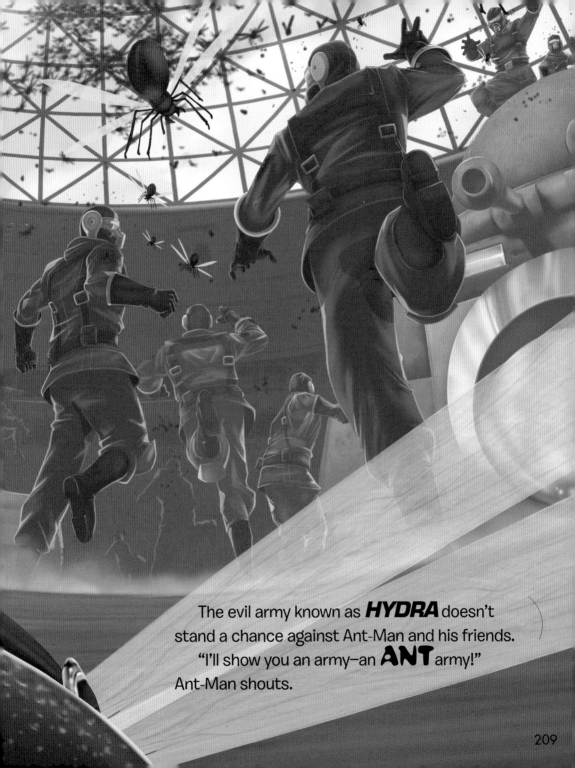

The evil army known as **HYDRA** doesn't stand a chance against Ant-Man and his friends. "I'll show you an army—an **ANT** army!" Ant-Man shouts.

Sometimes it takes Ant-Man and all the Avengers to fight one villain, such as ***COUNT NEFARIA***, who has many superpowers . . .

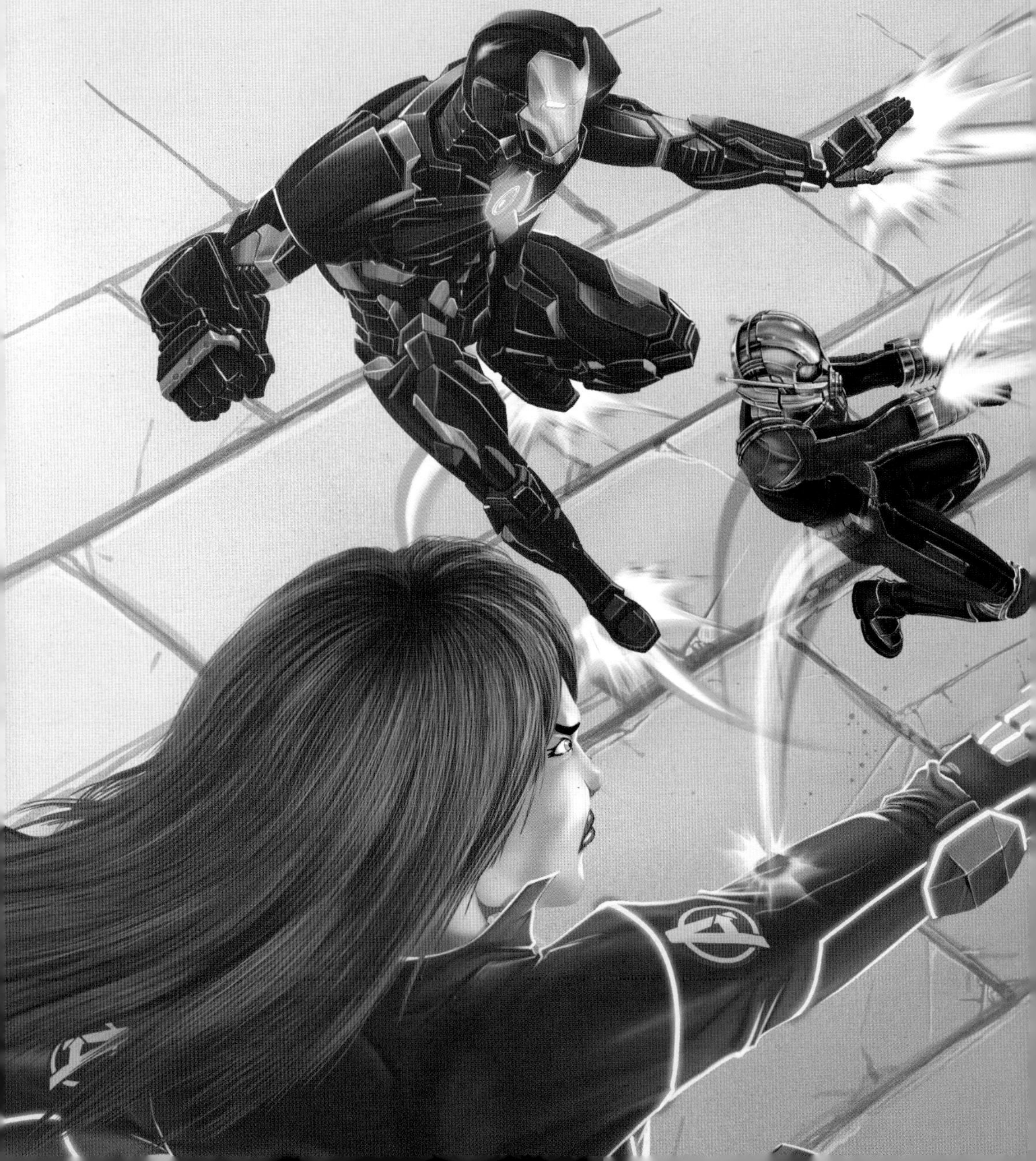

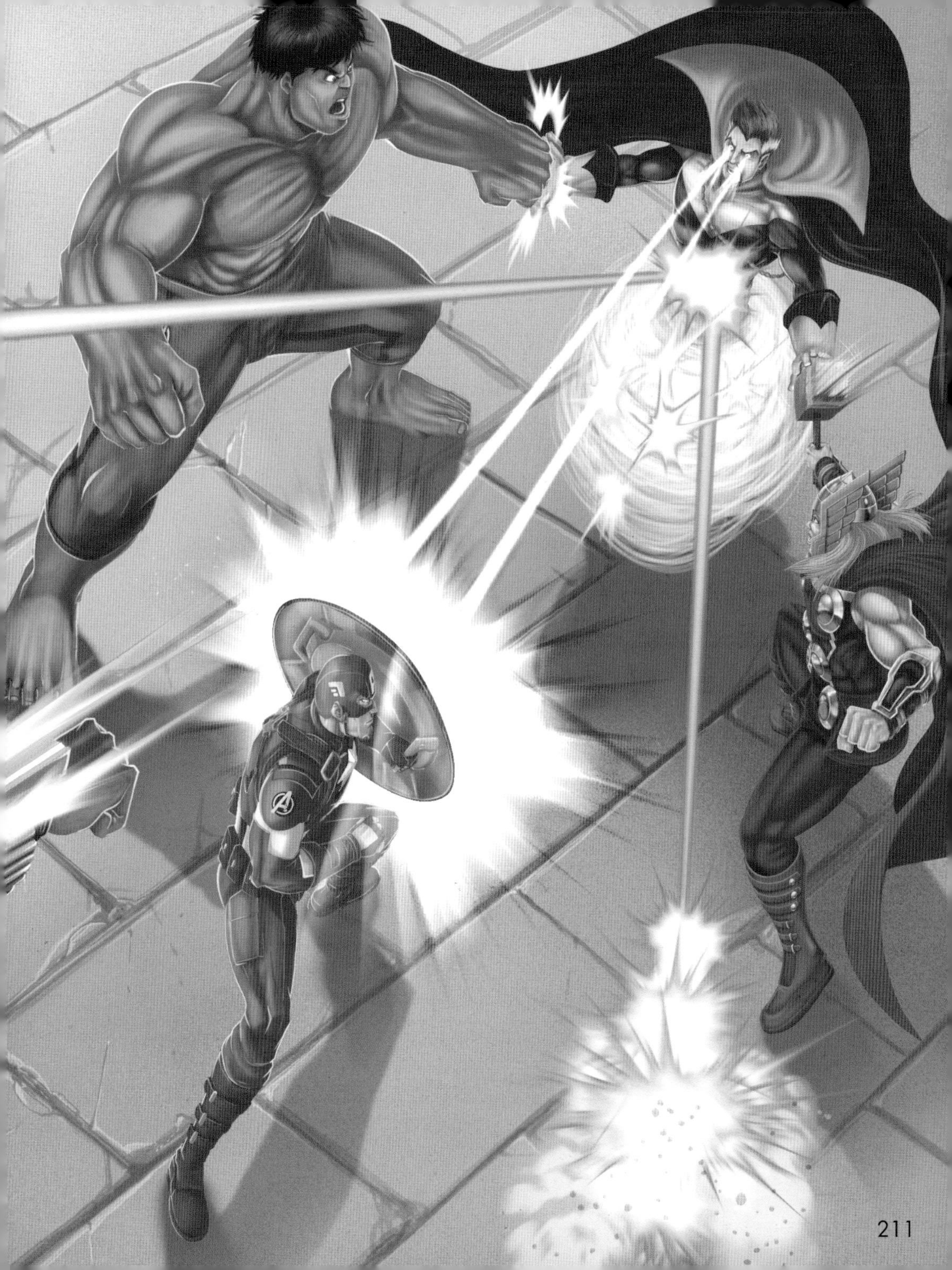

. . . and sometimes they fight whole teams of super villains, such as the ***MASTERS OF EVIL***, who combine their powers in hopes of defeating the heroes and taking over the world.

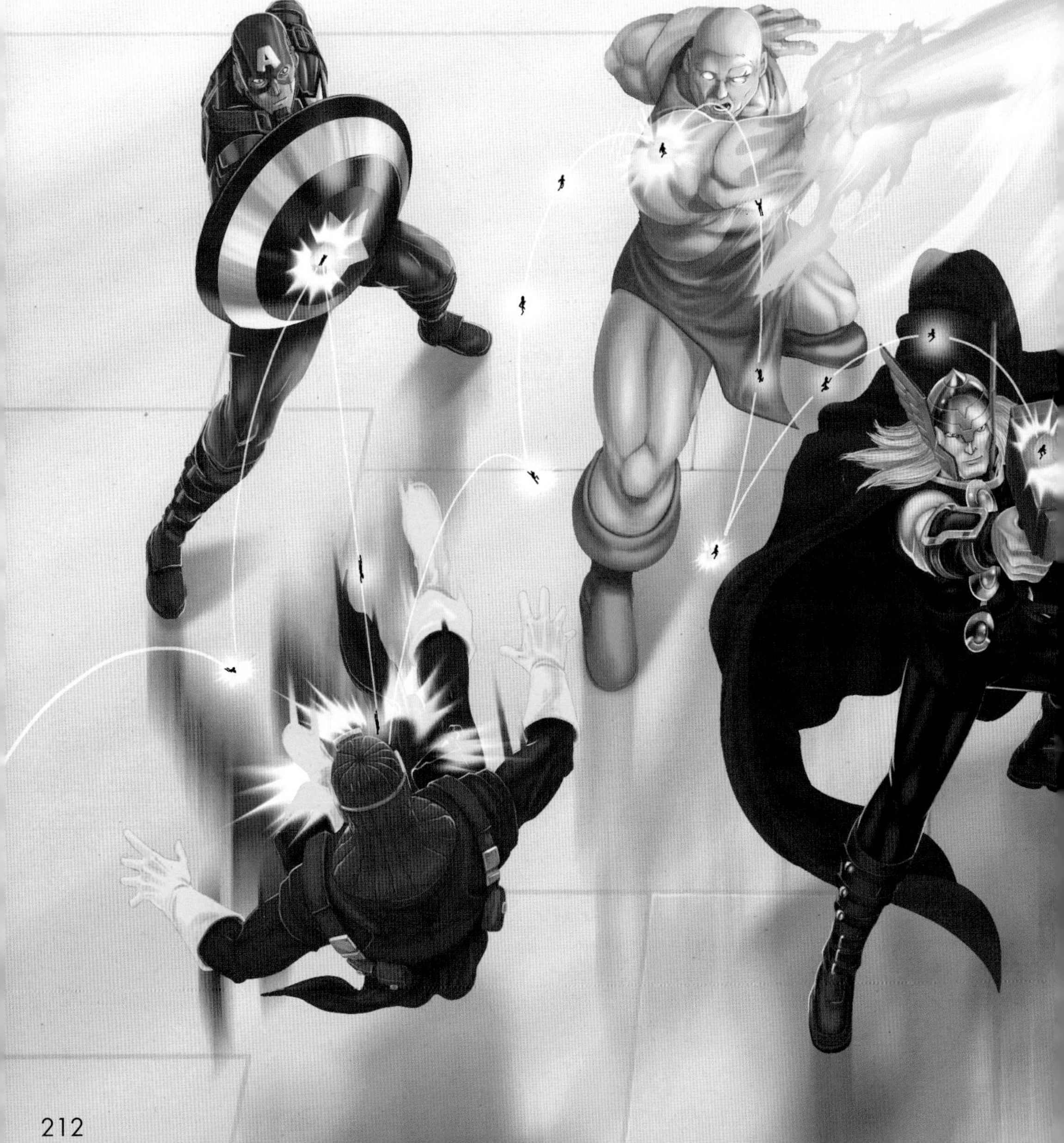

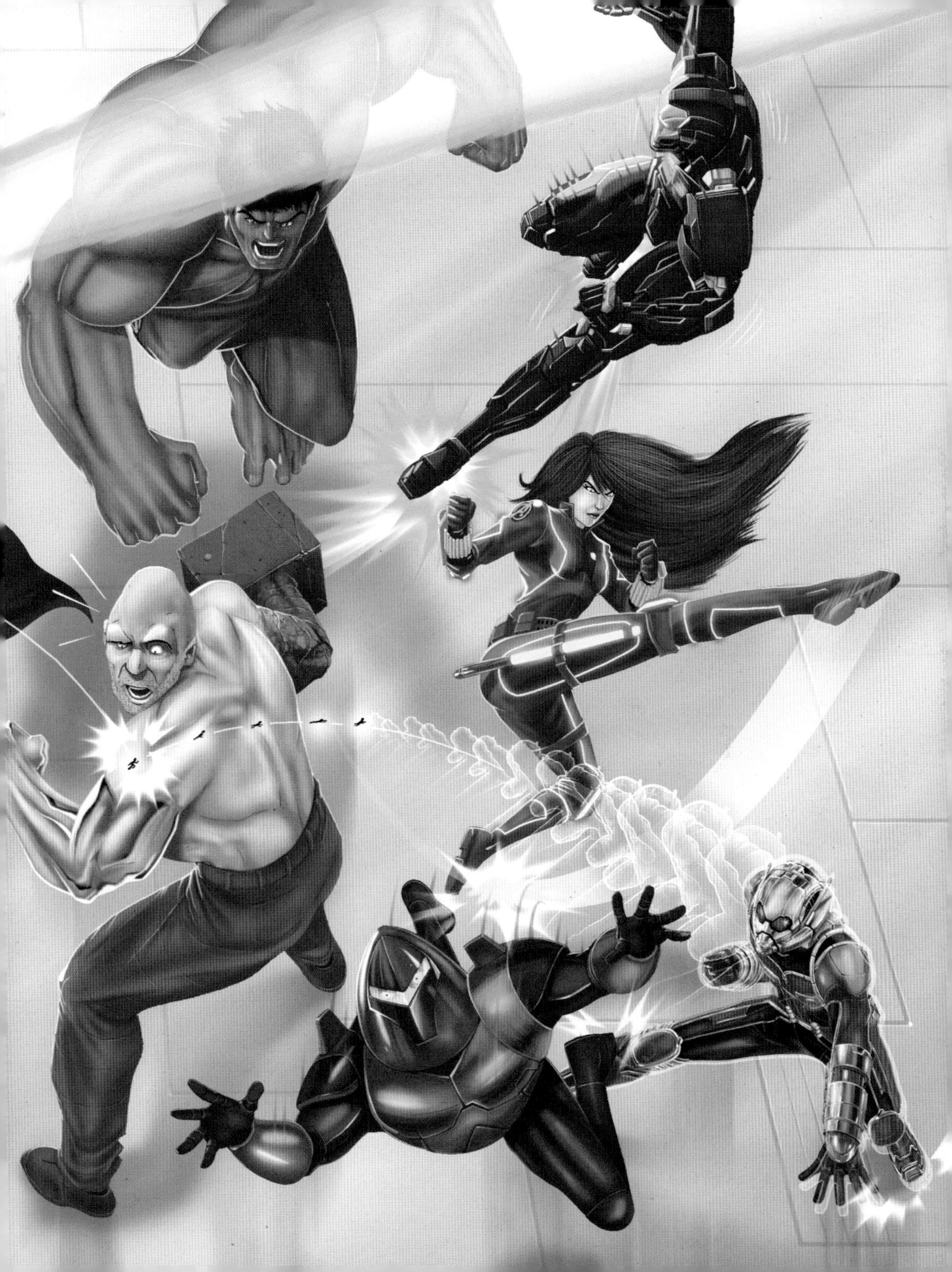

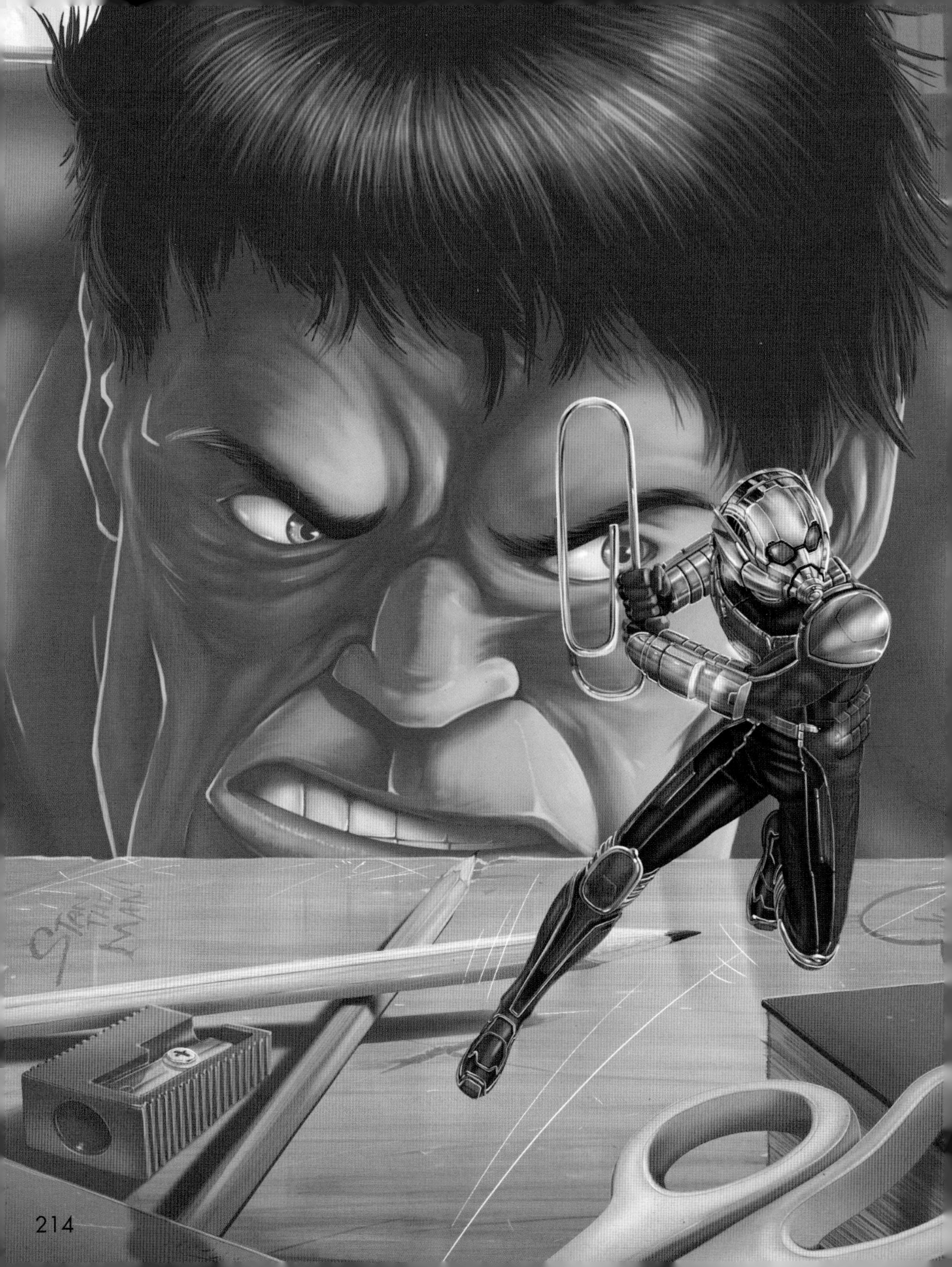

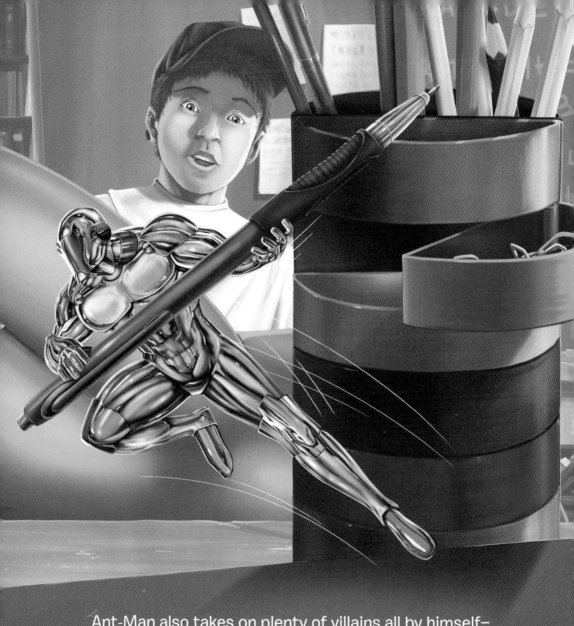

Ant-Man also takes on plenty of villains all by himself—
even ones like the **SUPER ADAPTOID**, who can mimic
any superhero's powers. The robot can shrink like Ant-Man!
    "This desk isn't big enough for the both of us,"
Ant-Man says.

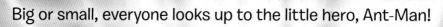

Big or small, everyone looks up to the little hero, Ant-Man!

GO, ANT-MAN!